Hakumei & Mikochi 7

Tiny Little Life in the Woods

Takuto Kashiki

Contents

Chapter 43

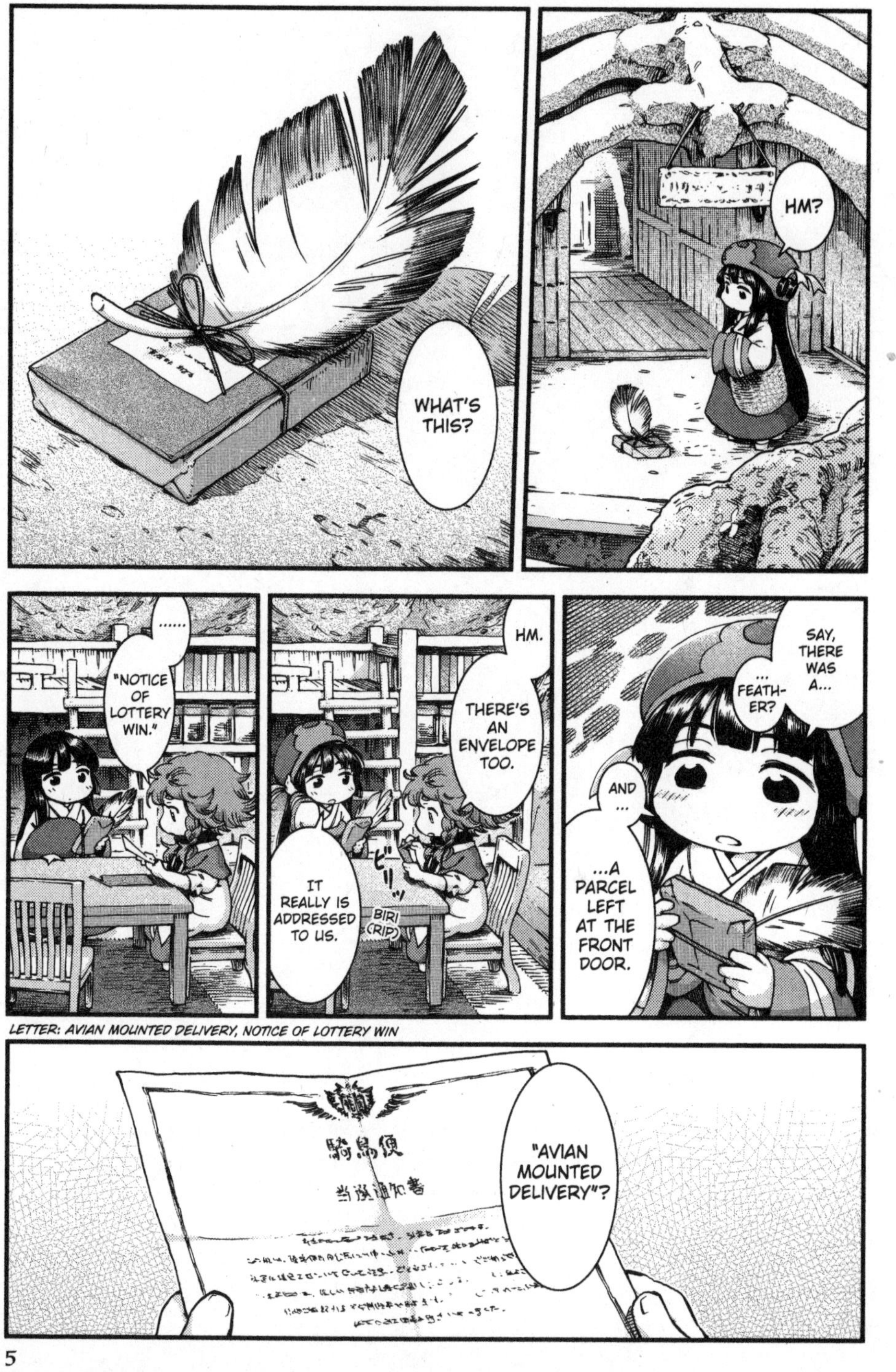
HM?
WHAT'S THIS?
SAY, THERE WAS A...
...FEATHER?
AND...
...A PARCEL LEFT AT THE FRONT DOOR.
HM.
THERE'S AN ENVELOPE TOO.
BIRI (RIP)
IT REALLY IS ADDRESSED TO US.
......
"NOTICE OF LOTTERY WIN."
LETTER: AVIAN MOUNTED DELIVERY, NOTICE OF LOTTERY WIN
騎鳥便
当選通知書
"AVIAN MOUNTED DELIVERY"?

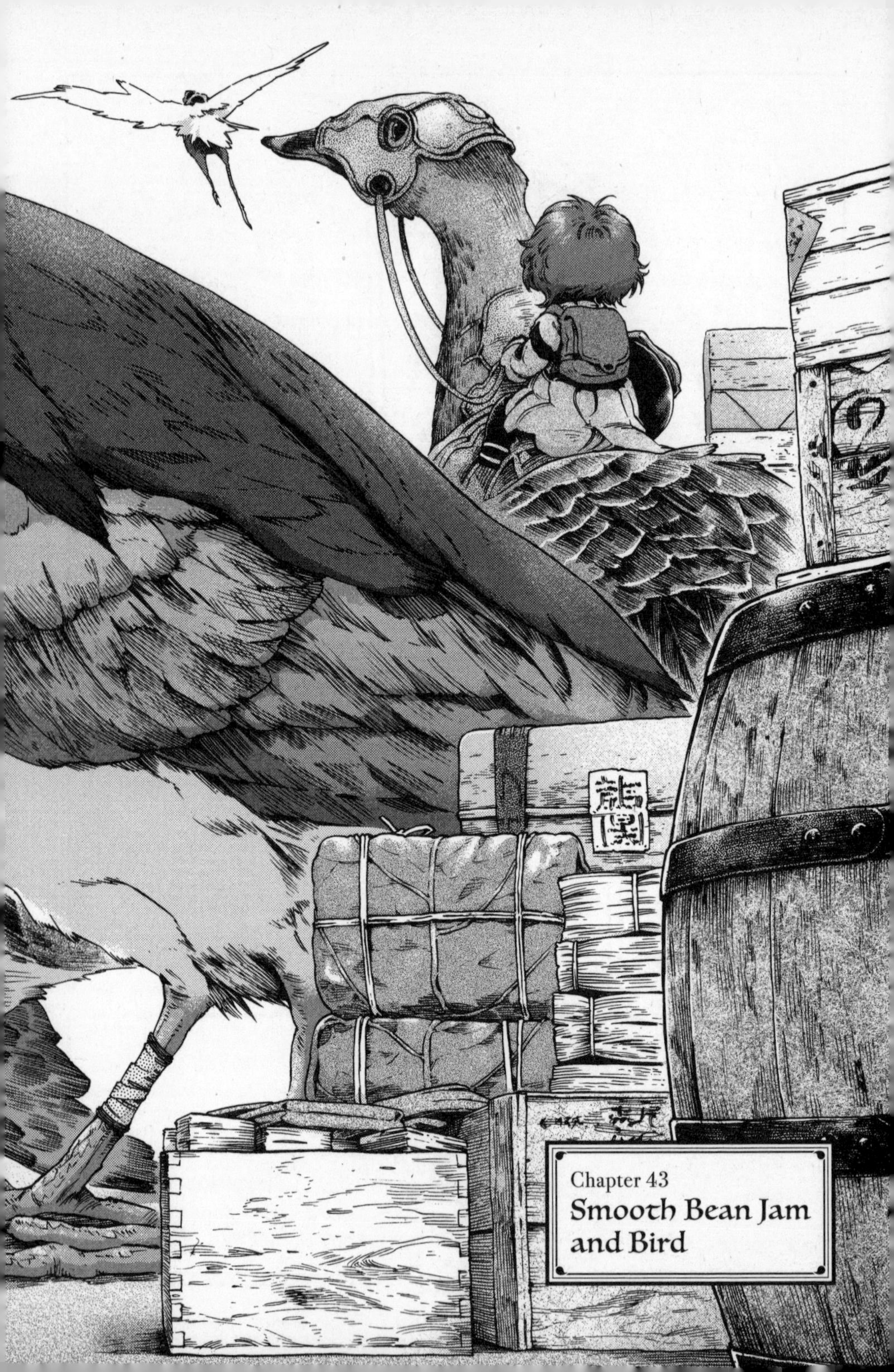

Chapter 43
Smooth Bean Jam and Bird

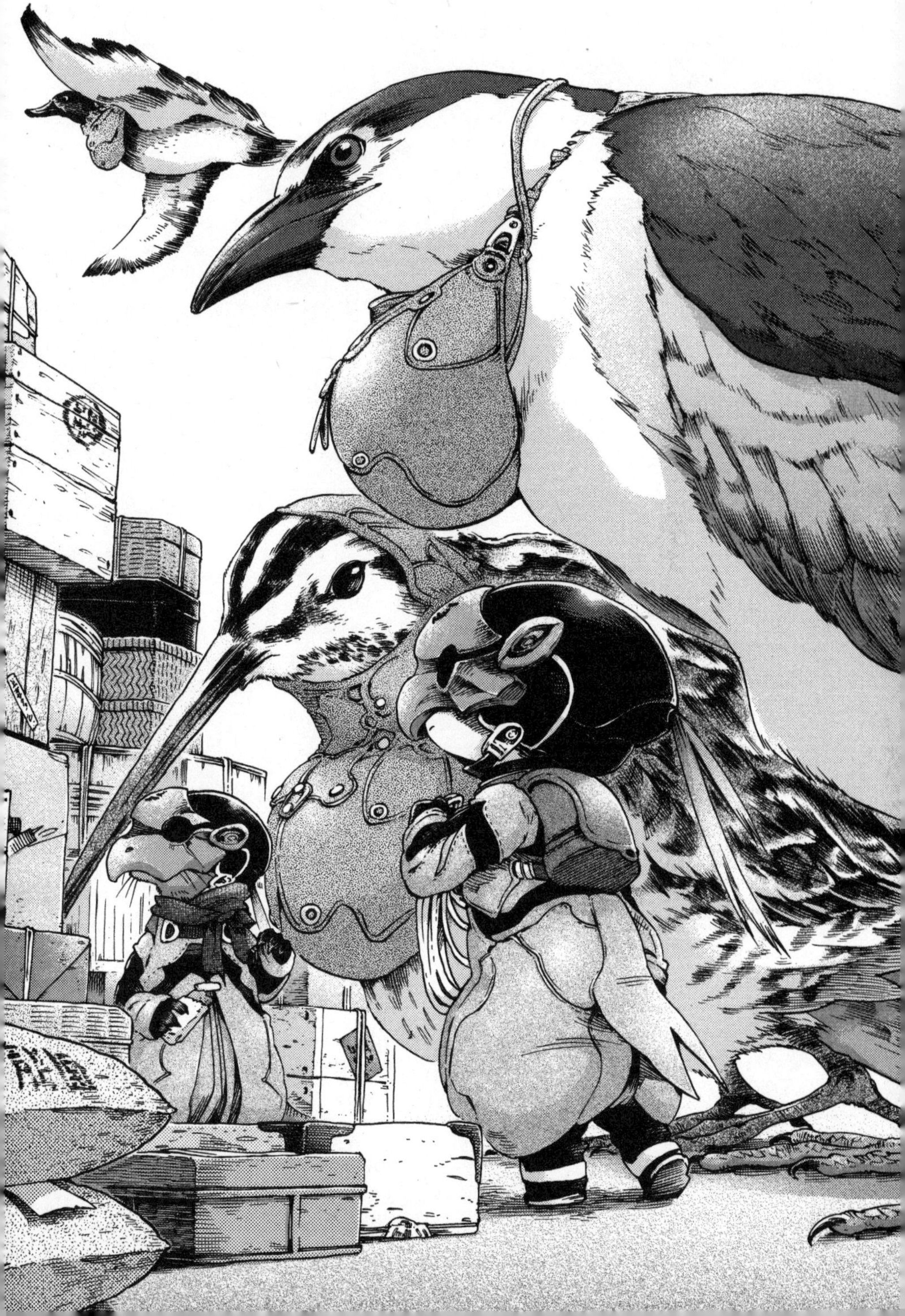

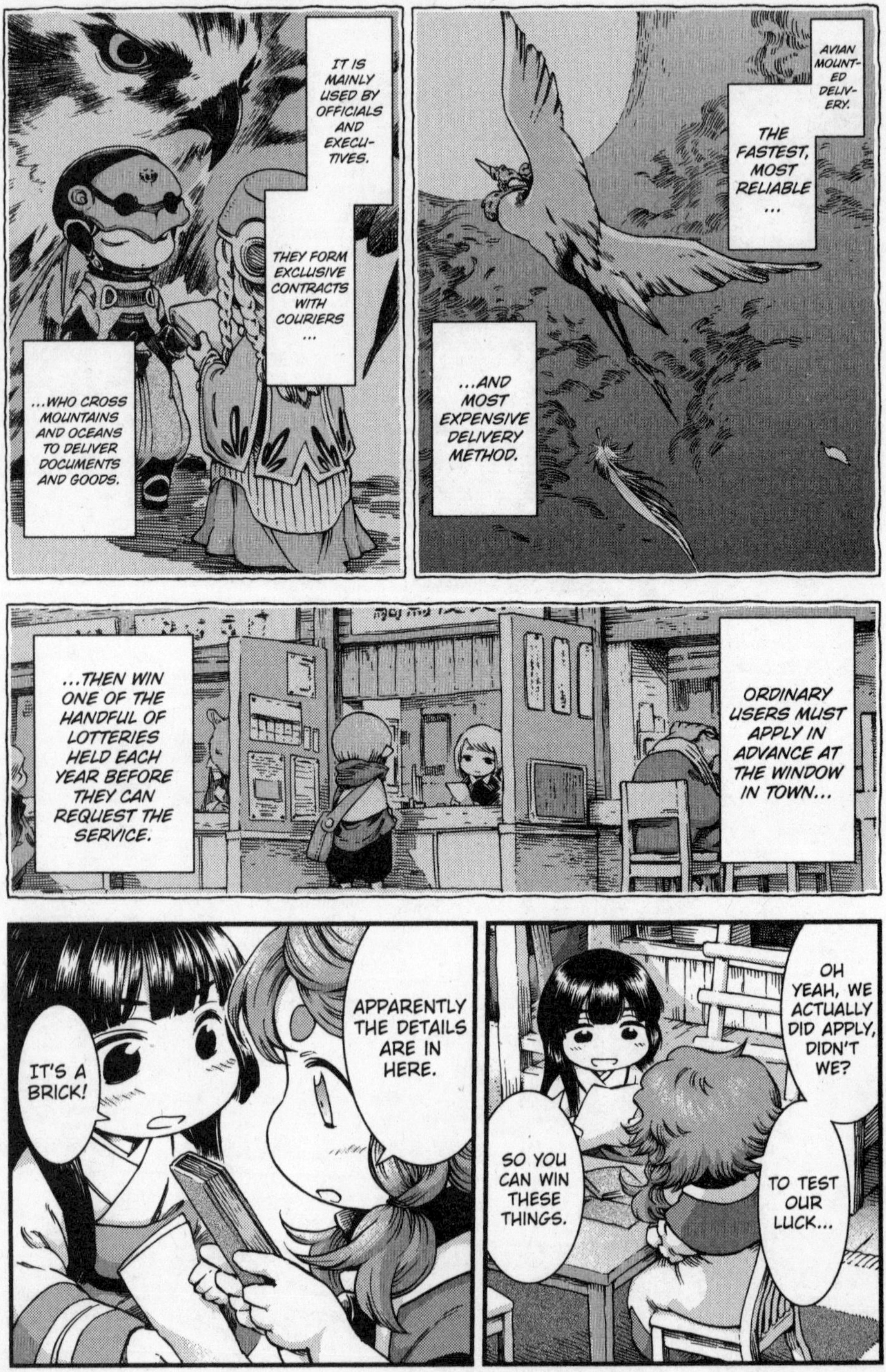
AVIAN MOUNTED DELIVERY.
THE FASTEST, MOST RELIABLE...
...AND MOST EXPENSIVE DELIVERY METHOD.
IT IS MAINLY USED BY OFFICIALS AND EXECUTIVES.
THEY FORM EXCLUSIVE CONTRACTS WITH COURIERS...
...WHO CROSS MOUNTAINS AND OCEANS TO DELIVER DOCUMENTS AND GOODS.
ORDINARY USERS MUST APPLY IN ADVANCE AT THE WINDOW IN TOWN...
...THEN WIN ONE OF THE HANDFUL OF LOTTERIES HELD EACH YEAR BEFORE THEY CAN REQUEST THE SERVICE.
OH YEAH, WE ACTUALLY DID APPLY, DIDN'T WE?
TO TEST OUR LUCK...
SO YOU CAN WIN THESE THINGS.
APPARENTLY THE DETAILS ARE IN HERE.
IT'S A BRICK!

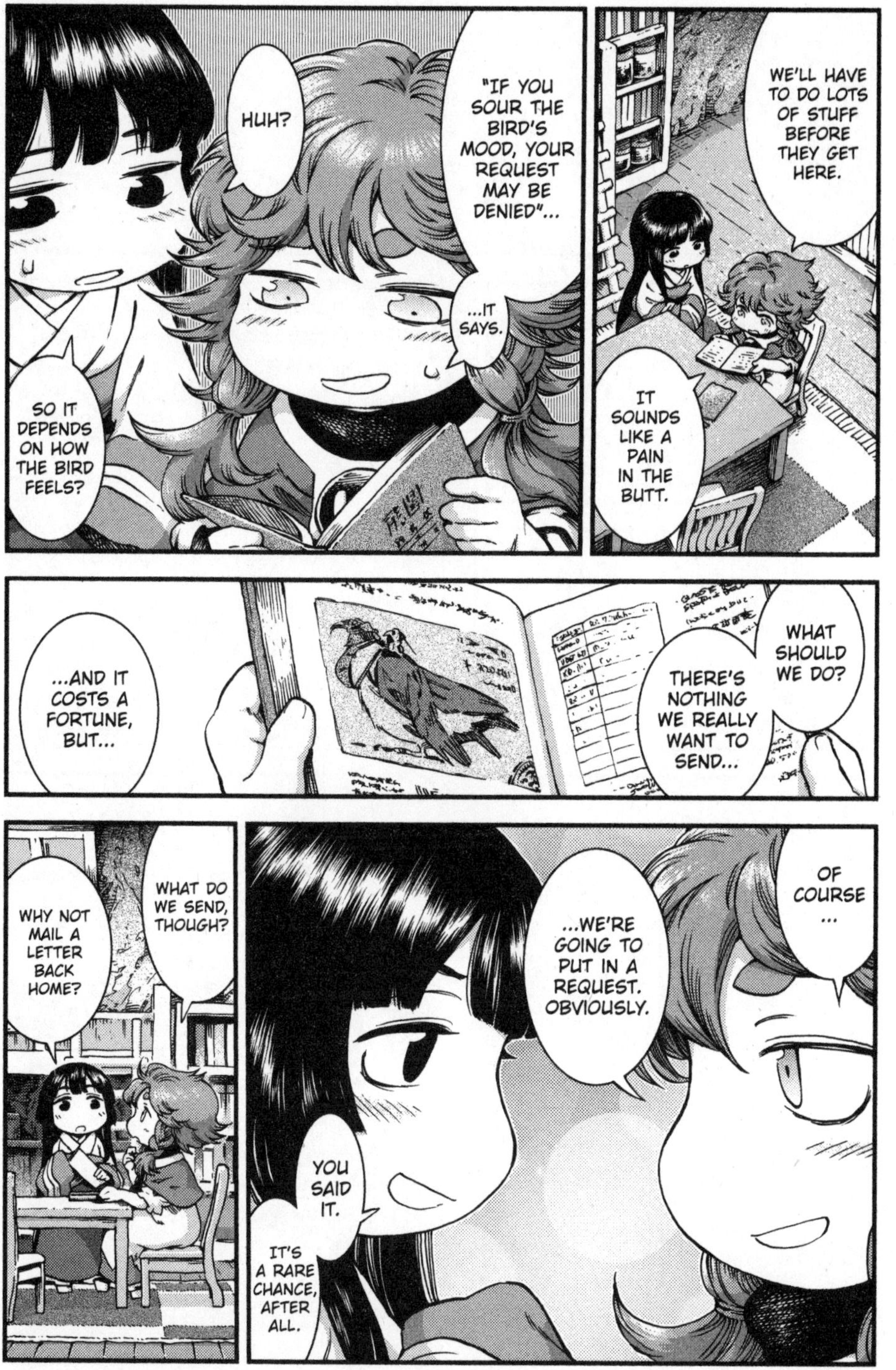
WE'LL HAVE TO DO LOTS OF STUFF BEFORE THEY GET HERE.
IT SOUNDS LIKE A PAIN IN THE BUTT.
"IF YOU SOUR THE BIRD'S MOOD, YOUR REQUEST MAY BE DENIED"...
...IT SAYS.
HUH?
SO IT DEPENDS ON HOW THE BIRD FEELS?
WHAT SHOULD WE DO?
THERE'S NOTHING WE REALLY WANT TO SEND...
...AND IT COSTS A FORTUNE, BUT...
OF COURSE ...
...WE'RE GOING TO PUT IN A REQUEST. OBVIOUSLY.
YOU SAID IT.
IT'S A RARE CHANCE, AFTER ALL.
WHAT DO WE SEND, THOUGH?
WHY NOT MAIL A LETTER BACK HOME?

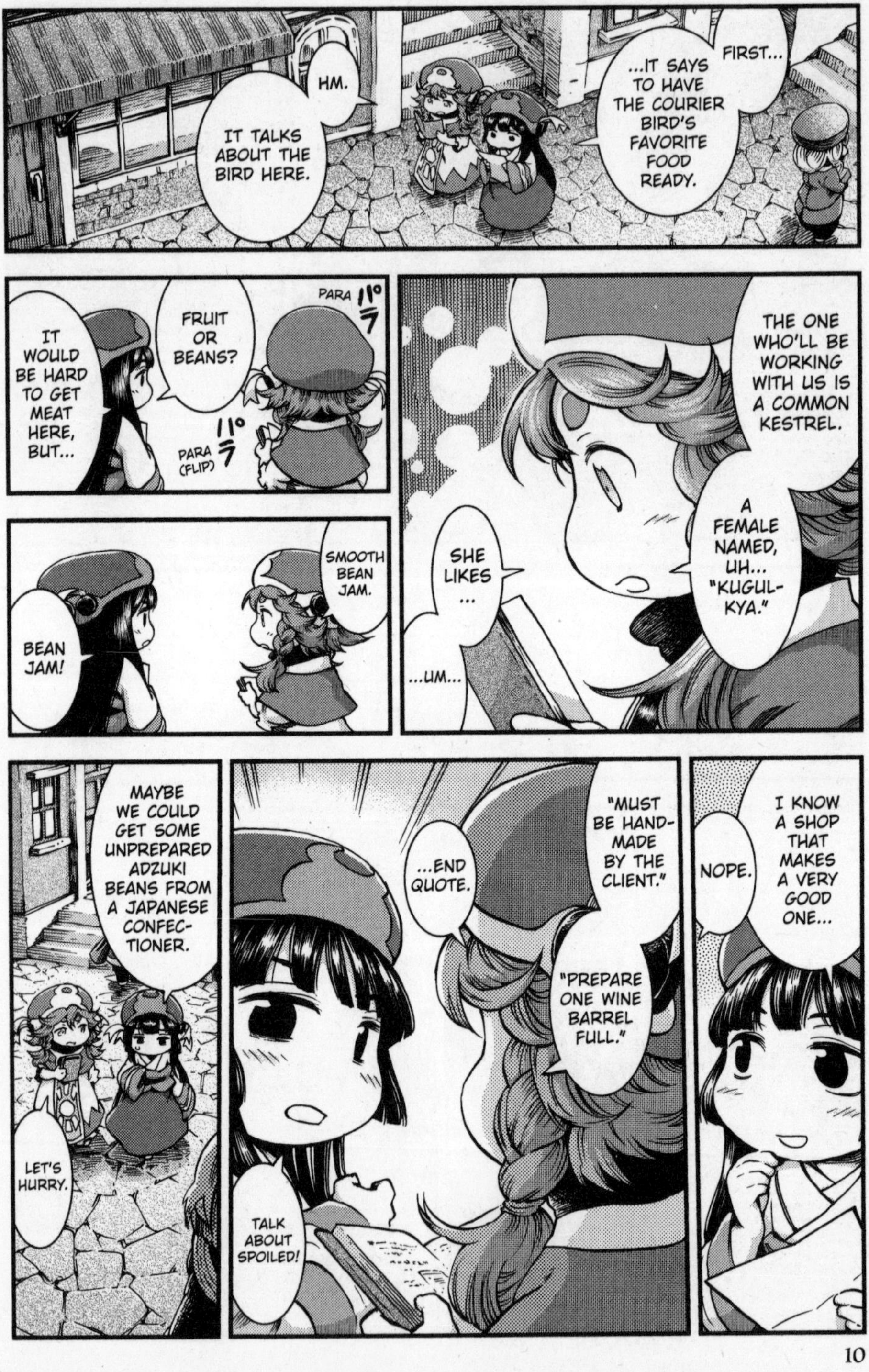
FIRST...
...IT SAYS TO HAVE THE COURIER BIRD'S FAVORITE FOOD READY.
HM.
IT TALKS ABOUT THE BIRD HERE.
THE ONE WHO'LL BE WORKING WITH US IS A COMMON KESTREL.
A FEMALE NAMED, UH... "KUGUL-KYA."
SHE LIKES...
...UM...
PARA パラ
PARA (FLIP) パラ
FRUIT OR BEANS?
IT WOULD BE HARD TO GET MEAT HERE, BUT...
SMOOTH BEAN JAM.
BEAN JAM!
I KNOW A SHOP THAT MAKES A VERY GOOD ONE...
NOPE.
"MUST BE HAND-MADE BY THE CLIENT."
...END QUOTE.
"PREPARE ONE WINE BARREL FULL."
TALK ABOUT SPOILED!
MAYBE WE COULD GET SOME UNPREPARED ADZUKI BEANS FROM A JAPANESE CONFECTIONER.
LET'S HURRY.

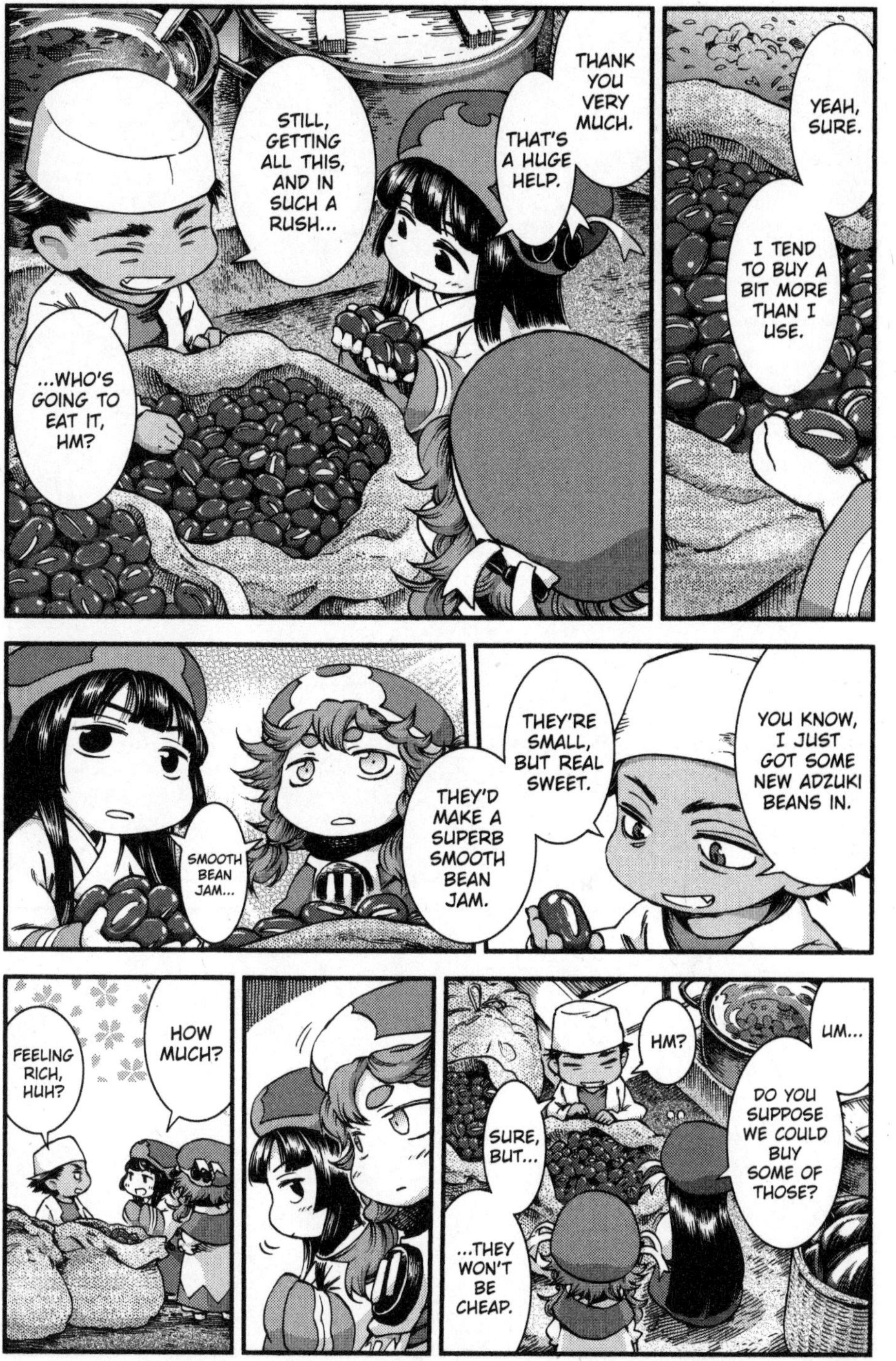
YEAH, SURE.
I TEND TO BUY A BIT MORE THAN I USE.
THANK YOU VERY MUCH.
THAT'S A HUGE HELP.
STILL, GETTING ALL THIS, AND IN SUCH A RUSH...
...WHO'S GOING TO EAT IT, HM?
YOU KNOW, I JUST GOT SOME NEW ADZUKI BEANS IN.
THEY'RE SMALL, BUT REAL SWEET.
THEY'D MAKE A SUPERB SMOOTH BEAN JAM.
SMOOTH BEAN JAM...
UM...
DO YOU SUPPOSE WE COULD BUY SOME OF THOSE?
HM?
SURE, BUT...
...THEY WON'T BE CHEAP.
HOW MUCH?
FEELING RICH, HUH?

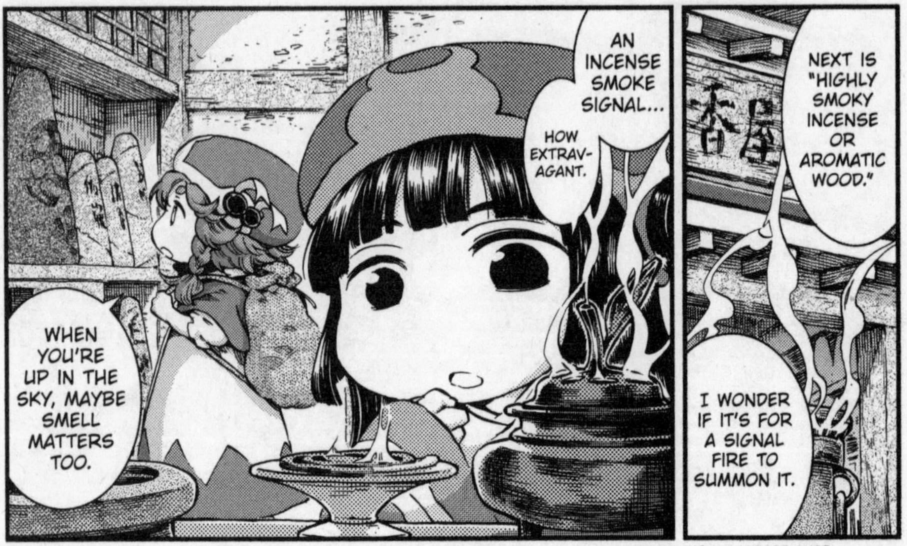
NEXT IS "HIGHLY SMOKY INCENSE OR AROMATIC WOOD."
I WONDER IF IT'S FOR A SIGNAL FIRE TO SUMMON IT.
AN INCENSE SMOKE SIGNAL...
HOW EXTRAVAGANT.
WHEN YOU'RE UP IN THE SKY, MAYBE SMELL MATTERS TOO.

SIGN: INCENSE SHOP

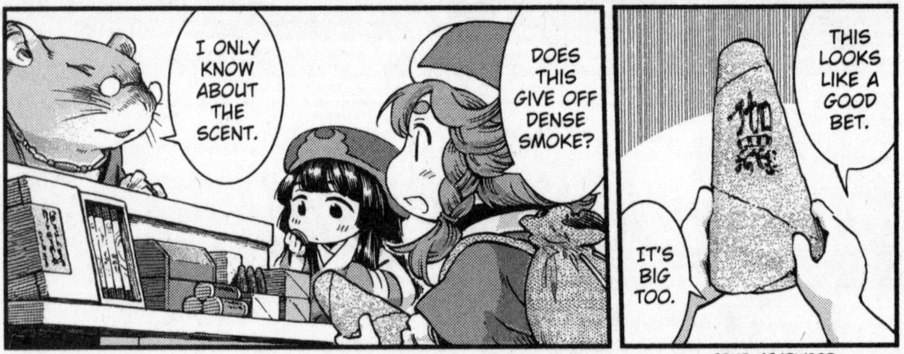
THIS LOOKS LIKE A GOOD BET.
IT'S BIG TOO.
DOES THIS GIVE OFF DENSE SMOKE?
I ONLY KNOW ABOUT THE SCENT.

CONE: AGARWOOD

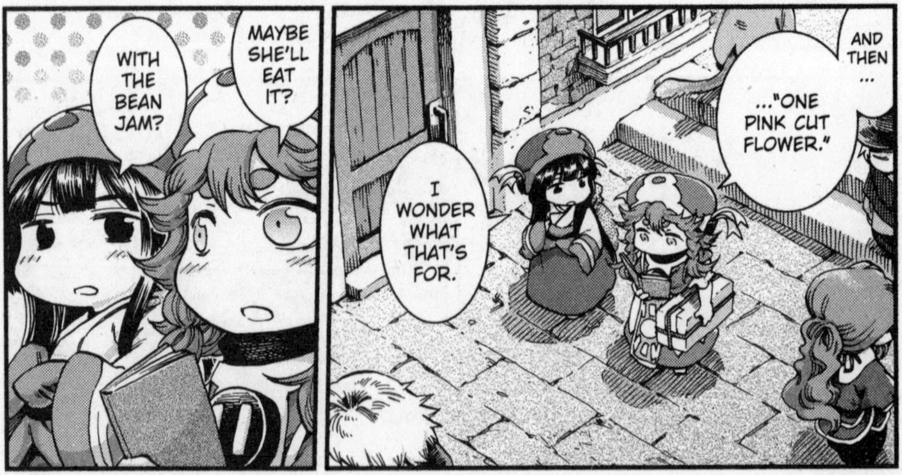
AND THEN...
..."ONE PINK CUT FLOWER."
I WONDER WHAT THAT'S FOR.
MAYBE SHE'LL EAT IT?
WITH THE BEAN JAM?

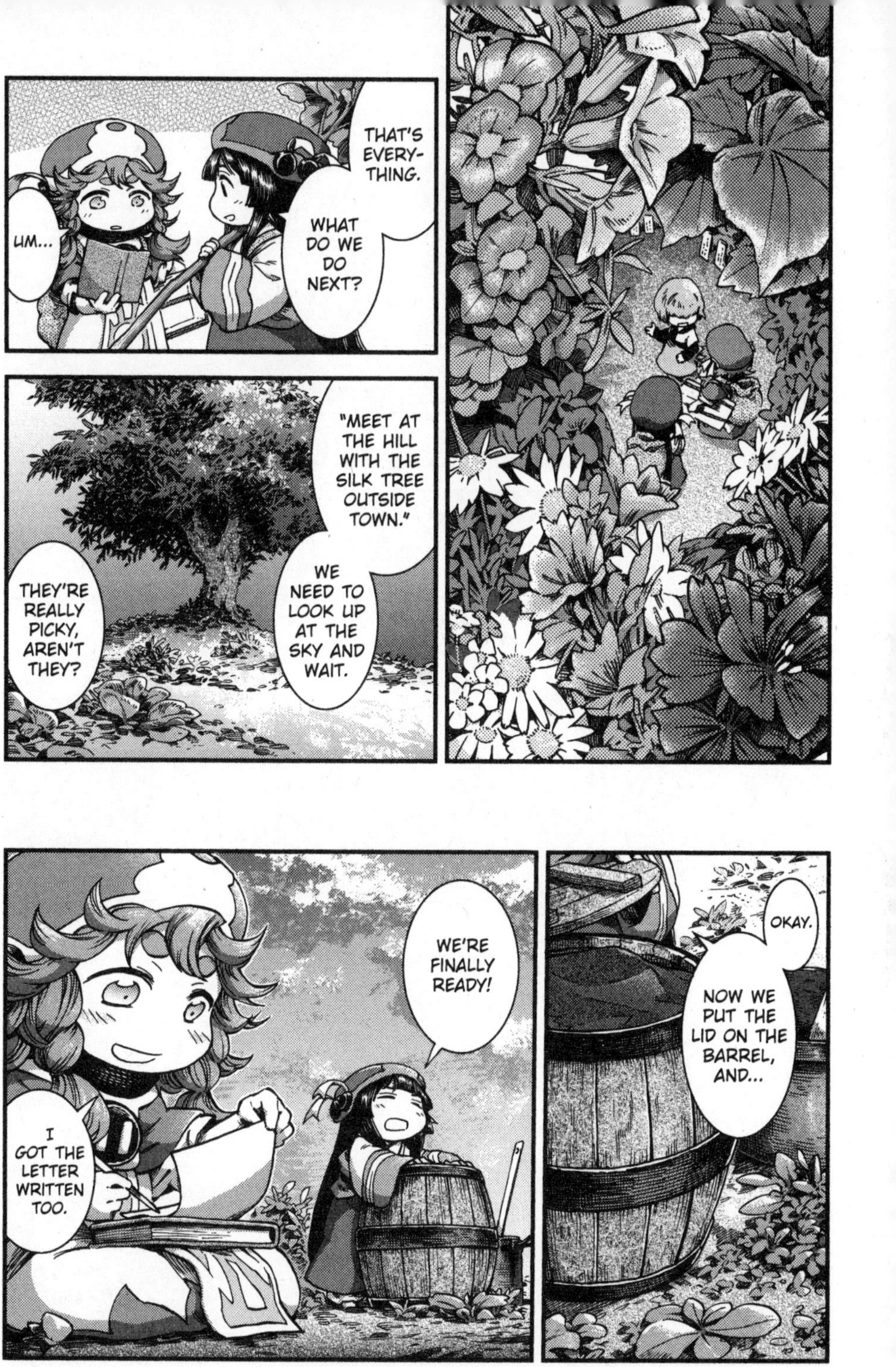
THAT'S EVERY-THING.
WHAT DO WE DO NEXT?
UM...
"MEET AT THE HILL WITH THE SILK TREE OUTSIDE TOWN."
WE NEED TO LOOK UP AT THE SKY AND WAIT.
THEY'RE REALLY PICKY, AREN'T THEY?
OKAY.
NOW WE PUT THE LID ON THE BARREL, AND...
WE'RE FINALLY READY!
I GOT THE LETTER WRITTEN TOO.

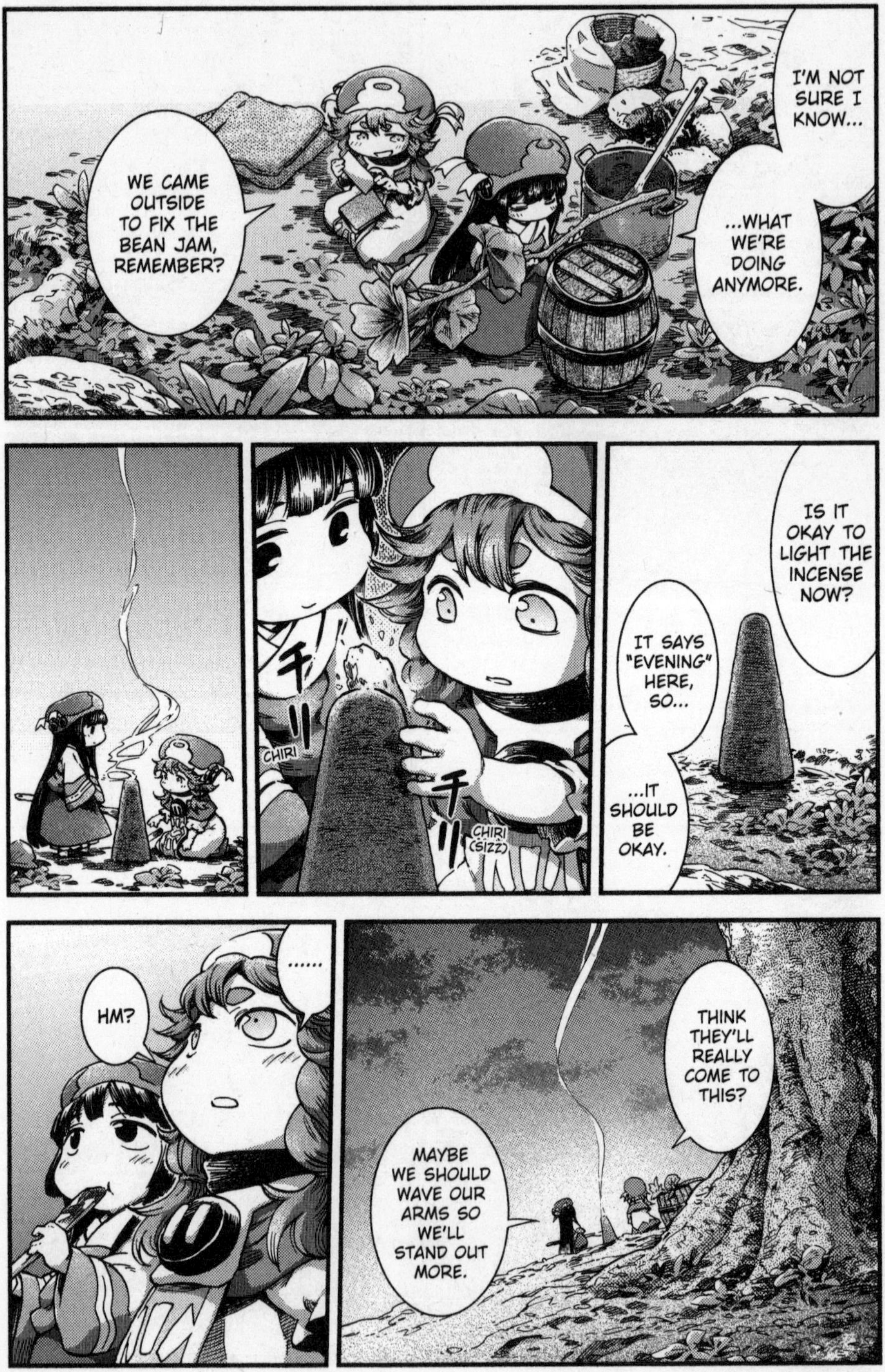
I'M NOT SURE I KNOW...
...WHAT WE'RE DOING ANYMORE.
WE CAME OUTSIDE TO FIX THE BEAN JAM, REMEMBER?
IS IT OKAY TO LIGHT THE INCENSE NOW?
IT SAYS "EVENING" HERE, SO...
...IT SHOULD BE OKAY.
チリ
CHIRI
チリ
CHIRI (SIZZ)
THINK THEY'LL REALLY COME TO THIS?
MAYBE WE SHOULD WAVE OUR ARMS SO WE'LL STAND OUT MORE.
......
HM?

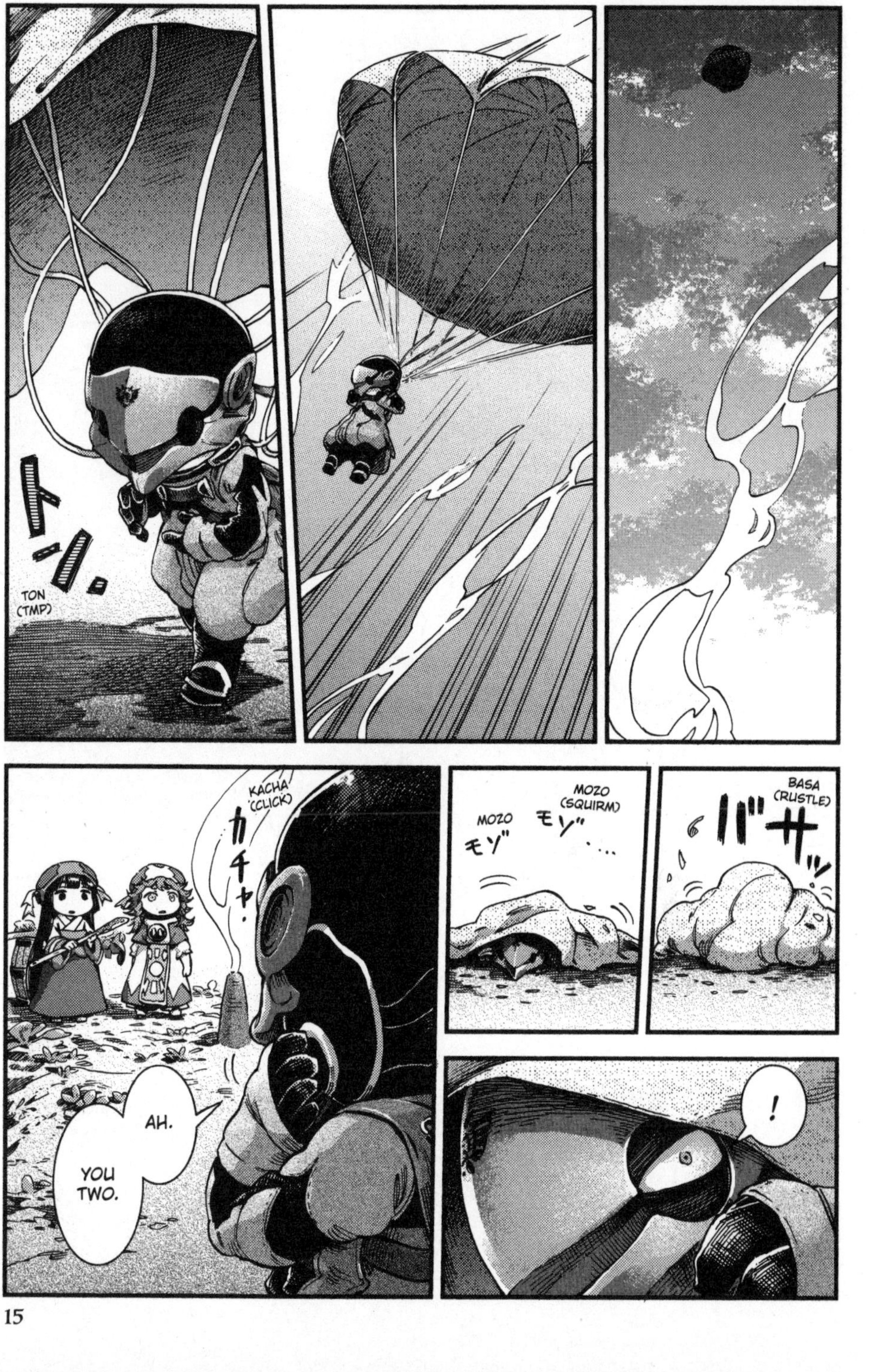

トン
TON
(TMP)
バサッ
BASA
(RUSTLE)
MOZO
(SQUIRM)
モゾ
MOZO
モゾ...
!
KACHA
(CLICK)
カチャ
AH.
YOU TWO.

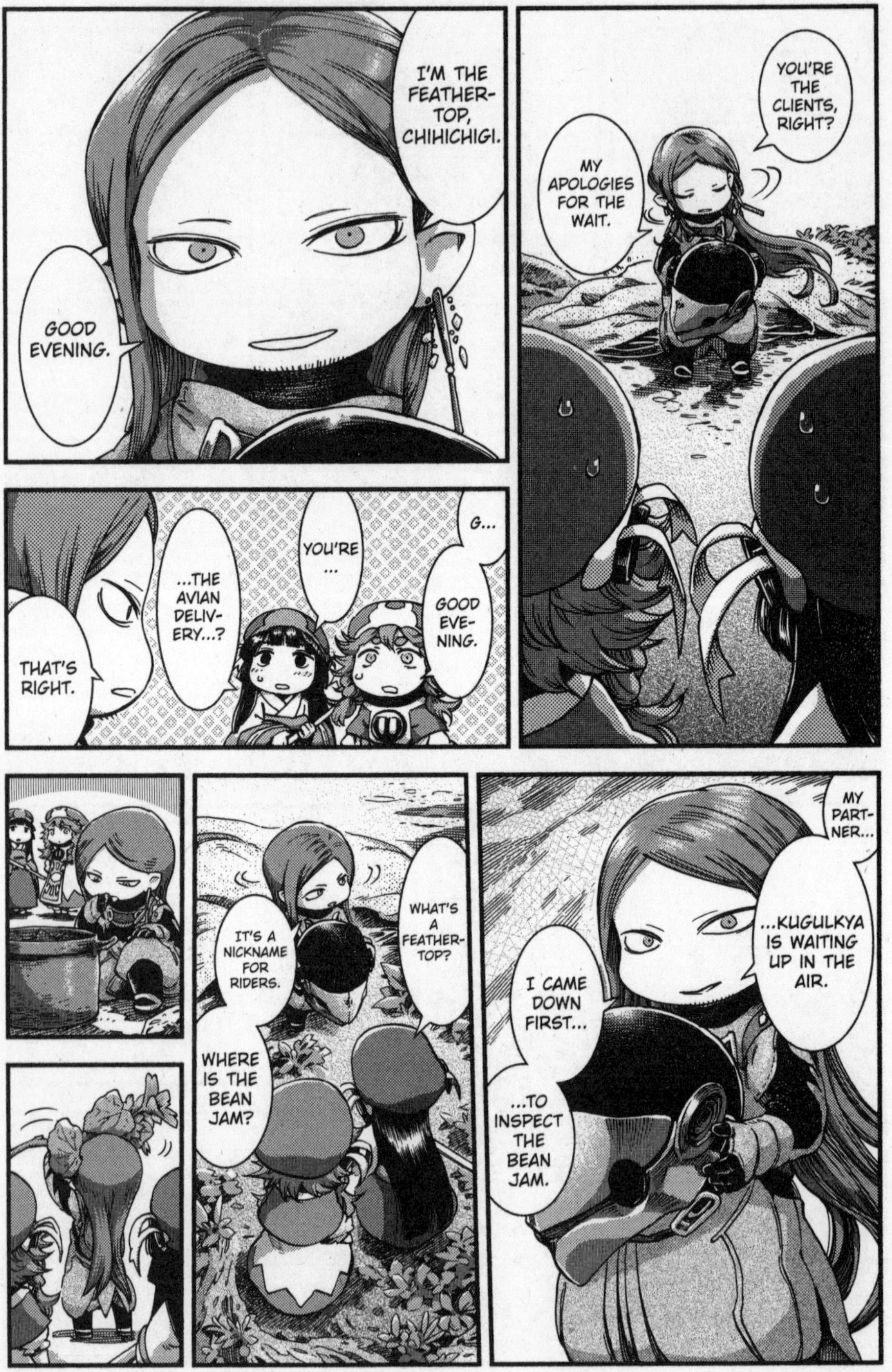
YOU'RE THE CLIENTS, RIGHT?
MY APOLOGIES FOR THE WAIT.
I'M THE FEATHER-TOP, CHIHICHIGI.
GOOD EVENING.
G... GOOD EVENING.
YOU'RE...
...THE AVIAN DELIVERY...?
THAT'S RIGHT.
MY PARTNER...
...KUGULKYA IS WAITING UP IN THE AIR.
I CAME DOWN FIRST...
...TO INSPECT THE BEAN JAM.
WHAT'S A FEATHER-TOP?
IT'S A NICKNAME FOR RIDERS.
WHERE IS THE BEAN JAM?

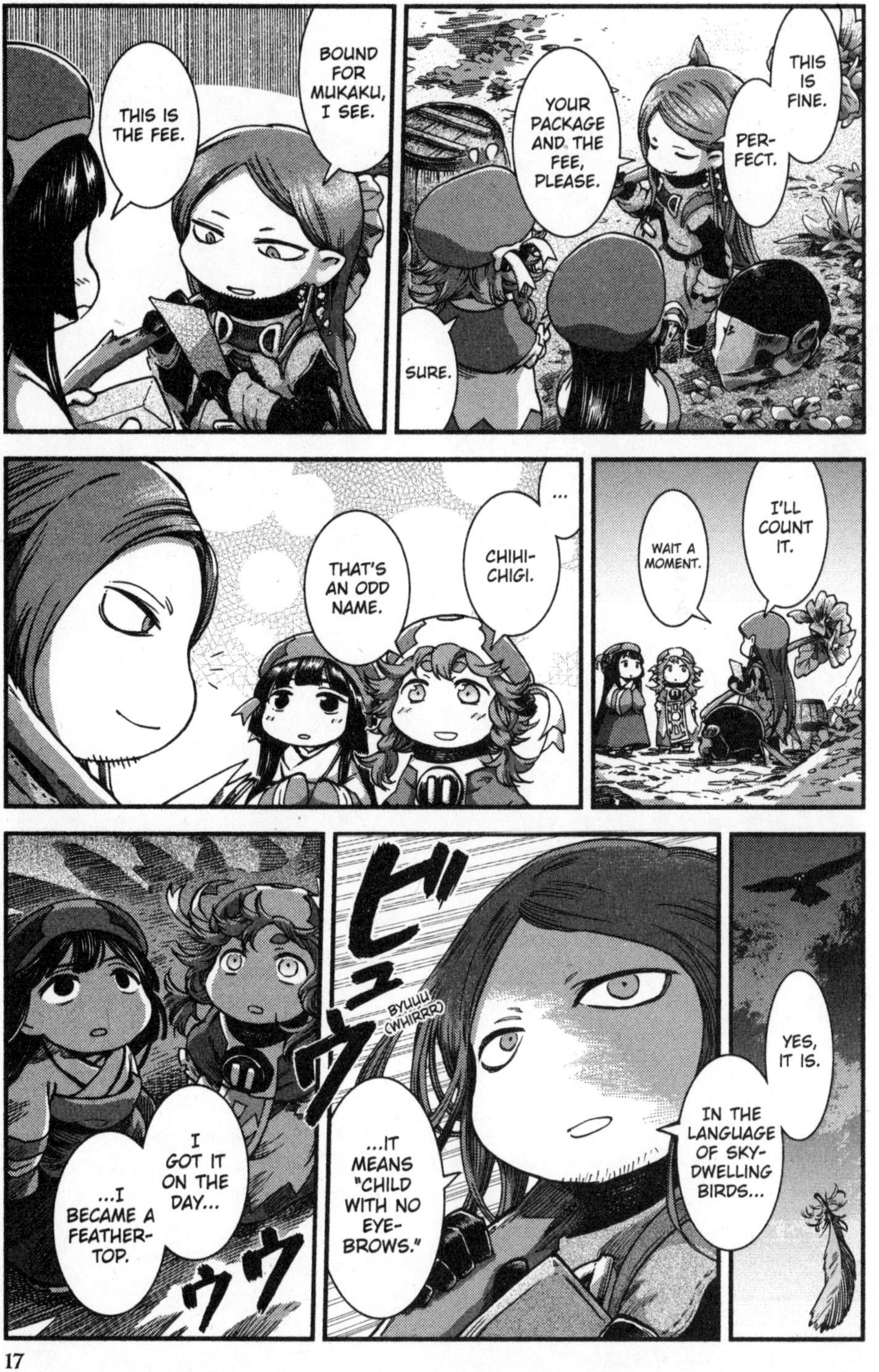
THIS IS FINE.
PER-FECT.
YOUR PACKAGE AND THE FEE, PLEASE.
SURE.
BOUND FOR MUKAKU, I SEE.
THIS IS THE FEE.
I'LL COUNT IT.
WAIT A MOMENT.
...
CHIHI-CHIGI.
THAT'S AN ODD NAME.
YES, IT IS.
IN THE LANGUAGE OF SKY-DWELLING BIRDS...
ビュウウ
BYUUU (WHIRRR)
...IT MEANS "CHILD WITH NO EYE-BROWS."
I GOT IT ON THE DAY...
...I BECAME A FEATHER-TOP.

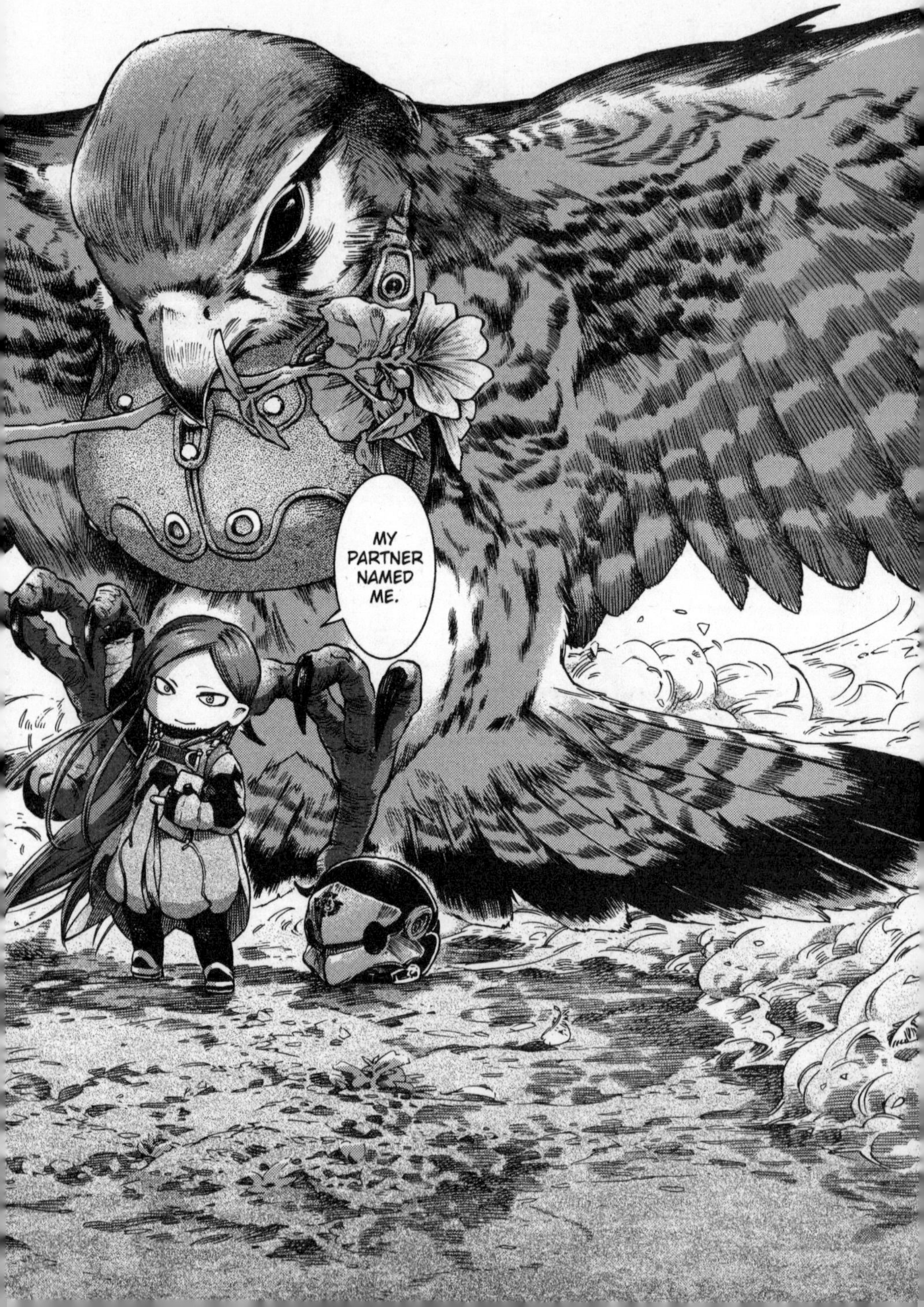
MY PARTNER NAMED ME.

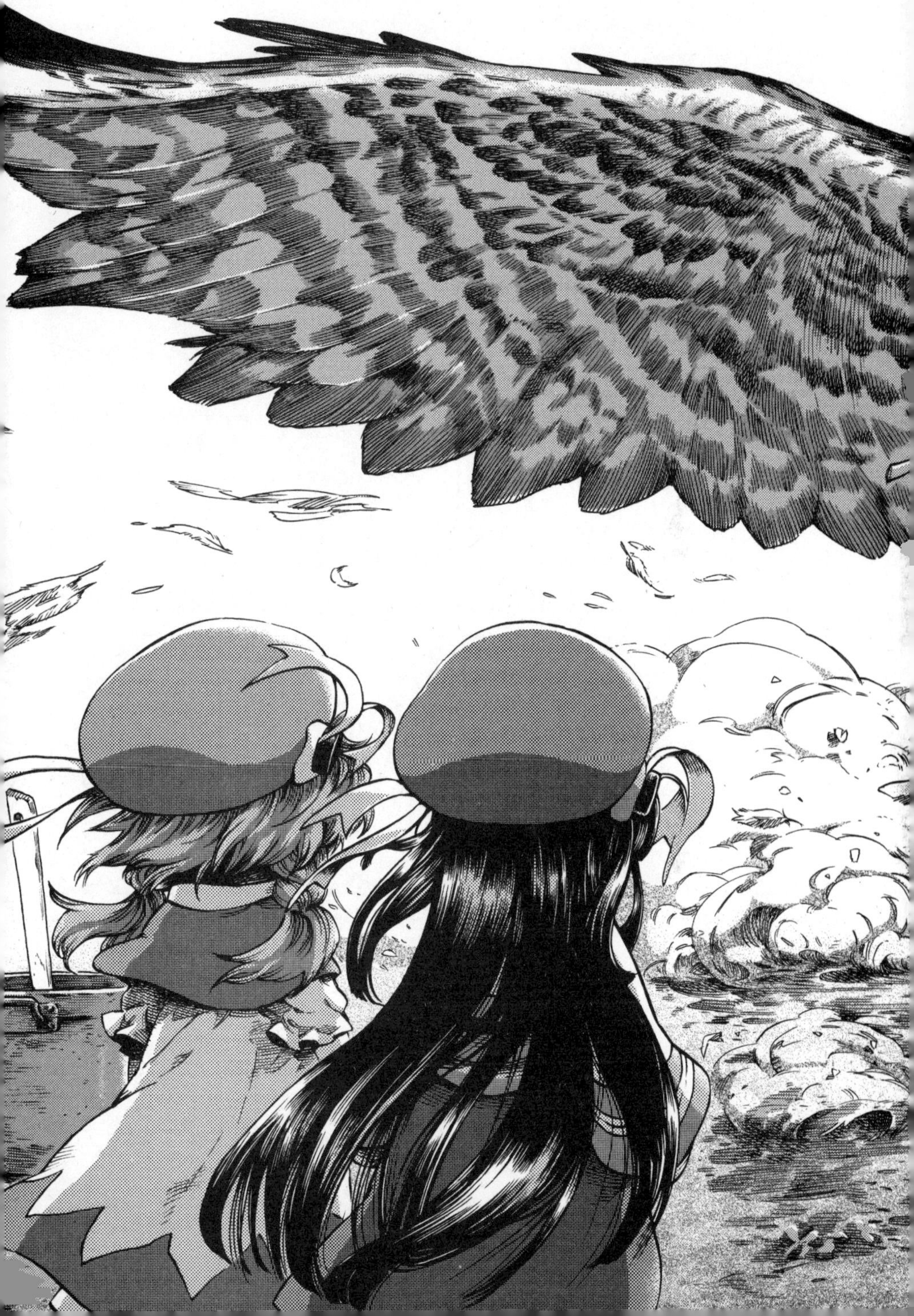

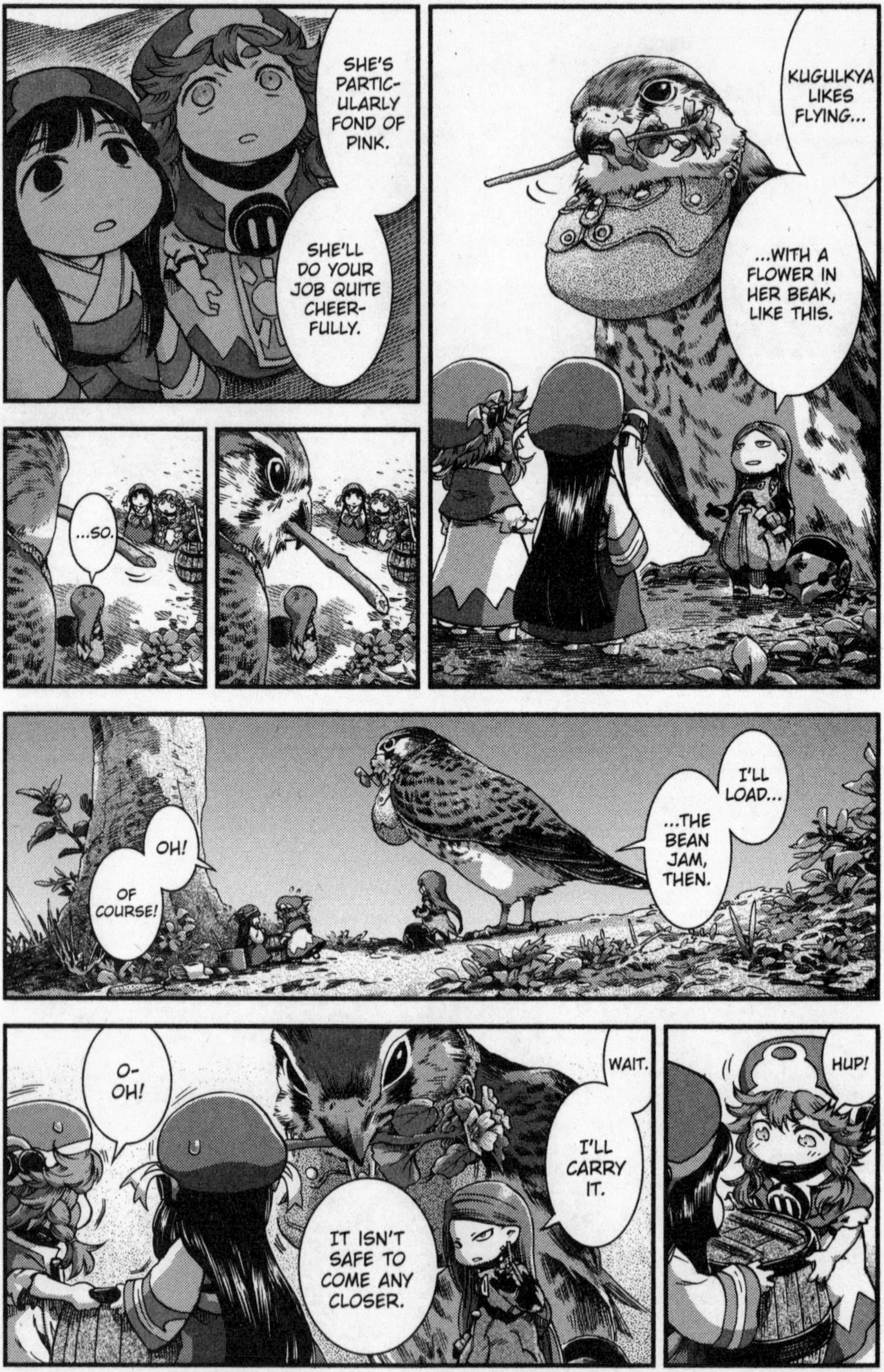
KUGULKYA LIKES FLYING...
...WITH A FLOWER IN HER BEAK, LIKE THIS.
SHE'S PARTICULARLY FOND OF PINK.
SHE'LL DO YOUR JOB QUITE CHEERFULLY.
...SO.
I'LL LOAD...
...THE BEAN JAM, THEN.
OH!
OF COURSE!
HUP!
WAIT.
I'LL CARRY IT.
IT ISN'T SAFE TO COME ANY CLOSER.
O-OH!

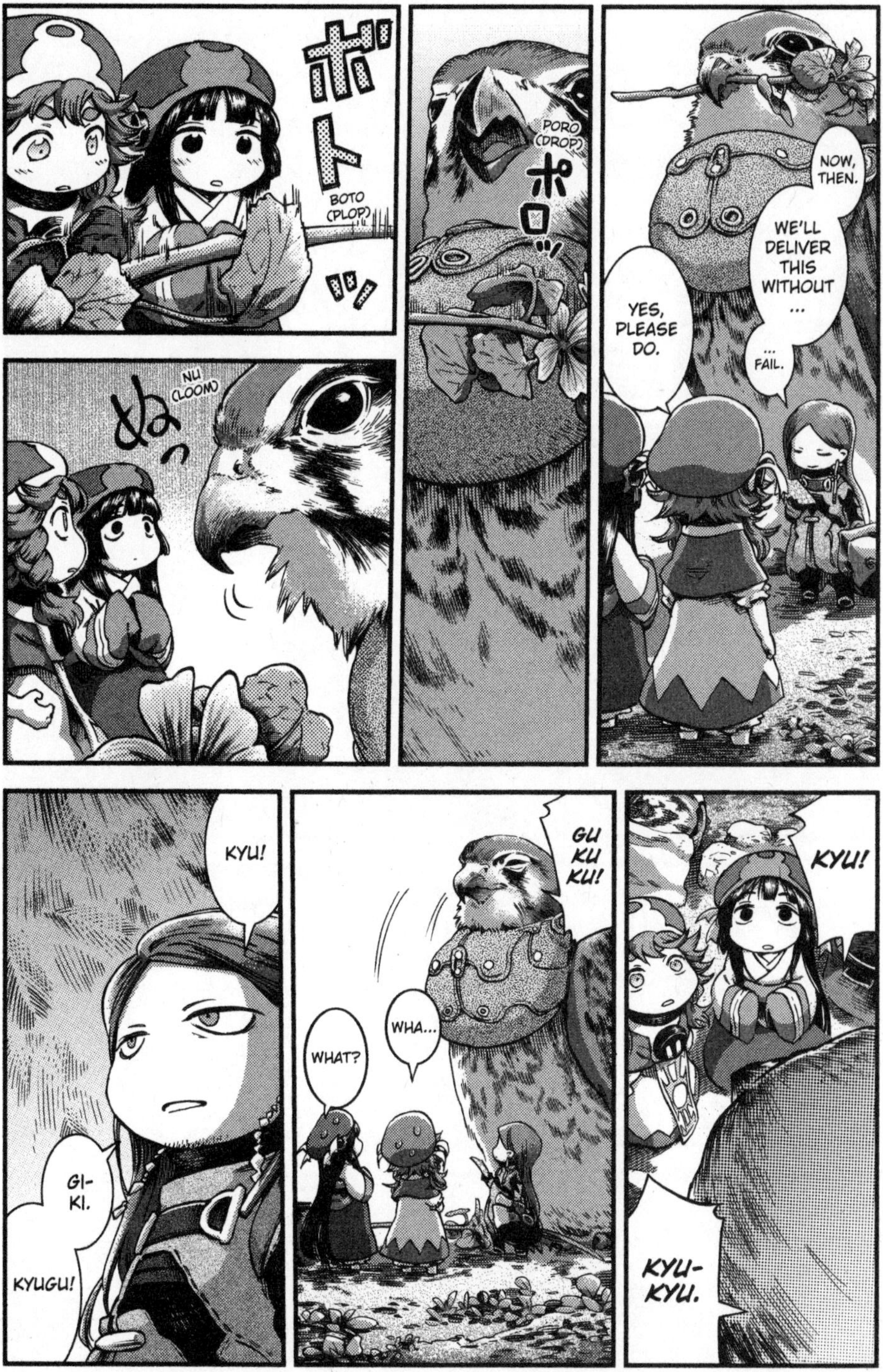
NOW, THEN.
WE'LL DELIVER THIS WITHOUT ...
... FAIL.
YES, PLEASE DO.
ポロッ
PORO (DROP)
ボト
BOTO (PLOP)
ッ!!
ぬっ
NU (LOOM)
KYU!
KYU-KYU.
GU KU KU!
WHA...
WHAT?
KYU!
GI-KI.
KYUGU!

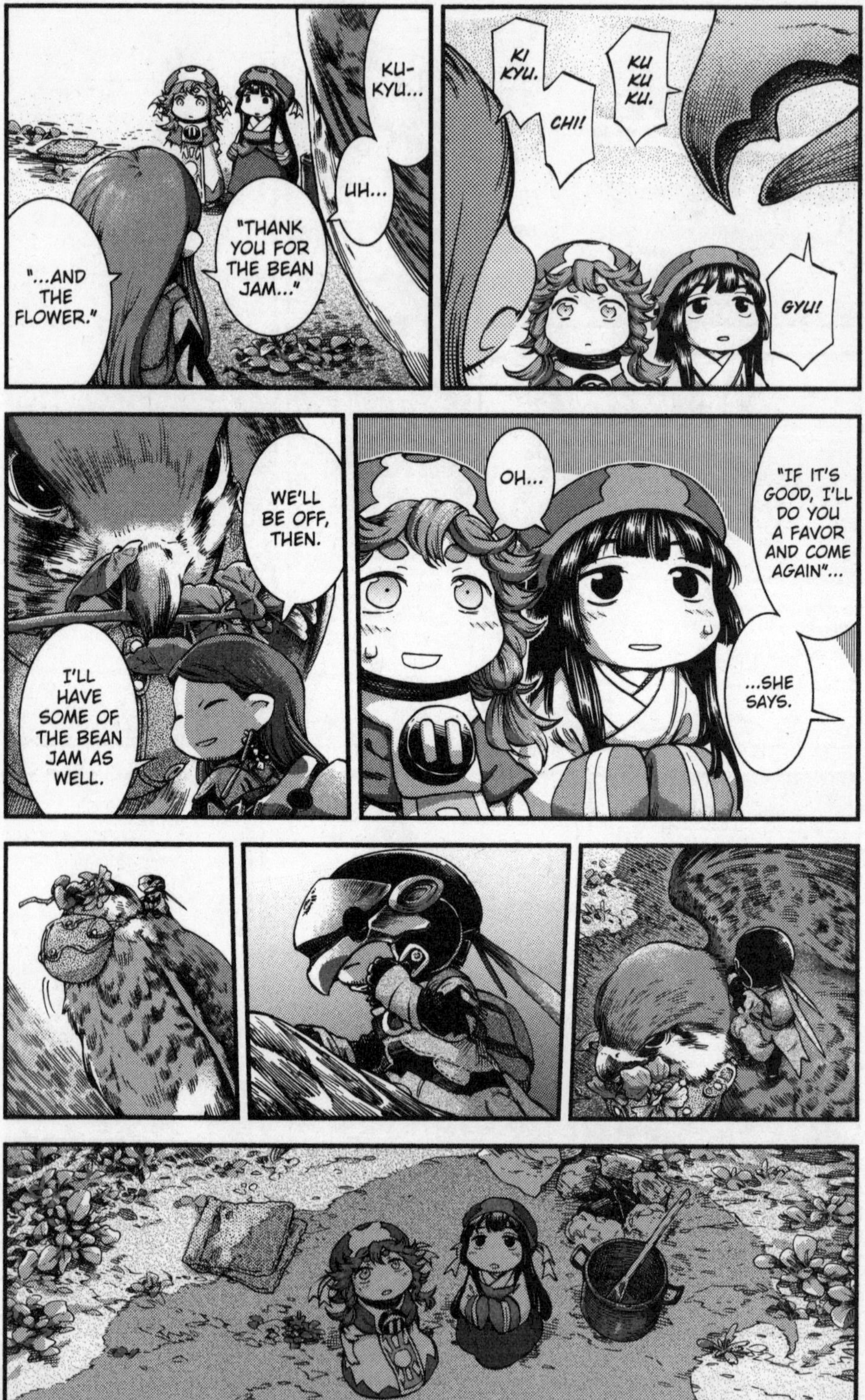
KU KU KU.
KI KYU.
CHI!
GYU!
KU-KYU...
UH...
"THANK YOU FOR THE BEAN JAM..."
"...AND THE FLOWER."
"IF IT'S GOOD, I'LL DO YOU A FAVOR AND COME AGAIN"...
OH...
...SHE SAYS.
WE'LL BE OFF, THEN.
I'LL HAVE SOME OF THE BEAN JAM AS WELL.

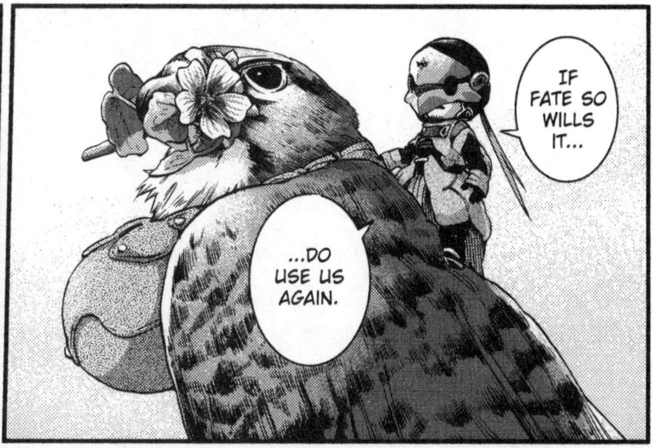
IF FATE SO WILLS IT...
...DO USE US AGAIN.
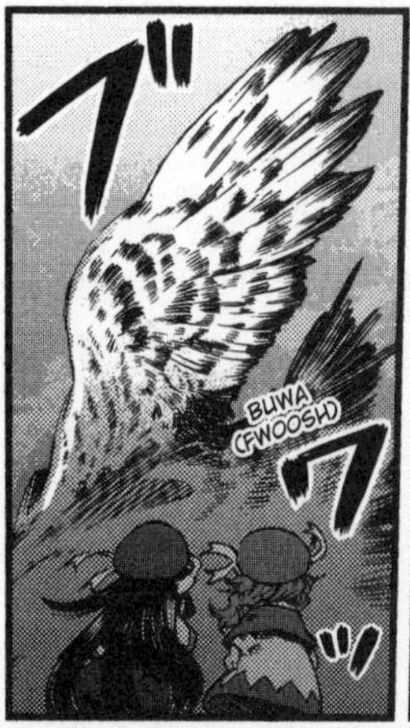
BUWA (FWOOSH)
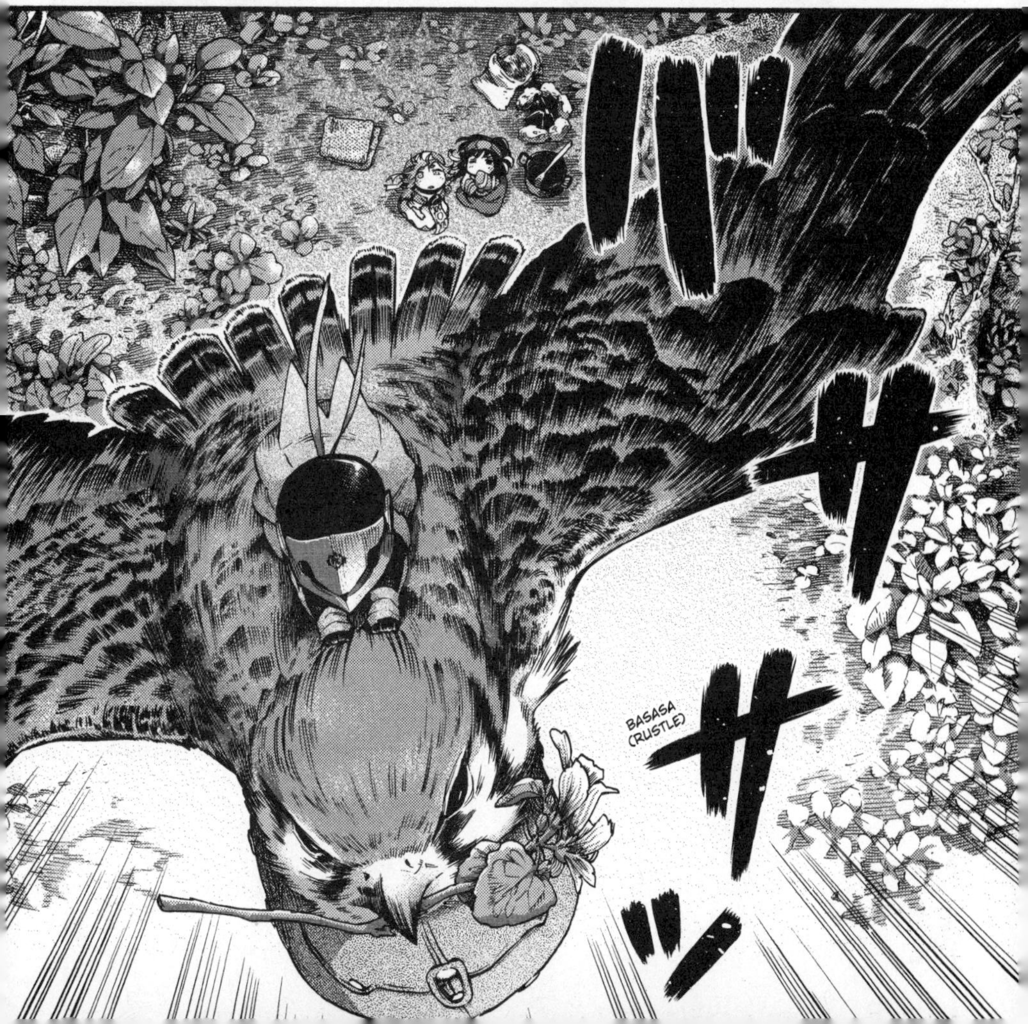
BASASA (RUSTLE)

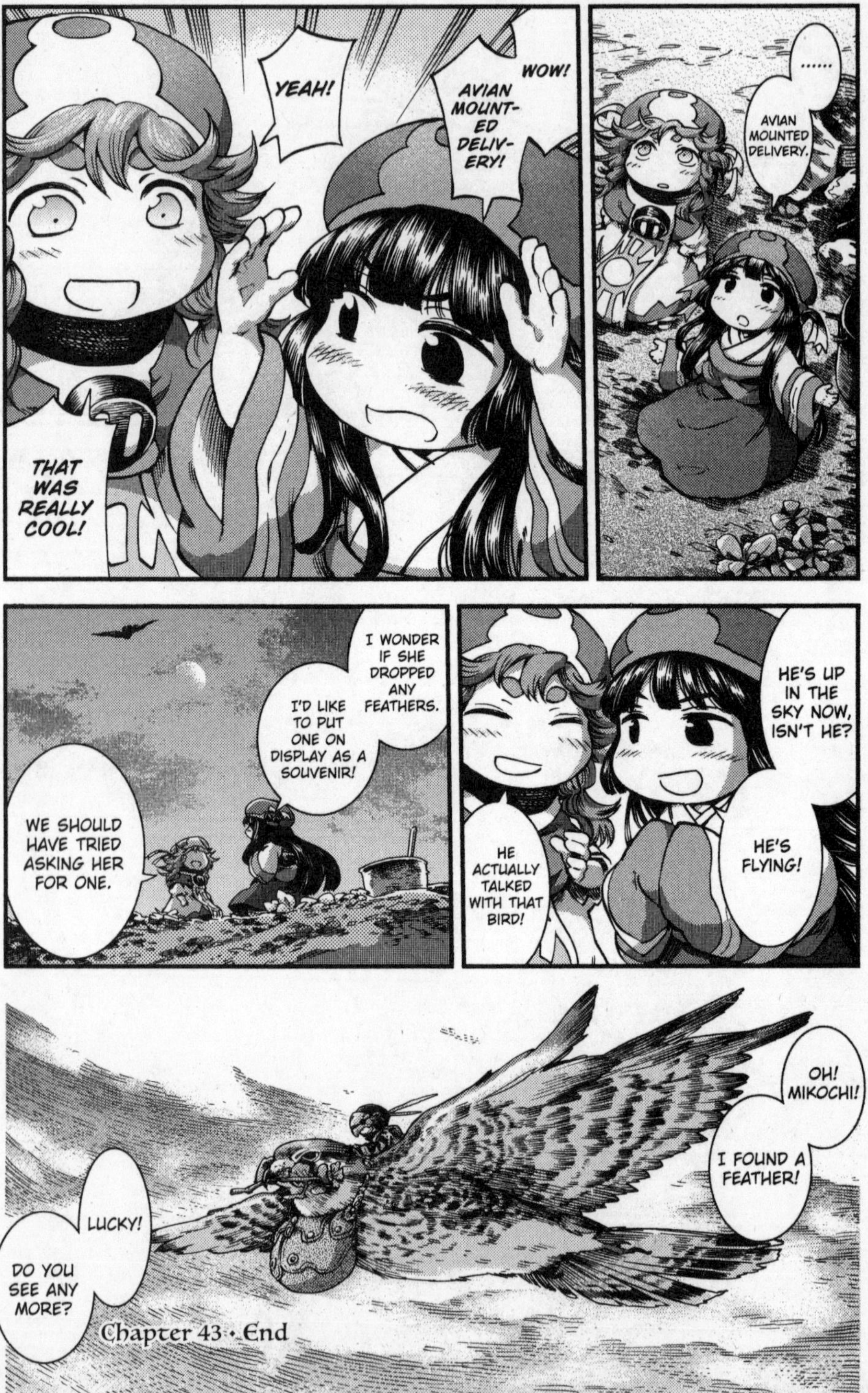
......
AVIAN MOUNTED DELIVERY.
WOW! AVIAN MOUNT-ED DELIV-ERY!
YEAH!
THAT WAS REALLY COOL!
HE'S UP IN THE SKY NOW, ISN'T HE?
HE'S FLYING!
HE ACTUALLY TALKED WITH THAT BIRD!
I WONDER IF SHE DROPPED ANY FEATHERS.
I'D LIKE TO PUT ONE ON DISPLAY AS A SOUVENIR!
WE SHOULD HAVE TRIED ASKING HER FOR ONE.
OH! MIKOCHI!
I FOUND A FEATHER!
LUCKY!
DO YOU SEE ANY MORE?
Chapter 43 • End

The term "feathertops" refers to the bird riders of
the Avian Mounted Delivery. Their main duties consist of
conversing with clients, interpreting the language of birds,
and managing the schedule.

In order to become a feathertop, a child under the age
of five must visit Sakazara, the Avian Mounted Delivery's
headquarters, and be chosen by a chick. Those who are
chosen begin training at Sakazara immediately, sleeping and
eating alongside the birds. When a feathertop masters the
language of birds, their bird gives them a name, and they are
registered as an official pair.

The term "feathertop" comes from the fact that, in the
distant past, riders stiffened their hair with wax and oil,
shaped it into wings, and used it to glide.

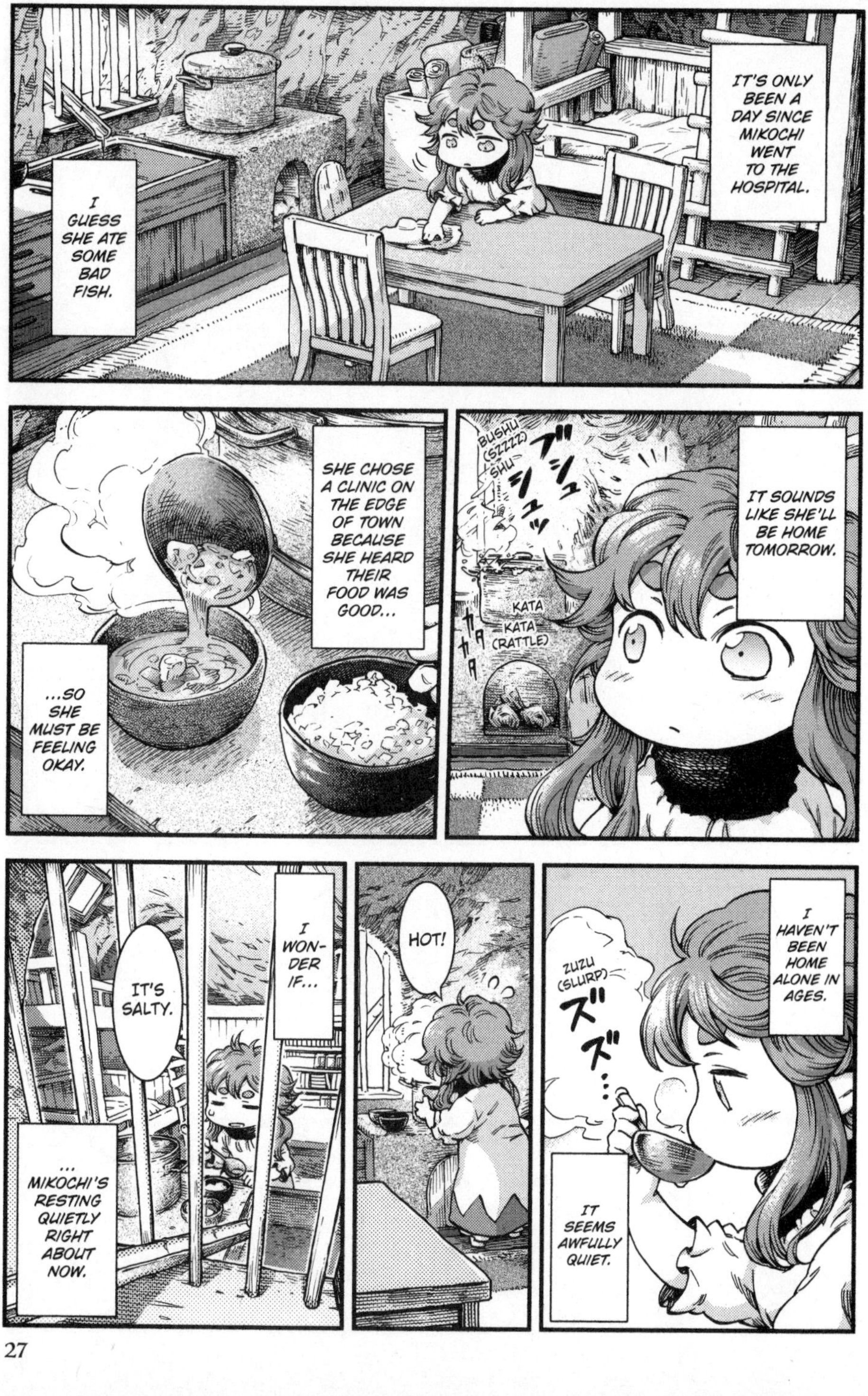
IT'S ONLY BEEN A DAY SINCE MIKOCHI WENT TO THE HOSPITAL.
I GUESS SHE ATE SOME BAD FISH.
IT SOUNDS LIKE SHE'LL BE HOME TOMORROW.
BUSHU (SZZZZ) SHU
ブシュ
シュッ
KATA KATA (RATTLE)
カタ
カタ
SHE CHOSE A CLINIC ON THE EDGE OF TOWN BECAUSE SHE HEARD THEIR FOOD WAS GOOD...
...SO SHE MUST BE FEELING OKAY.
I HAVEN'T BEEN HOME ALONE IN AGES.
ZUZU (SLURP)
ズズ...
IT SEEMS AWFULLY QUIET.
HOT!
I WONDER IF...
IT'S SALTY.
...MIKOCHI'S RESTING QUIETLY RIGHT ABOUT NOW.

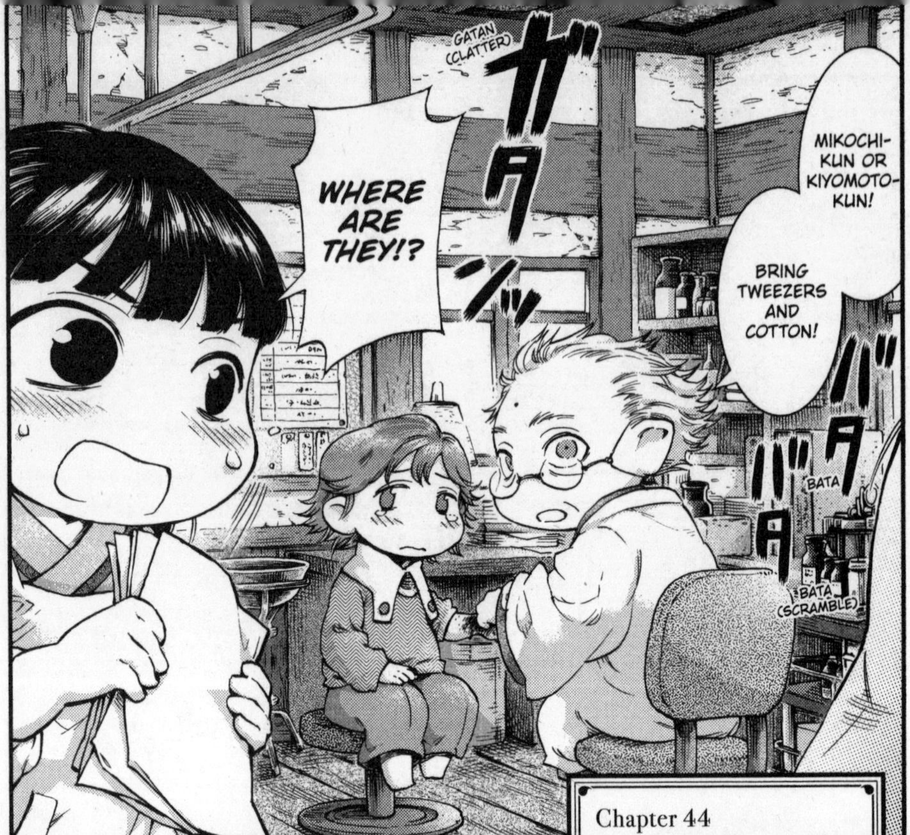
GATAN (CLATTER)
MIKOCHI-KUN OR KIYOMOTO-KUN!
BRING TWEEZERS AND COTTON!
BATA
BATA (SCRAMBLE)
WHERE ARE THEY!?

Chapter 44

The Clinic on the Edge of Town

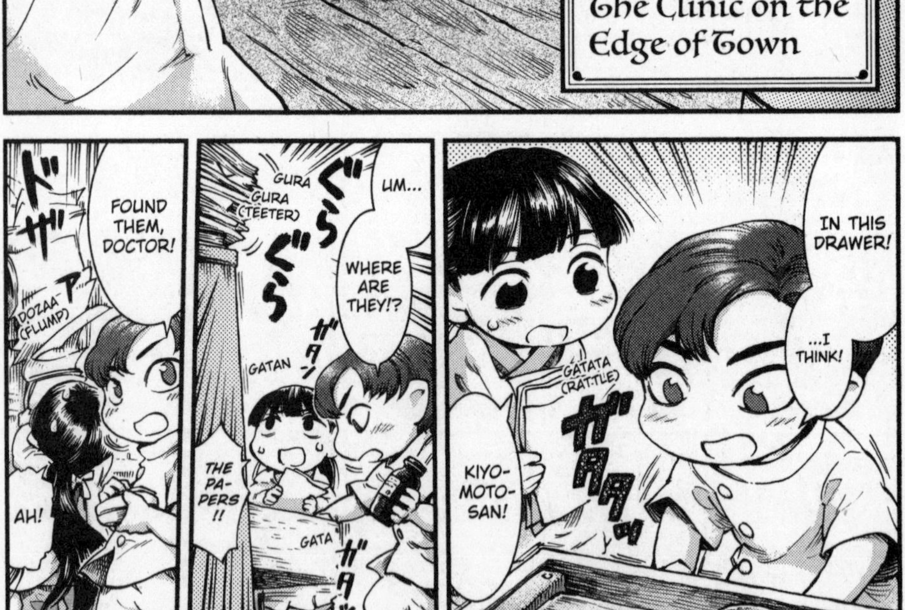
IN THIS DRAWER!
...I THINK!
GATATA (RATTLE)
KIYOMOTO-SAN!
UM...
WHERE ARE THEY!?
GURA GURA (TEETER)
GATAN
THE PAPERS!!
GATA
FOUND THEM, DOCTOR!
DOZAA (FLUMP)
AH!

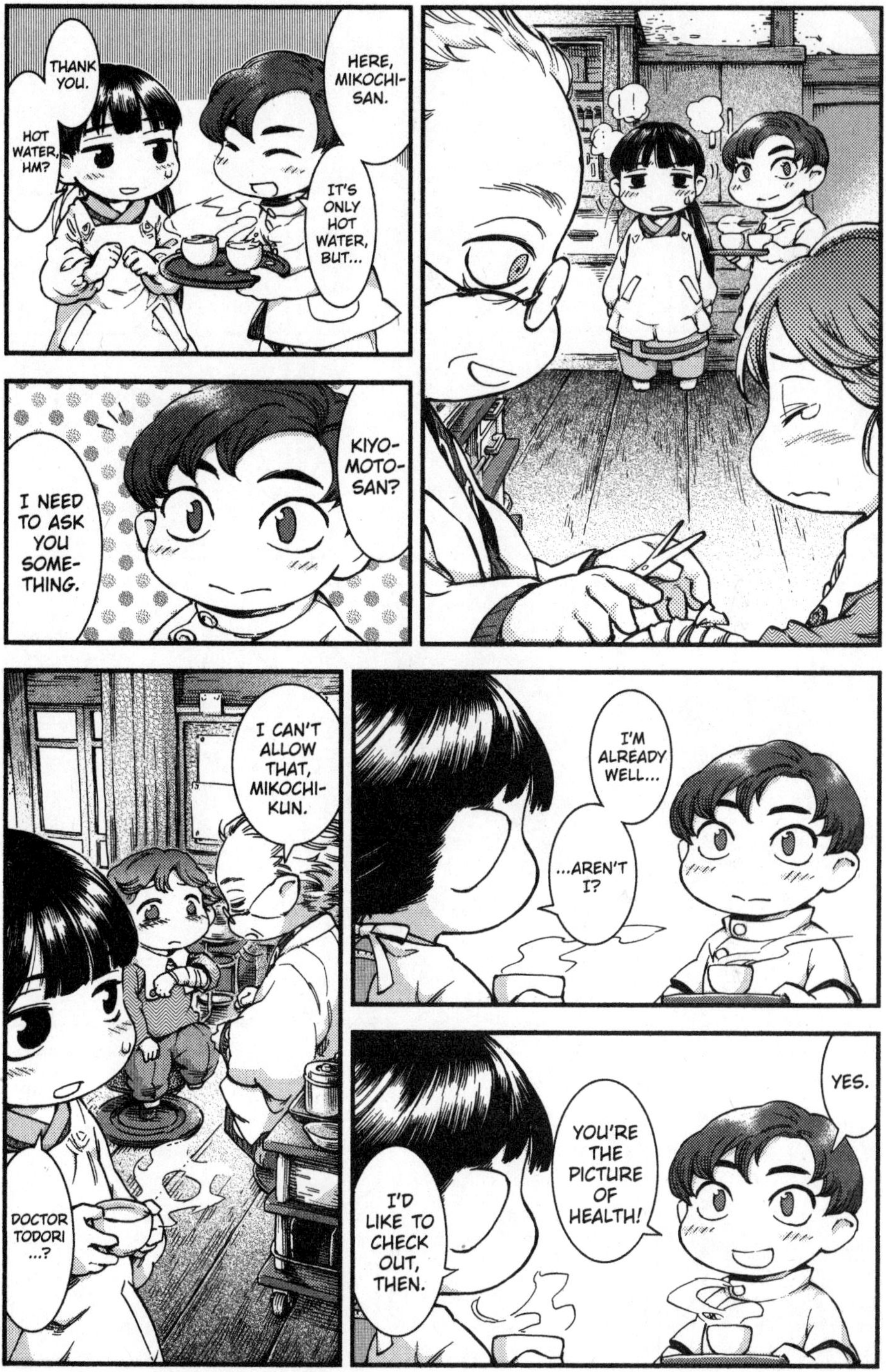
HERE, MIKOCHI-SAN.
IT'S ONLY HOT WATER, BUT...
THANK YOU.
HOT WATER, HM?
KIYOMOTO-SAN?
I NEED TO ASK YOU SOMETHING.
I'M ALREADY WELL...
...AREN'T I?
YES.
YOU'RE THE PICTURE OF HEALTH!
I'D LIKE TO CHECK OUT, THEN.
I CAN'T ALLOW THAT, MIKOCHI-KUN.
DOCTOR TODORI ...?

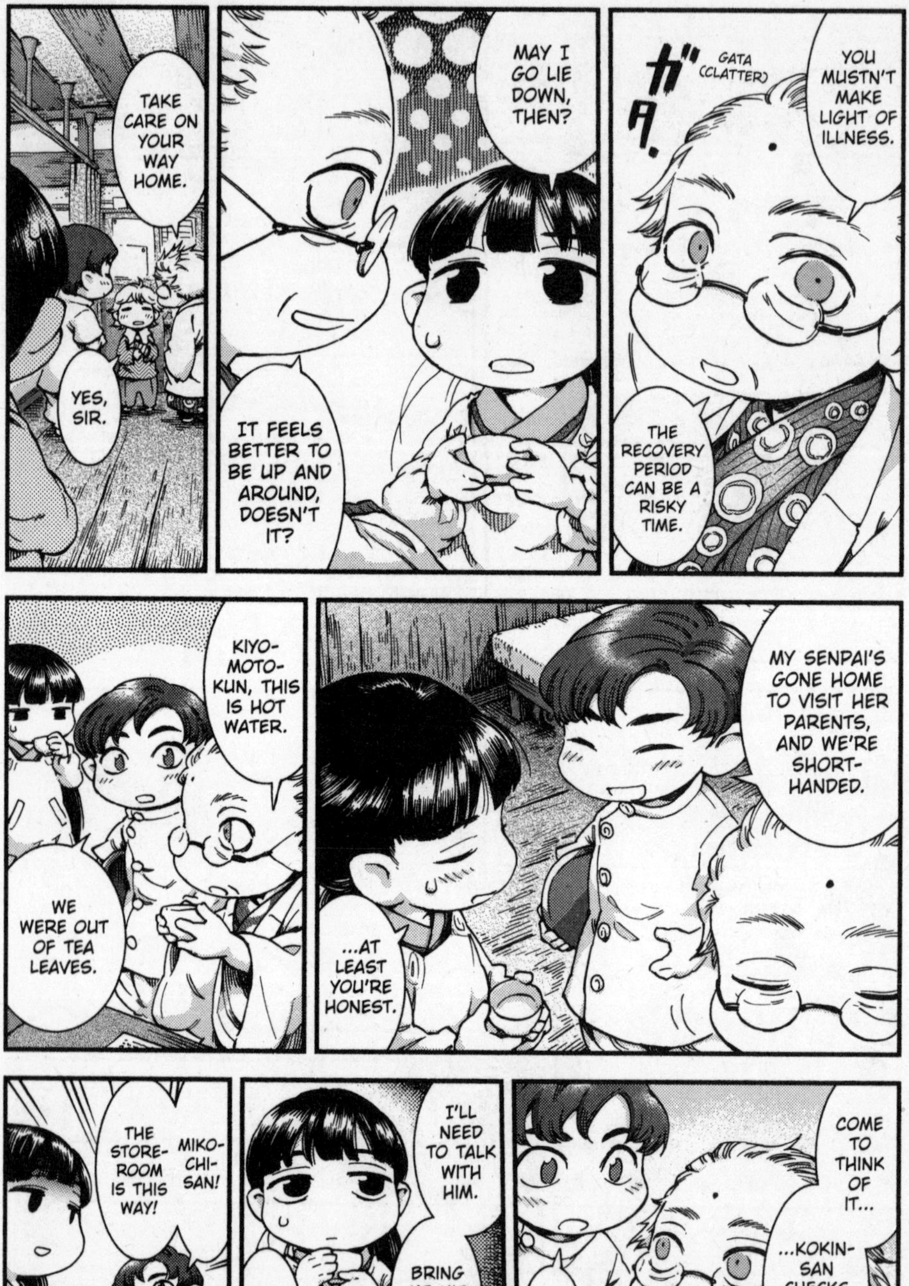
ガタ
GATA (CLATTER)
YOU MUSTN'T MAKE LIGHT OF ILLNESS.
THE RECOVERY PERIOD CAN BE A RISKY TIME.
MAY I GO LIE DOWN, THEN?
IT FEELS BETTER TO BE UP AND AROUND, DOESN'T IT?
TAKE CARE ON YOUR WAY HOME.
YES, SIR.
MY SENPAI'S GONE HOME TO VISIT HER PARENTS, AND WE'RE SHORT-HANDED.
...AT LEAST YOU'RE HONEST.
KIYO-MOTO-KUN, THIS IS HOT WATER.
WE WERE OUT OF TEA LEAVES.
COME TO THINK OF IT...
...KOKIN-SAN CHECKS OUT TODAY.
YES.
I'LL NEED TO TALK WITH HIM.
BRING ME HIS HEALTH REPORT.
YES, SIR!
MIKO-CHI-SAN!
THE STORE-ROOM IS THIS WAY!
RIGHT.

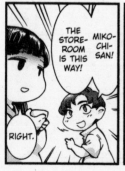

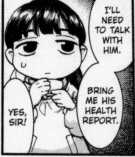

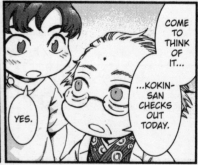

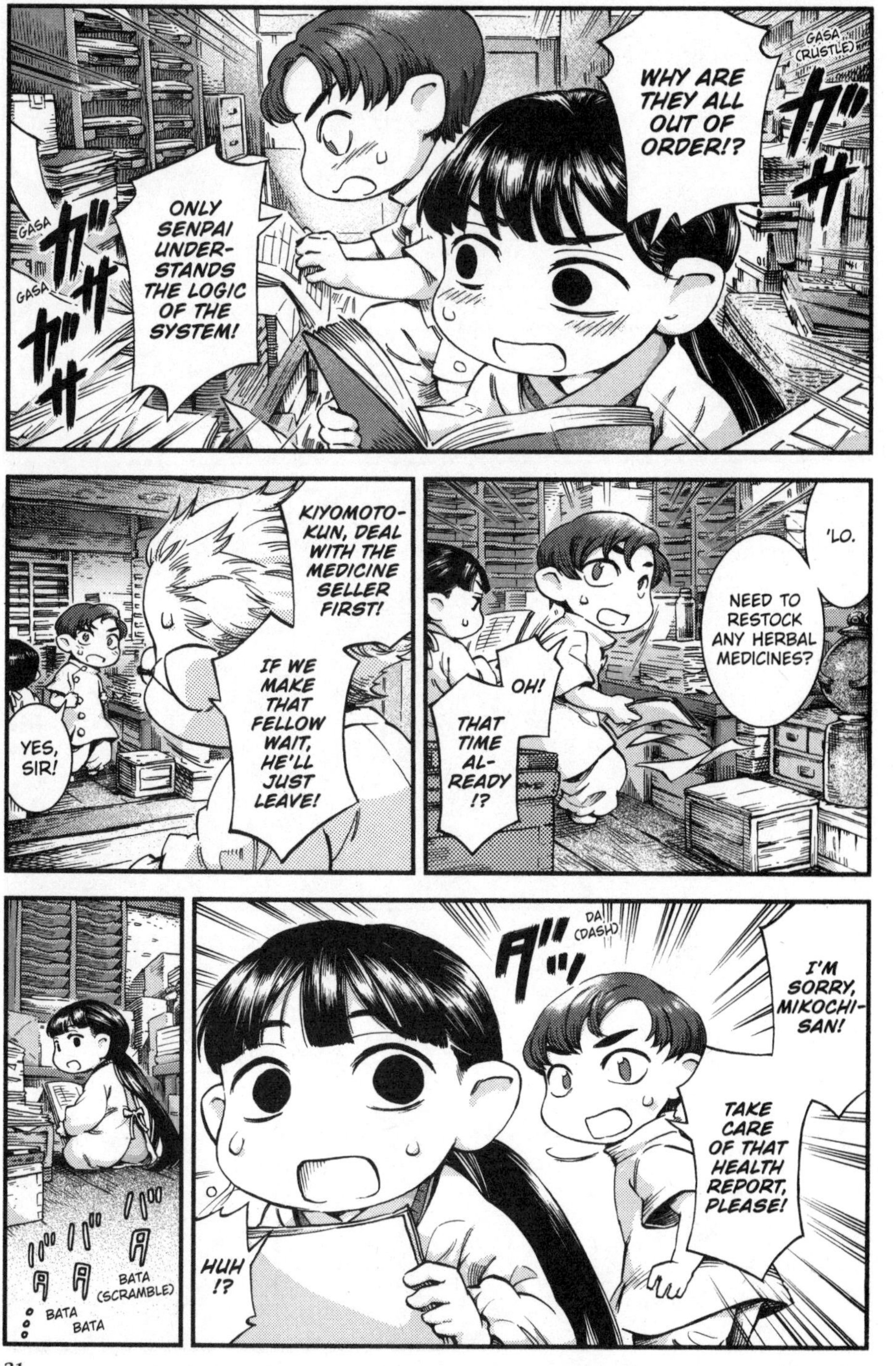
GASA (RUSTLE)
WHY ARE THEY ALL OUT OF ORDER!?
ONLY SENPAI UNDERSTANDS THE LOGIC OF THE SYSTEM!
GASA
GASA
'LO.
NEED TO RESTOCK ANY HERBAL MEDICINES?
OH!
THAT TIME ALREADY!?
KIYOMOTO-KUN, DEAL WITH THE MEDICINE SELLER FIRST!
IF WE MAKE THAT FELLOW WAIT, HE'LL JUST LEAVE!
YES, SIR!
DA (DASH)
I'M SORRY, MIKOCHI-SAN!
TAKE CARE OF THAT HEALTH REPORT, PLEASE!
HUH!?
BATA (SCRAMBLE)
BATA BATA

BOX: READY-ACCESS BOX FOR HEALTH REPORTS

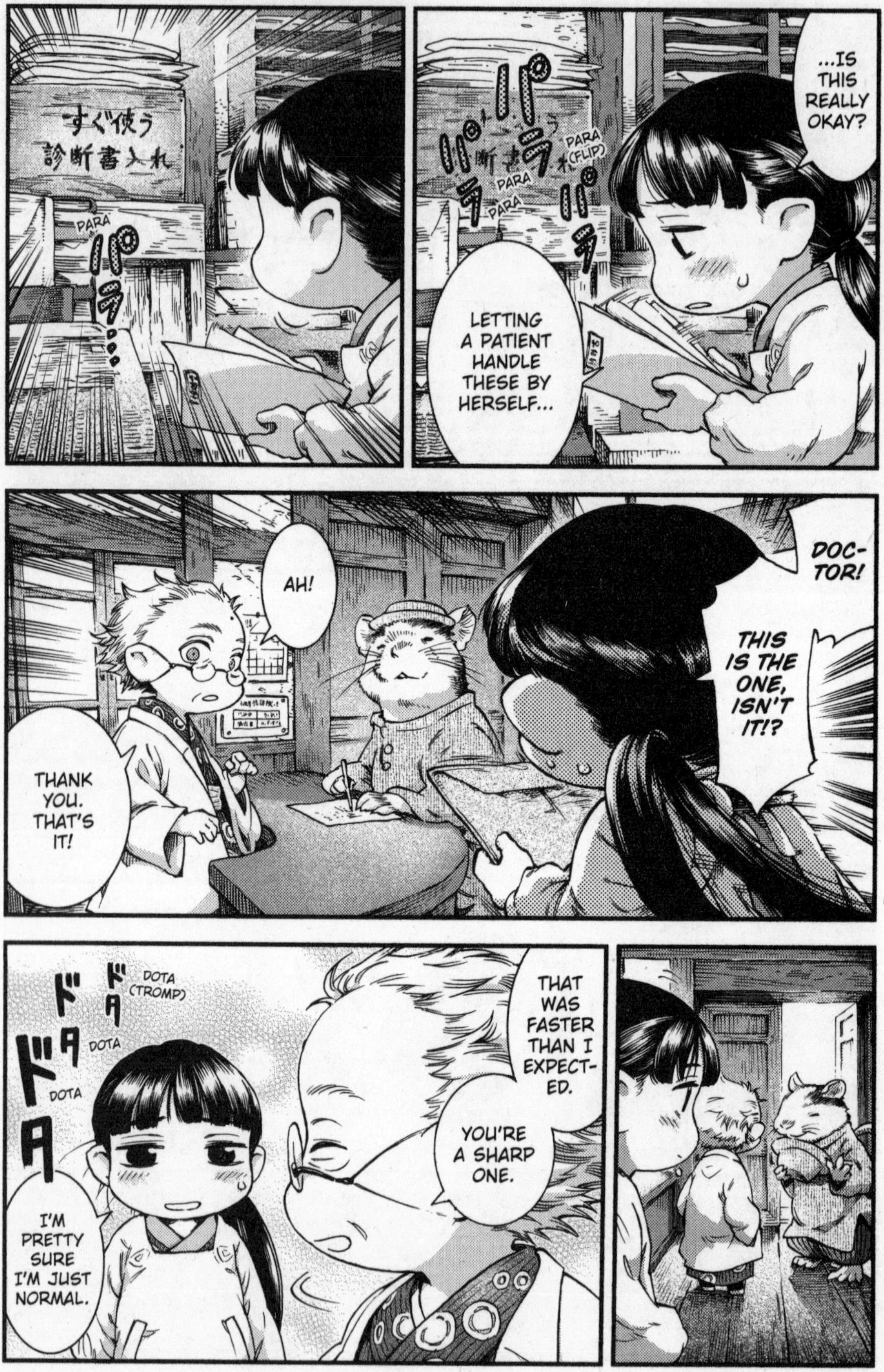
...IS THIS REALLY OKAY?
PARA (FLIP)
PARA
PARA
LETTING A PATIENT HANDLE THESE BY HERSELF...
すぐ使う
診断書入れ
PARA
DOCTOR!
THIS IS THE ONE, ISN'T IT!?
AH!
THANK YOU. THAT'S IT!
THAT WAS FASTER THAN I EXPECTED.
YOU'RE A SHARP ONE.
DOTA (TROMP)
DOTA
DOTA
I'M PRETTY SURE I'M JUST NORMAL.

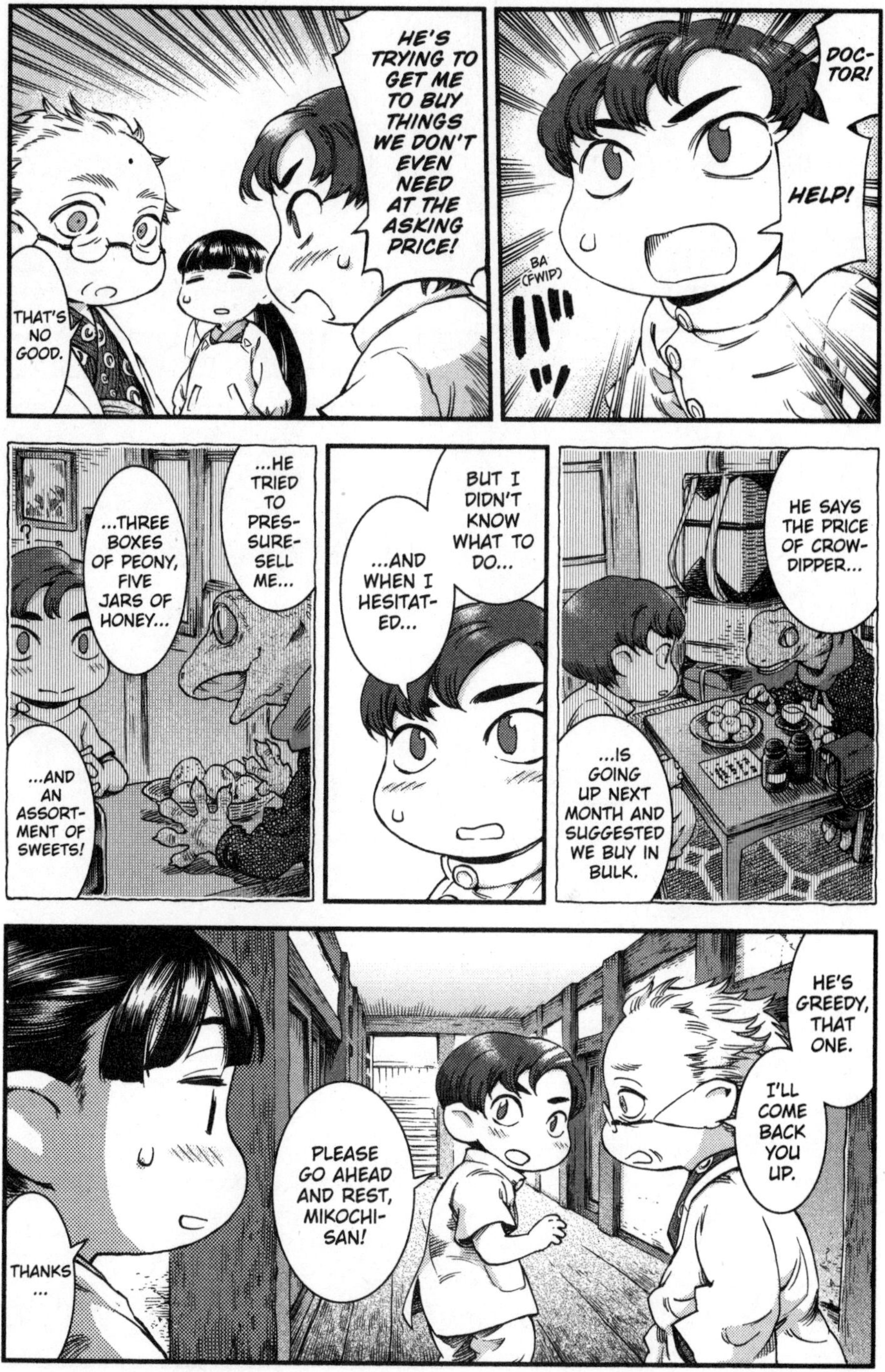
DOCTOR!
HELP!
BA (FWIP)
HE'S TRYING TO GET ME TO BUY THINGS WE DON'T EVEN NEED AT THE ASKING PRICE!
THAT'S NO GOOD.
HE SAYS THE PRICE OF CROW-DIPPER...
...IS GOING UP NEXT MONTH AND SUGGESTED WE BUY IN BULK.
BUT I DIDN'T KNOW WHAT TO DO...
...AND WHEN I HESITATED...
...HE TRIED TO PRESSURE-SELL ME...
...THREE BOXES OF PEONY, FIVE JARS OF HONEY...
...AND AN ASSORTMENT OF SWEETS!
HE'S GREEDY, THAT ONE.
I'LL COME BACK YOU UP.
PLEASE GO AHEAD AND REST, MIKOCHI-SAN!
THANKS...

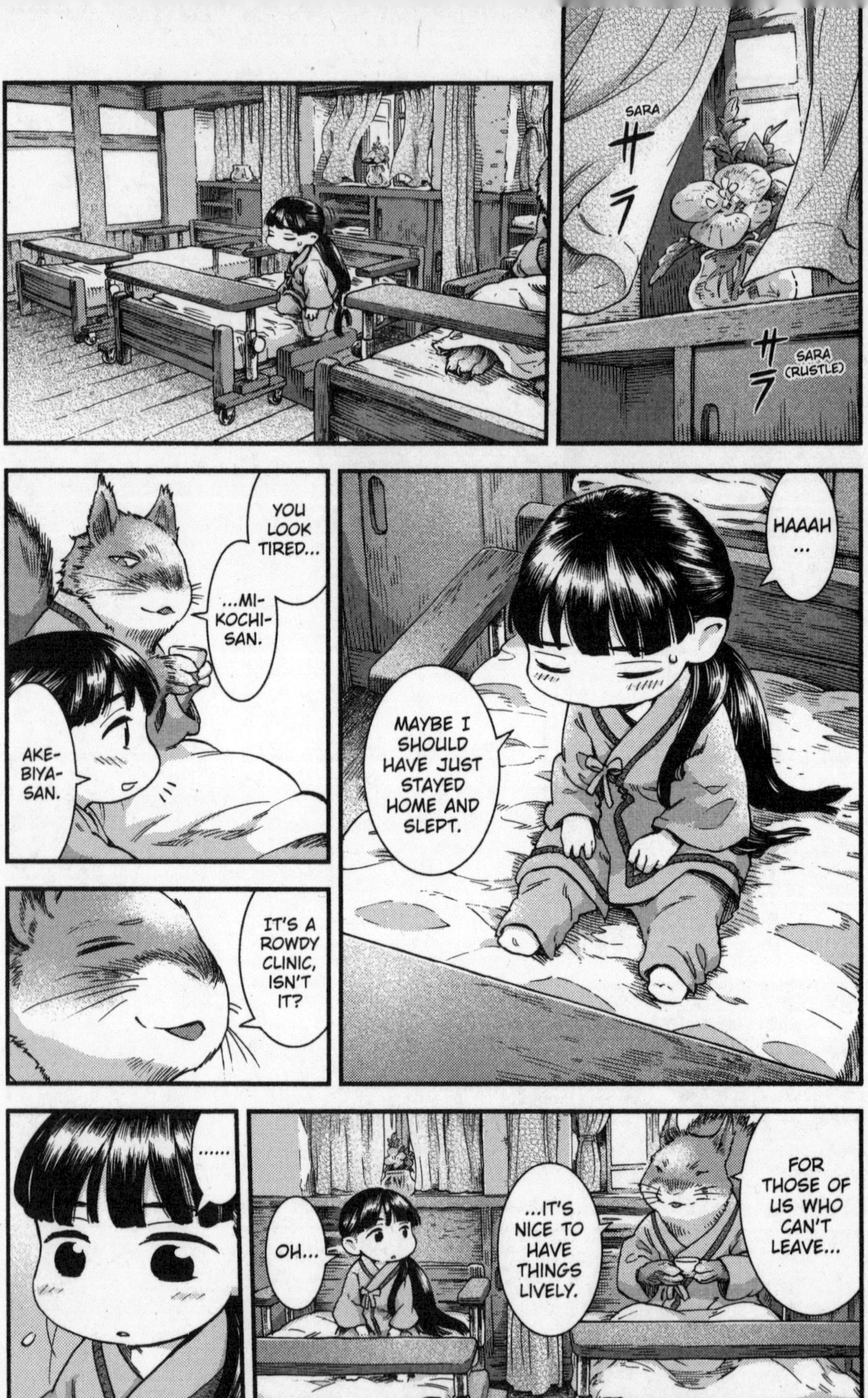
SARA
サラ
サラ
SARA (RUSTLE)
HAAAH...
MAYBE I SHOULD HAVE JUST STAYED HOME AND SLEPT.
YOU LOOK TIRED...
...MI-KOCHI-SAN.
AKE-BIYA-SAN.
IT'S A ROWDY CLINIC, ISN'T IT?
FOR THOSE OF US WHO CAN'T LEAVE...
...IT'S NICE TO HAVE THINGS LIVELY.
OH...
......

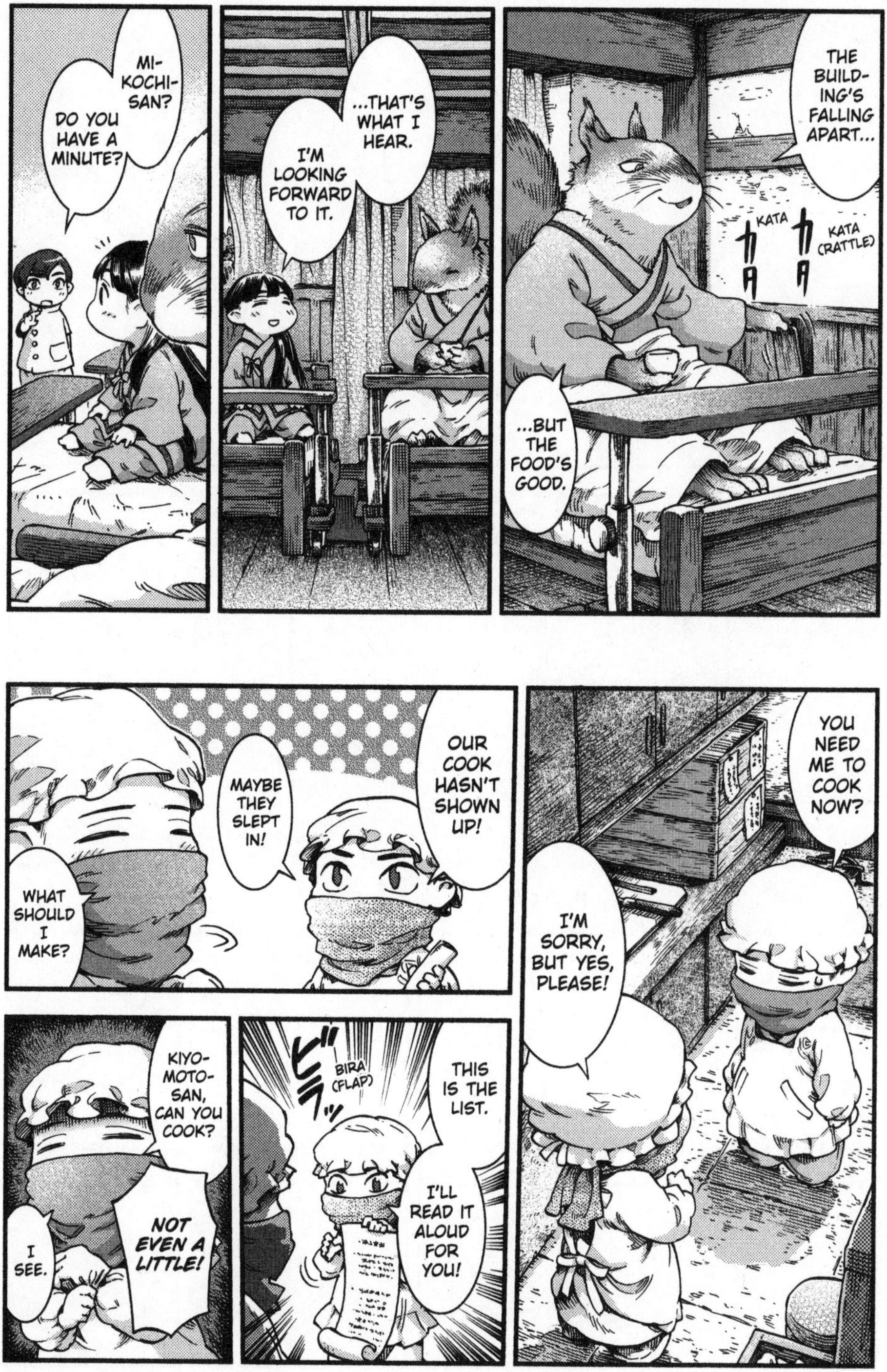
THE BUILDING'S FALLING APART...
カタ KATA
カタ KATA (RATTLE)
...BUT THE FOOD'S GOOD.
...THAT'S WHAT I HEAR.
I'M LOOKING FORWARD TO IT.
MI-KOCHI-SAN?
DO YOU HAVE A MINUTE?
YOU NEED ME TO COOK NOW?
I'M SORRY, BUT YES, PLEASE!
OUR COOK HASN'T SHOWN UP!
MAYBE THEY SLEPT IN!
WHAT SHOULD I MAKE?
ビラッ BIRA (FLAP)
THIS IS THE LIST.
I'LL READ IT ALOUD FOR YOU!
KIYO-MOTO-SAN, CAN YOU COOK?
NOT EVEN A LITTLE!
I SEE.

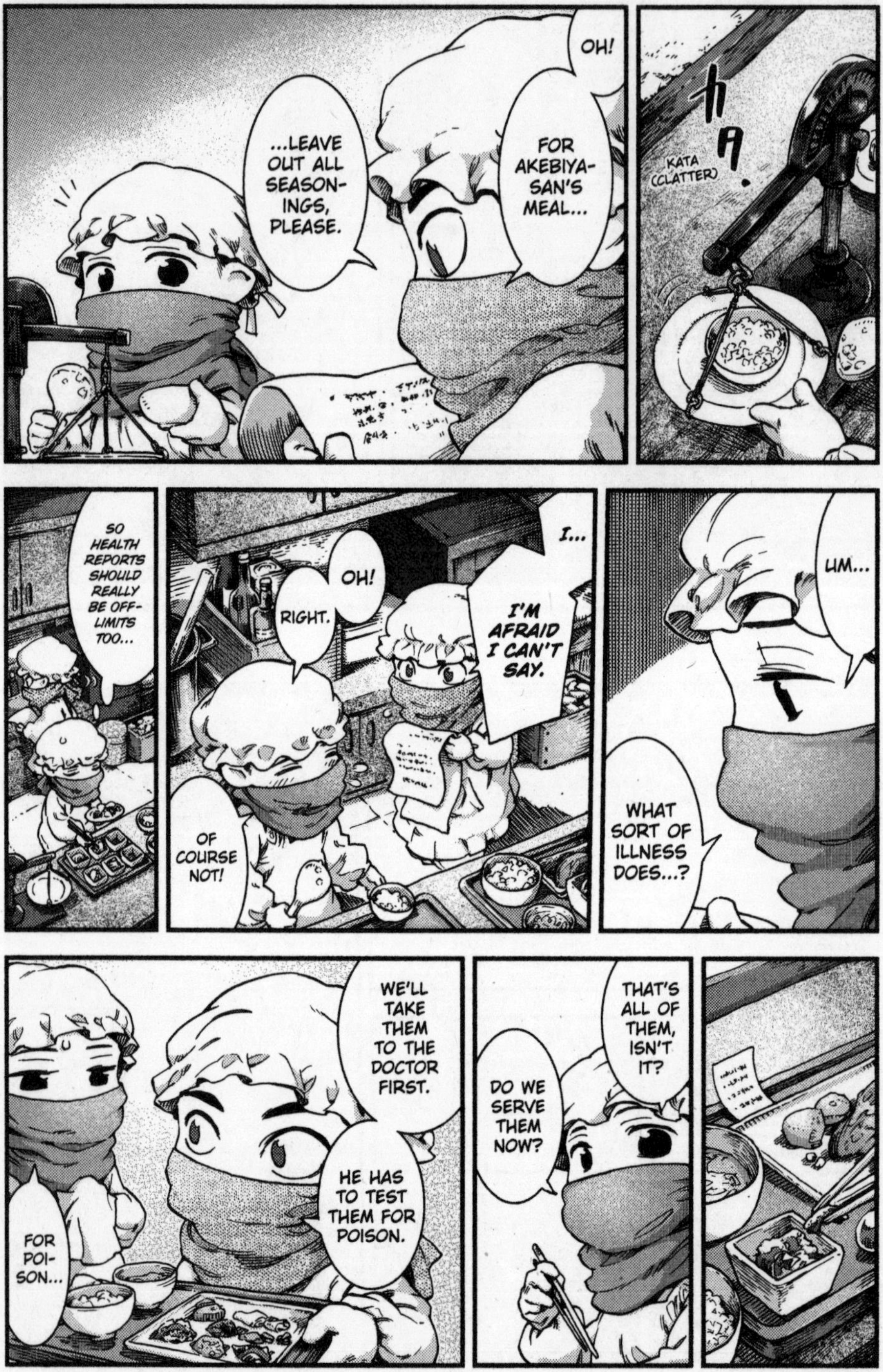
カタ
KATA (CLATTER)
OH!
FOR AKEBIYA-SAN'S MEAL...
...LEAVE OUT ALL SEASONINGS, PLEASE.
UM...
WHAT SORT OF ILLNESS DOES...?
I...
I'M AFRAID I CAN'T SAY.
OH!
RIGHT.
OF COURSE NOT!
SO HEALTH REPORTS SHOULD REALLY BE OFF-LIMITS TOO...
THAT'S ALL OF THEM, ISN'T IT?
DO WE SERVE THEM NOW?
WE'LL TAKE THEM TO THE DOCTOR FIRST.
HE HAS TO TEST THEM FOR POISON.
FOR POISON...

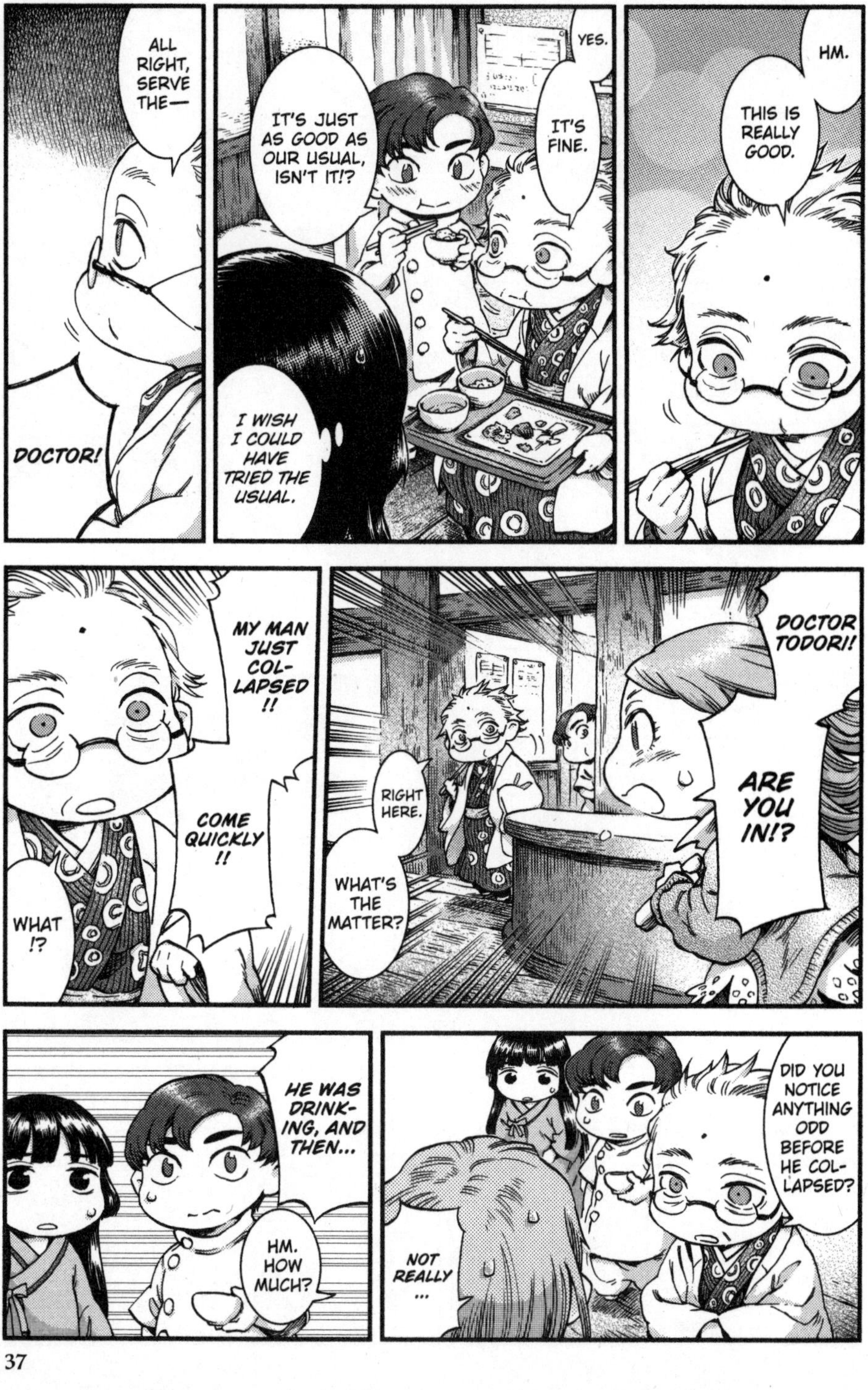
HM.
THIS IS REALLY GOOD.
YES.
IT'S FINE.
IT'S JUST AS GOOD AS OUR USUAL, ISN'T IT!?
I WISH I COULD HAVE TRIED THE USUAL.
ALL RIGHT, SERVE THE—
DOCTOR!
DOCTOR TODORI!
ARE YOU IN!?
RIGHT HERE.
WHAT'S THE MATTER?
MY MAN JUST COLLAPSED!!
COME QUICKLY!!
WHAT!?
DID YOU NOTICE ANYTHING ODD BEFORE HE COLLAPSED?
NOT REALLY...
HE WAS DRINKING, AND THEN...
HM. HOW MUCH?

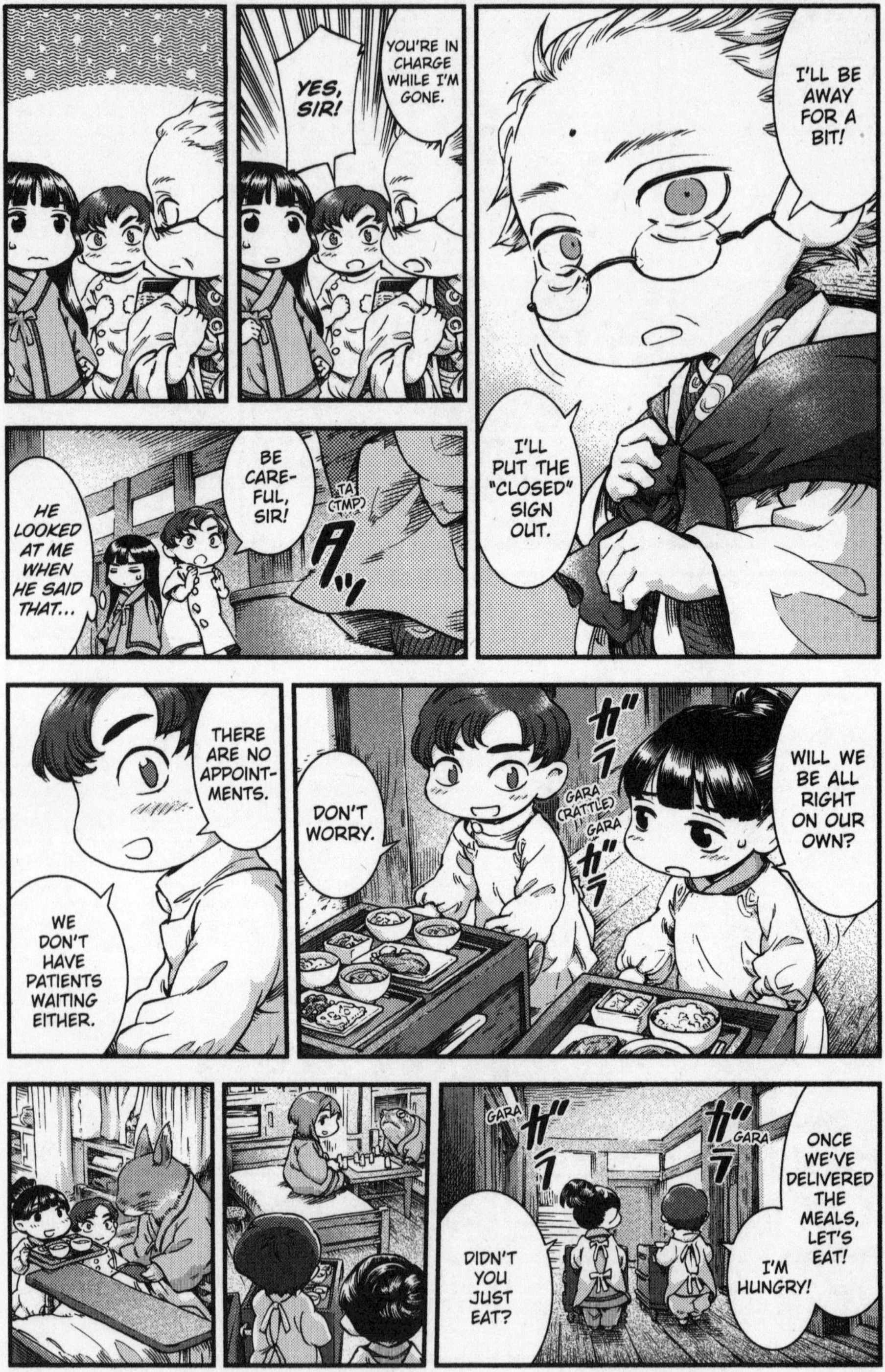
I'LL BE AWAY FOR A BIT!
I'LL PUT THE "CLOSED" SIGN OUT.
YOU'RE IN CHARGE WHILE I'M GONE.
YES, SIR!
BE CAREFUL, SIR!
TA (TMP)
HE LOOKED AT ME WHEN HE SAID THAT...
WILL WE BE ALL RIGHT ON OUR OWN?
GARA (RATTLE) GARA
DON'T WORRY.
THERE ARE NO APPOINTMENTS.
WE DON'T HAVE PATIENTS WAITING EITHER.
GARA
ONCE WE'VE DELIVERED THE MEALS, LET'S EAT!
I'M HUNGRY!
GARA
DIDN'T YOU JUST EAT?

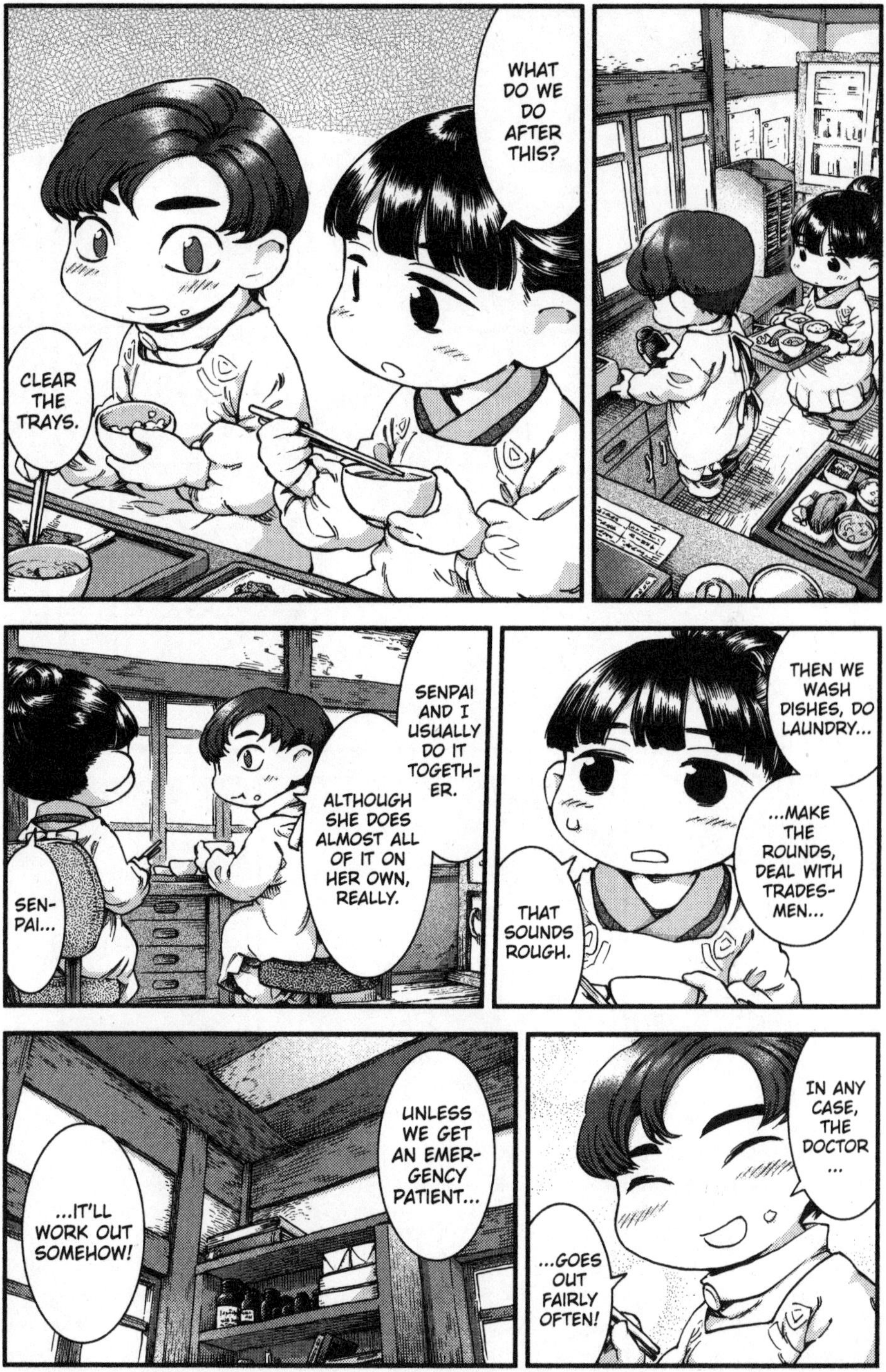
WHAT DO WE DO AFTER THIS?
CLEAR THE TRAYS.
THEN WE WASH DISHES, DO LAUNDRY...
...MAKE THE ROUNDS, DEAL WITH TRADES-MEN...
THAT SOUNDS ROUGH.
SENPAI AND I USUALLY DO IT TOGETH-ER.
ALTHOUGH SHE DOES ALMOST ALL OF IT ON HER OWN, REALLY.
SEN-PAI...
IN ANY CASE, THE DOCTOR ...
...GOES OUT FAIRLY OFTEN!
UNLESS WE GET AN EMER-GENCY PATIENT...
...IT'LL WORK OUT SOMEHOW!

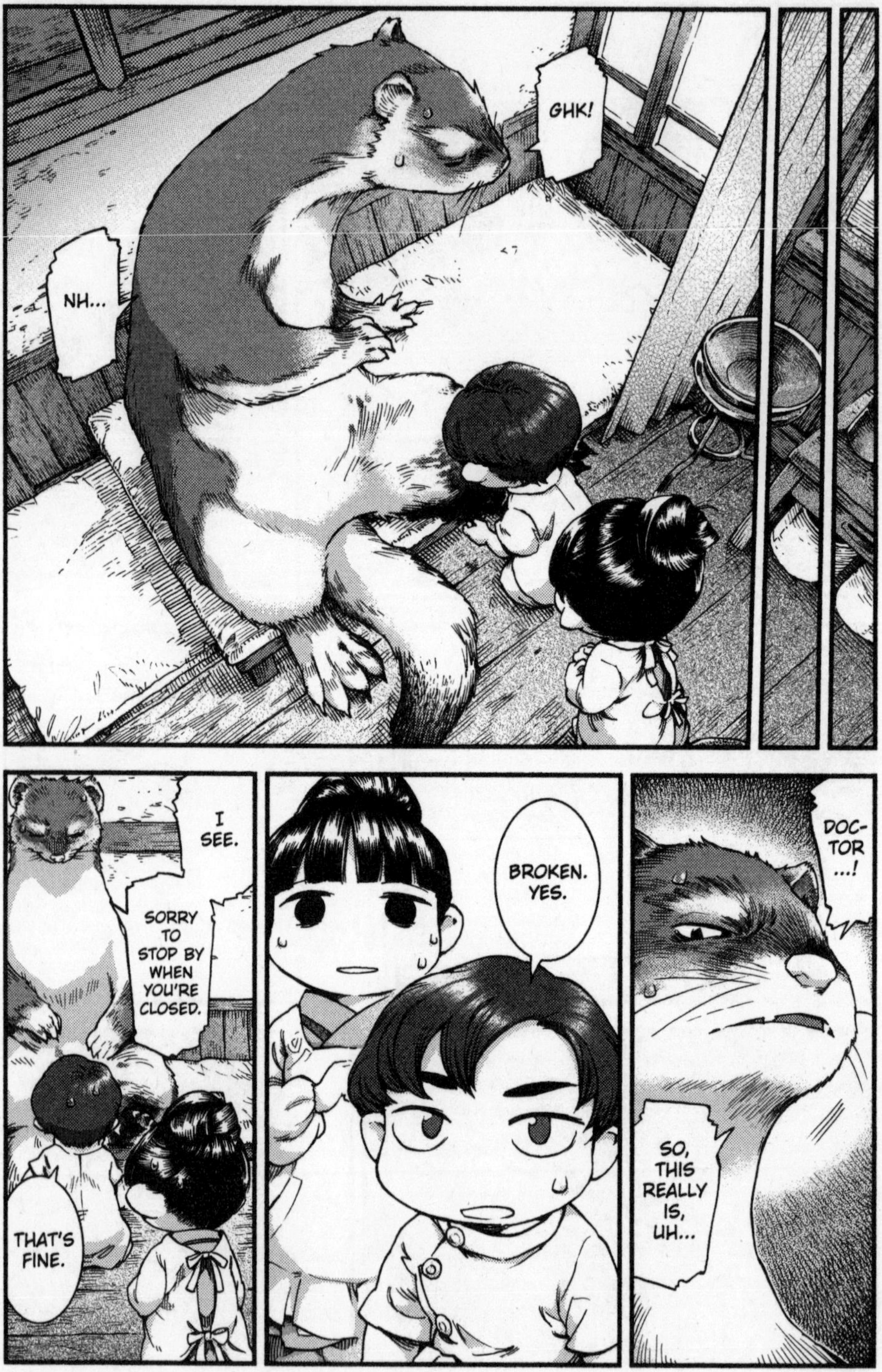
GHK!
NH...
DOC-TOR ...!
SO, THIS REALLY IS, UH...
BROKEN. YES.
I SEE.
SORRY TO STOP BY WHEN YOU'RE CLOSED.
THAT'S FINE.

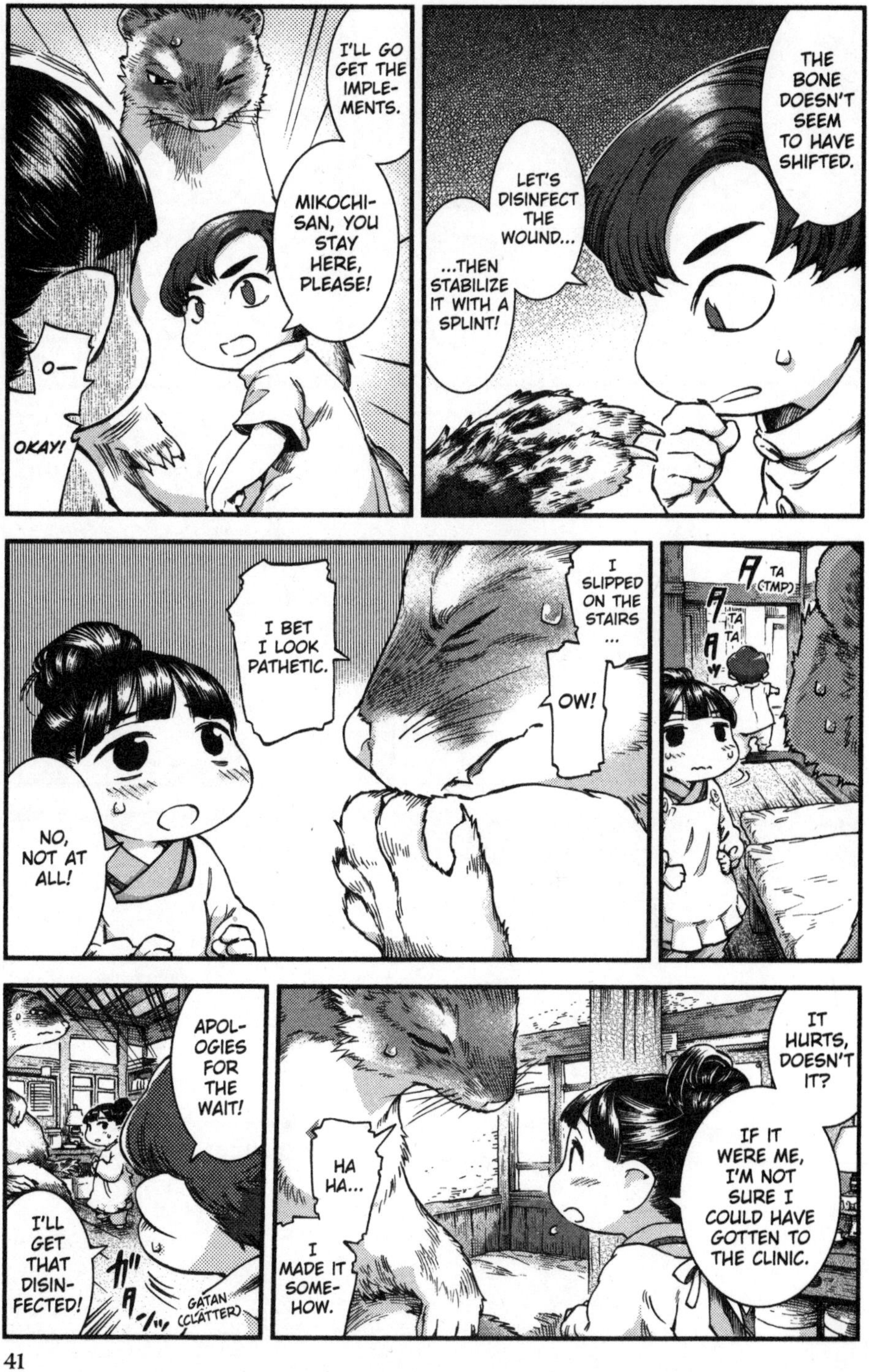
THE BONE DOESN'T SEEM TO HAVE SHIFTED.
LET'S DISINFECT THE WOUND...
...THEN STABILIZE IT WITH A SPLINT!
I'LL GO GET THE IMPLEMENTS.
MIKOCHI-SAN, YOU STAY HERE, PLEASE!
O—
OKAY!
TA (TMP)
TA
TA
I SLIPPED ON THE STAIRS ...
OW!
I BET I LOOK PATHETIC.
NO, NOT AT ALL!
IT HURTS, DOESN'T IT?
IF IT WERE ME, I'M NOT SURE I COULD HAVE GOTTEN TO THE CLINIC.
HA HA...
I MADE IT SOMEHOW.
APOLOGIES FOR THE WAIT!
I'LL GET THAT DISINFECTED!
GATAN (CLATTER)

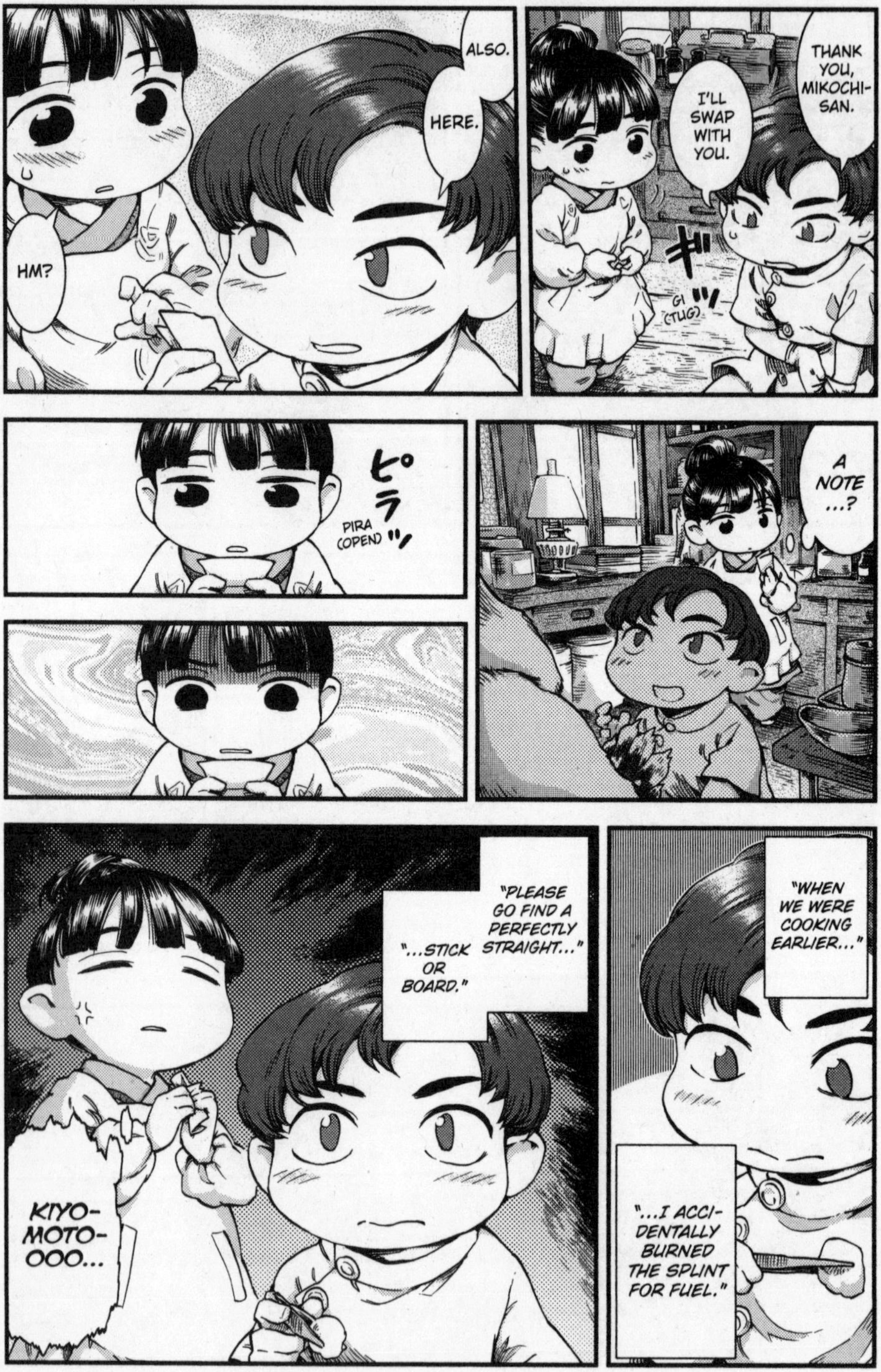
THANK YOU, MIKOCHI-SAN.
I'LL SWAP WITH YOU.
ギッ
GI (TUG)
ALSO.
HERE.
HM?
A NOTE ...?
ピラッ
PIRA (OPEN)
"WHEN WE WERE COOKING EARLIER..."
"...I ACCIDENTALLY BURNED THE SPLINT FOR FUEL."
"PLEASE GO FIND A PERFECTLY STRAIGHT..."
"...STICK OR BOARD."
KIYO-MOTO-OOO...

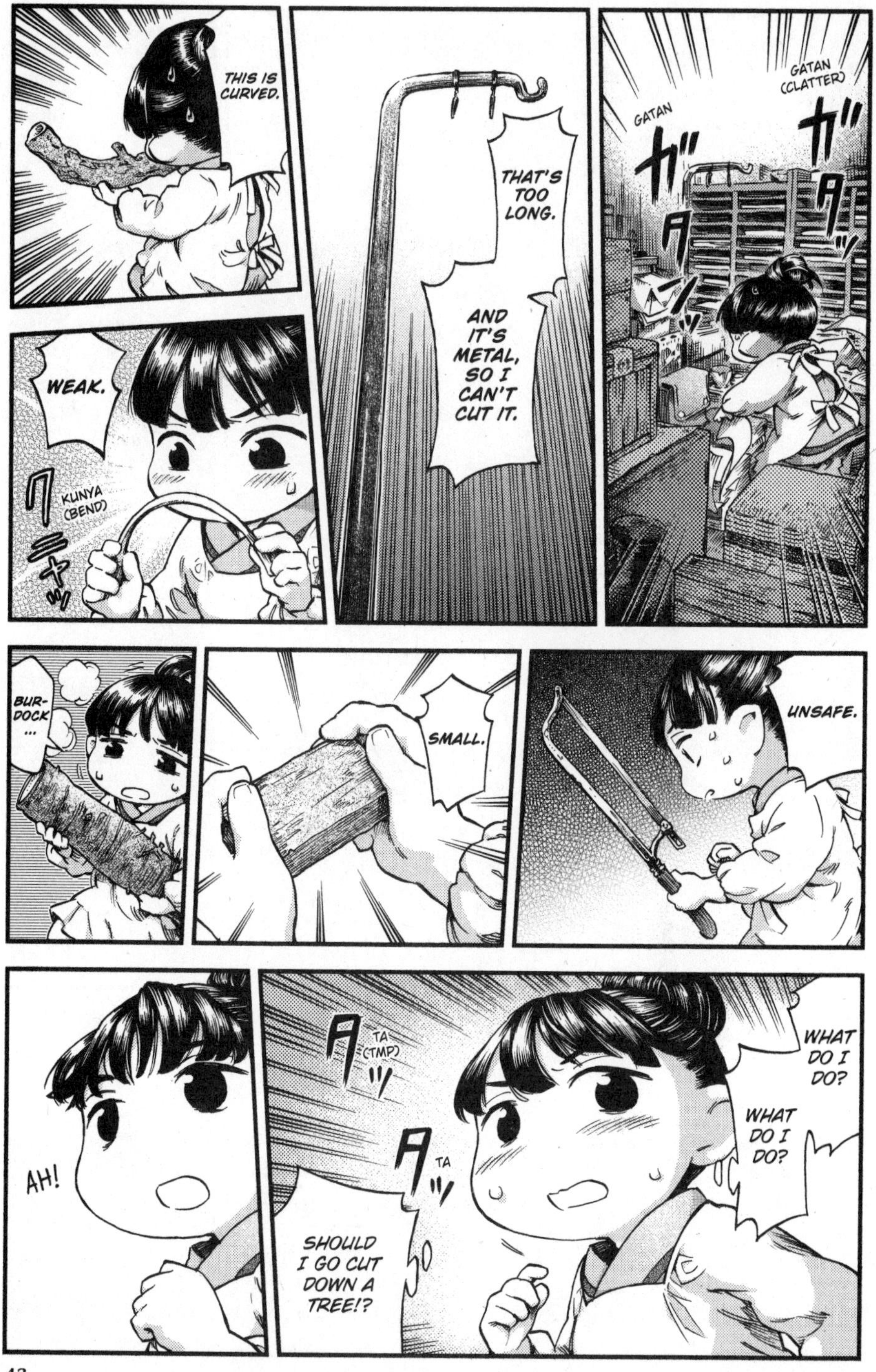

GATAN (CLATTER)
GATAN
THAT'S TOO LONG.
AND IT'S METAL, SO I CAN'T CUT IT.
THIS IS CURVED.
WEAK.
KUNYA (BEND)
UNSAFE.
SMALL.
BURDOCK...
WHAT DO I DO?
WHAT DO I DO?
TA (TMP)
TA
SHOULD I GO CUT DOWN A TREE!?
AH!

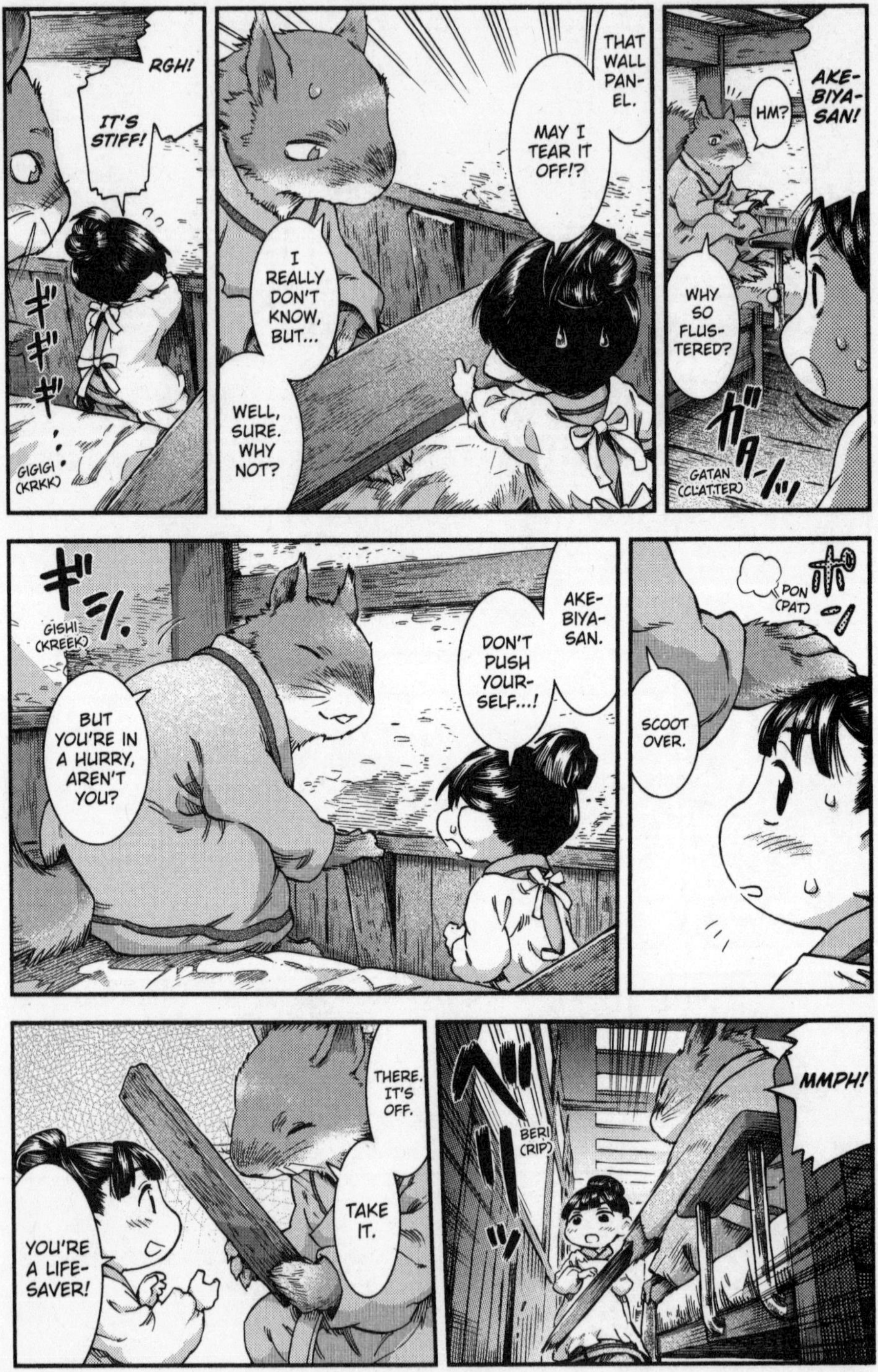
AKEBIYA-SAN!
HM?
WHY SO FLUSTERED?
GATAN (CLATTER)
THAT WALL PANEL. MAY I TEAR IT OFF!?
I REALLY DON'T KNOW, BUT...
WELL, SURE. WHY NOT?
RGH!
IT'S STIFF!
GIGIGI (KRKK)
PON (PAT)
SCOOT OVER.
AKEBIYA-SAN. DON'T PUSH YOURSELF...!
BUT YOU'RE IN A HURRY, AREN'T YOU?
GISHI (KREEK)
MMPH!
BERI (RIP)
THERE. IT'S OFF.
TAKE IT.
YOU'RE A LIFE-SAVER!

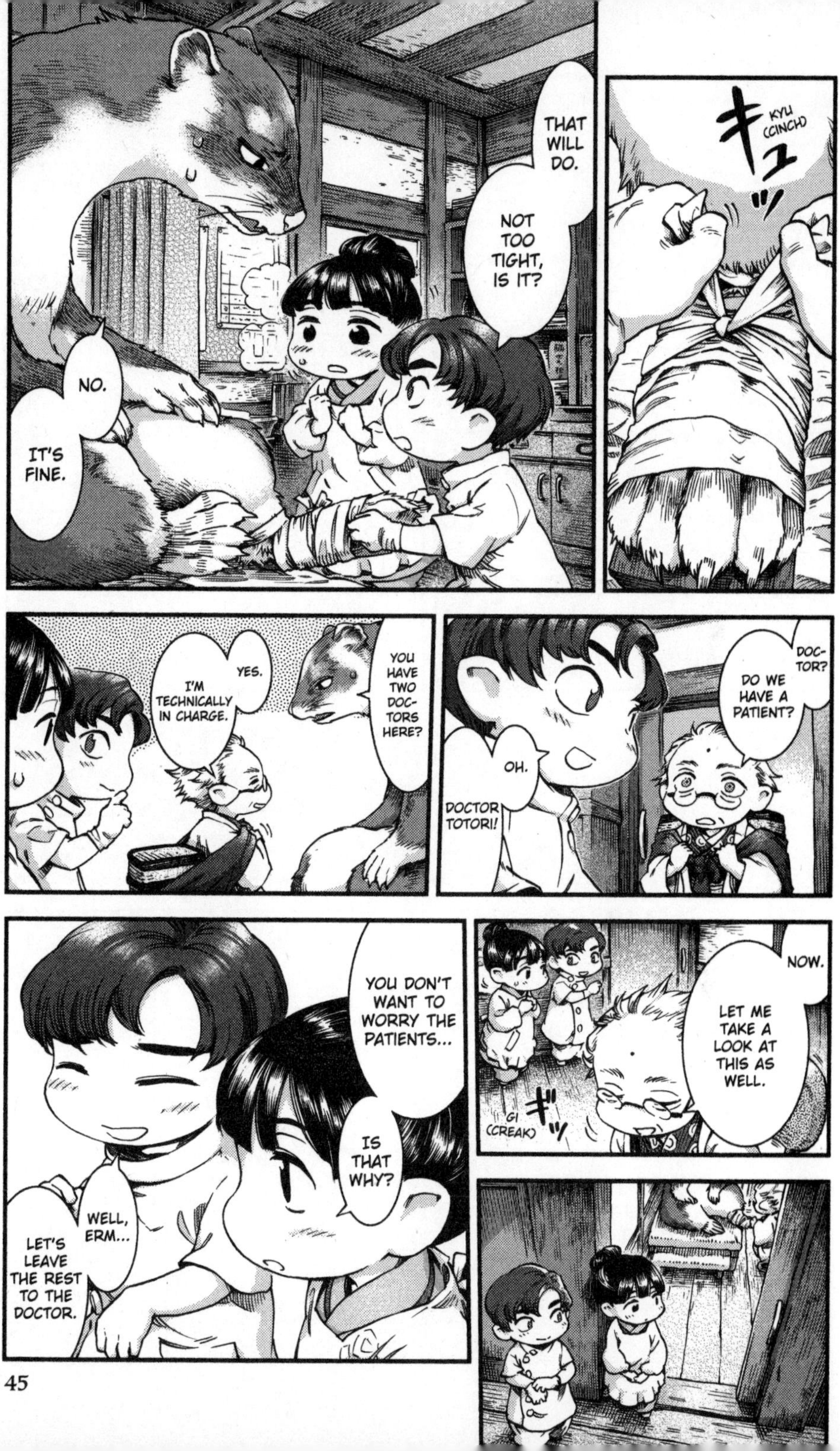
KYU (CINCH)
THAT WILL DO.
NOT TOO TIGHT, IS IT?
NO.
IT'S FINE.
DOC-TOR?
DO WE HAVE A PATIENT?
OH.
DOCTOR TOTORI!
YOU HAVE TWO DOC-TORS HERE?
YES.
I'M TECHNICALLY IN CHARGE.
NOW.
LET ME TAKE A LOOK AT THIS AS WELL.
GI (CREAK)
YOU DON'T WANT TO WORRY THE PATIENTS...
IS THAT WHY?
WELL, ERM...
LET'S LEAVE THE REST TO THE DOCTOR.

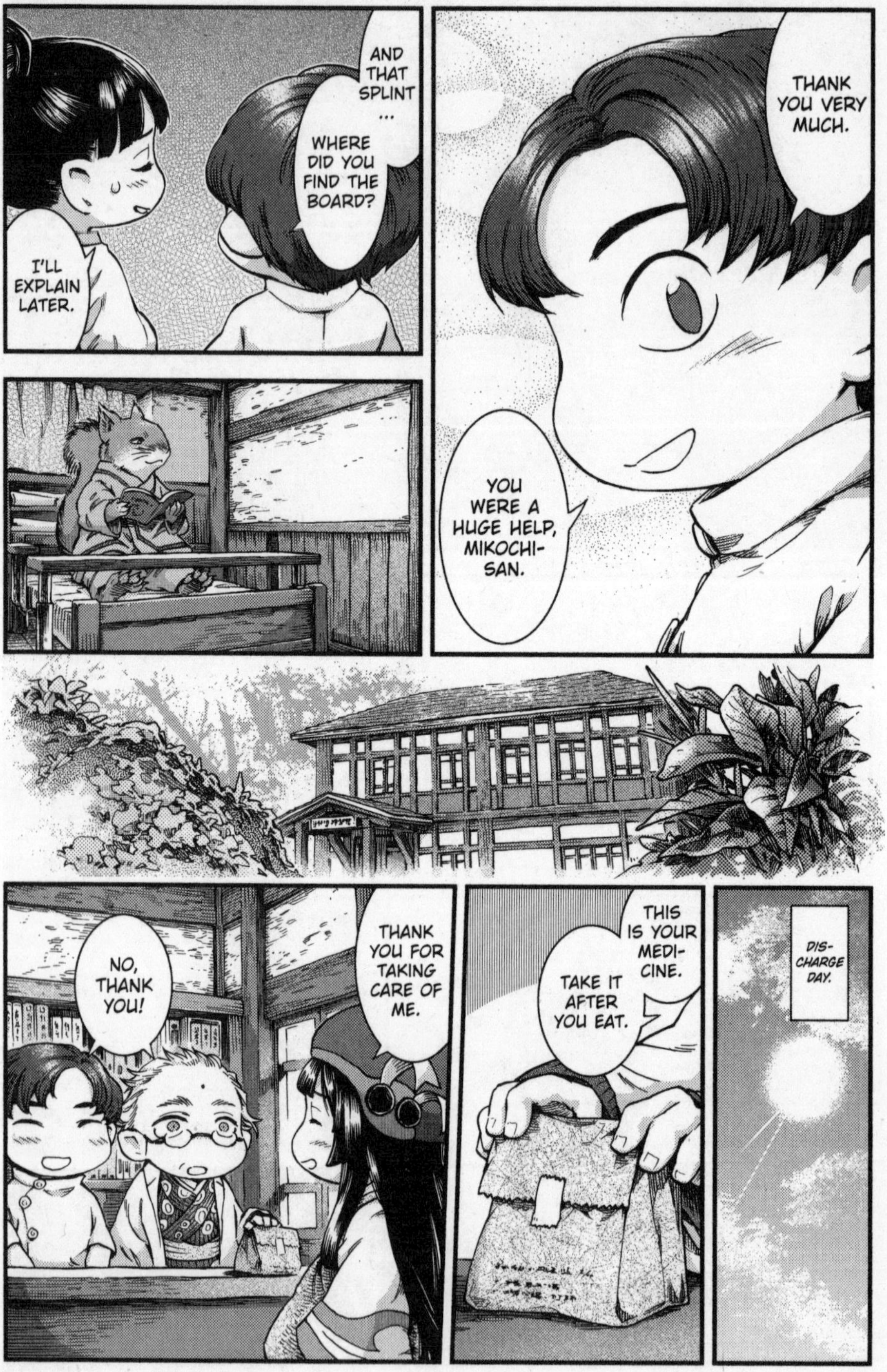
THANK YOU VERY MUCH.
YOU WERE A HUGE HELP, MIKOCHI-SAN.
AND THAT SPLINT ...
WHERE DID YOU FIND THE BOARD?
I'LL EXPLAIN LATER.
DIS-CHARGE DAY.
THIS IS YOUR MEDI-CINE.
TAKE IT AFTER YOU EAT.
THANK YOU FOR TAKING CARE OF ME.
NO, THANK YOU!

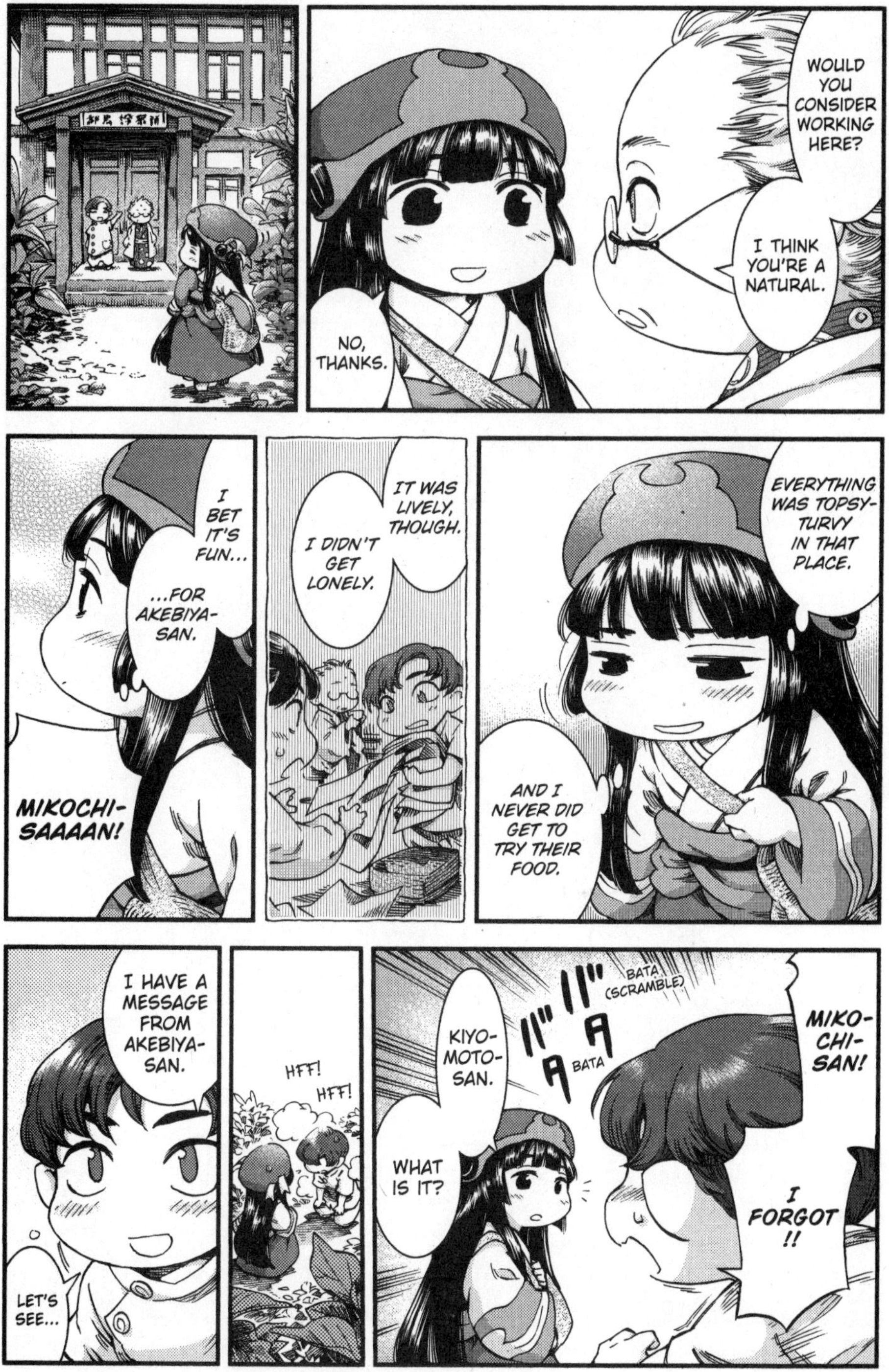
WOULD YOU CONSIDER WORKING HERE?
I THINK YOU'RE A NATURAL.
NO, THANKS.
EVERYTHING WAS TOPSY-TURVY IN THAT PLACE.
AND I NEVER DID GET TO TRY THEIR FOOD.
IT WAS LIVELY, THOUGH.
I DIDN'T GET LONELY.
I BET IT'S FUN...
...FOR AKEBIYA-SAN.
MIKOCHI-SAAAAN!
MIKO-CHI-SAN!
BATA (SCRAMBLE)
BATA
KIYO-MOTO-SAN.
WHAT IS IT?
I FORGOT!!
HFF!
HFF!
I HAVE A MESSAGE FROM AKEBIYA-SAN.
LET'S SEE...

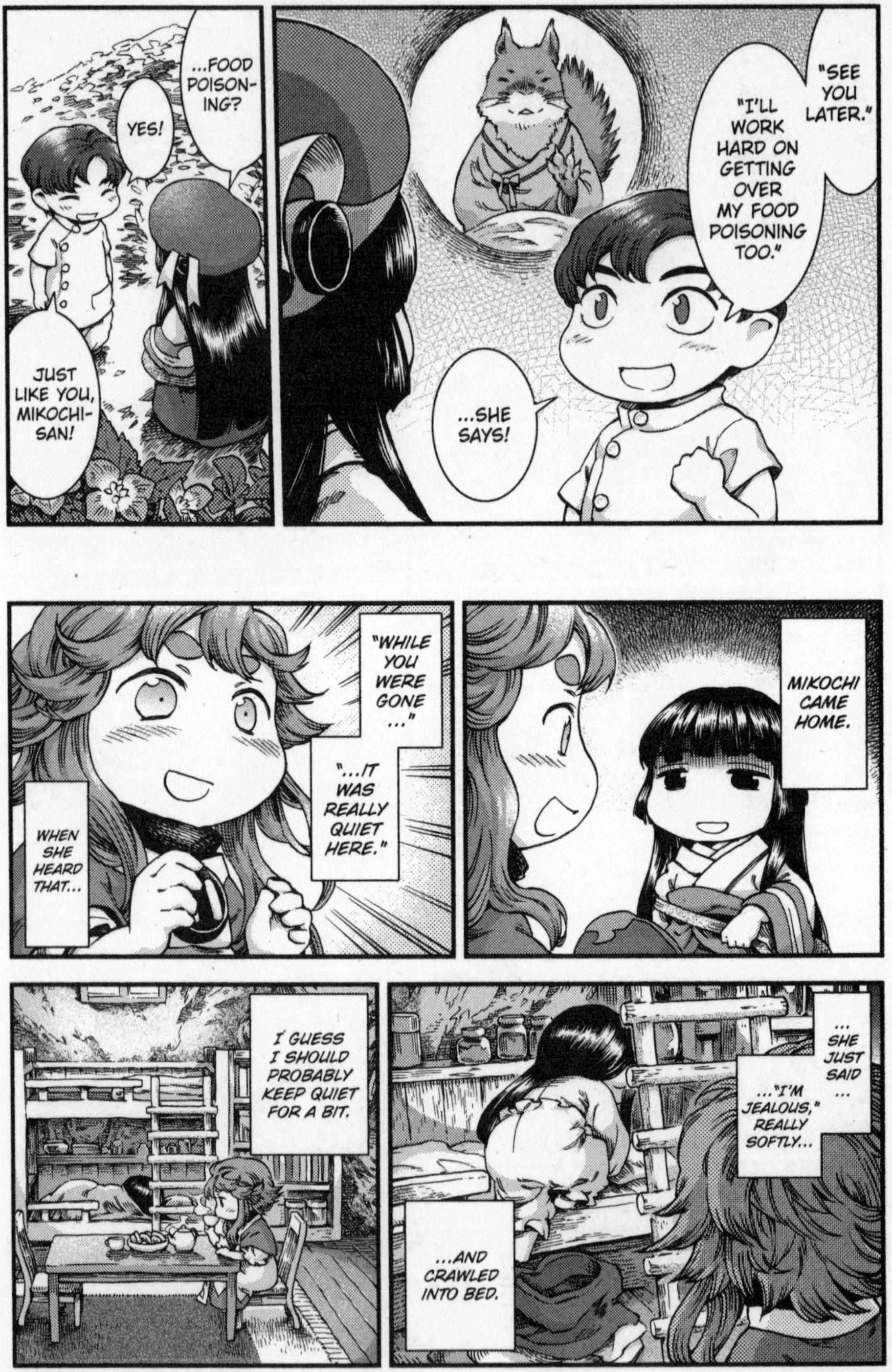
"SEE YOU LATER."
"I'LL WORK HARD ON GETTING OVER MY FOOD POISONING TOO."
...SHE SAYS!
...FOOD POISON-ING?
YES!
JUST LIKE YOU, MIKOCHI-SAN!
MIKOCHI CAME HOME.
"WHILE YOU WERE GONE ..."
"...IT WAS REALLY QUIET HERE."
WHEN SHE HEARD THAT...
... SHE JUST SAID ...
..."I'M JEALOUS," REALLY SOFTLY...
...AND CRAWLED INTO BED.
I GUESS I SHOULD PROBABLY KEEP QUIET FOR A BIT.

"Welcome back, Senpai! How was your trip?"

"Oh, the stories will keep. Tell me about the backlog of work and the damages."

"There aren't any to speak of!"

"Don't bother trying to look good, all right? I even bought boxes of sweets to take to people when we go around apologizing."

"It's true. One of the patients helped us out."

"...Helped *you*, Kiyo? Single-handedly? Why did you let that one get away?"

"The doctor and I both tried to recruit her, but she turned us down."

"Well, I suppose she would have. ...Hm? There's a wall panel missing here. What happened?"

"Huh!? Good question. I just now noticed it!"

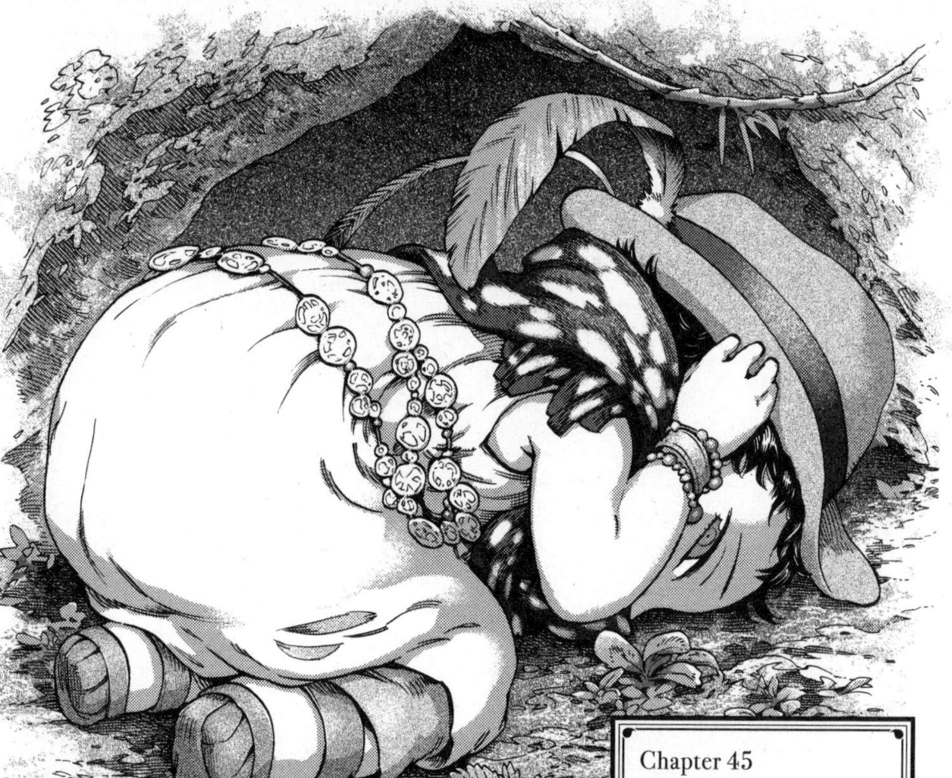

Chapter 45
The Thunder Sleepover Party

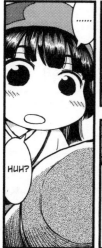

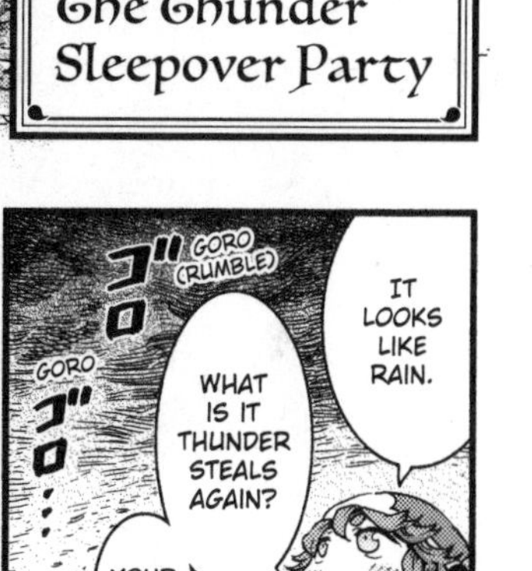
IT LOOKS LIKE RAIN.
GORO (RUMBLE)
ゴロ
GORO
ゴロ…
WHAT IS IT THUNDER STEALS AGAIN?
YOUR EYES?
BELLY BUTTON.

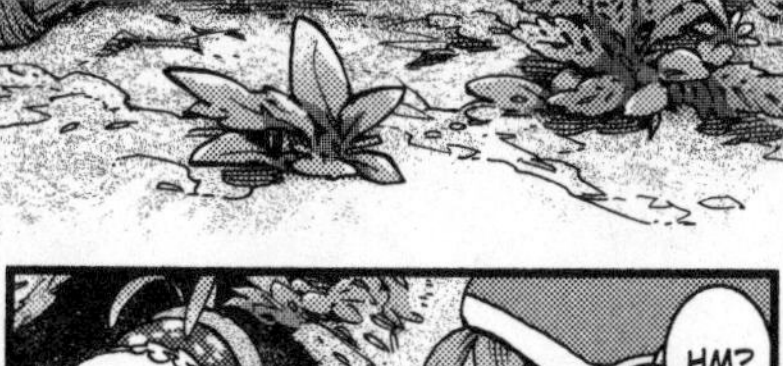
HM?
WHAT'S THAT?

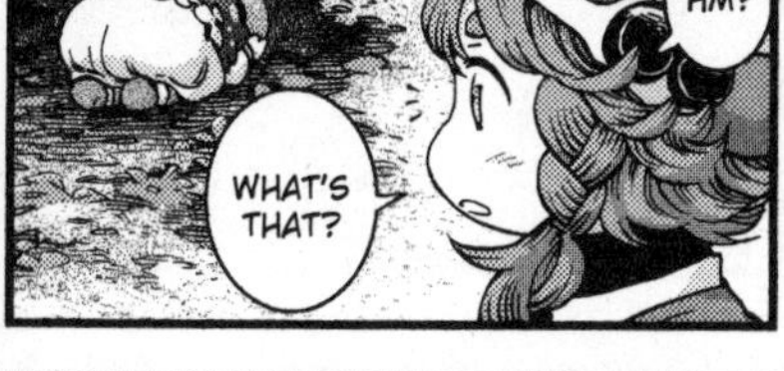
A PERSON?
ARE YOU ALL RIGHT?
DO YOU FEEL SICK, OR…?

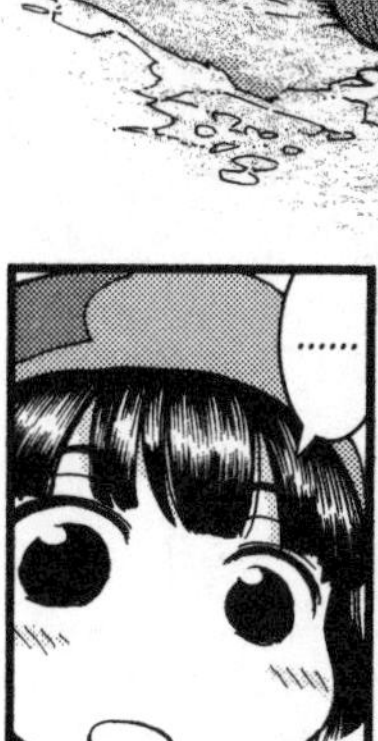
……
HUH?

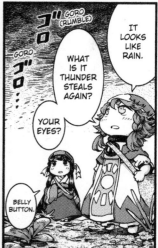

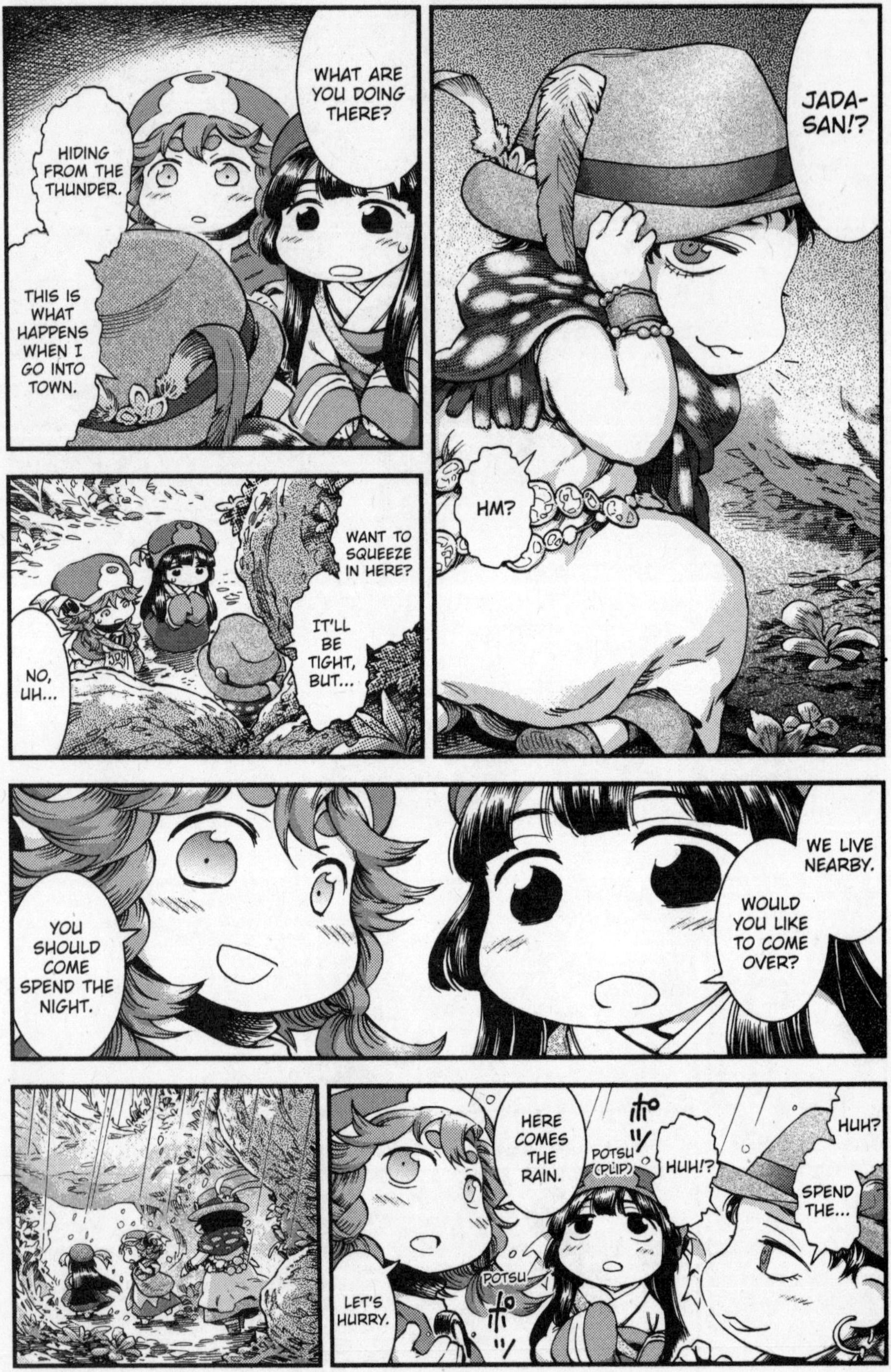
JADA-SAN!?
HM?
WHAT ARE YOU DOING THERE?
HIDING FROM THE THUNDER.
THIS IS WHAT HAPPENS WHEN I GO INTO TOWN.
WANT TO SQUEEZE IN HERE?
IT'LL BE TIGHT, BUT...
NO, UH...
WE LIVE NEARBY.
WOULD YOU LIKE TO COME OVER?
YOU SHOULD COME SPEND THE NIGHT.
HUH?
SPEND THE...
HUH!?
ポツ
POTSU (PLIP)
HERE COMES THE RAIN.
POTSU
ポツ
LET'S HURRY.

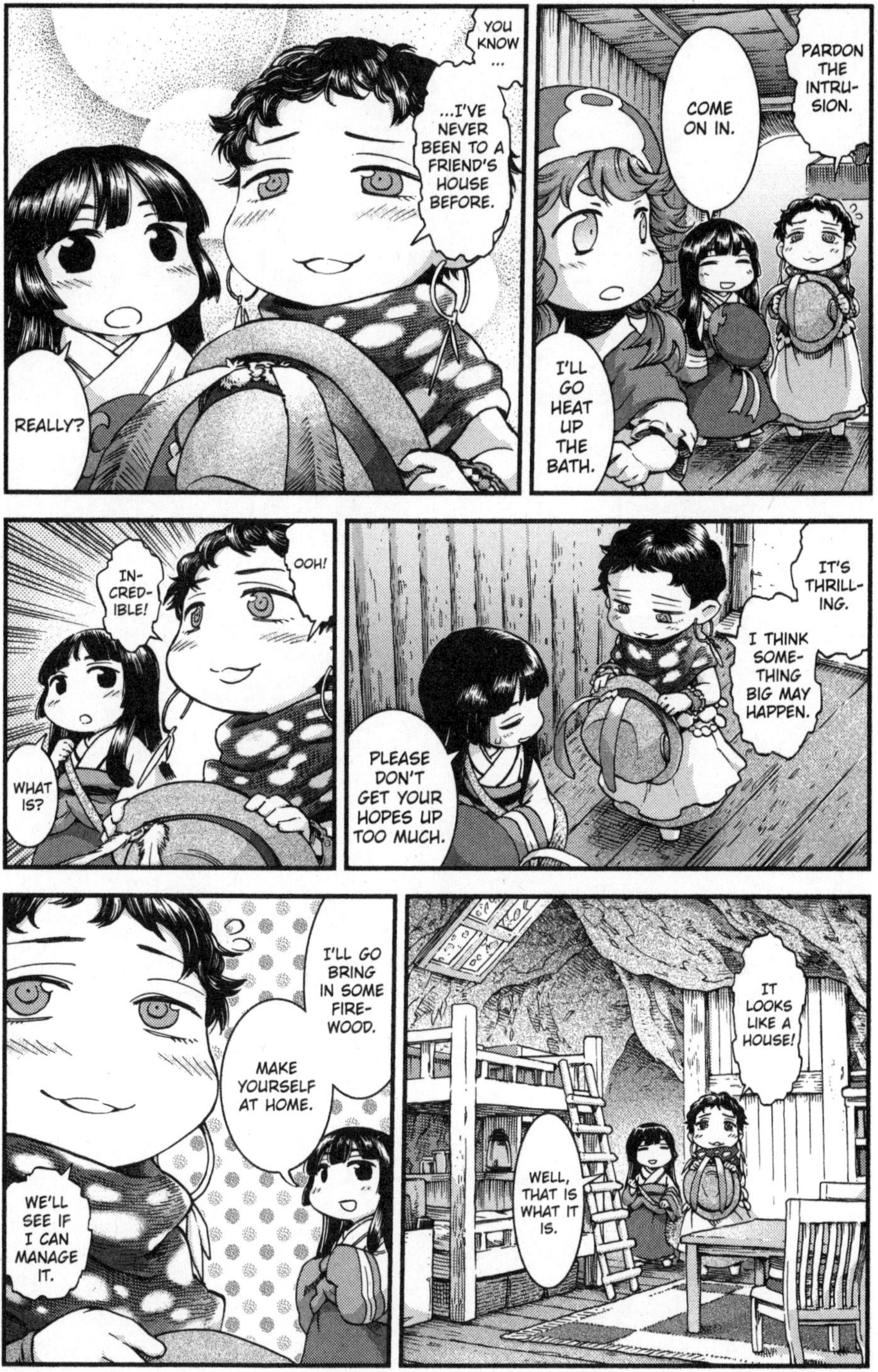
PARDON THE INTRU-SION.
COME ON IN.
I'LL GO HEAT UP THE BATH.
YOU KNOW ...
...I'VE NEVER BEEN TO A FRIEND'S HOUSE BEFORE.
REALLY?
IT'S THRILL-ING.
I THINK SOME-THING BIG MAY HAPPEN.
PLEASE DON'T GET YOUR HOPES UP TOO MUCH.
OOH!
IN-CRED-IBLE!
WHAT IS?
IT LOOKS LIKE A HOUSE!
WELL, THAT IS WHAT IT IS.
I'LL GO BRING IN SOME FIRE-WOOD.
MAKE YOURSELF AT HOME.
WE'LL SEE IF I CAN MANAGE IT.

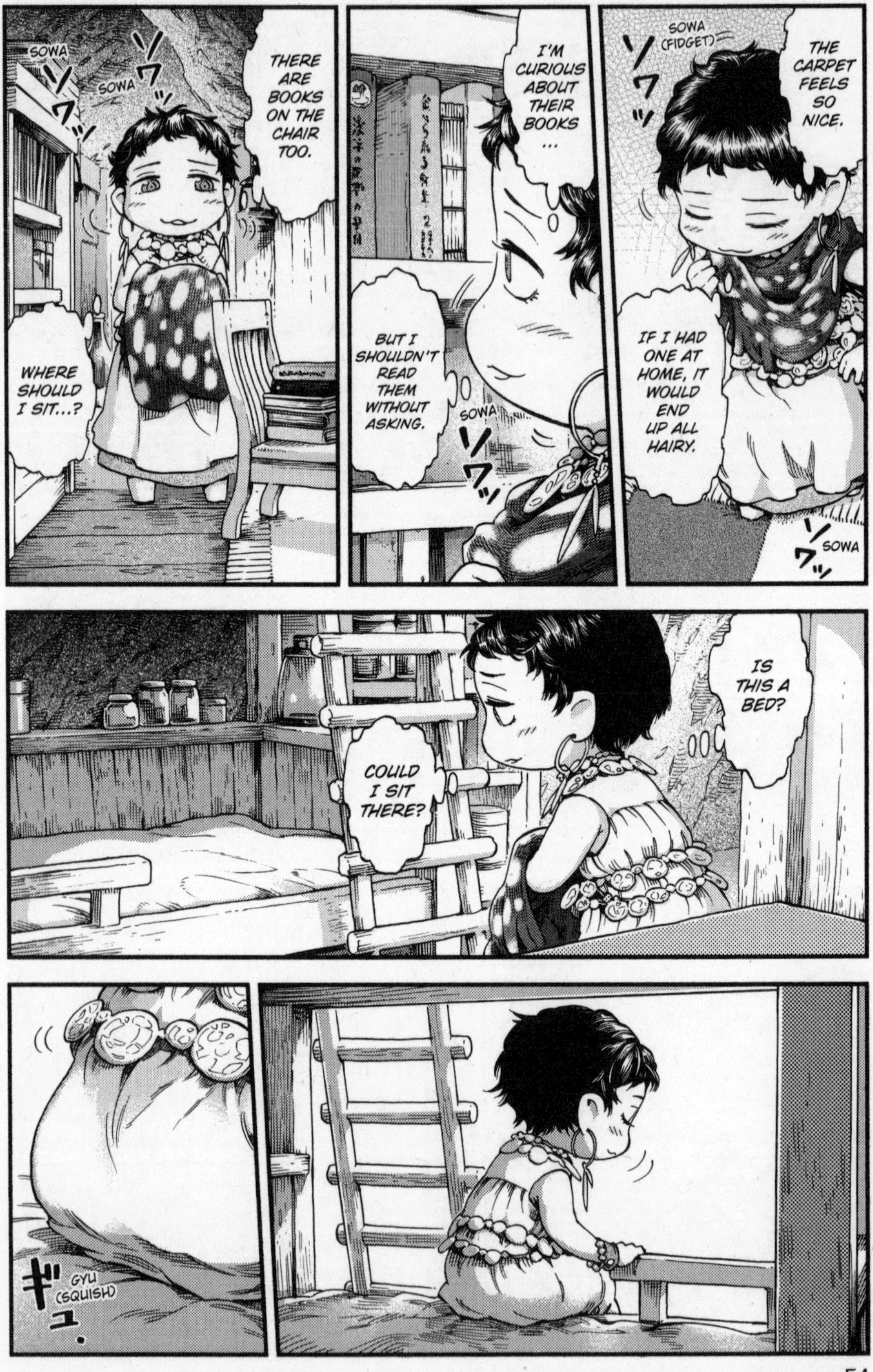
THE CARPET FEELS SO NICE.
SOWA (FIDGET)
IF I HAD ONE AT HOME, IT WOULD END UP ALL HAIRY.
SOWA
I'M CURIOUS ABOUT THEIR BOOKS...
BUT I SHOULDN'T READ THEM WITHOUT ASKING.
SOWA
THERE ARE BOOKS ON THE CHAIR TOO.
SOWA
SOWA
WHERE SHOULD I SIT...?
IS THIS A BED?
COULD I SIT THERE?
GYU (SQUISH)

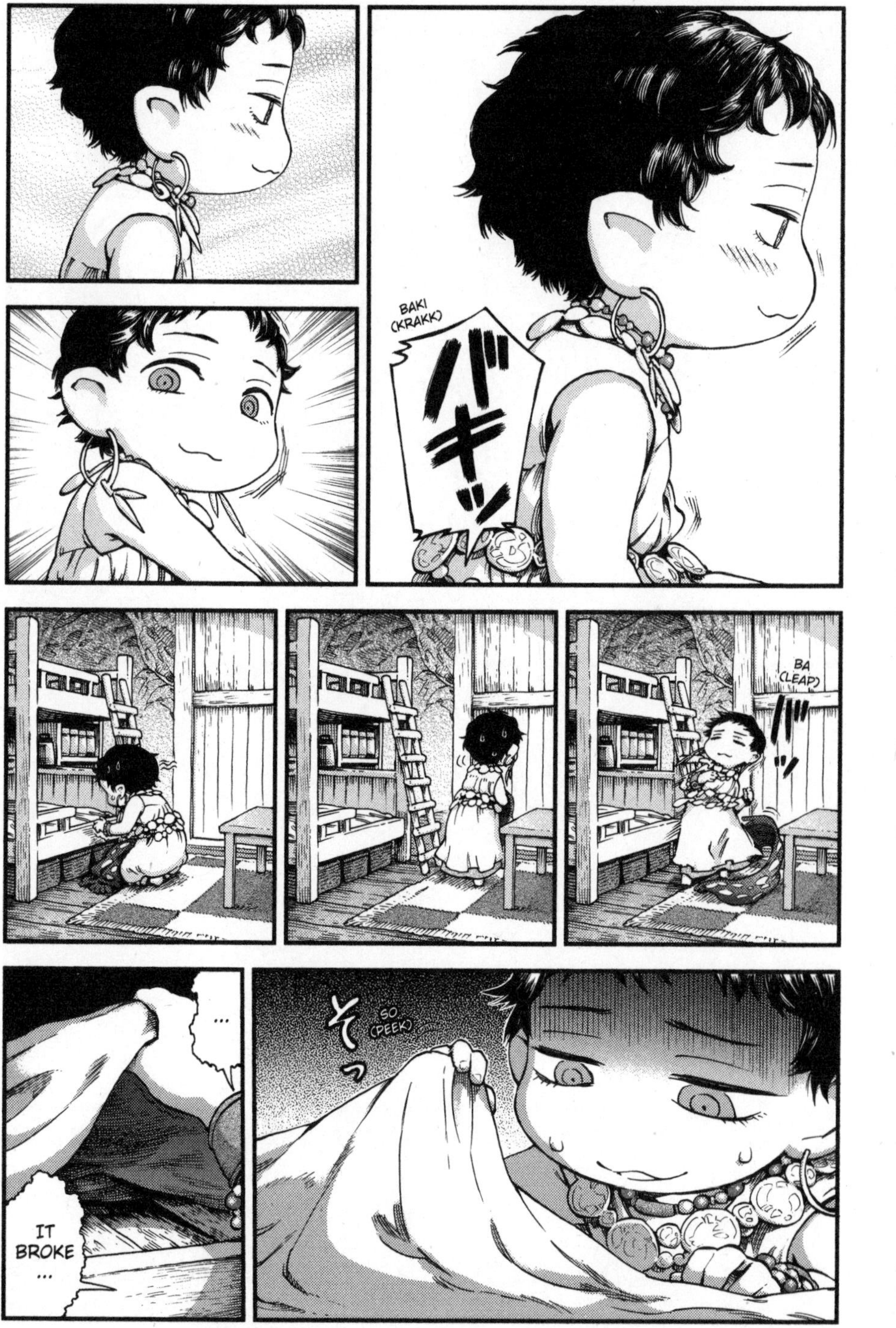
バキッ
BAKI (KRAKK)
バッ
BA (LEAP)
そっ
SO (PEEK)
...
IT BROKE ...

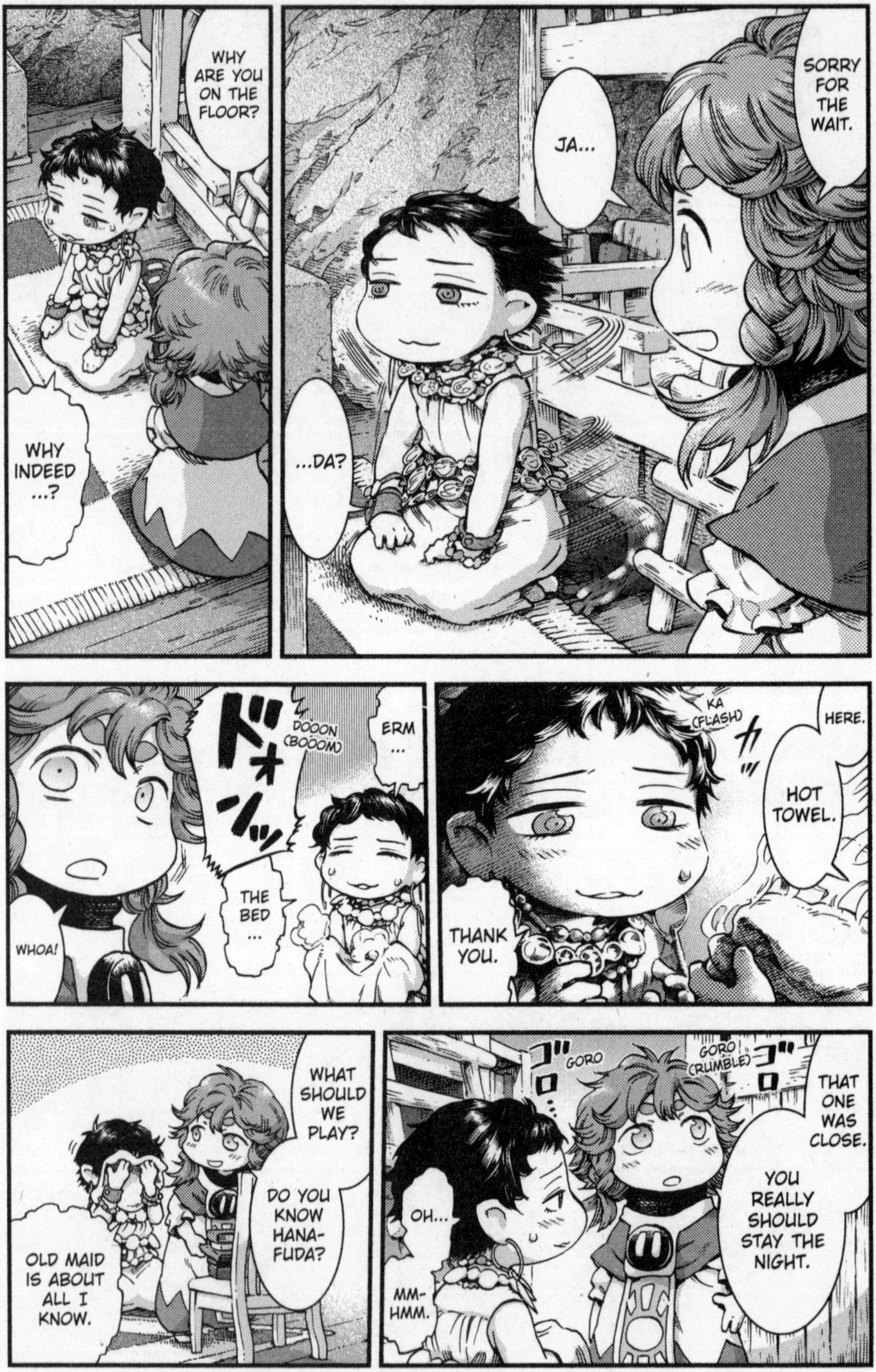
SORRY FOR THE WAIT.
JA...
...DA?
WHY ARE YOU ON THE FLOOR?
WHY INDEED ...?
KA (FLASH)
カッ
HERE.
HOT TOWEL.
THANK YOU.
ERM ...
ドォンッ
DOOON (BOOOM)
THE BED ...
WHOA!
ゴロ
GORO (RUMBLE)
ゴロ
GORO
THAT ONE WAS CLOSE.
YOU REALLY SHOULD STAY THE NIGHT.
OH...
MM-HMM.
WHAT SHOULD WE PLAY?
DO YOU KNOW HANA-FUDA?
OLD MAID IS ABOUT ALL I KNOW.

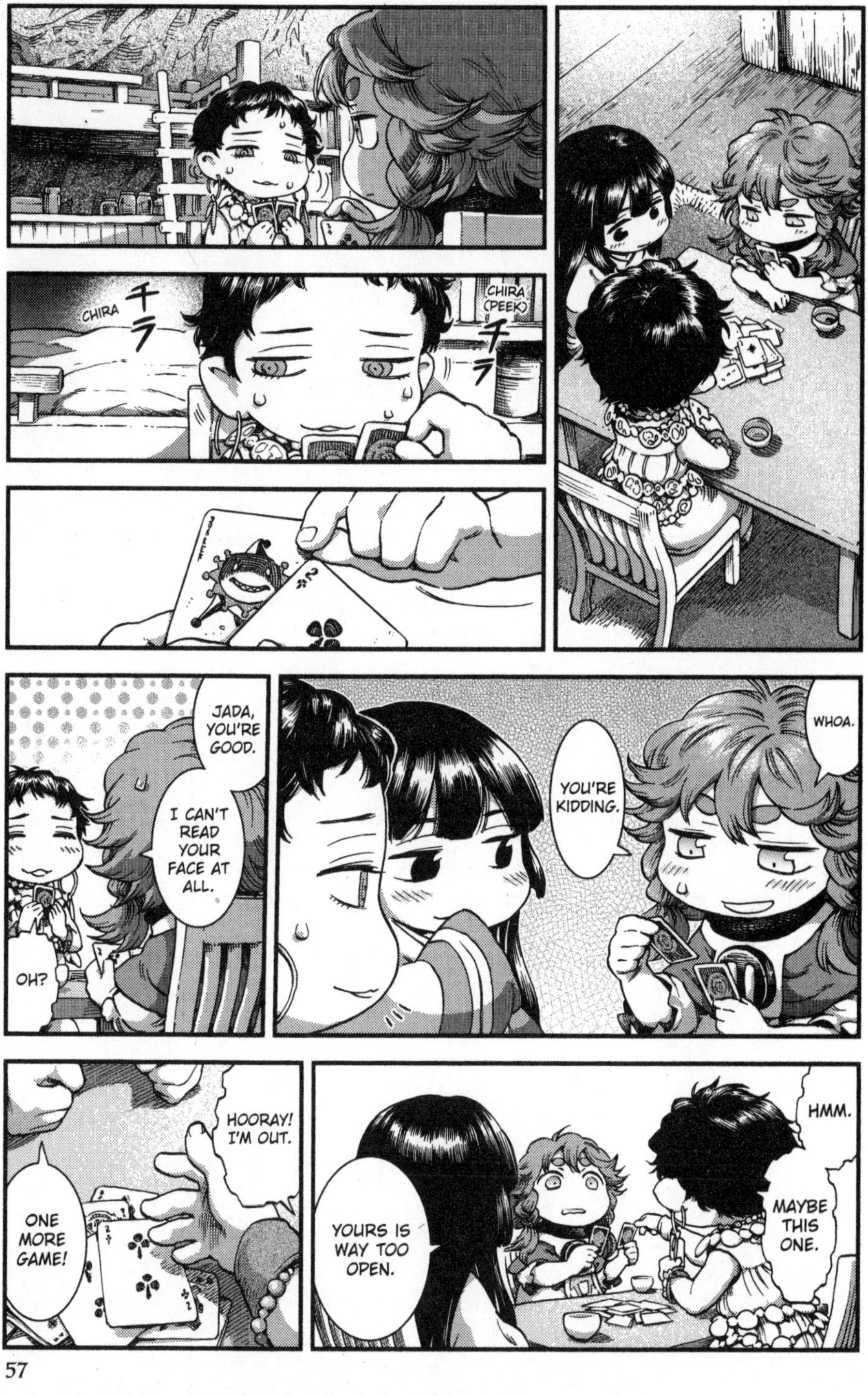
CHIRA (PEEK)
チラ
CHIRA
チラ
WHOA.
YOU'RE KIDDING.
JADA, YOU'RE GOOD.
I CAN'T READ YOUR FACE AT ALL.
OH?
HMM.
MAYBE THIS ONE.
YOURS IS WAY TOO OPEN.
HOORAY! I'M OUT.
ONE MORE GAME!

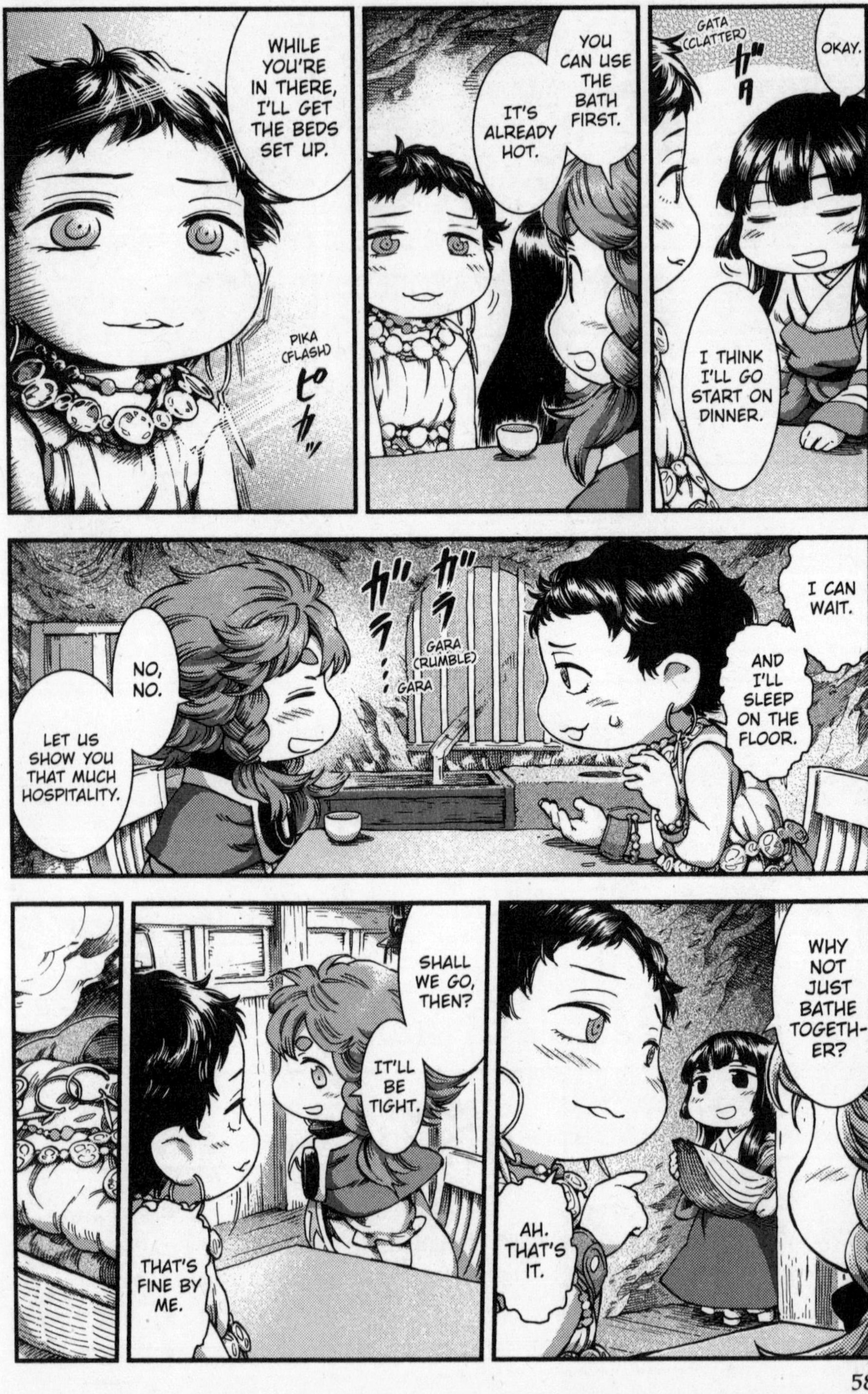
GATA (CLATTER)
ガタ
OKAY.
I THINK I'LL GO START ON DINNER.
YOU CAN USE THE BATH FIRST.
IT'S ALREADY HOT.
WHILE YOU'RE IN THERE, I'LL GET THE BEDS SET UP.
PIKA (FLASH)
ピカッ
I CAN WAIT.
AND I'LL SLEEP ON THE FLOOR.
ガラ
GARA (RUMBLE)
ガラ
GARA
NO, NO.
LET US SHOW YOU THAT MUCH HOSPITALITY.
WHY NOT JUST BATHE TOGETHER?
AH. THAT'S IT.
SHALL WE GO, THEN?
IT'LL BE TIGHT.
THAT'S FINE BY ME.

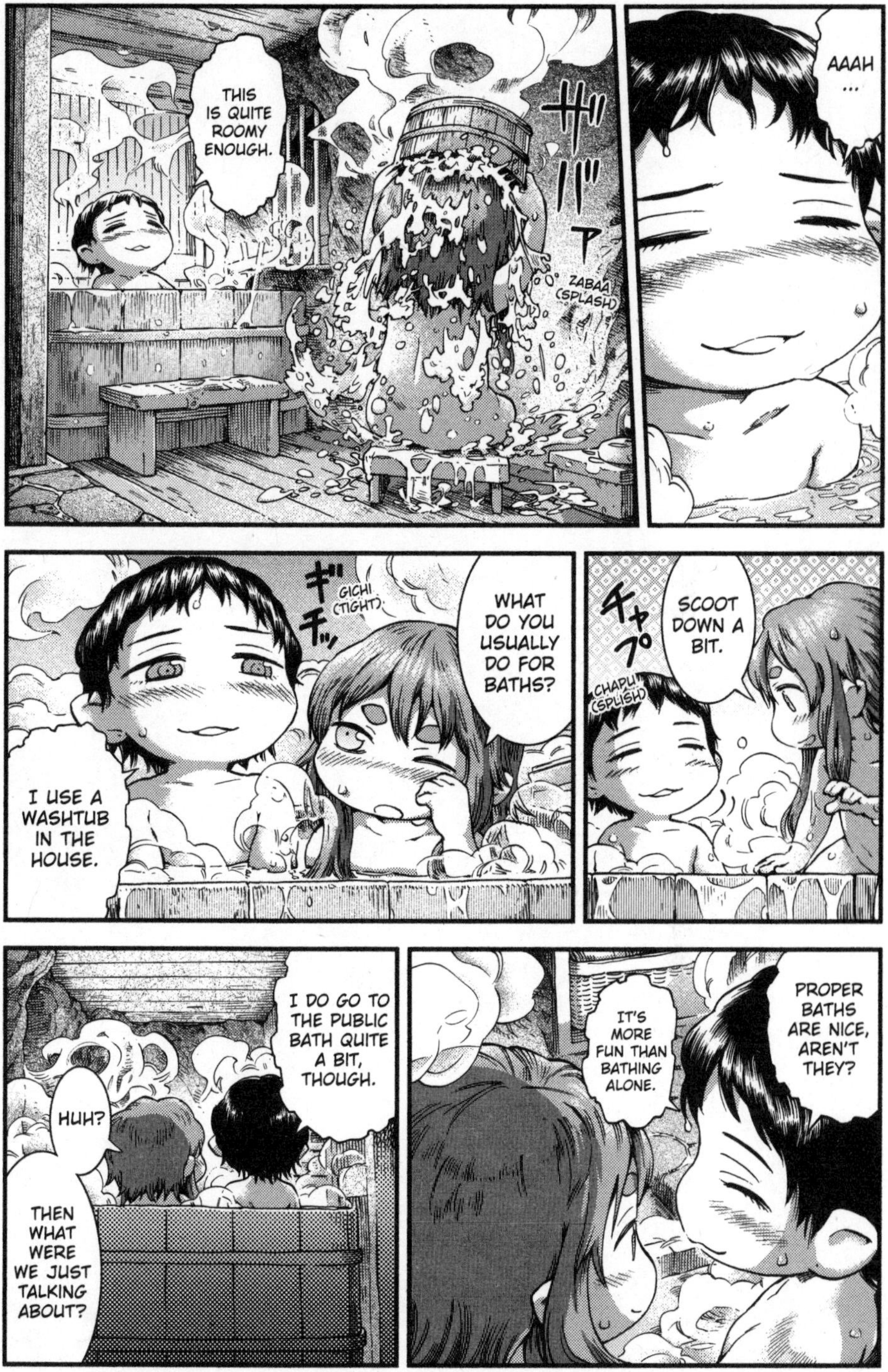
AAAH ...
ザバァ
ZABAA (SPLASH)
THIS IS QUITE ROOMY ENOUGH.
SCOOT DOWN A BIT.
チャプ
CHAPU (SPLASH)
WHAT DO YOU USUALLY DO FOR BATHS?
ギチッ
GICHI (TIGHT)
I USE A WASHTUB IN THE HOUSE.
PROPER BATHS ARE NICE, AREN'T THEY?
IT'S MORE FUN THAN BATHING ALONE.
I DO GO TO THE PUBLIC BATH QUITE A BIT, THOUGH.
HUH?
THEN WHAT WERE WE JUST TALKING ABOUT?

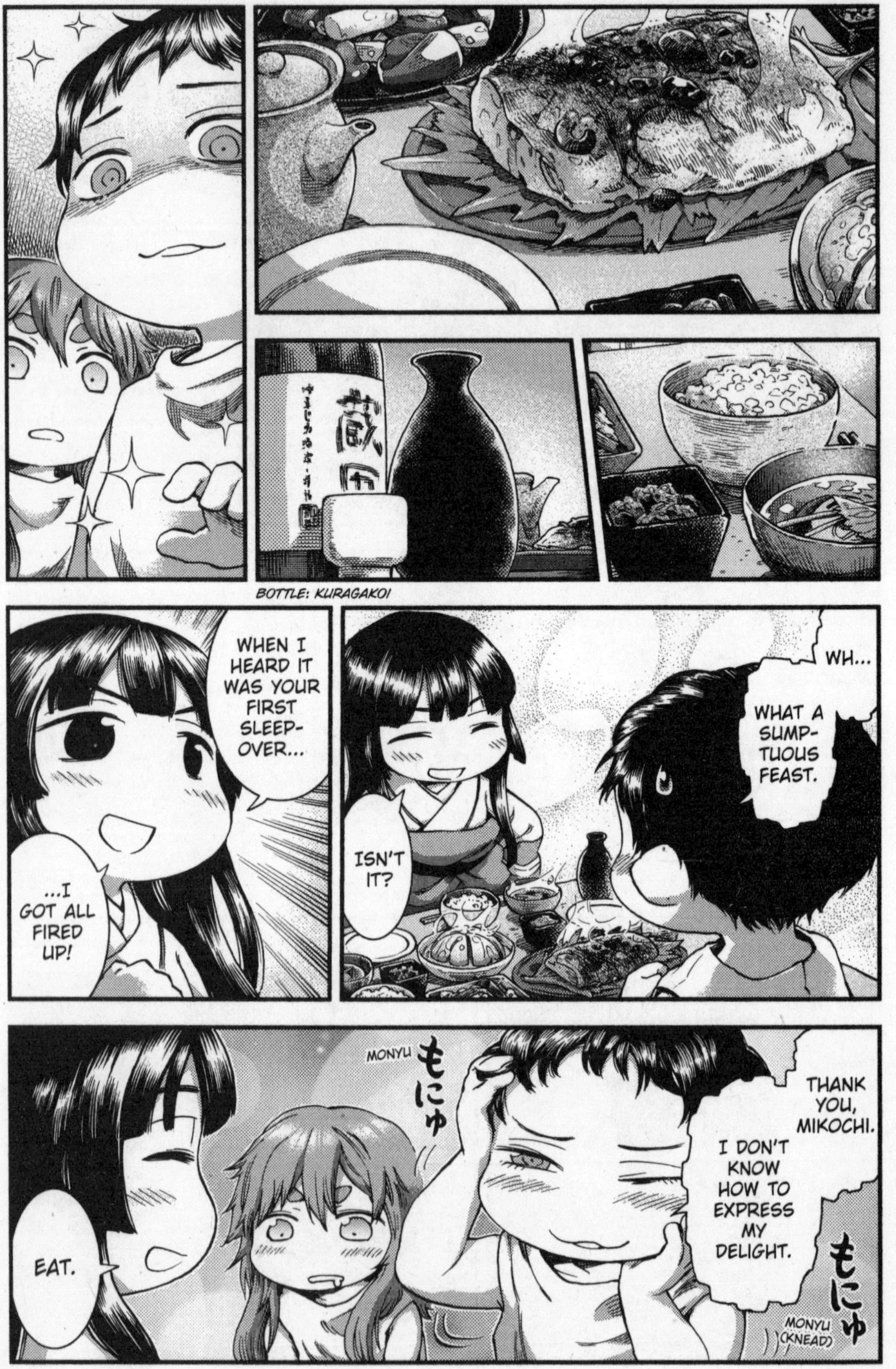

BOTTLE: KURAGAKOI
WH...
WHAT A SUMPTUOUS FEAST.
ISN'T IT?
WHEN I HEARD IT WAS YOUR FIRST SLEEPOVER...
...I GOT ALL FIRED UP!
THANK YOU, MIKOCHI.
I DON'T KNOW HOW TO EXPRESS MY DELIGHT.
もにゅ
MONYU (KNEAD)
もにゅ
MONYU
EAT.

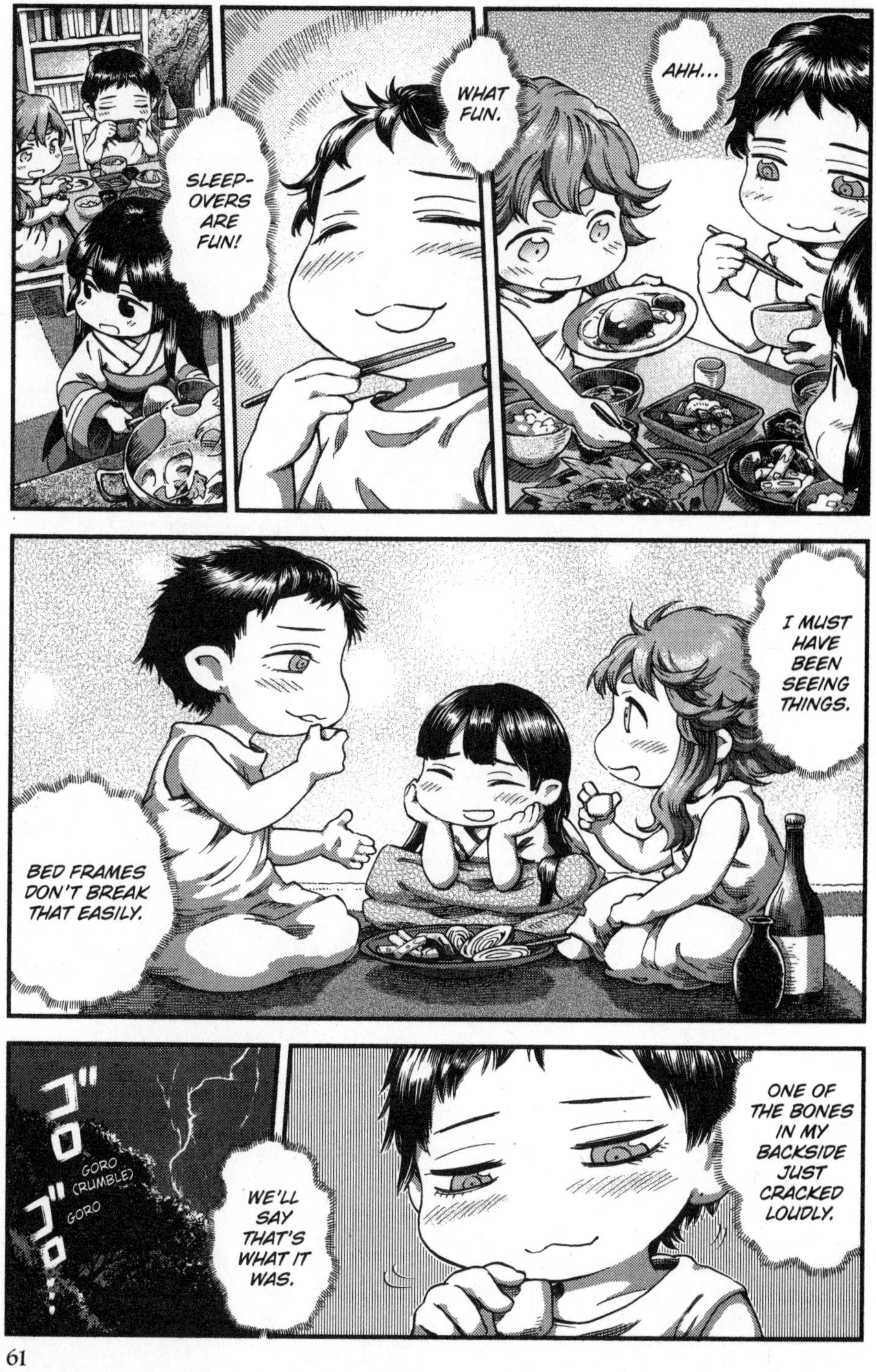
AHH...
WHAT FUN.
SLEEP-OVERS ARE FUN!
I MUST HAVE BEEN SEEING THINGS.
BED FRAMES DON'T BREAK THAT EASILY.
ONE OF THE BONES IN MY BACKSIDE JUST CRACKED LOUDLY.
WE'LL SAY THAT'S WHAT IT WAS.
ゴロ
GORO (RUMBLE)
ゴロ…
GORO

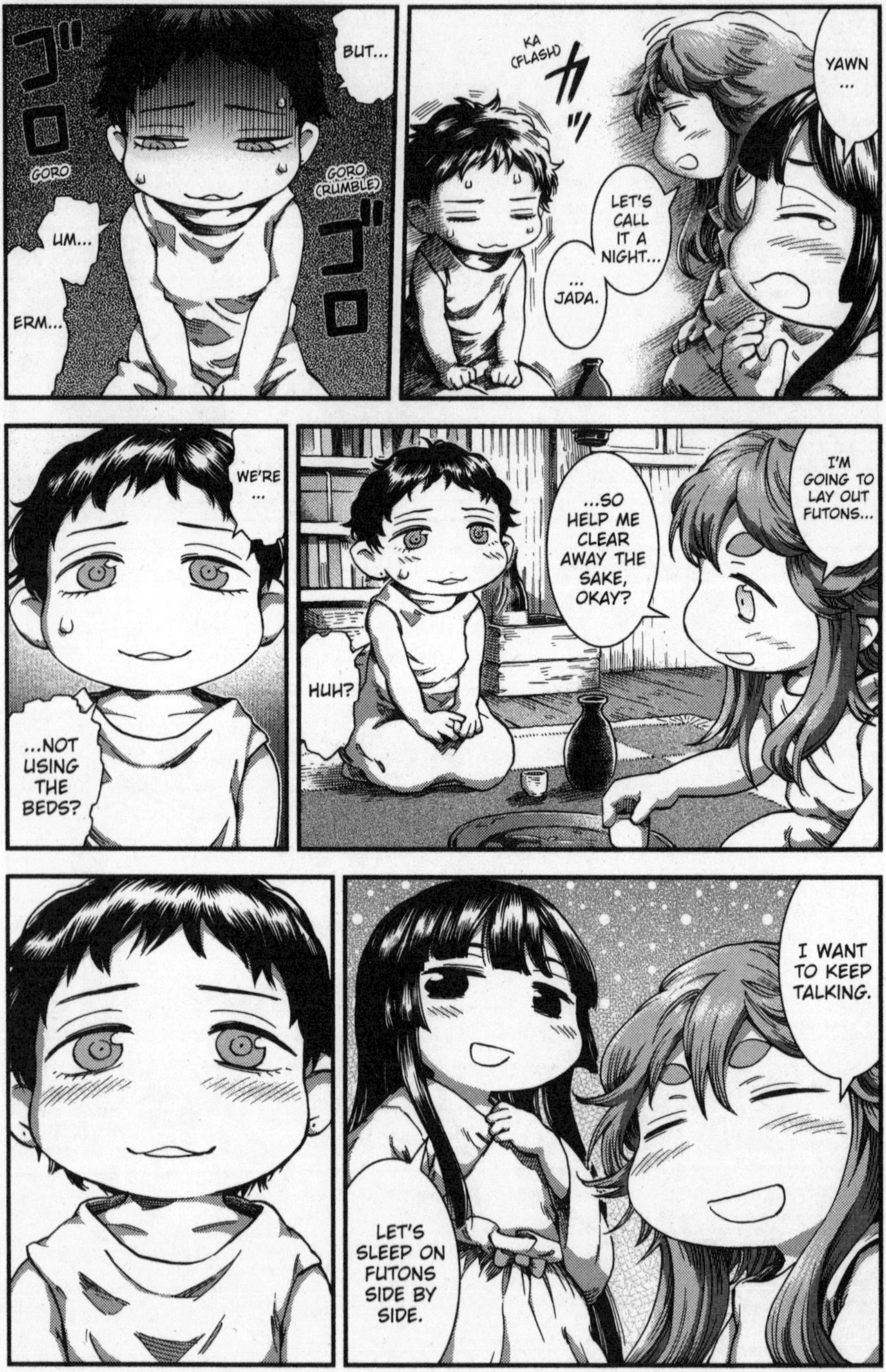
YAWN...
KA (FLASH)
LET'S CALL IT A NIGHT...
...JADA.
BUT...
GORO
GORO (RUMBLE)
UM...
ERM...
I'M GOING TO LAY OUT FUTONS...
...SO HELP ME CLEAR AWAY THE SAKE, OKAY?
HUH?
WE'RE...
...NOT USING THE BEDS?
I WANT TO KEEP TALKING.
LET'S SLEEP ON FUTONS SIDE BY SIDE.

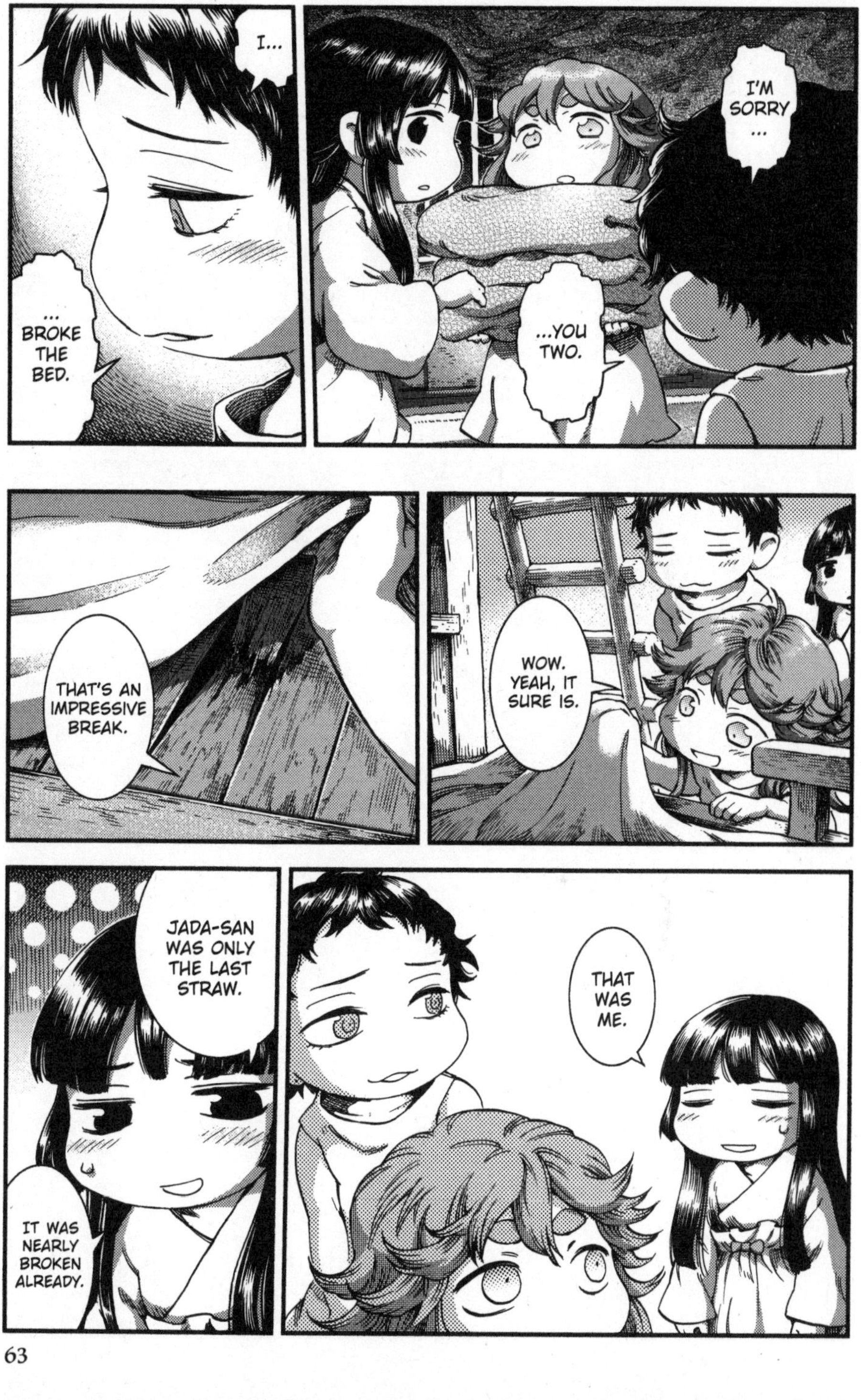
I'M SORRY ...
...YOU TWO.
I...
... BROKE THE BED.
WOW. YEAH, IT SURE IS.
THAT'S AN IMPRESSIVE BREAK.
THAT WAS ME.
JADA-SAN WAS ONLY THE LAST STRAW.
IT WAS NEARLY BROKEN ALREADY.

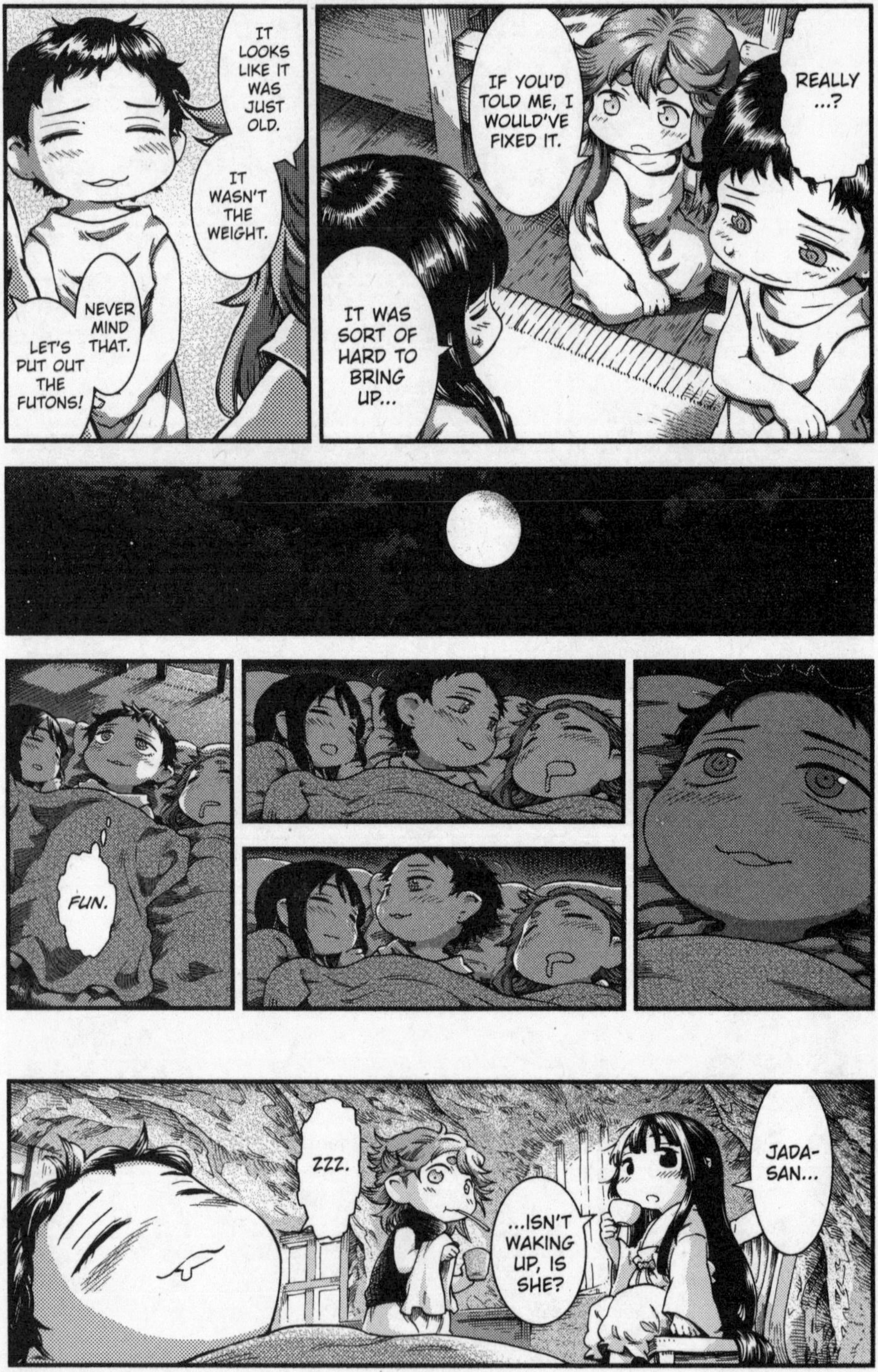
REALLY ...?
IF YOU'D TOLD ME, I WOULD'VE FIXED IT.
IT WAS SORT OF HARD TO BRING UP...
IT LOOKS LIKE IT WAS JUST OLD.
IT WASN'T THE WEIGHT.
NEVER MIND THAT.
LET'S PUT OUT THE FUTONS!
FUN.
JADA-SAN...
...ISN'T WAKING UP, IS SHE?
ZZZ.

•*Column*• Underfoot Steps 45 / Gifts of the Sea Cards

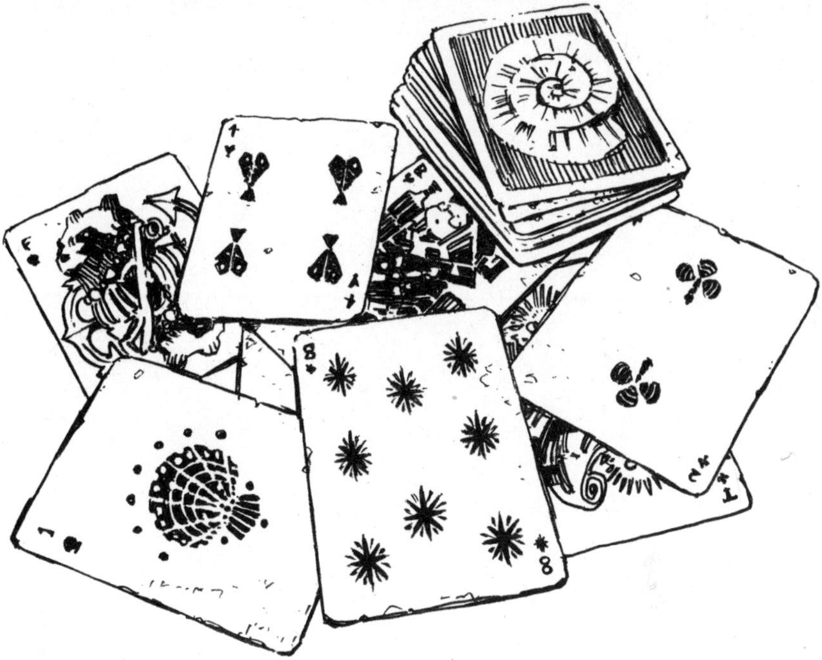

In the souvenir shops of Arabi, "Gifts of the Sea" card decks are nearly ubiquitous.

The four suits are sea urchins, bivalves, dried fish and conchs. There are three different types of picture cards—anchors, sails, and liquors—and the special cards have sharks on them.

Genuine products issued by the merchant association have the Arabi town emblem printed on the back. On knockoff versions, the emblem is slightly warped. Hakumei and Mikochi's deck is genuine; the Ossicle owner gave it to Hakumei to commemorate her string of ten losses after they played together.

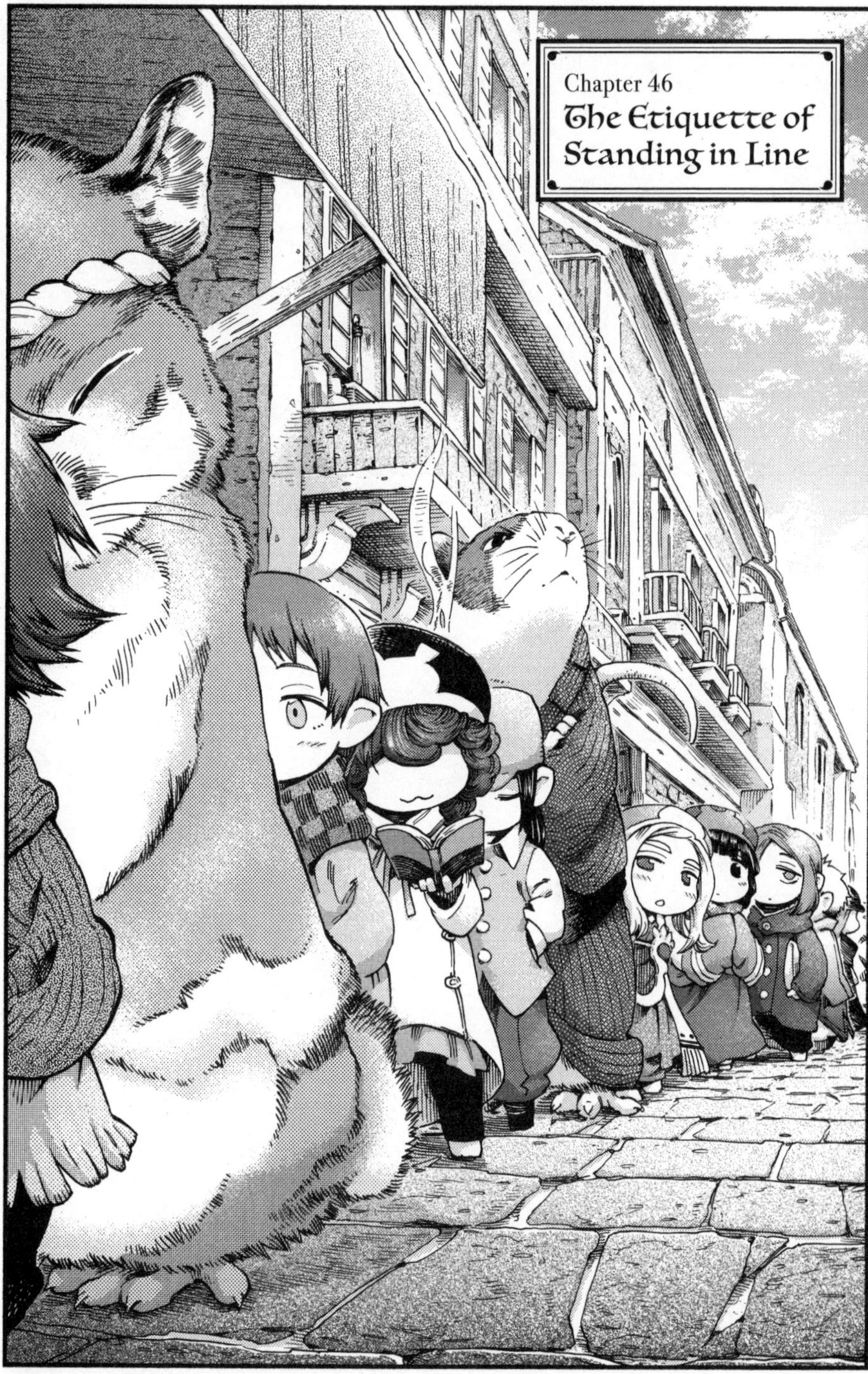
Chapter 46
The Etiquette of Standing in Line

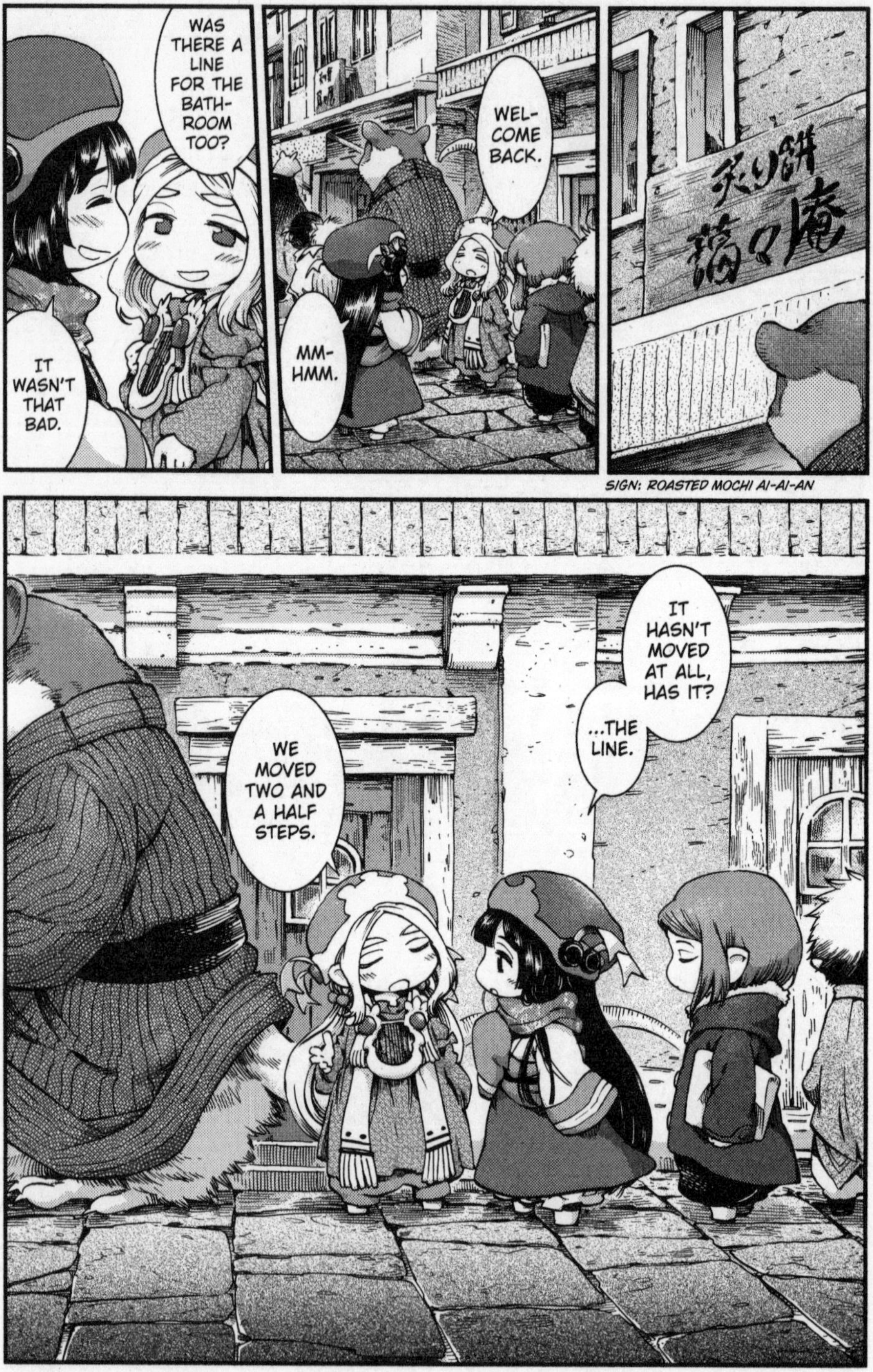
炙り餅
藹々庵
SIGN: ROASTED MOCHI AI-AI-AN
WEL-COME BACK.
MM-HMM.
WAS THERE A LINE FOR THE BATH-ROOM TOO?
IT WASN'T THAT BAD.
IT HASN'T MOVED AT ALL, HAS IT?
...THE LINE.
WE MOVED TWO AND A HALF STEPS.

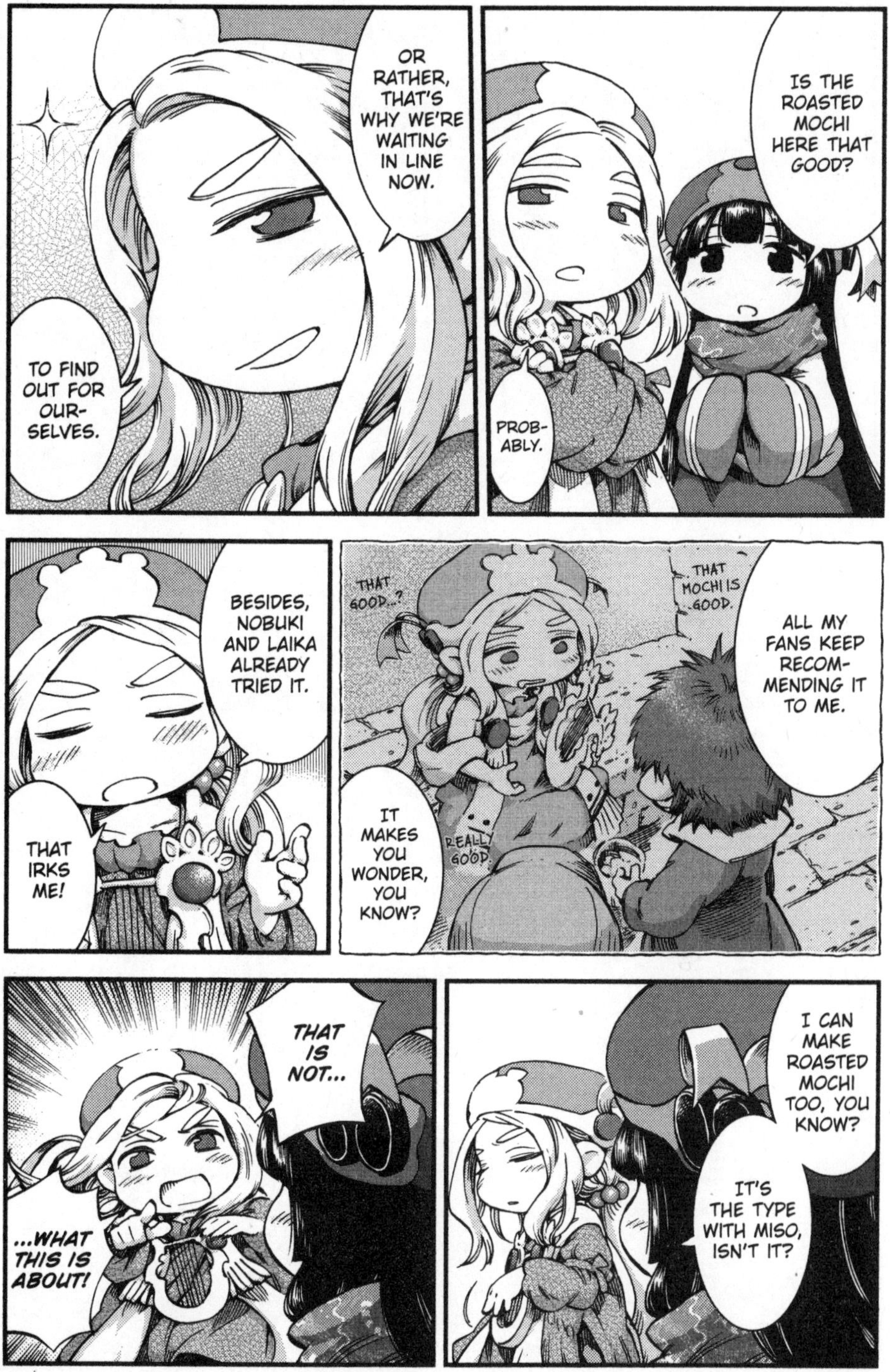
IS THE ROASTED MOCHI HERE THAT GOOD?
PROB-ABLY.
OR RATHER, THAT'S WHY WE'RE WAITING IN LINE NOW.
TO FIND OUT FOR OUR-SELVES.
ALL MY FANS KEEP RECOM-MENDING IT TO ME.
...THAT MOCHI IS ...GOOD.
THAT GOOD...?
REALL GOOD.
IT MAKES YOU WONDER, YOU KNOW?
BESIDES, NOBUKI AND LAIKA ALREADY TRIED IT.
THAT IRKS ME!
I CAN MAKE ROASTED MOCHI TOO, YOU KNOW?
IT'S THE TYPE WITH MISO, ISN'T IT?
THAT IS NOT...
...WHAT THIS IS ABOUT!

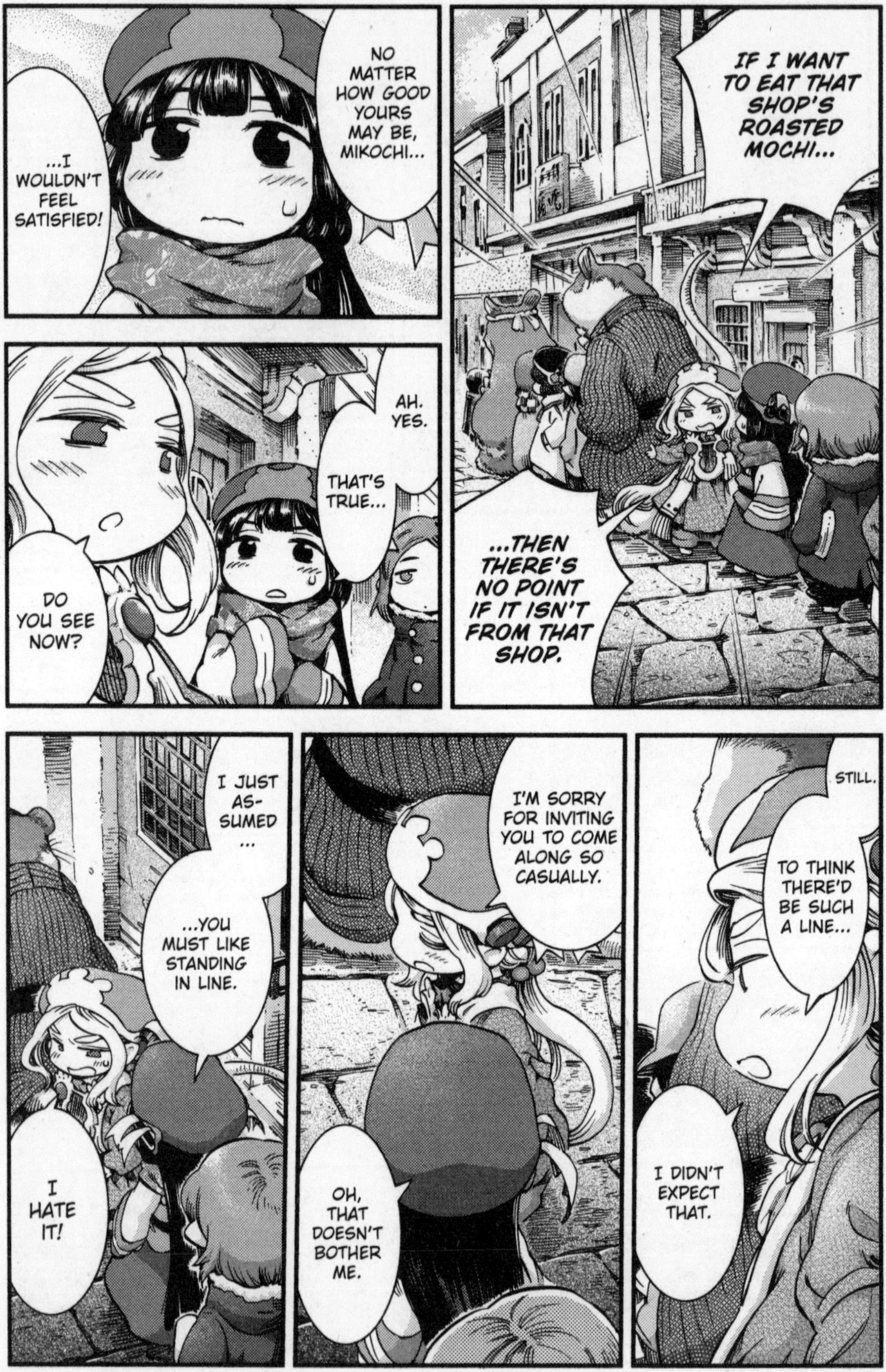
IF I WANT TO EAT THAT SHOP'S ROASTED MOCHI...
...THEN THERE'S NO POINT IF IT ISN'T FROM THAT SHOP.
NO MATTER HOW GOOD YOURS MAY BE, MIKOCHI...
...I WOULDN'T FEEL SATISFIED!
AH. YES.
THAT'S TRUE...
DO YOU SEE NOW?
STILL.
TO THINK THERE'D BE SUCH A LINE...
I DIDN'T EXPECT THAT.
I'M SORRY FOR INVITING YOU TO COME ALONG SO CASUALLY.
OH, THAT DOESN'T BOTHER ME.
I JUST AS-SUMED...
...YOU MUST LIKE STANDING IN LINE.
I HATE IT!

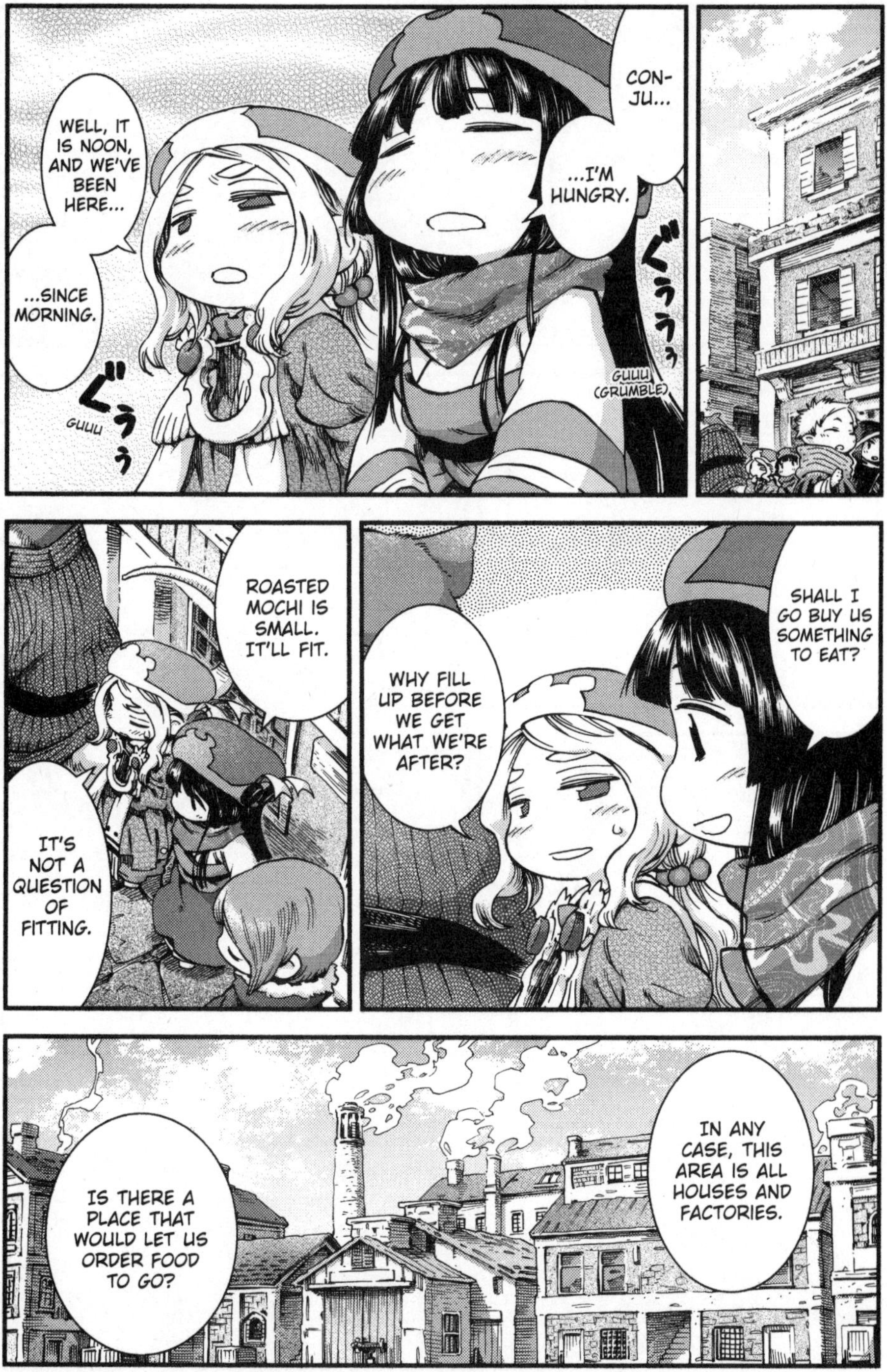
CON-JU...
...I'M HUNGRY.
ぐううぅ
GUUU (GRUMBLE)
WELL, IT IS NOON, AND WE'VE BEEN HERE...
...SINCE MORNING.
ぐうう
GUUU
SHALL I GO BUY US SOMETHING TO EAT?
WHY FILL UP BEFORE WE GET WHAT WE'RE AFTER?
ROASTED MOCHI IS SMALL. IT'LL FIT.
IT'S NOT A QUESTION OF FITTING.
IN ANY CASE, THIS AREA IS ALL HOUSES AND FACTORIES.
IS THERE A PLACE THAT WOULD LET US ORDER FOOD TO GO?

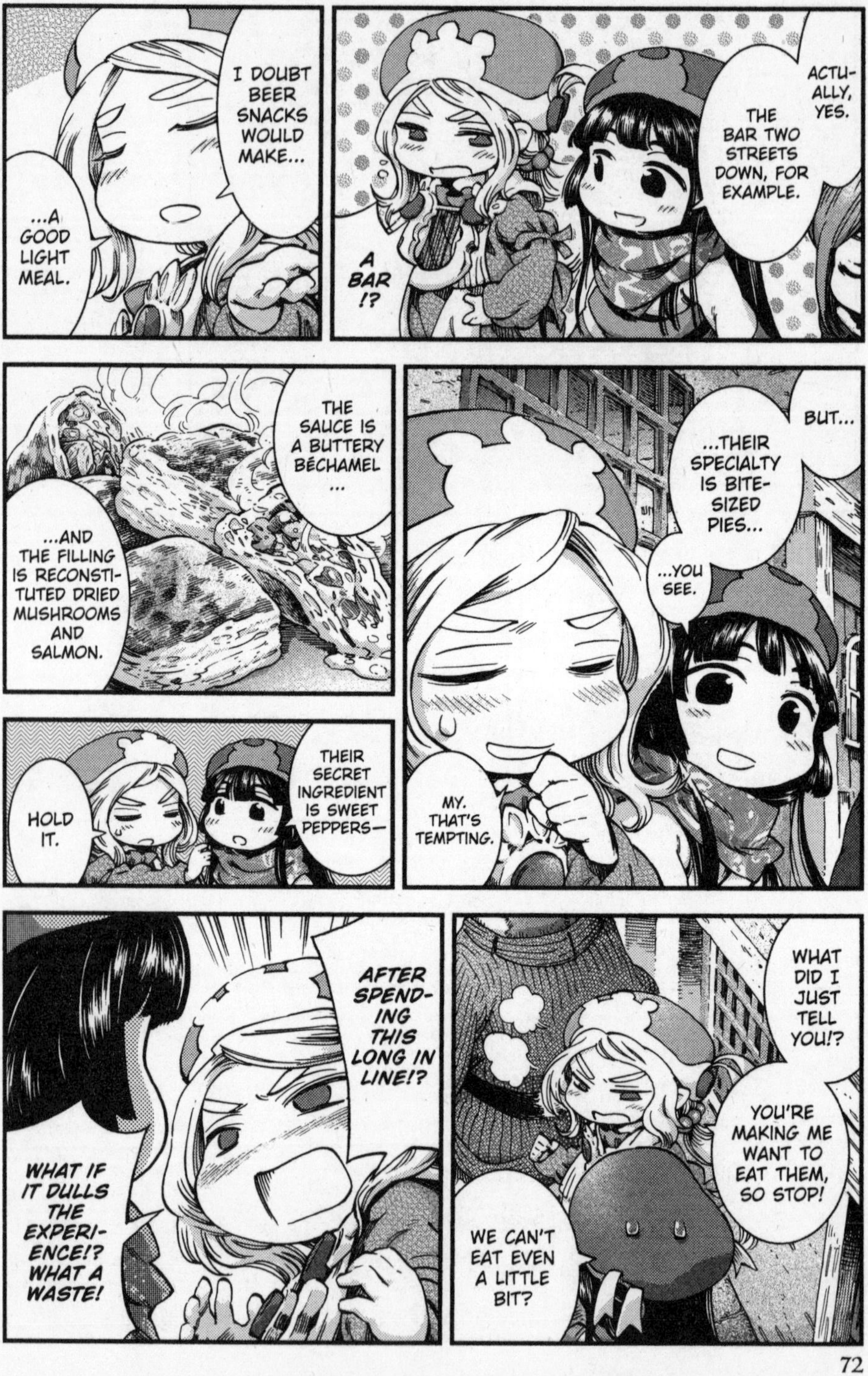
ACTUALLY, YES.
THE BAR TWO STREETS DOWN, FOR EXAMPLE.
A BAR!?
I DOUBT BEER SNACKS WOULD MAKE...
...A GOOD LIGHT MEAL.
BUT...
...THEIR SPECIALTY IS BITE-SIZED PIES...
...YOU SEE.
MY. THAT'S TEMPTING.
THE SAUCE IS A BUTTERY BÉCHAMEL...
...AND THE FILLING IS RECONSTITUTED DRIED MUSHROOMS AND SALMON.
THEIR SECRET INGREDIENT IS SWEET PEPPERS—
HOLD IT.
WHAT DID I JUST TELL YOU!?
YOU'RE MAKING ME WANT TO EAT THEM, SO STOP!
WE CAN'T EAT EVEN A LITTLE BIT?
AFTER SPENDING THIS LONG IN LINE!?
WHAT IF IT DULLS THE EXPERIENCE!? WHAT A WASTE!

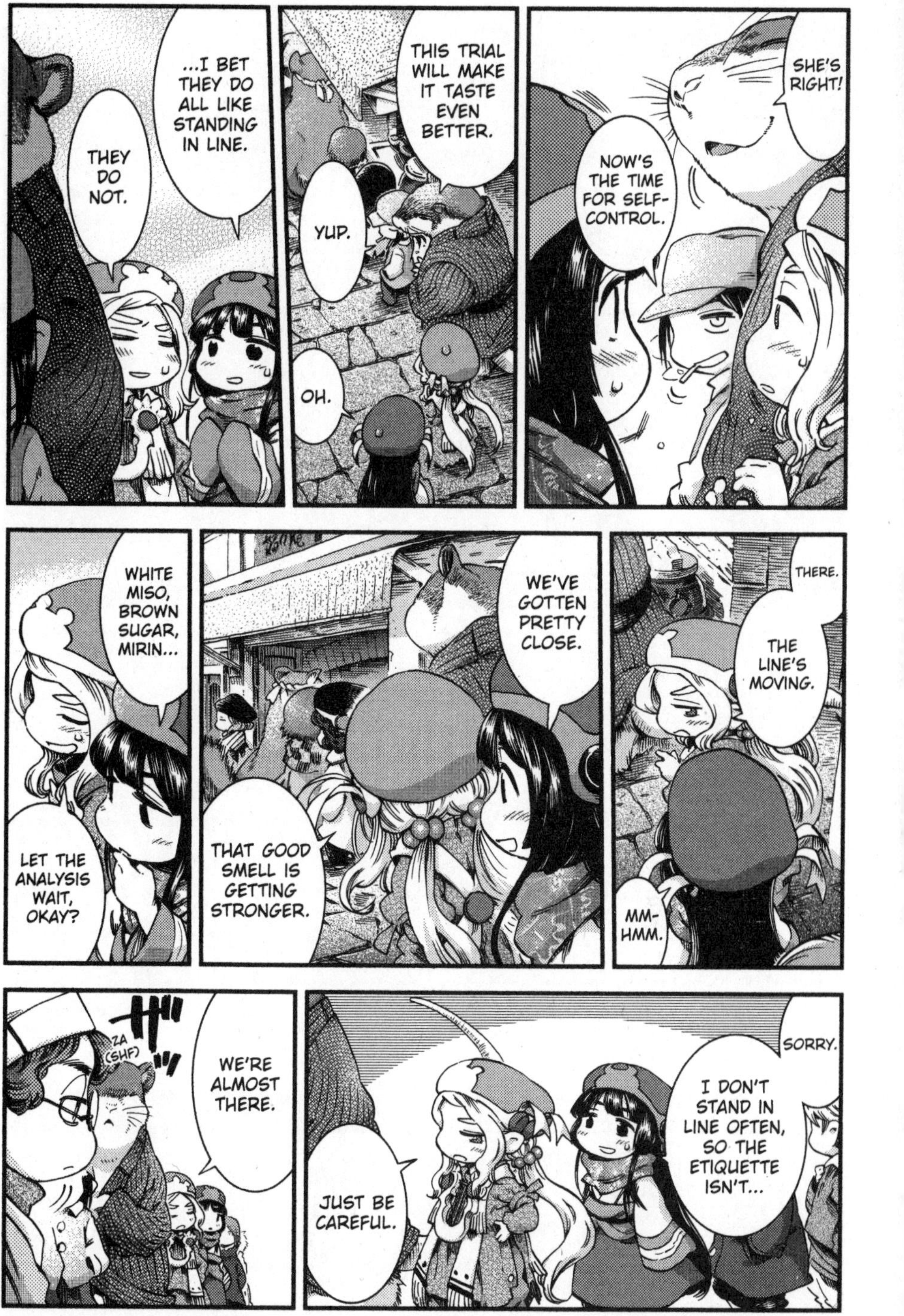
SHE'S RIGHT!
NOW'S THE TIME FOR SELF-CONTROL.
THIS TRIAL WILL MAKE IT TASTE EVEN BETTER.
YUP.
OH.
...I BET THEY DO ALL LIKE STANDING IN LINE.
THEY DO NOT.
THERE.
THE LINE'S MOVING.
MM-HMM.
WE'VE GOTTEN PRETTY CLOSE.
THAT GOOD SMELL IS GETTING STRONGER.
WHITE MISO, BROWN SUGAR, MIRIN...
LET THE ANALYSIS WAIT, OKAY?
SORRY.
I DON'T STAND IN LINE OFTEN, SO THE ETIQUETTE ISN'T...
JUST BE CAREFUL.
ZA (SHF)
WE'RE ALMOST THERE.

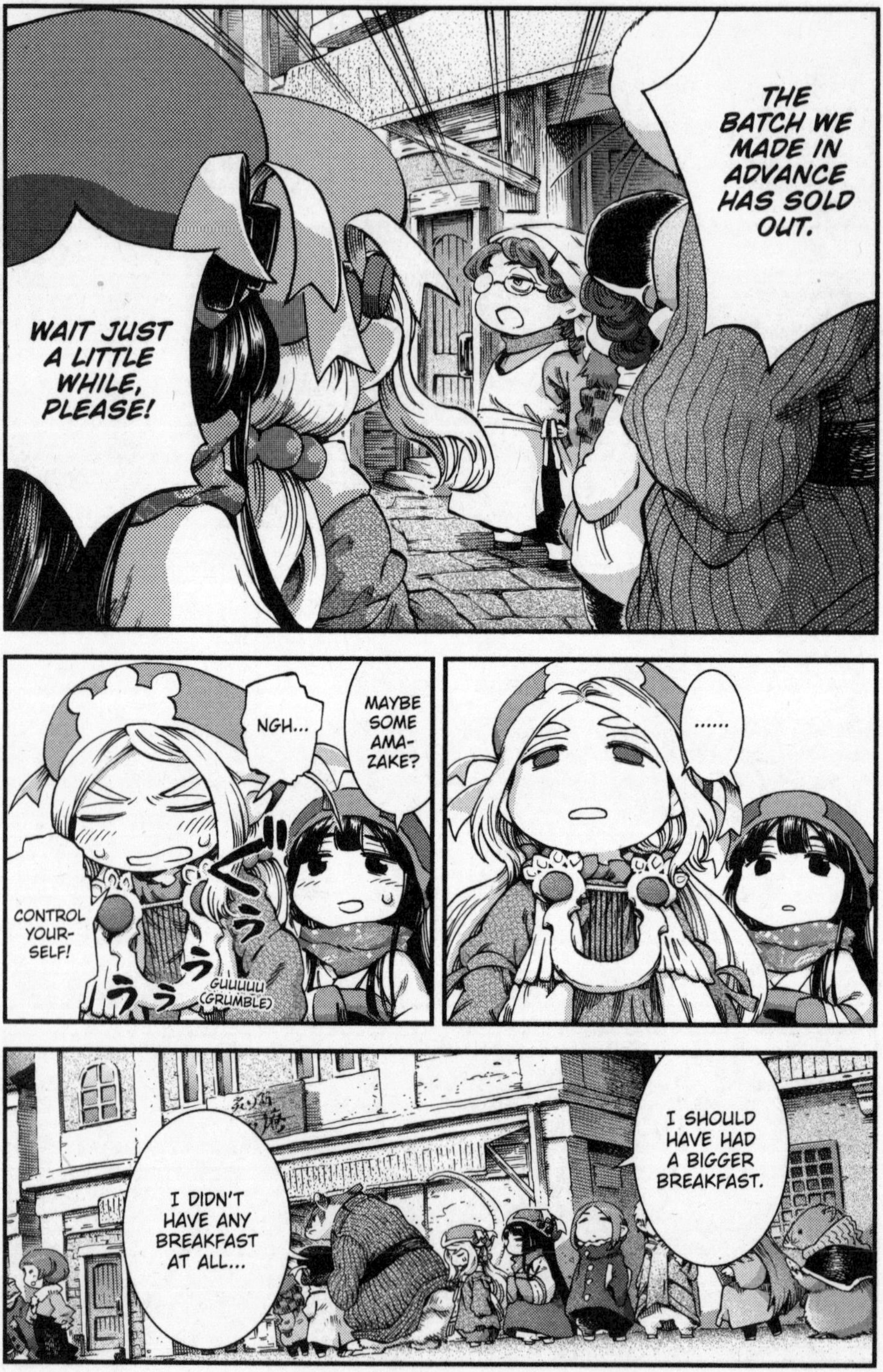
THE BATCH WE MADE IN ADVANCE HAS SOLD OUT.
WAIT JUST A LITTLE WHILE, PLEASE!
......
MAYBE SOME AMA-ZAKE?
NGH...
CONTROL YOUR-SELF!
GUUUUU (GRUMBLE)
I SHOULD HAVE HAD A BIGGER BREAKFAST.
I DIDN'T HAVE ANY BREAKFAST AT ALL...

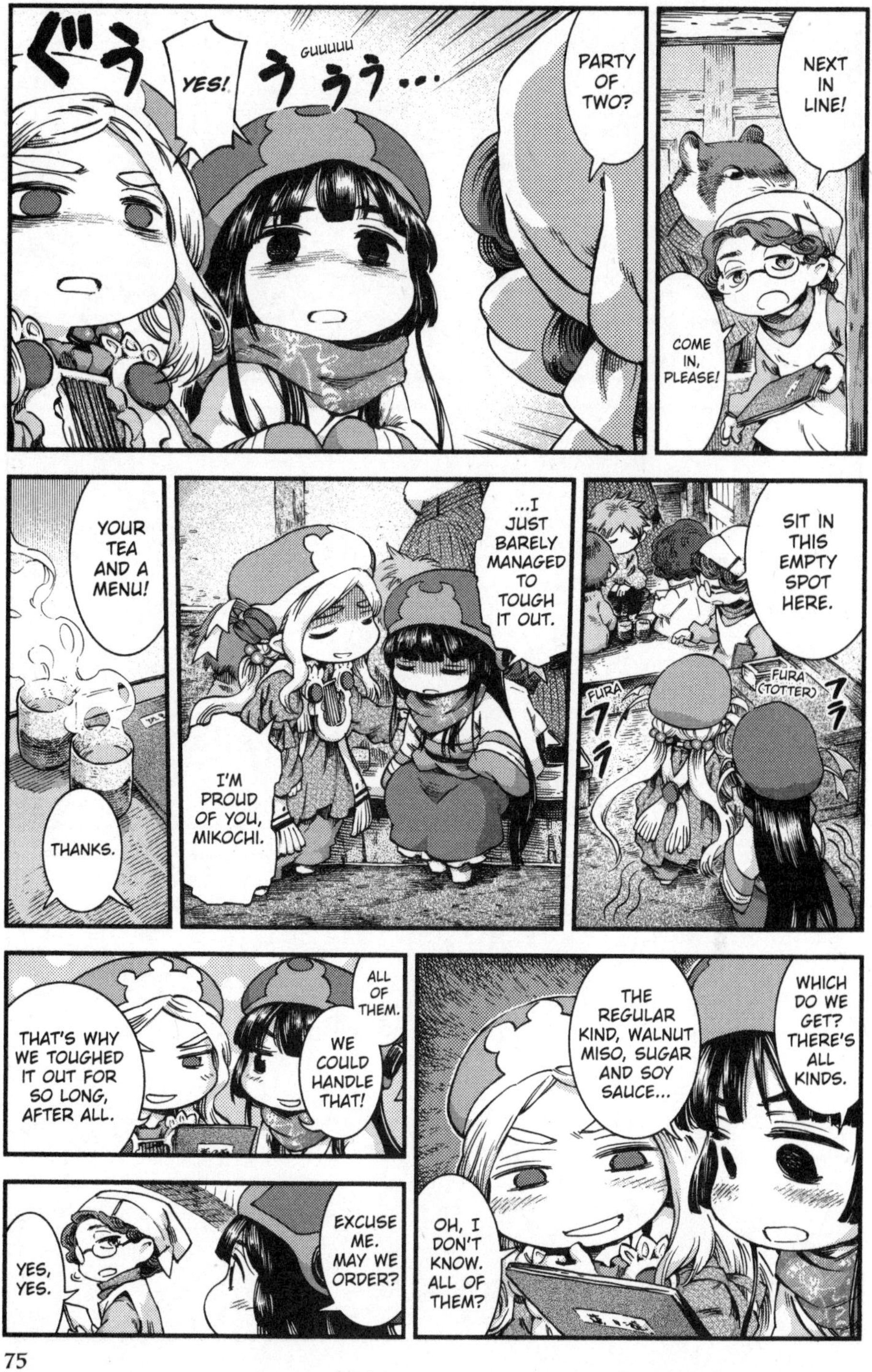
NEXT IN LINE!
COME IN, PLEASE!
PARTY OF TWO?
ううう…
GUUUUU
YES!
ぐう
SIT IN THIS EMPTY SPOT HERE.
FURA (TOTTER)
フラ
FURA
フラ
...I JUST BARELY MANAGED TO TOUGH IT OUT.
I'M PROUD OF YOU, MIKOCHI.
YOUR TEA AND A MENU!
THANKS.
WHICH DO WE GET? THERE'S ALL KINDS.
THE REGULAR KIND, WALNUT MISO, SUGAR AND SOY SAUCE...
OH, I DON'T KNOW. ALL OF THEM?
ALL OF THEM.
WE COULD HANDLE THAT!
THAT'S WHY WE TOUGHED IT OUT FOR SO LONG, AFTER ALL.
EXCUSE ME. MAY WE ORDER?
YES, YES.

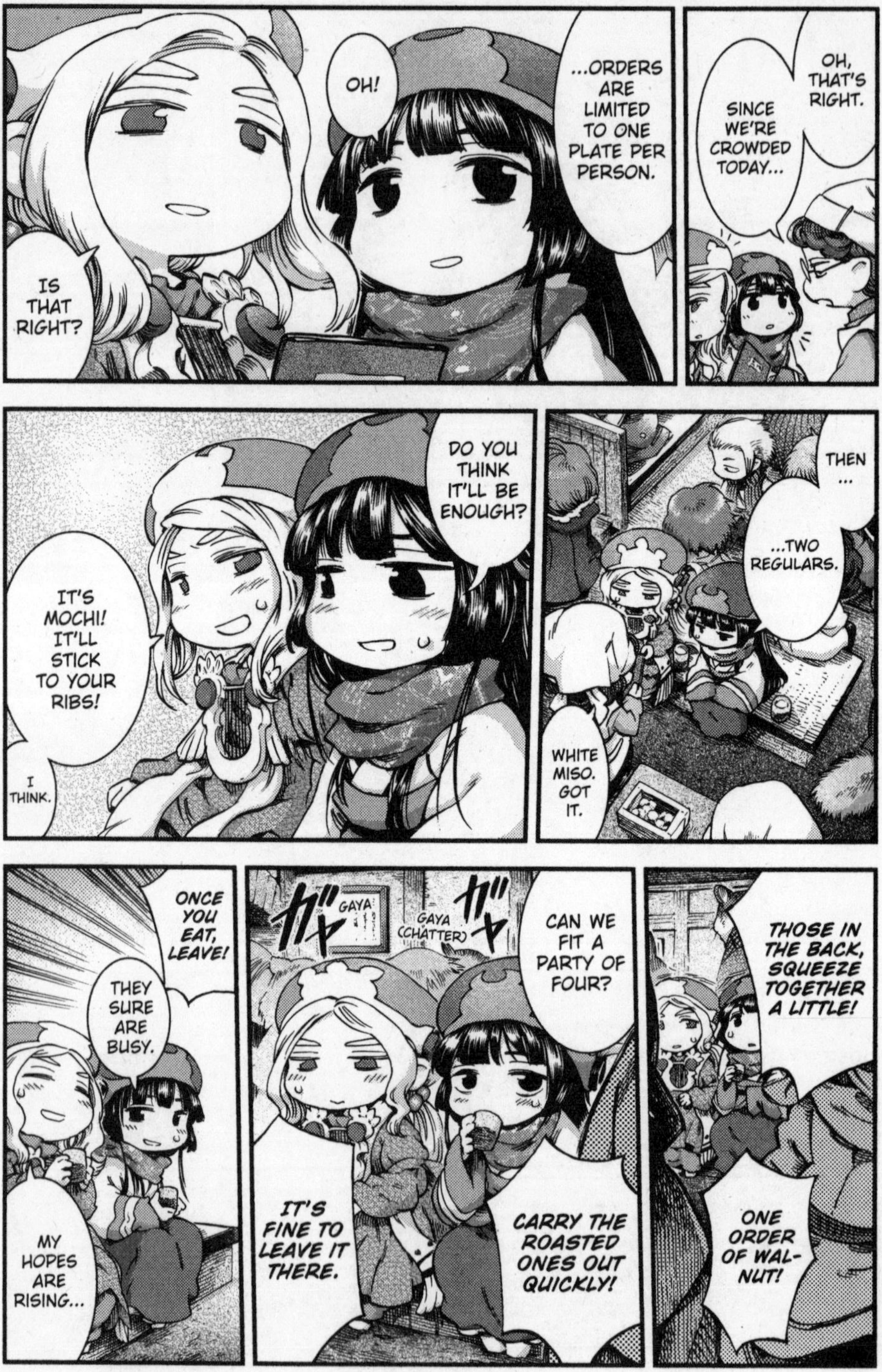
OH, THAT'S RIGHT.
SINCE WE'RE CROWDED TODAY...
...ORDERS ARE LIMITED TO ONE PLATE PER PERSON.
OH!
IS THAT RIGHT?
THEN ...
...TWO REGULARS.
WHITE MISO. GOT IT.
DO YOU THINK IT'LL BE ENOUGH?
IT'S MOCHI! IT'LL STICK TO YOUR RIBS!
I THINK.
THOSE IN THE BACK, SQUEEZE TOGETHER A LITTLE!
ONE ORDER OF WAL-NUT!
CAN WE FIT A PARTY OF FOUR?
GAYA
GAYA (CHATTER)
CARRY THE ROASTED ONES OUT QUICKLY!
IT'S FINE TO LEAVE IT THERE.
ONCE YOU EAT, LEAVE!
THEY SURE ARE BUSY.
MY HOPES ARE RISING...

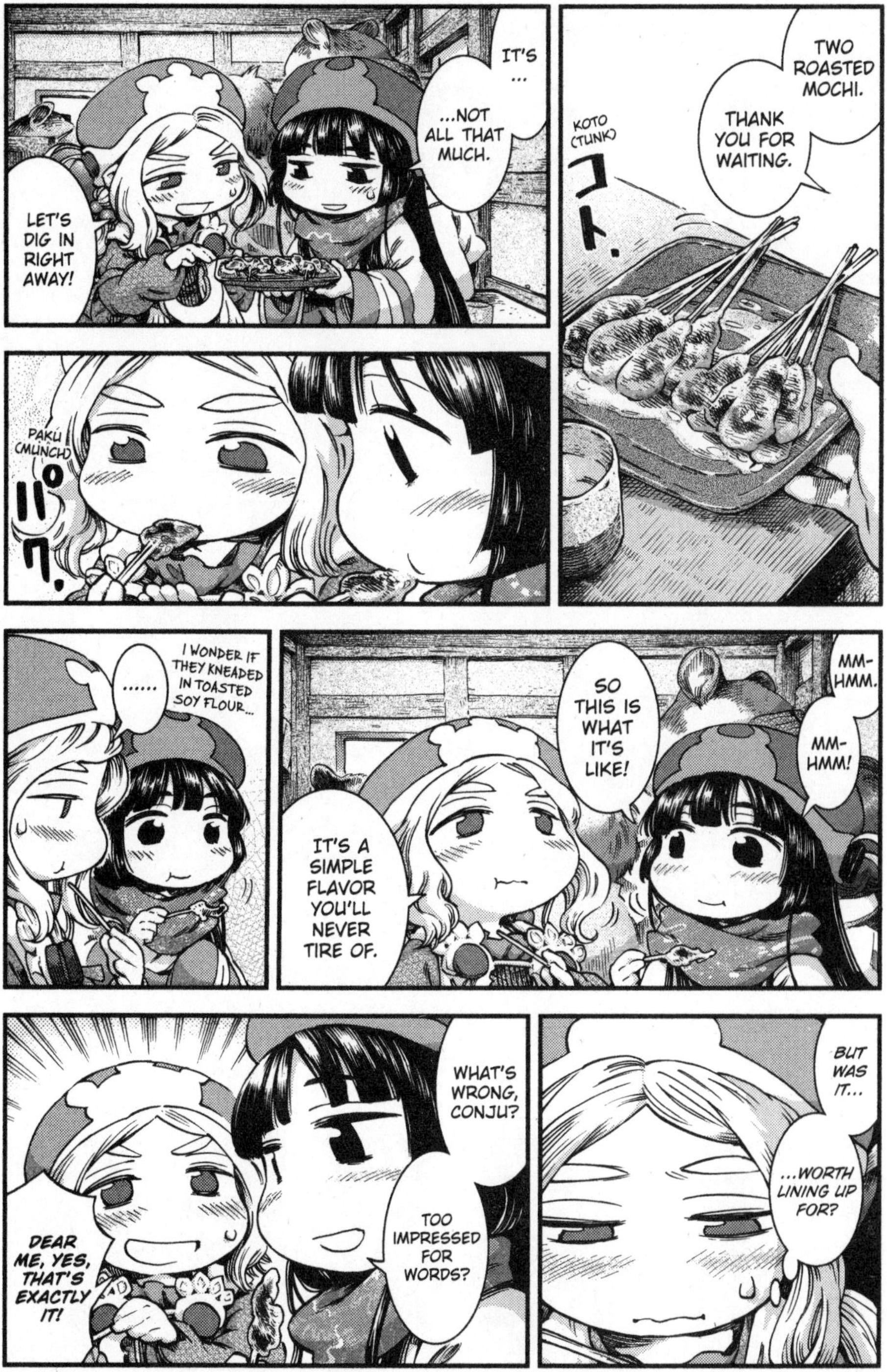
TWO ROASTED MOCHI.
THANK YOU FOR WAITING.
KOTO (TUNK)
コト.
IT'S ...
...NOT ALL THAT MUCH.
LET'S DIG IN RIGHT AWAY!
PAKU (MUNCH)
パク.
MM-HMM.
MM-HMM!
SO THIS IS WHAT IT'S LIKE!
IT'S A SIMPLE FLAVOR YOU'LL NEVER TIRE OF.
......
I WONDER IF THEY KNEADED IN TOASTED SOY FLOUR...
BUT WAS IT...
...WORTH LINING UP FOR?
WHAT'S WRONG, CONJU?
TOO IMPRESSED FOR WORDS?
DEAR ME, YES, THAT'S EXACTLY IT!

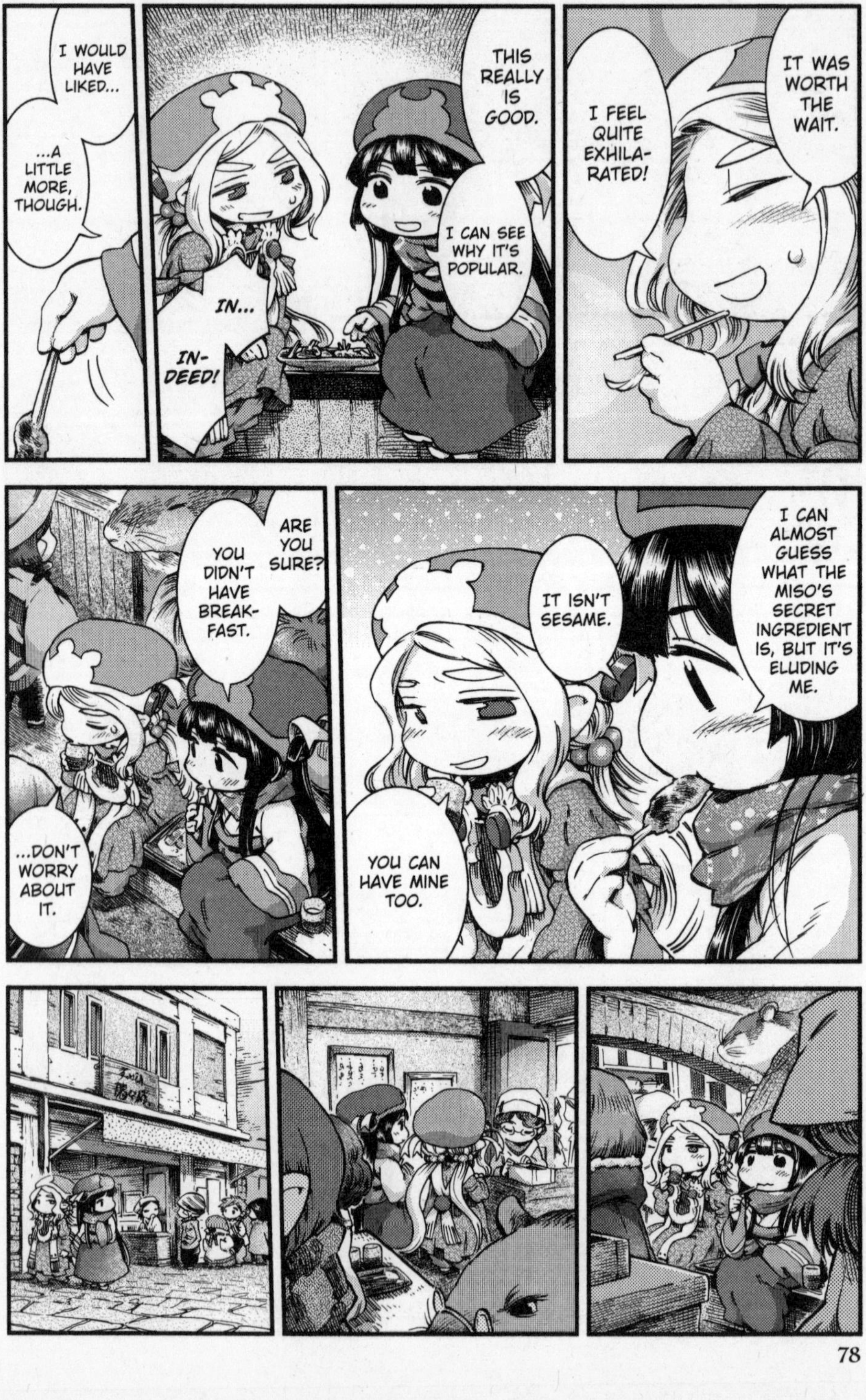
IT WAS WORTH THE WAIT.
I FEEL QUITE EXHILA-RATED!
THIS REALLY IS GOOD.
I CAN SEE WHY IT'S POPULAR.
IN...
IN-DEED!
I WOULD HAVE LIKED...
...A LITTLE MORE, THOUGH.
I CAN ALMOST GUESS WHAT THE MISO'S SECRET INGREDIENT IS, BUT IT'S ELUDING ME.
IT ISN'T SESAME.
YOU CAN HAVE MINE TOO.
ARE YOU SURE?
YOU DIDN'T HAVE BREAK-FAST.
...DON'T WORRY ABOUT IT.

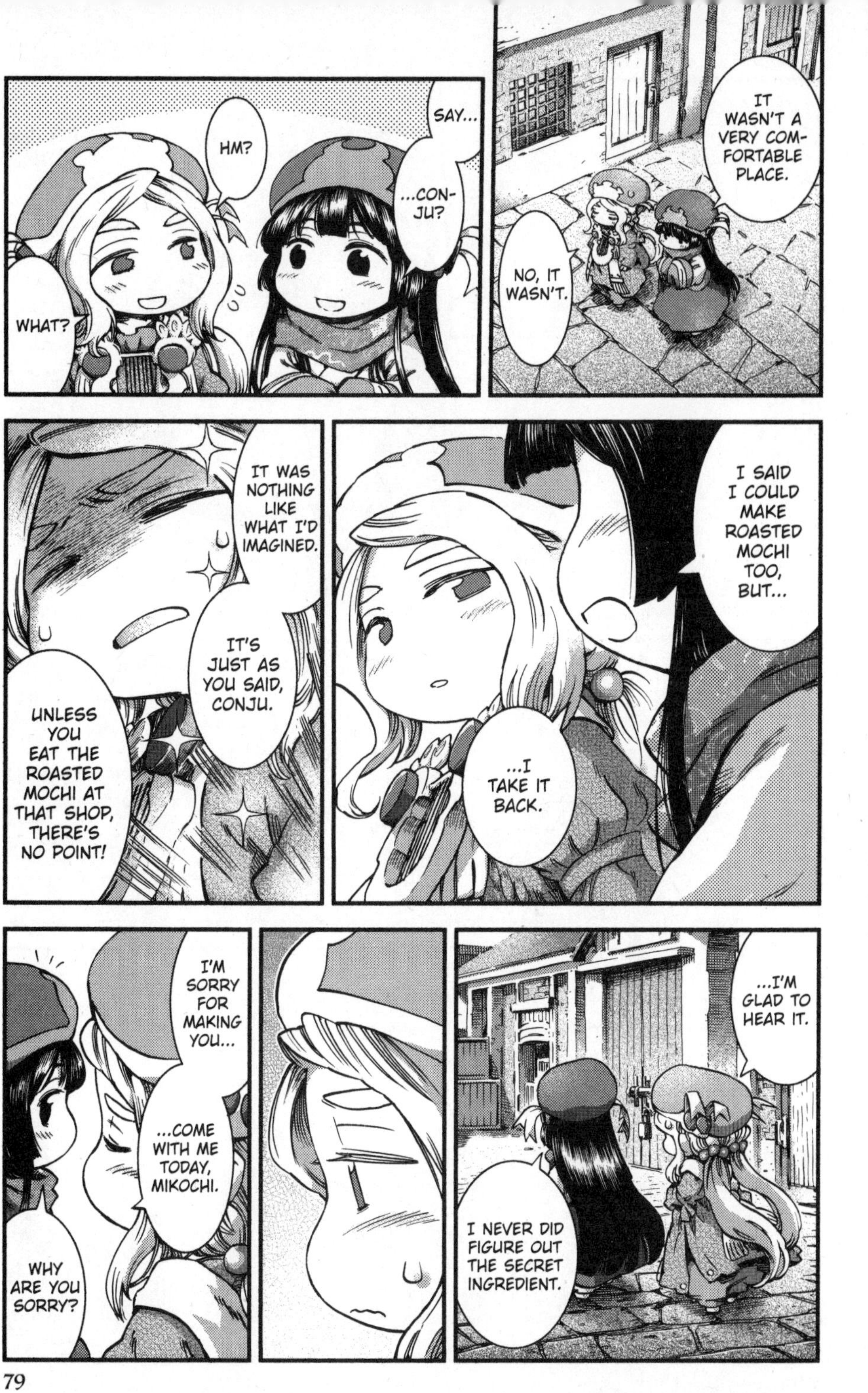
IT WASN'T A VERY COM-FORTABLE PLACE.
NO, IT WASN'T.
SAY...
...CON-JU?
HM?
WHAT?
I SAID I COULD MAKE ROASTED MOCHI TOO, BUT...
...I TAKE IT BACK.
IT WAS NOTHING LIKE WHAT I'D IMAGINED.
IT'S JUST AS YOU SAID, CONJU.
UNLESS YOU EAT THE ROASTED MOCHI AT THAT SHOP, THERE'S NO POINT!
...I'M GLAD TO HEAR IT.
I NEVER DID FIGURE OUT THE SECRET INGREDIENT.
I'M SORRY FOR MAKING YOU...
...COME WITH ME TODAY, MIKOCHI.
WHY ARE YOU SORRY?

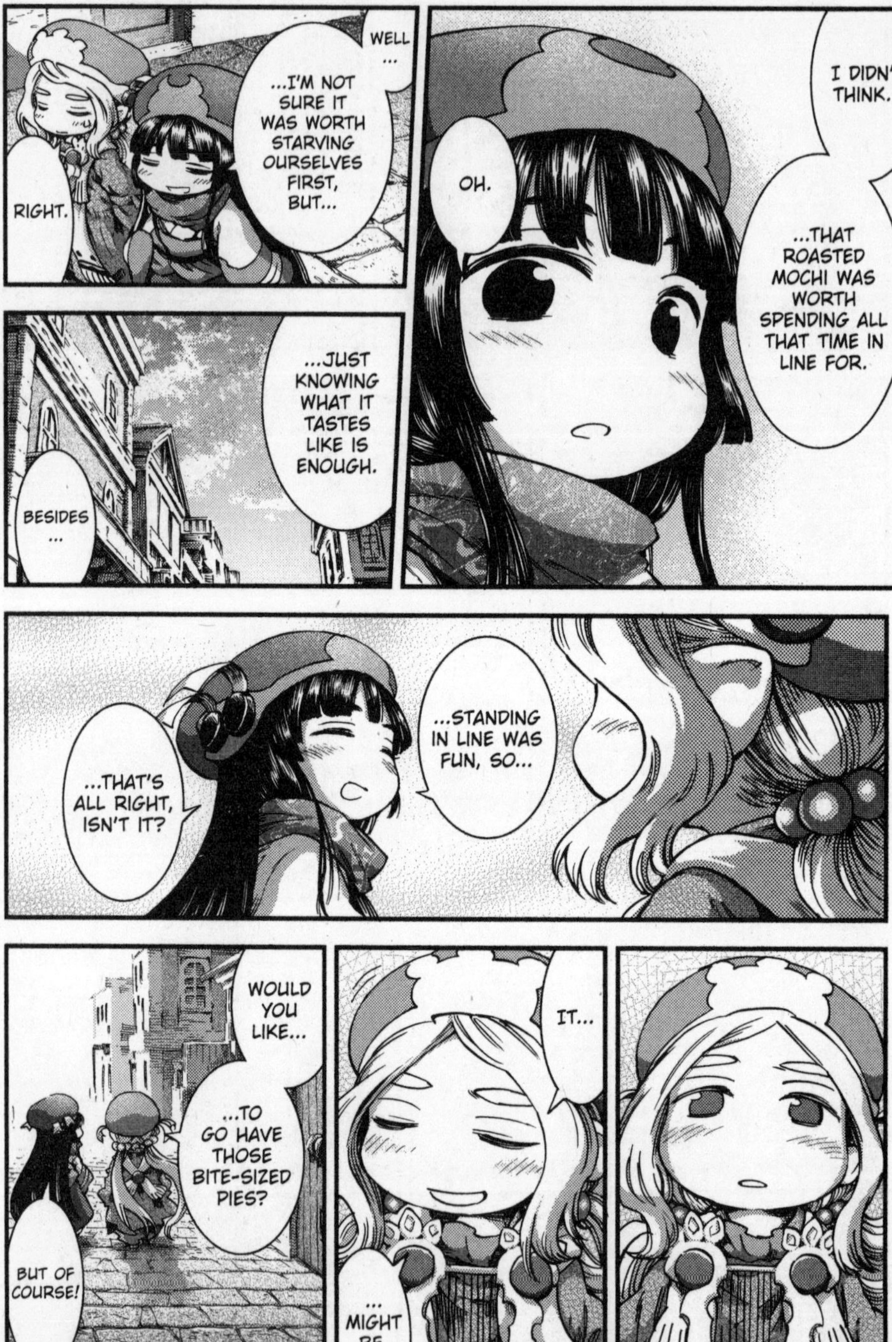
I DIDN'T THINK...
...THAT ROASTED MOCHI WAS WORTH SPENDING ALL THAT TIME IN LINE FOR.
OH.
WELL ...
...I'M NOT SURE IT WAS WORTH STARVING OURSELVES FIRST, BUT...
RIGHT.
...JUST KNOWING WHAT IT TASTES LIKE IS ENOUGH.
BESIDES ...
...STANDING IN LINE WAS FUN, SO...
...THAT'S ALL RIGHT, ISN'T IT?
IT...
... MIGHT BE.
WOULD YOU LIKE...
...TO GO HAVE THOSE BITE-SIZED PIES?
BUT OF COURSE!

A traditional Japanese sweetshop located on the southeast edge of Makinata. Originally, it was a wholesale rice merchant that had been handed down through the generations since before Makinata was cultivated. However, eight years ago, it reinvented itself as an eatery with a menu focused on different types of mochi. Its star product—roasted mochi—is simple, fragrant, and soft, and has been a best seller for years. It's said to be a re-creation of a dish the first shop owner made for himself using leftover mochi rice.

The simply furnished, quiet restaurant is located in a remodeled warehouse, but lately word of mouth has increased its clientele dramatically, and it's suddenly grown lively.

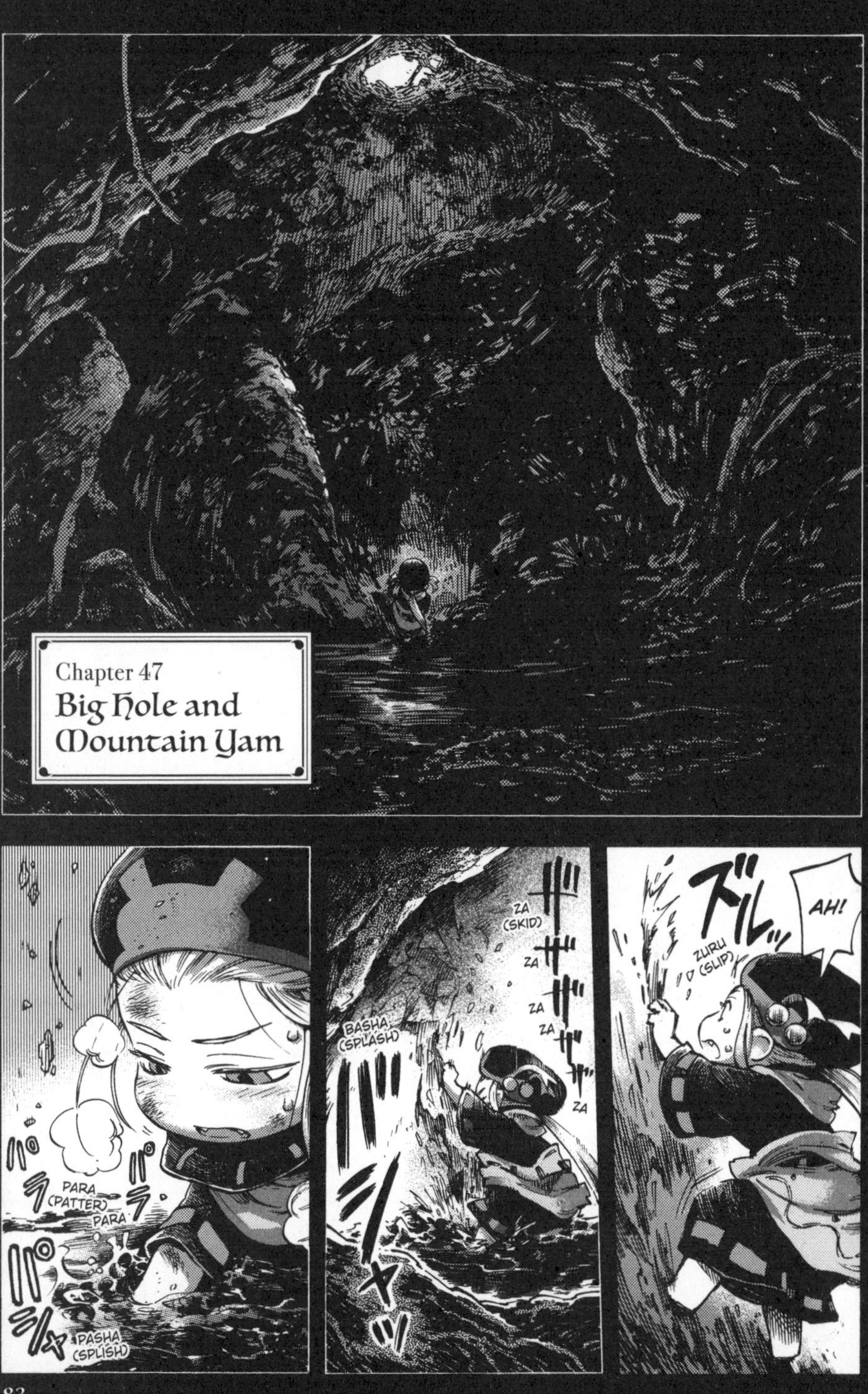
Chapter 47
Big Hole and Mountain Yam
ズル
ZURU (SLIP)
AH!
ZA (SKID)
ZA
ZA
ZA
ZA
BASHA (SPLASH)
PARA (PATTER) PARA
PASHA (SPLISH)

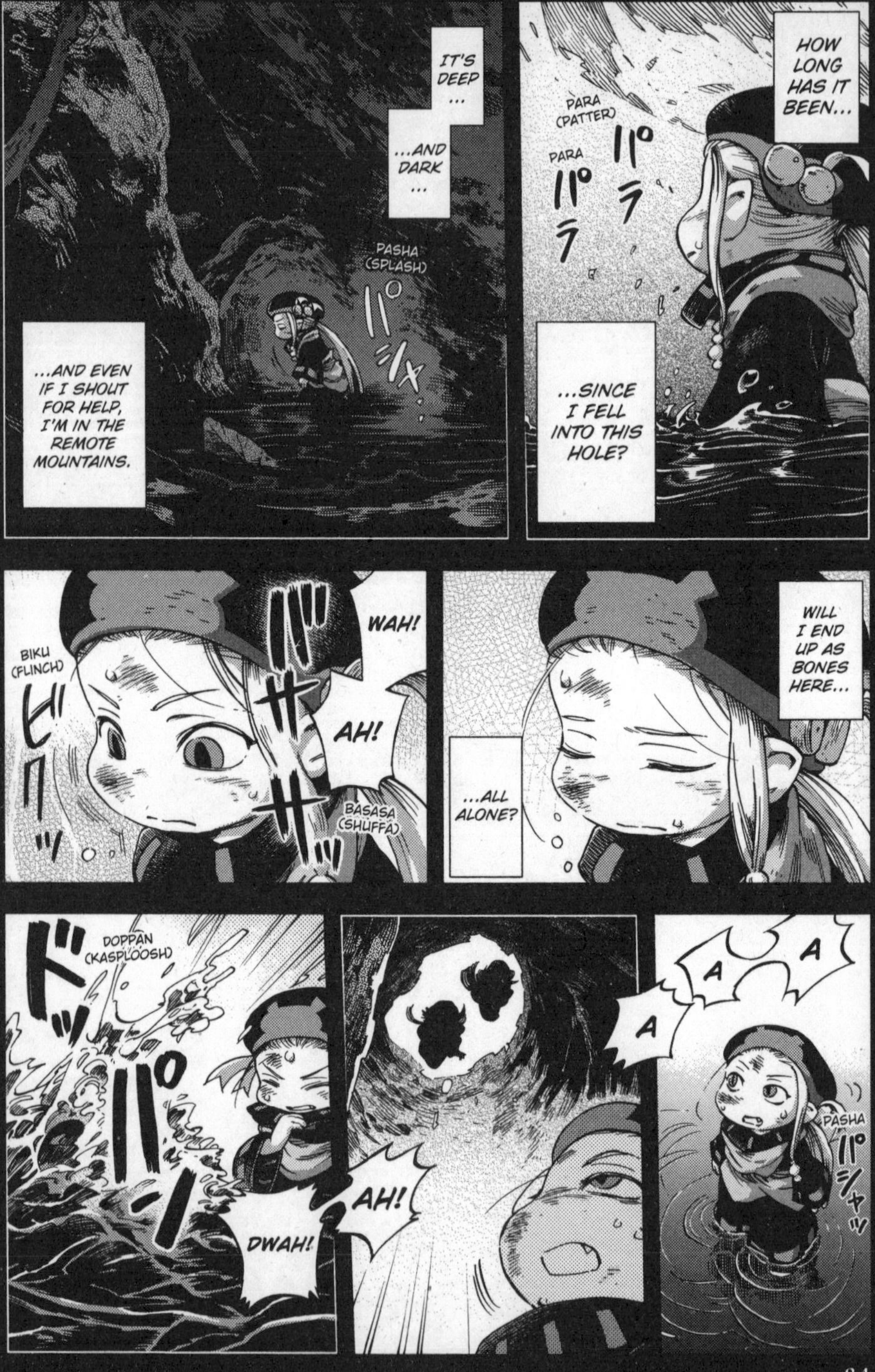
HOW LONG HAS IT BEEN...
PARA (PATTER)
PARA
...SINCE I FELL INTO THIS HOLE?
IT'S DEEP...
...AND DARK...
PASHA (SPLASH)
...AND EVEN IF I SHOUT FOR HELP, I'M IN THE REMOTE MOUNTAINS.
WILL I END UP AS BONES HERE...
...ALL ALONE?
WAH!
BIKU (FLINCH)
AH!
BASASA (SHUFFA)
A
A
A
PASHA
AH!
DOPPAN (KASPLOOSH)
DWAH!

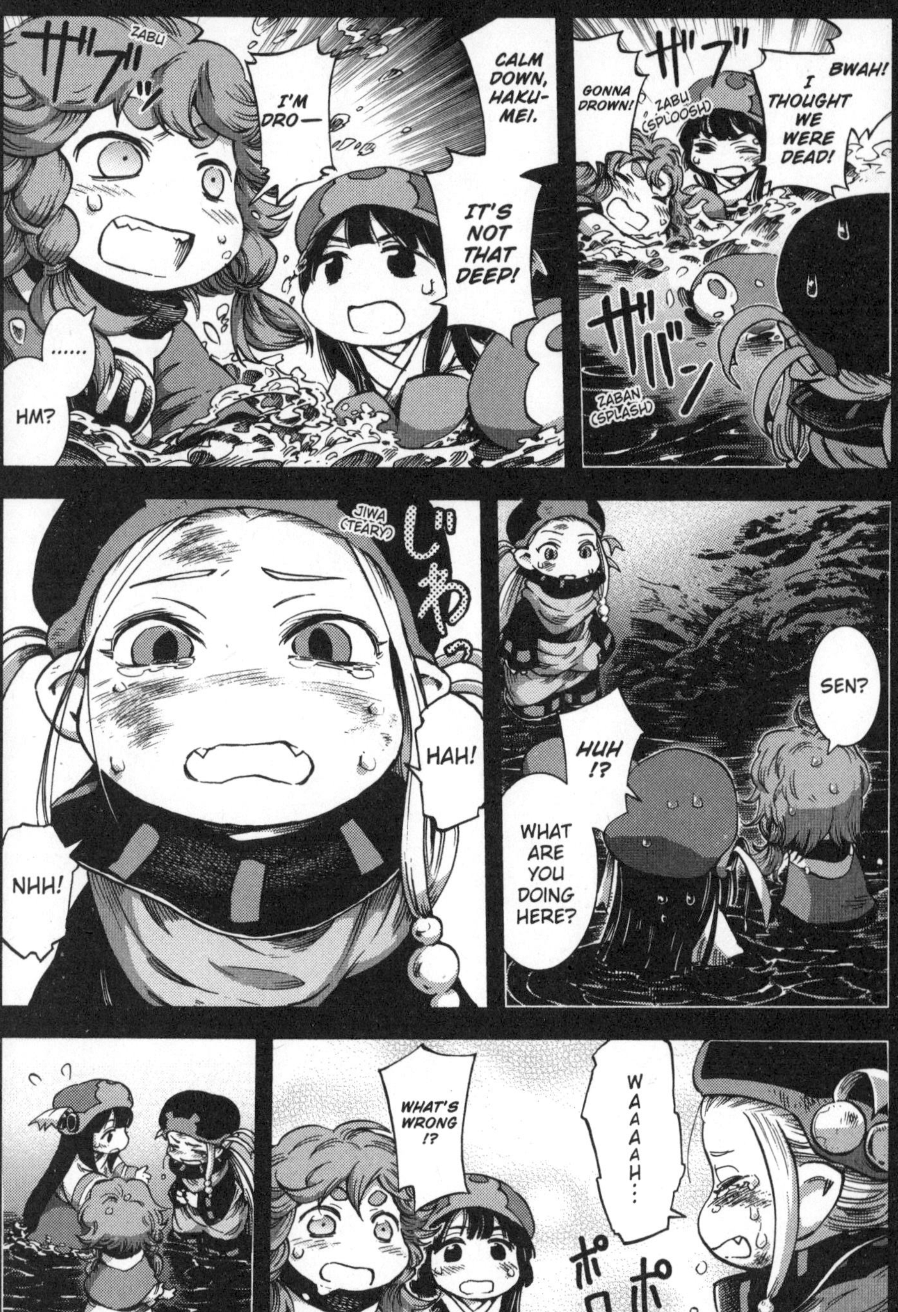
BWAH! I THOUGHT WE WERE DEAD!
ZABU (SPLOOSH)
GONNA DROWN!
ZABAN (SPLASH)
ZABU
CALM DOWN, HAKU-MEI.
I'M DRO—
IT'S NOT THAT DEEP!
......
HM?
SEN?
HUH!?
WHAT ARE YOU DOING HERE?
JIWA (TEARY)
HAH!
NHH!
WAAAAAH...
WHAT'S WRONG!?
PORO
PORO (PLIP)

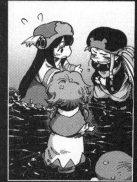

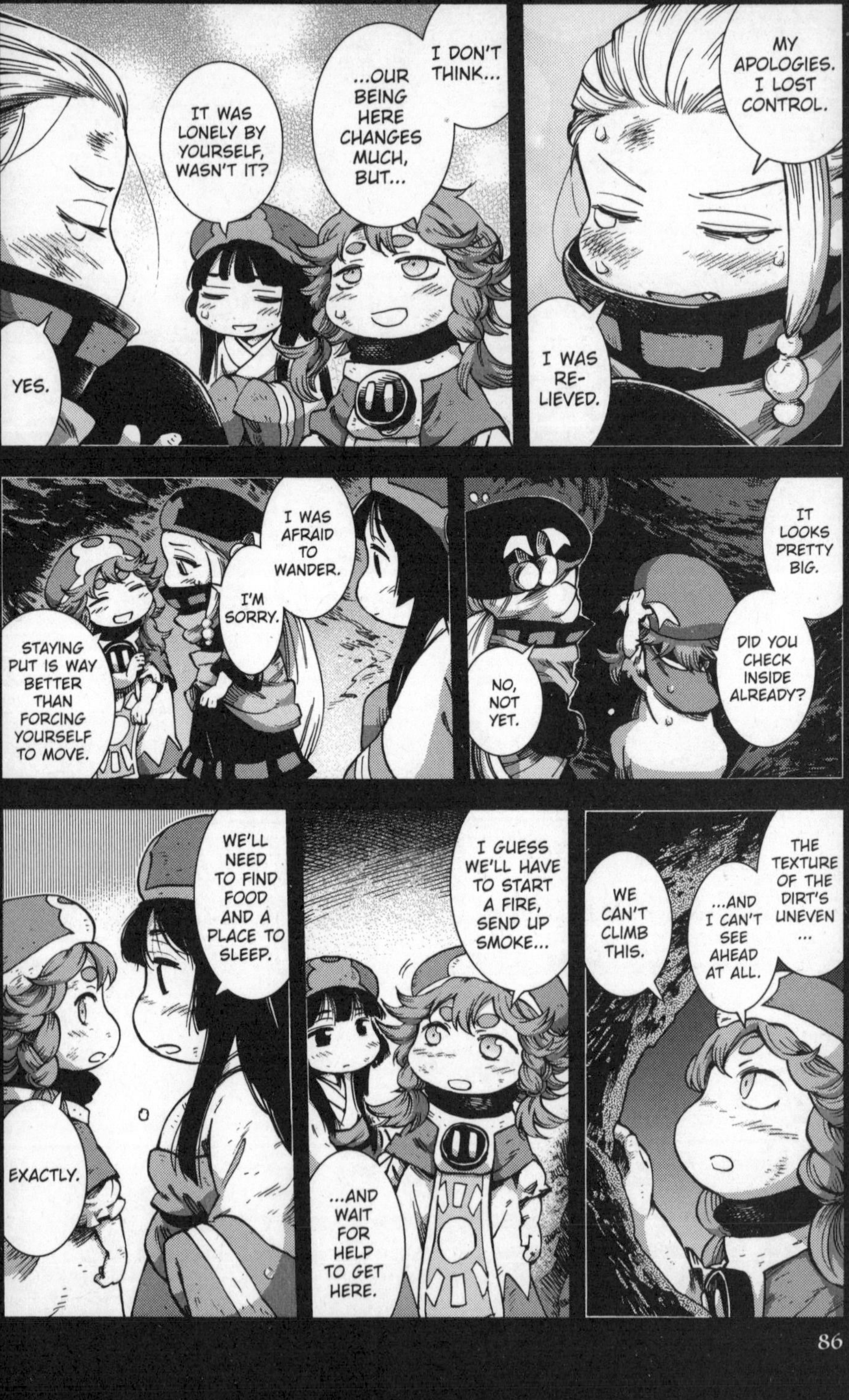
MY APOLOGIES. I LOST CONTROL.
I WAS RE-LIEVED.
I DON'T THINK...
...OUR BEING HERE CHANGES MUCH, BUT...
IT WAS LONELY BY YOURSELF, WASN'T IT?
YES.
IT LOOKS PRETTY BIG.
DID YOU CHECK INSIDE ALREADY?
NO, NOT YET.
I WAS AFRAID TO WANDER.
I'M SORRY.
STAYING PUT IS WAY BETTER THAN FORCING YOURSELF TO MOVE.
THE TEXTURE OF THE DIRT'S UNEVEN ...
...AND I CAN'T SEE AHEAD AT ALL.
WE CAN'T CLIMB THIS.
I GUESS WE'LL HAVE TO START A FIRE, SEND UP SMOKE...
...AND WAIT FOR HELP TO GET HERE.
WE'LL NEED TO FIND FOOD AND A PLACE TO SLEEP.
EXACTLY.

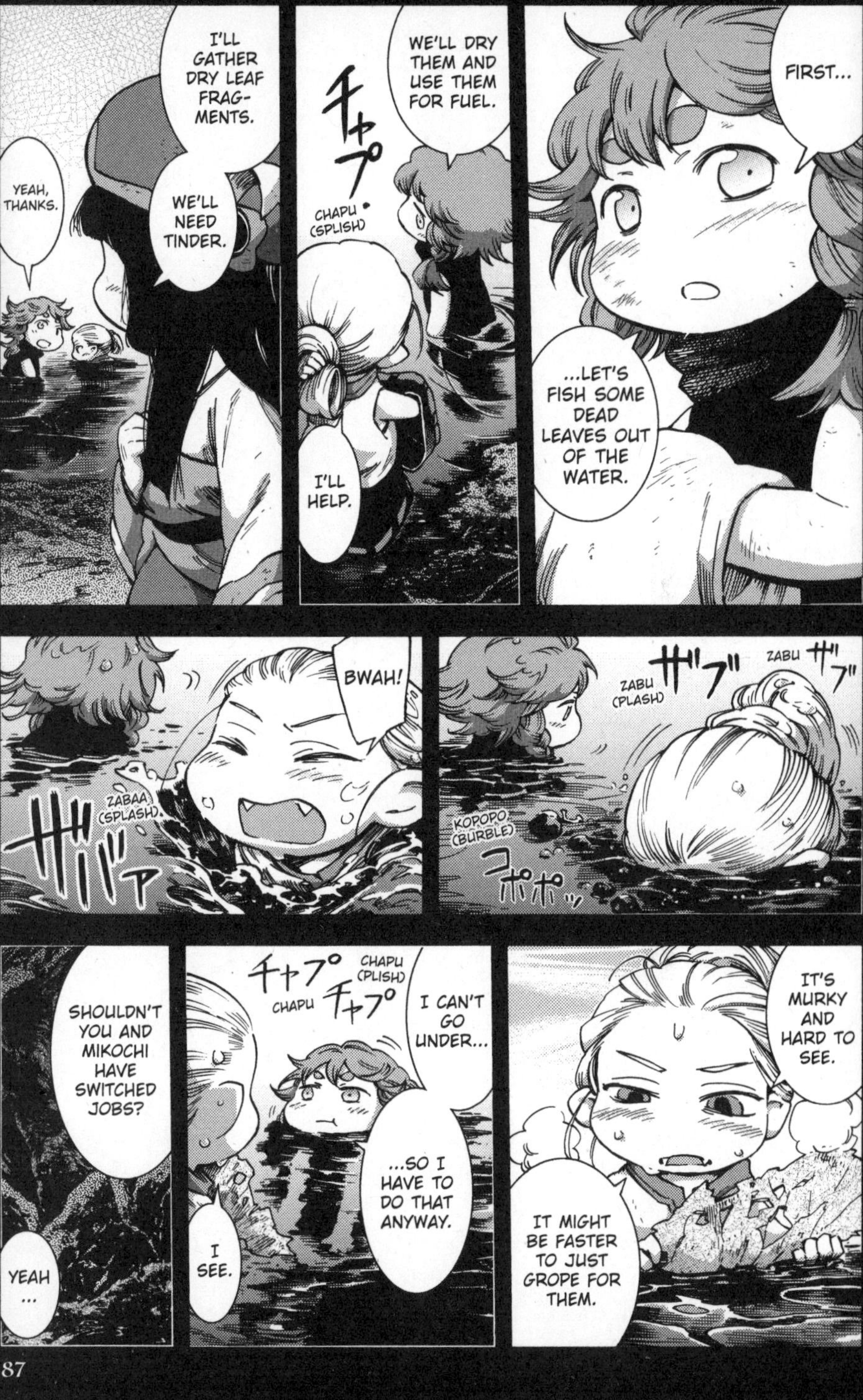
FIRST...
...LET'S FISH SOME DEAD LEAVES OUT OF THE WATER.
WE'LL DRY THEM AND USE THEM FOR FUEL.
チャプ
CHAPU (SPLISH)
I'LL HELP.
I'LL GATHER DRY LEAF FRAG-MENTS.
WE'LL NEED TINDER.
YEAH, THANKS.
ザブ
ZABU (PLASH)
ZABU
ザブ
KOPOPO (BURBLE)
コポポッ
BWAH!
ZABAA (SPLASH)
ザバァ
IT'S MURKY AND HARD TO SEE.
IT MIGHT BE FASTER TO JUST GROPE FOR THEM.
チャプ
CHAPU (PLISH)
CHAPU
チャプ
I CAN'T GO UNDER...
...SO I HAVE TO DO THAT ANYWAY.
I SEE.
SHOULDN'T YOU AND MIKOCHI HAVE SWITCHED JOBS?
YEAH...

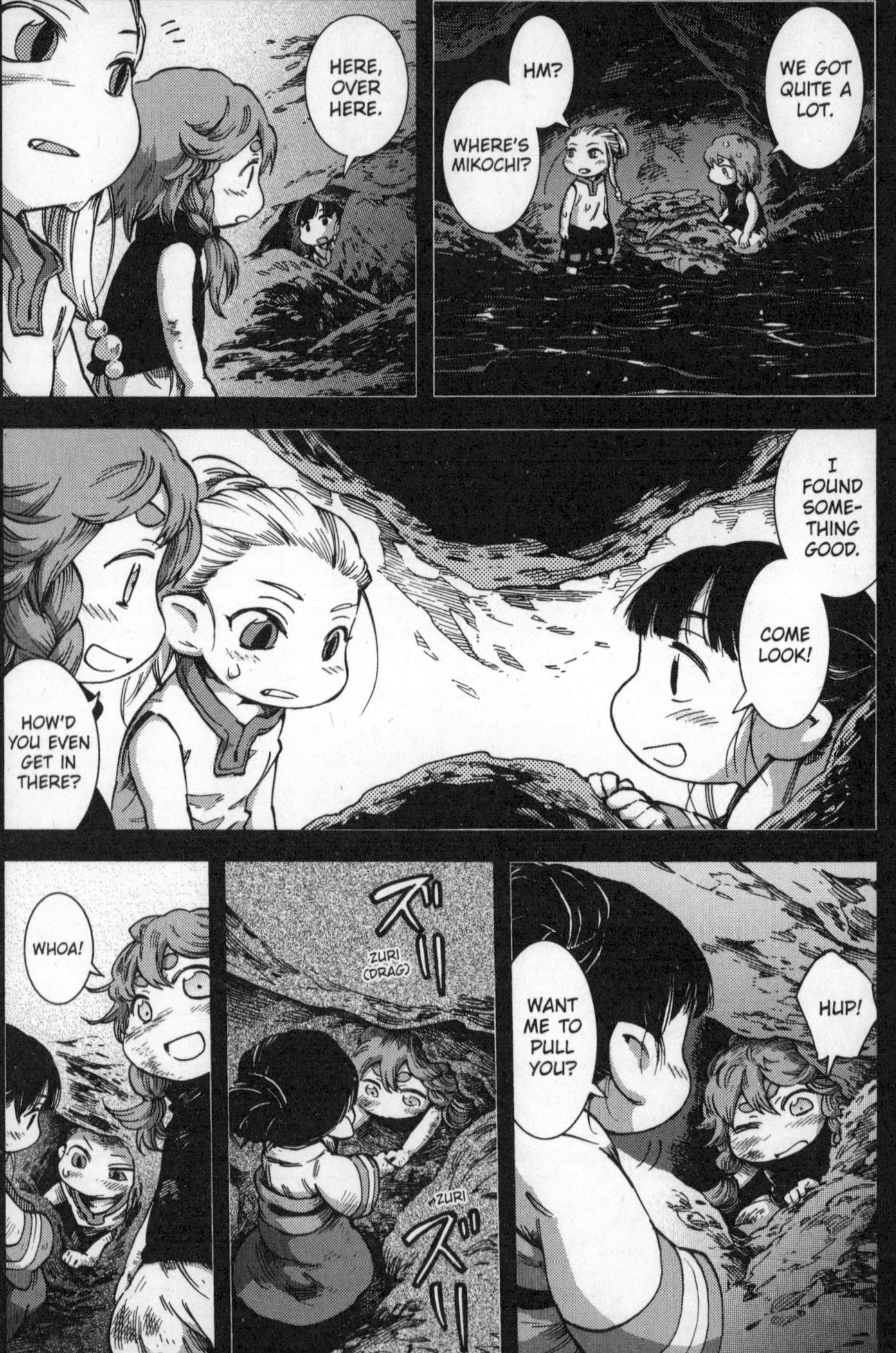
WE GOT QUITE A LOT.
HM?
WHERE'S MIKOCHI?
HERE, OVER HERE.
I FOUND SOME-THING GOOD.
COME LOOK!
HOW'D YOU EVEN GET IN THERE?
HUP!
WANT ME TO PULL YOU?
ズリ
ZURI (DRAG)
ズリ
ZURI
WHOA!

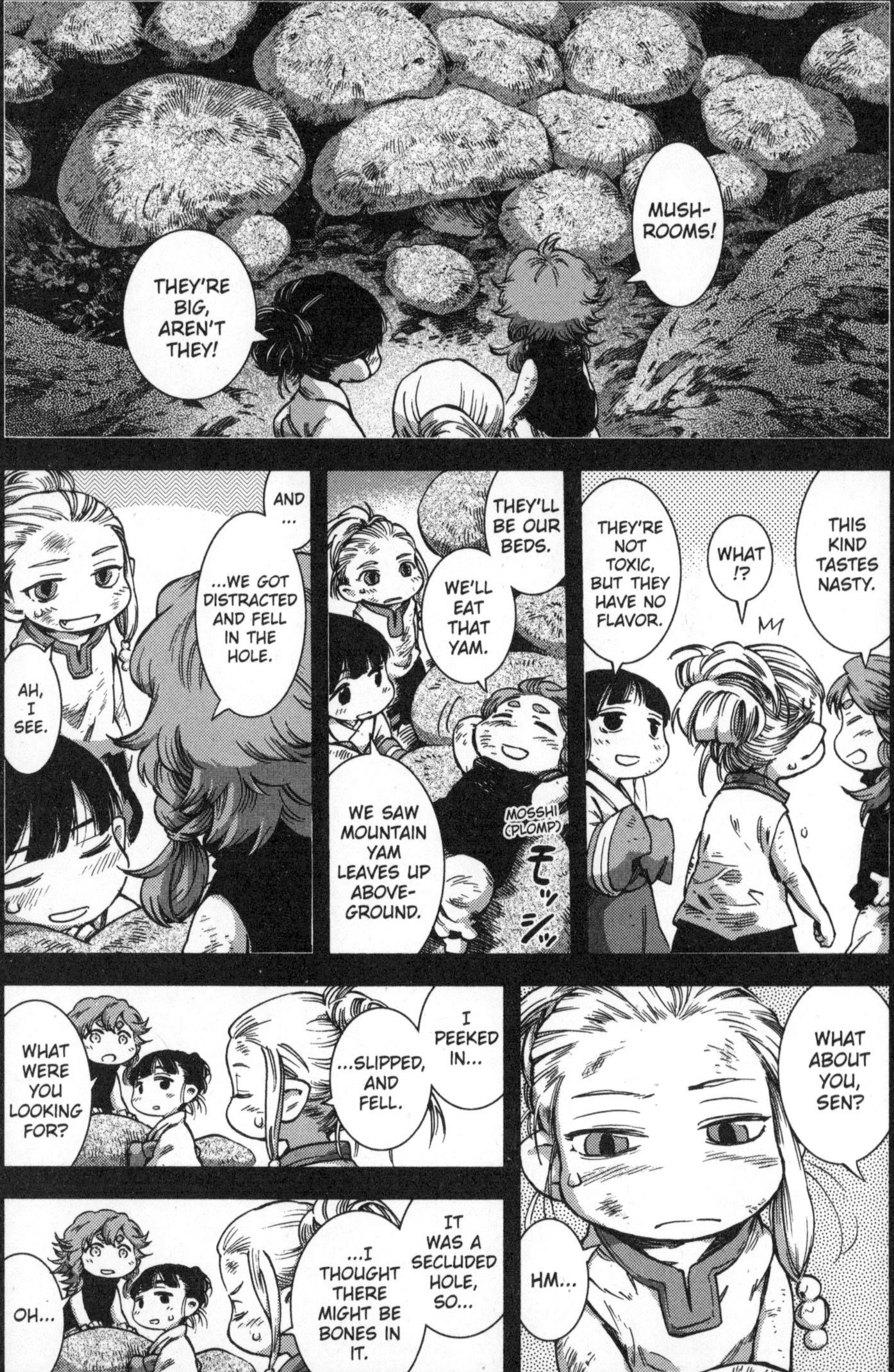
MUSH-ROOMS!
THEY'RE BIG, AREN'T THEY!
THIS KIND TASTES NASTY.
WHAT!?
THEY'RE NOT TOXIC, BUT THEY HAVE NO FLAVOR.
THEY'LL BE OUR BEDS.
WE'LL EAT THAT YAM.
WE SAW MOUNTAIN YAM LEAVES UP ABOVE-GROUND.
MOSSHI (PLOMP)
モッシッ
AND ...
...WE GOT DISTRACTED AND FELL IN THE HOLE.
AH, I SEE.
WHAT ABOUT YOU, SEN?
HM...
I PEEKED IN...
...SLIPPED, AND FELL.
WHAT WERE YOU LOOKING FOR?
IT WAS A SECLUDED HOLE, SO...
...I THOUGHT THERE MIGHT BE BONES IN IT.
OH...

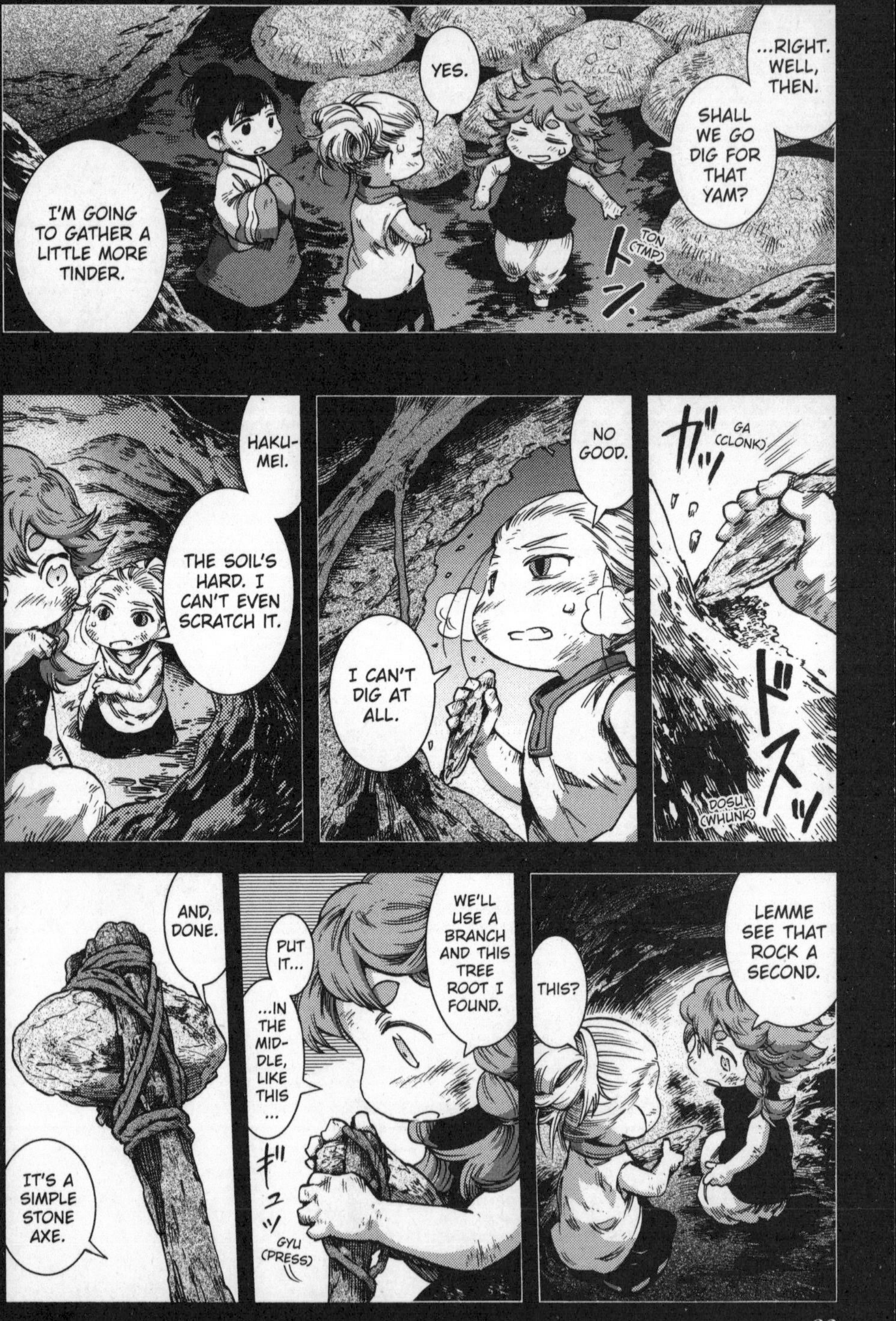
...RIGHT. WELL, THEN.
SHALL WE GO DIG FOR THAT YAM?
YES.
TON (TMP)
I'M GOING TO GATHER A LITTLE MORE TINDER.
GA (CLONK)
DOSU (WHUNK)
NO GOOD.
I CAN'T DIG AT ALL.
HAKU-MEI.
THE SOIL'S HARD. I CAN'T EVEN SCRATCH IT.
LEMME SEE THAT ROCK A SECOND.
THIS?
WE'LL USE A BRANCH AND THIS TREE ROOT I FOUND.
PUT IT...
...IN THE MIDDLE, LIKE THIS...
GYU (PRESS)
AND, DONE.
IT'S A SIMPLE STONE AXE.

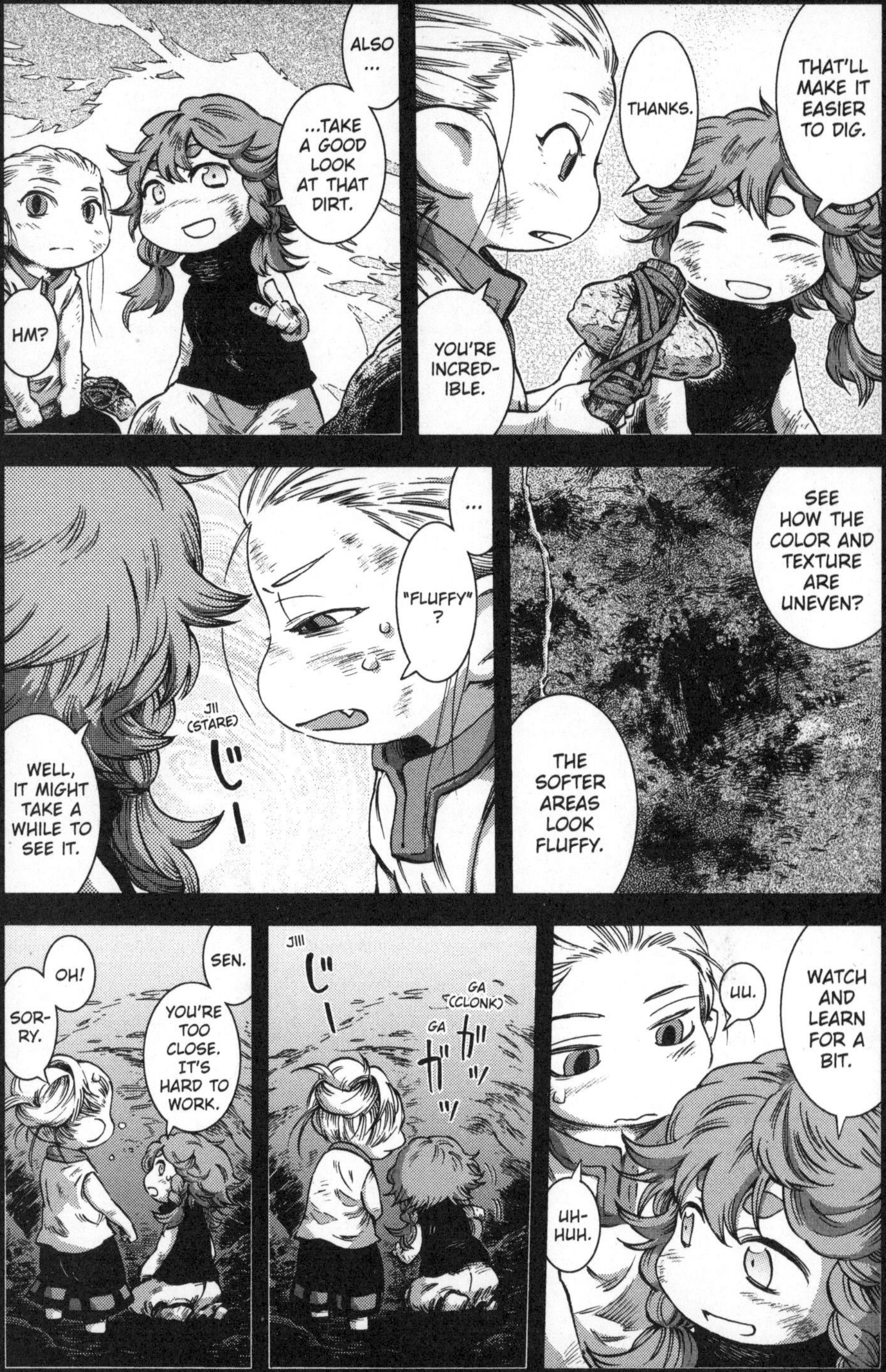
THAT'LL MAKE IT EASIER TO DIG.
THANKS.
YOU'RE INCREDIBLE.
ALSO ...
...TAKE A GOOD LOOK AT THAT DIRT.
HM?
SEE HOW THE COLOR AND TEXTURE ARE UNEVEN?
THE SOFTER AREAS LOOK FLUFFY.
...
"FLUFFY"?
JII (STARE)
じー
WELL, IT MIGHT TAKE A WHILE TO SEE IT.
WATCH AND LEARN FOR A BIT.
UU.
UH-HUH.
JIII
じー
GA (CLONK)
ガッ
GA
ガッ
SEN.
YOU'RE TOO CLOSE. IT'S HARD TO WORK.
OH!
SORRY.

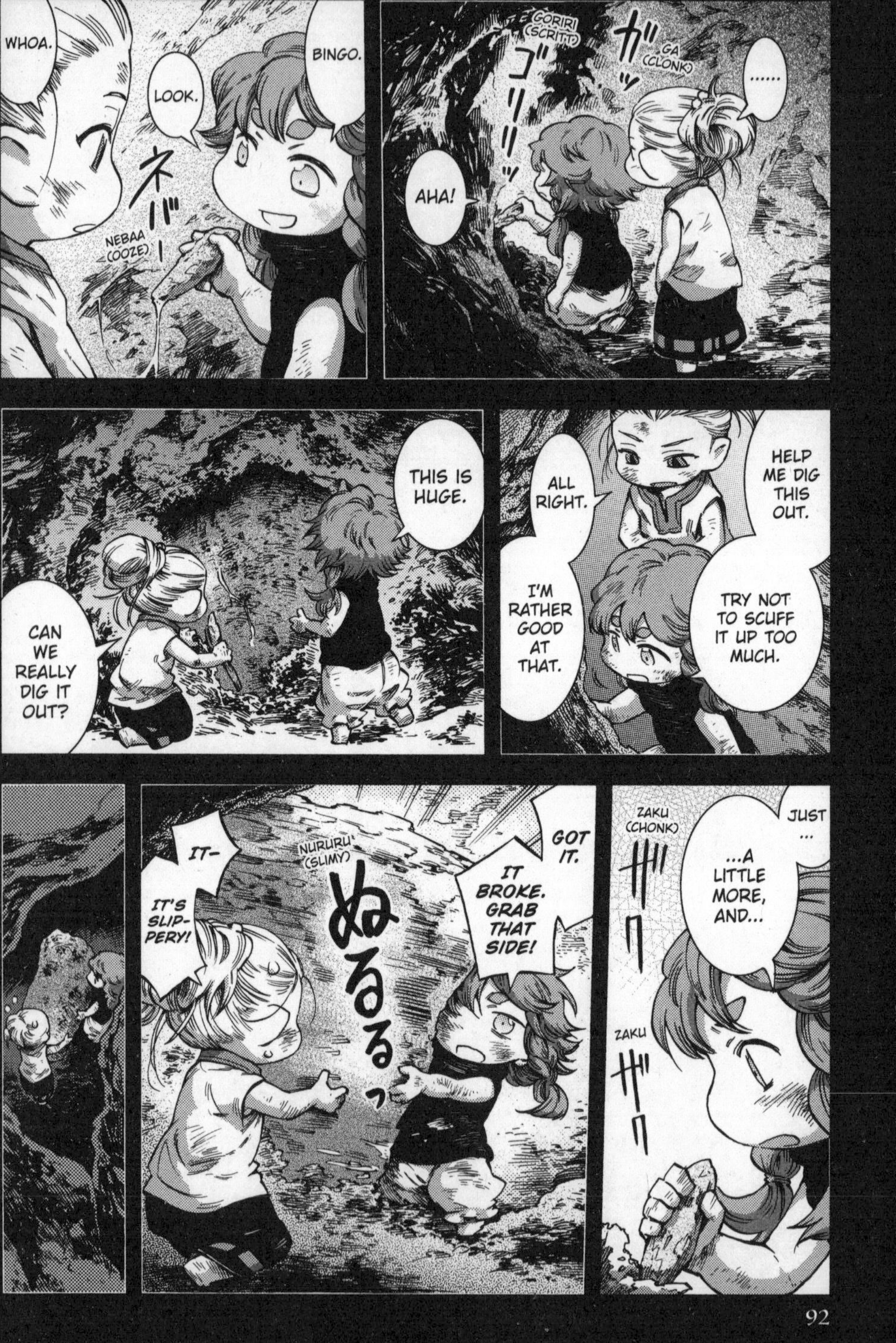
......
GA (CLONK)
GORIRI (SCRITT)
AHA!
BINGO.
LOOK.
WHOA.
NEBAA (OOZE)
HELP ME DIG THIS OUT.
ALL RIGHT.
TRY NOT TO SCUFF IT UP TOO MUCH.
I'M RATHER GOOD AT THAT.
THIS IS HUGE.
CAN WE REALLY DIG IT OUT?
JUST...
ZAKU (CHONK)
...A LITTLE MORE, AND...
ZAKU
GOT IT.
IT BROKE. GRAB THAT SIDE!
NURURU (SLIMY)
IT-
IT'S SLIP-PERY!

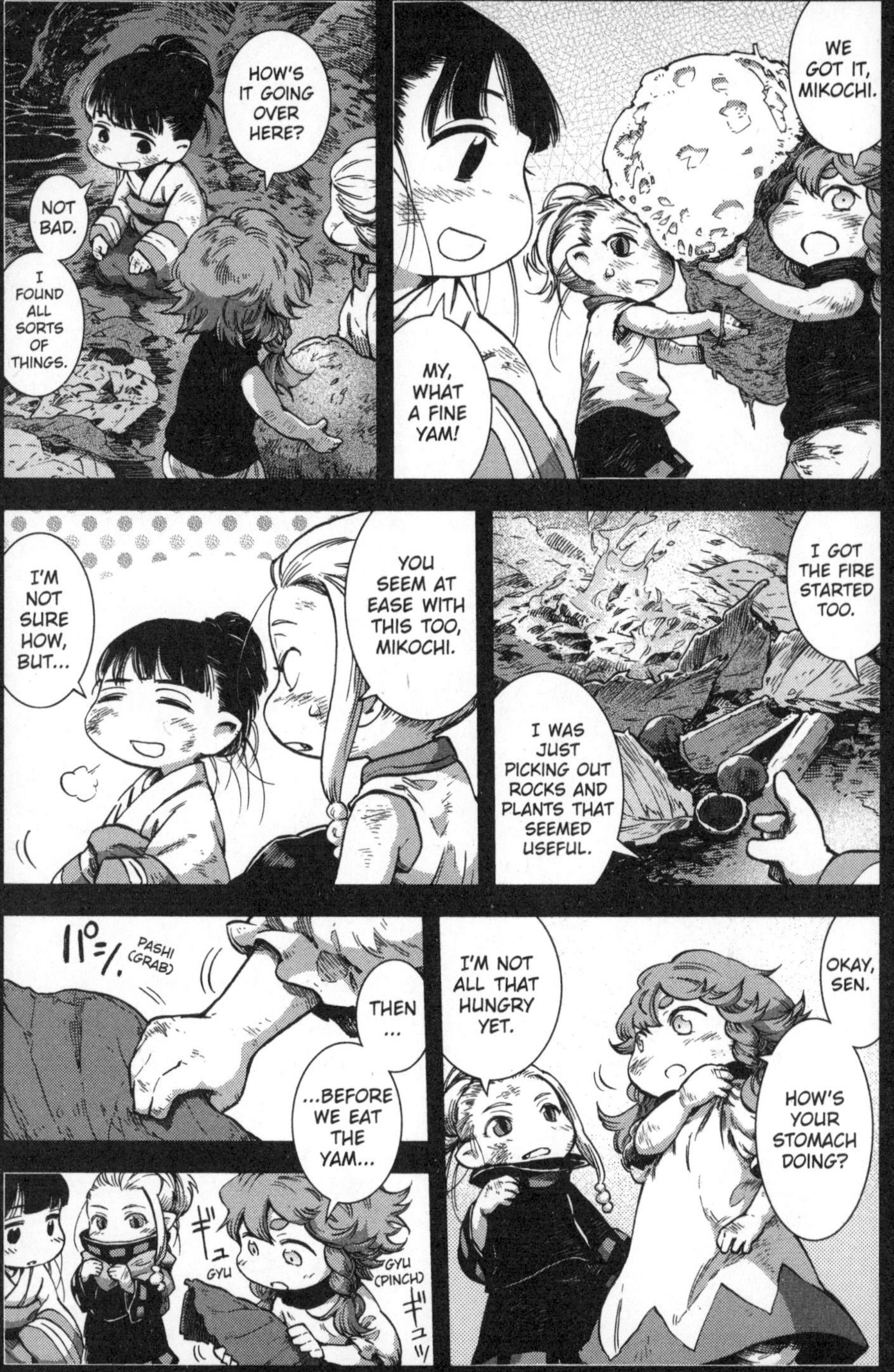
WE GOT IT, MIKOCHI.
MY, WHAT A FINE YAM!
HOW'S IT GOING OVER HERE?
NOT BAD.
I FOUND ALL SORTS OF THINGS.
I GOT THE FIRE STARTED TOO.
I WAS JUST PICKING OUT ROCKS AND PLANTS THAT SEEMED USEFUL.
YOU SEEM AT EASE WITH THIS TOO, MIKOCHI.
I'M NOT SURE HOW, BUT...
OKAY, SEN.
HOW'S YOUR STOMACH DOING?
I'M NOT ALL THAT HUNGRY YET.
THEN ...
...BEFORE WE EAT THE YAM...
パシッ
PASHI (GRAB)
ギュ
GYU
GYU (PINCH)
ギュッ

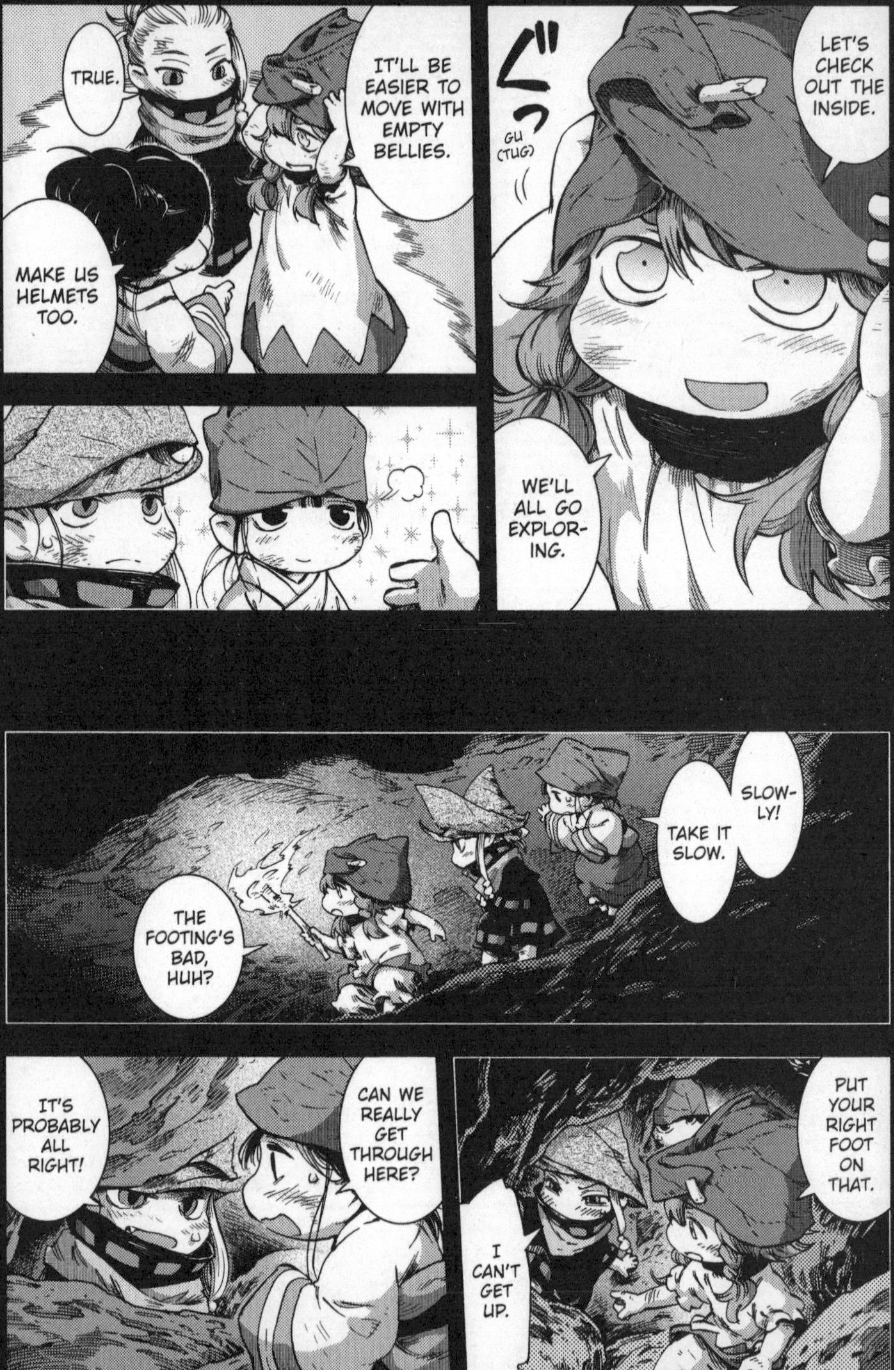
ぐっ
GU (TUG)
LET'S CHECK OUT THE INSIDE.
WE'LL ALL GO EXPLORING.
IT'LL BE EASIER TO MOVE WITH EMPTY BELLIES.
TRUE.
MAKE US HELMETS TOO.
SLOWLY!
TAKE IT SLOW.
THE FOOTING'S BAD, HUH?
PUT YOUR RIGHT FOOT ON THAT.
I CAN'T GET UP.
CAN WE REALLY GET THROUGH HERE?
IT'S PROBABLY ALL RIGHT!

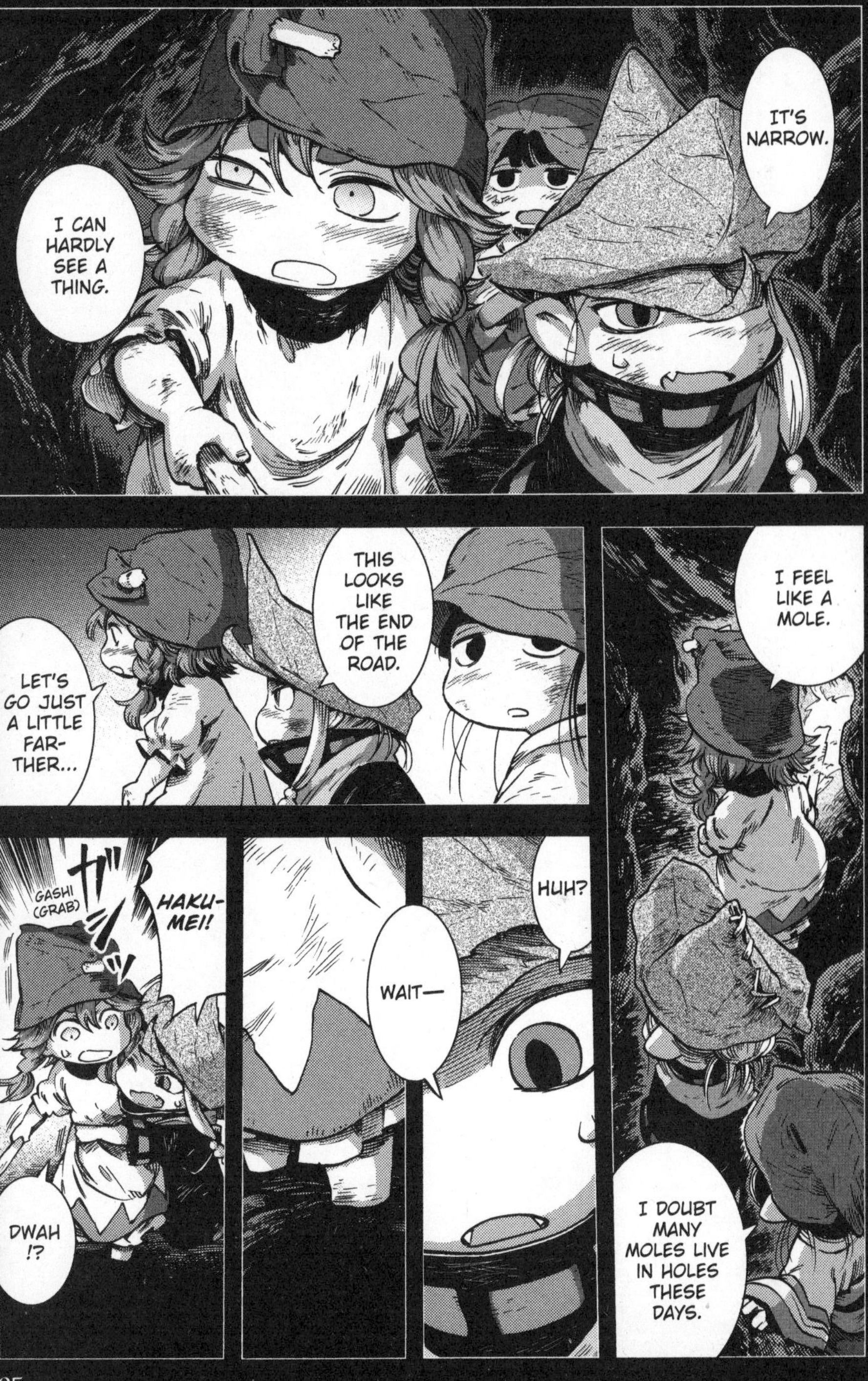
IT'S NARROW.
I CAN HARDLY SEE A THING.
I FEEL LIKE A MOLE.
I DOUBT MANY MOLES LIVE IN HOLES THESE DAYS.
THIS LOOKS LIKE THE END OF THE ROAD.
LET'S GO JUST A LITTLE FAR-THER...
HUH?
WAIT—
GASHI (GRAB)
HAKU-MEI!
DWAH !?

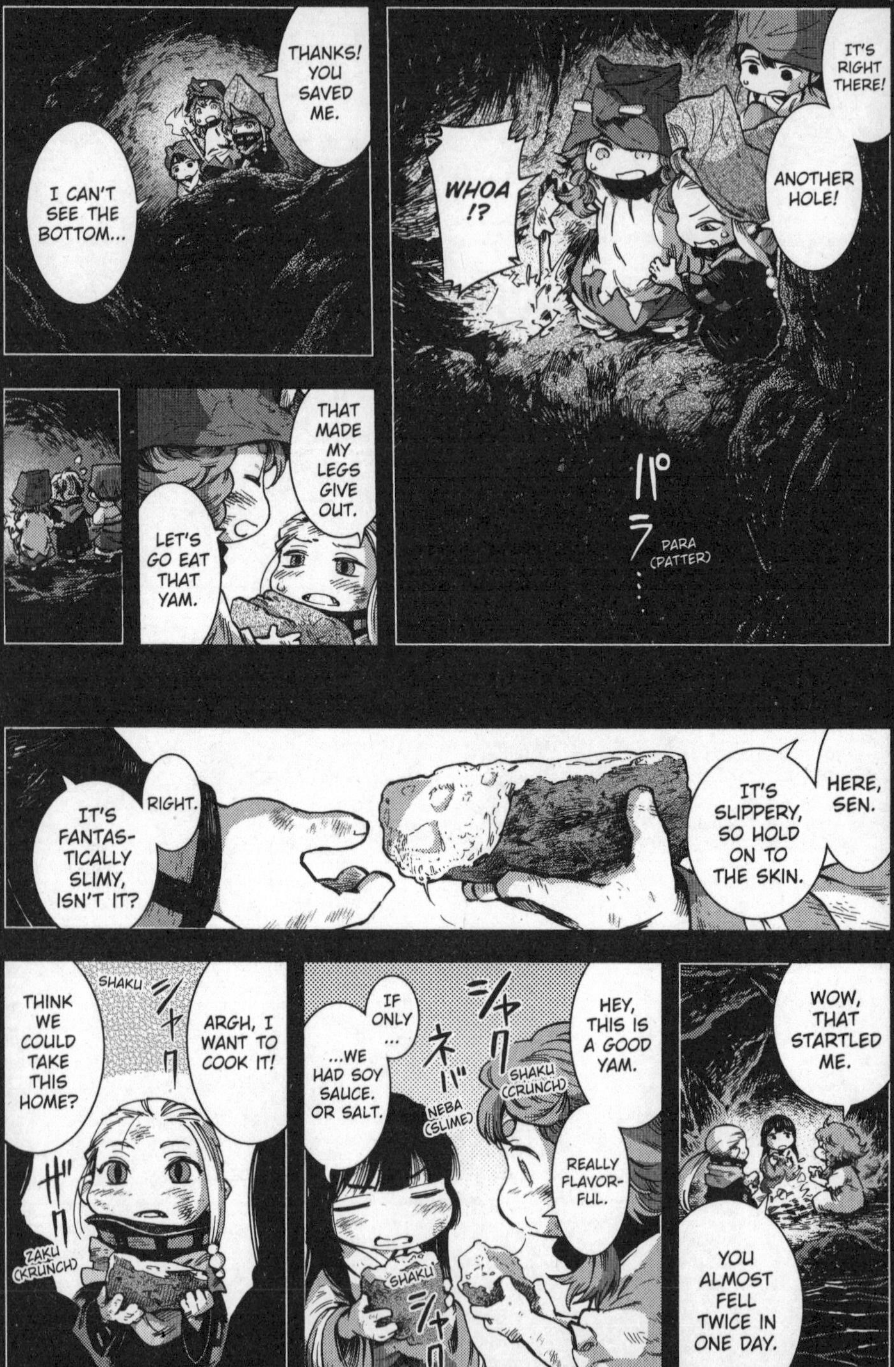
IT'S RIGHT THERE!
ANOTHER HOLE!
WHOA !?
PARA (PATTER)
THANKS! YOU SAVED ME.
I CAN'T SEE THE BOTTOM...
THAT MADE MY LEGS GIVE OUT.
LET'S GO EAT THAT YAM.
HERE, SEN.
IT'S SLIPPERY, SO HOLD ON TO THE SKIN.
RIGHT.
IT'S FANTASTICALLY SLIMY, ISN'T IT?
WOW, THAT STARTLED ME.
YOU ALMOST FELL TWICE IN ONE DAY.
HEY, THIS IS A GOOD YAM.
SHAKU (CRUNCH)
REALLY FLAVORFUL.
IF ONLY...
...WE HAD SOY SAUCE. OR SALT.
NEBA (SLIME)
SHAKU
ARGH, I WANT TO COOK IT!
SHAKU
THINK WE COULD TAKE THIS HOME?
ZAKU (KRUNCH)

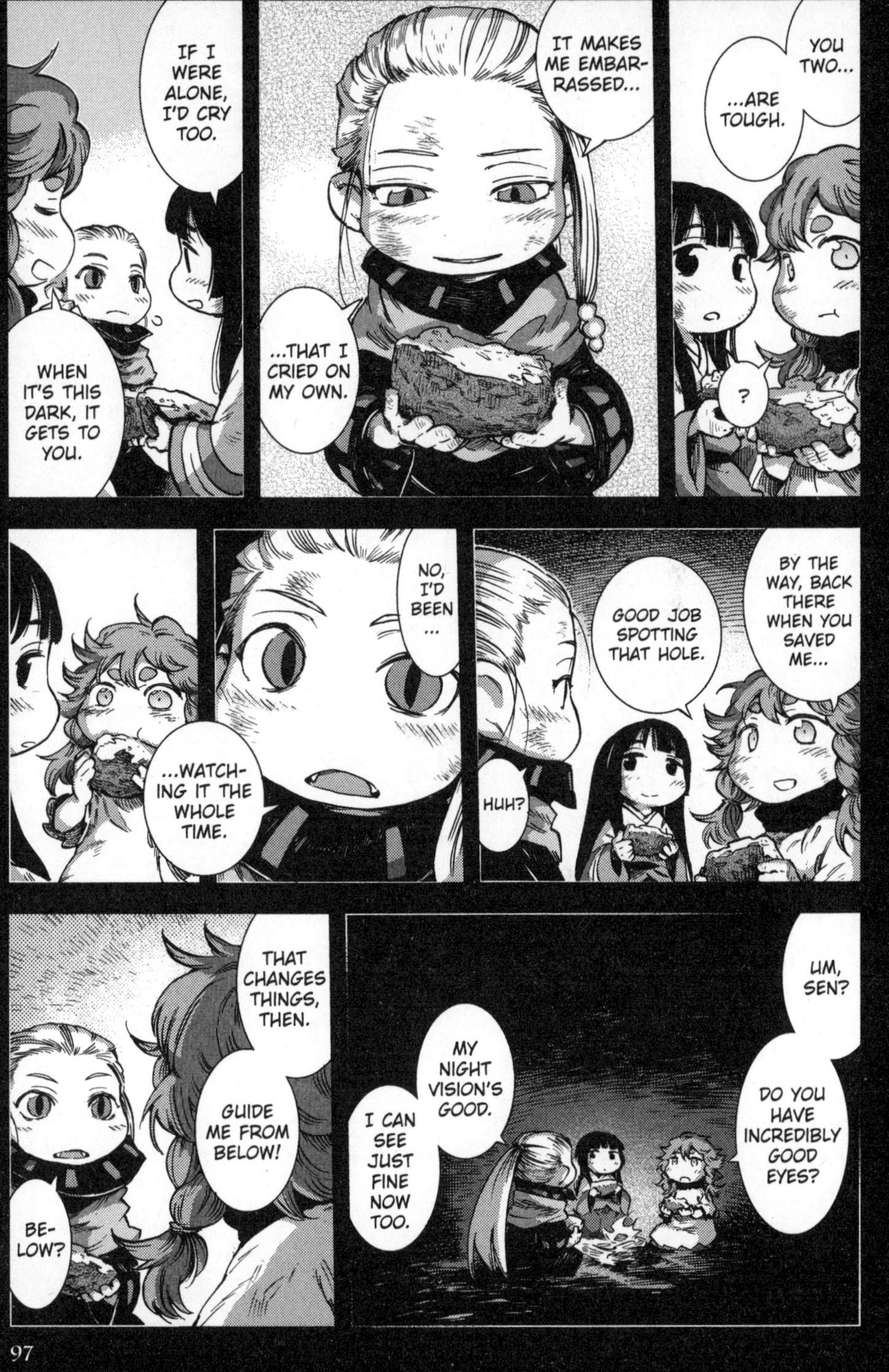
YOU TWO...
...ARE TOUGH.
?
IT MAKES ME EMBARRASSED...
...THAT I CRIED ON MY OWN.
IF I WERE ALONE, I'D CRY TOO.
WHEN IT'S THIS DARK, IT GETS TO YOU.
BY THE WAY, BACK THERE WHEN YOU SAVED ME...
GOOD JOB SPOTTING THAT HOLE.
HUH?
NO, I'D BEEN ...
...WATCHING IT THE WHOLE TIME.
UM, SEN?
DO YOU HAVE INCREDIBLY GOOD EYES?
MY NIGHT VISION'S GOOD.
I CAN SEE JUST FINE NOW TOO.
THAT CHANGES THINGS, THEN.
GUIDE ME FROM BELOW!
BE-LOW?

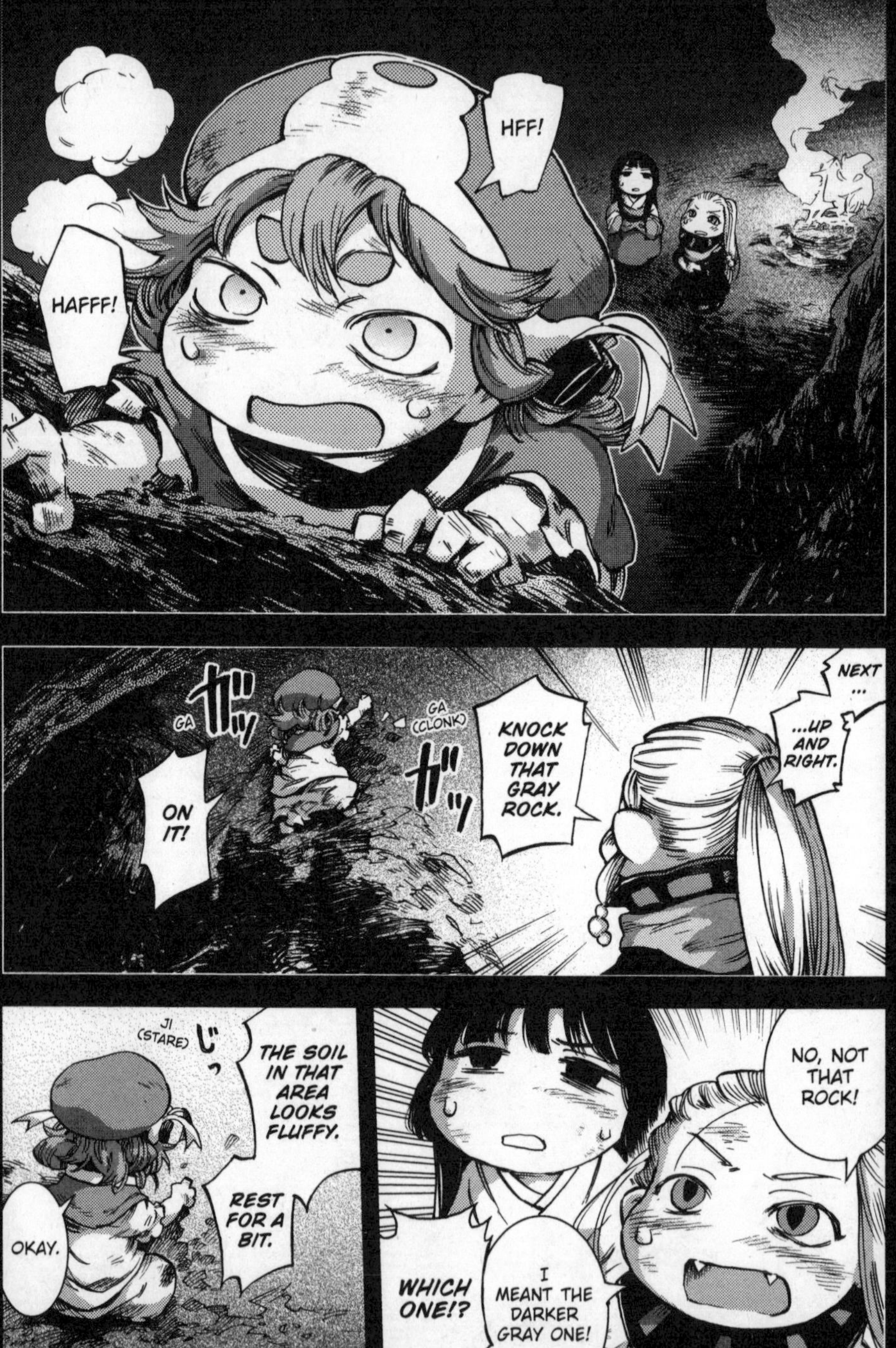
HFF!
HAFFF!
NEXT...
...UP AND RIGHT.
KNOCK DOWN THAT GRAY ROCK.
GA (CLONK)
GA
ON IT!
NO, NOT THAT ROCK!
I MEANT THE DARKER GRAY ONE!
WHICH ONE!?
JI (STARE)
THE SOIL IN THAT AREA LOOKS FLUFFY.
REST FOR A BIT.
OKAY.

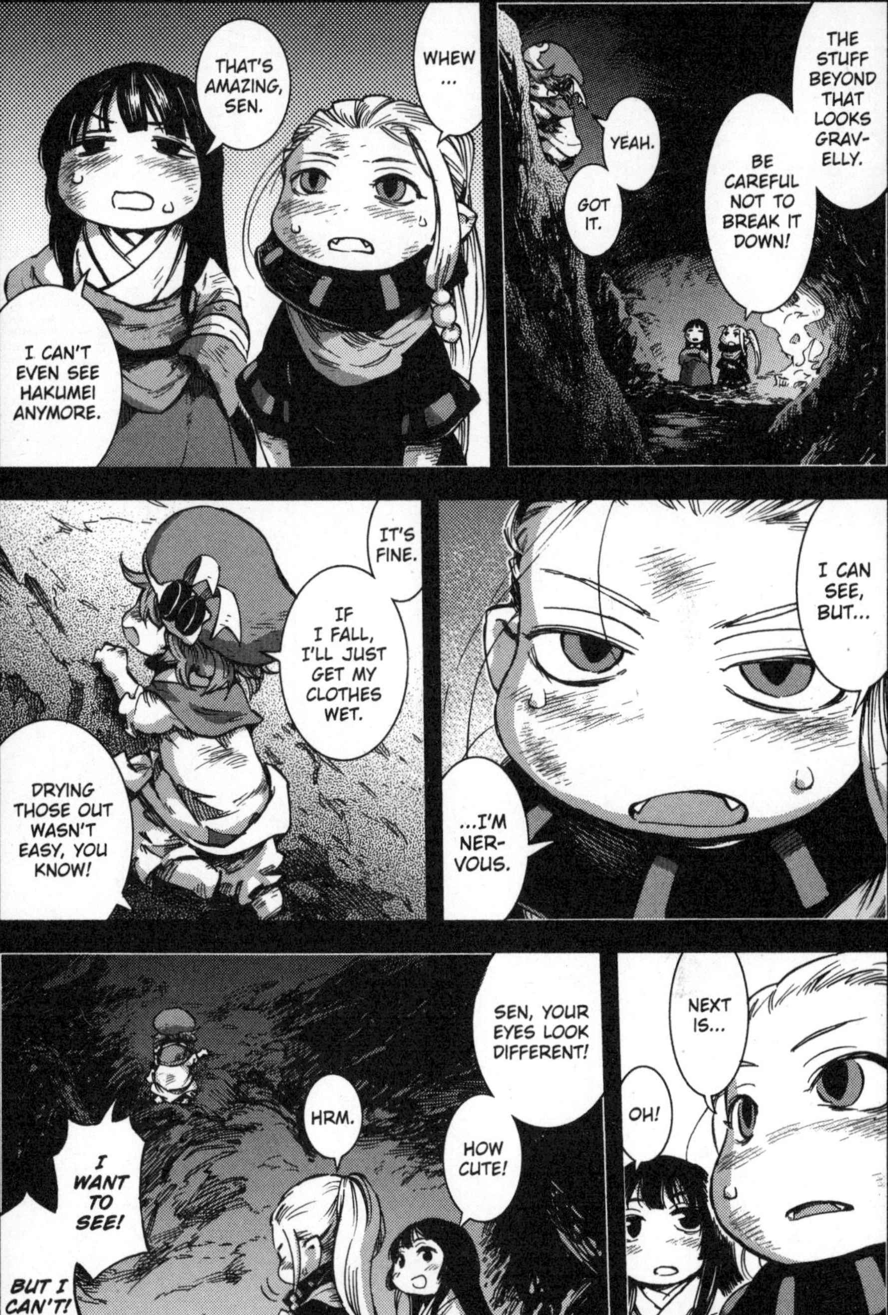
THE STUFF BEYOND THAT LOOKS GRAV-ELLY.
YEAH.
BE CAREFUL NOT TO BREAK IT DOWN!
GOT IT.
WHEW ...
THAT'S AMAZING, SEN.
I CAN'T EVEN SEE HAKUMEI ANYMORE.
I CAN SEE, BUT...
...I'M NER-VOUS.
IT'S FINE.
IF I FALL, I'LL JUST GET MY CLOTHES WET.
DRYING THOSE OUT WASN'T EASY, YOU KNOW!
NEXT IS...
OH!
SEN, YOUR EYES LOOK DIFFERENT!
HRM.
HOW CUTE!
I WANT TO SEE!
BUT I CAN'T!

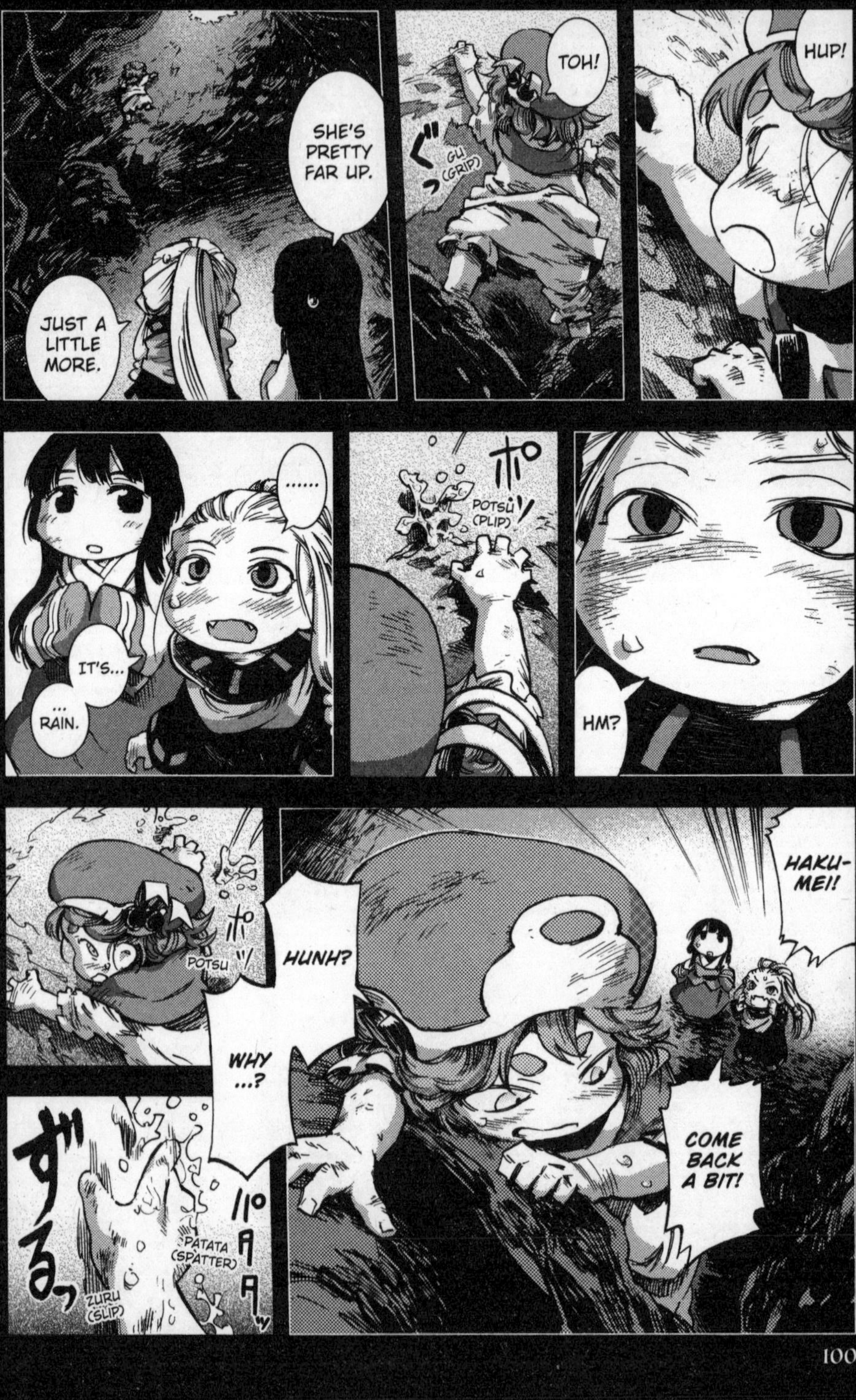
HUP!
TOH!
ぐっ
GU (GRIP)
SHE'S PRETTY FAR UP.
JUST A LITTLE MORE.
HM?
ポツッ
POTSU (PLIP)
......
IT'S...
... RAIN.
HAKU-MEI!
HUNH?
WHY ...?
COME BACK A BIT!
ポツ
POTSU
パタタ
PATATA (SPATTER)
ずるっ
ZURU (SLIP)

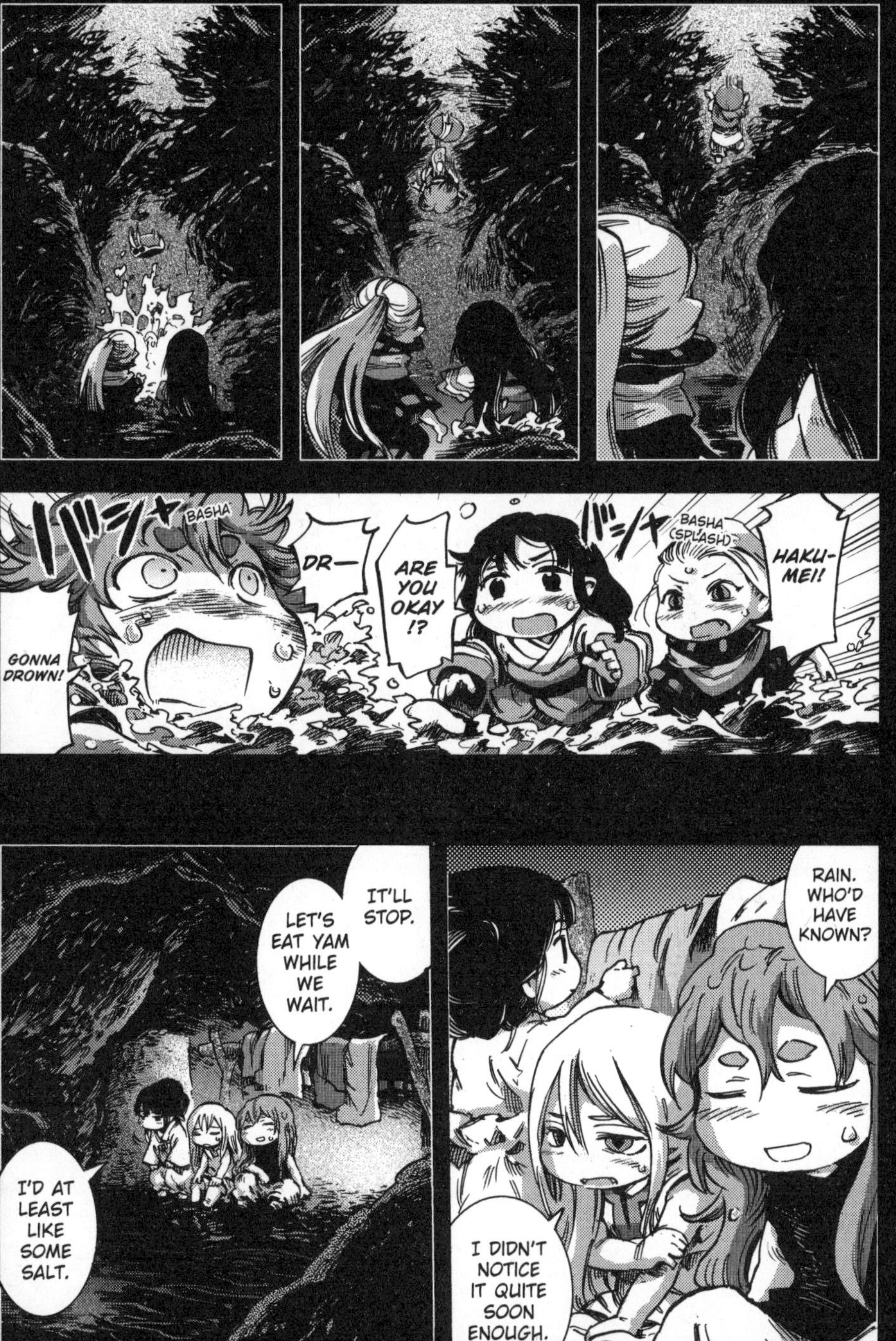
HAKU-MEI!
BASHA (SPLASH)
ARE YOU OKAY !?
DR—
BASHA
GONNA DROWN!
RAIN. WHO'D HAVE KNOWN?
I DIDN'T NOTICE IT QUITE SOON ENOUGH.
IT'LL STOP.
LET'S EAT YAM WHILE WE WAIT.
I'D AT LEAST LIKE SOME SALT.

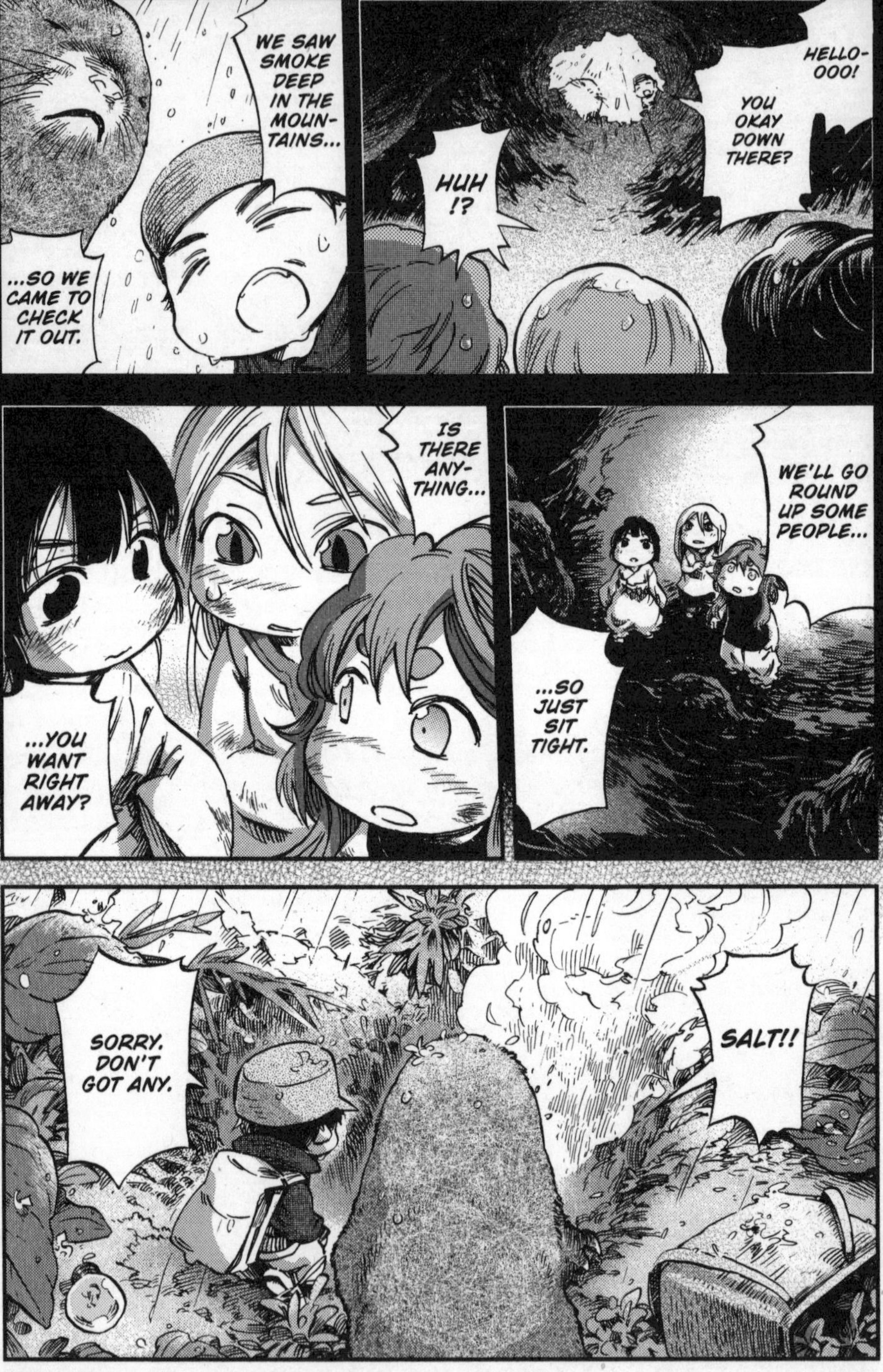
HELLO-OOO!
YOU OKAY DOWN THERE?
HUH!?
WE SAW SMOKE DEEP IN THE MOUNTAINS...
...SO WE CAME TO CHECK IT OUT.
WE'LL GO ROUND UP SOME PEOPLE...
...SO JUST SIT TIGHT.
IS THERE ANYTHING...
...YOU WANT RIGHT AWAY?
SALT!!
SORRY. DON'T GOT ANY.

Chapter 47 • End

•Column• Underfoot Steps 47 / Dead Leaf Helmets

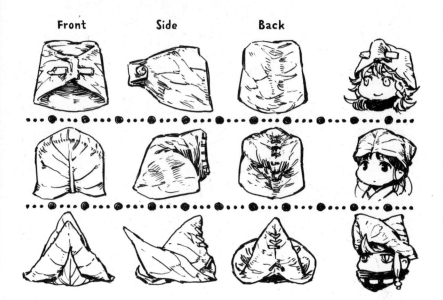

Front
Side
Back

"This one's yours, Sen. The crown's nice and pointy."

"Th-thanks."

"Mine looks a bit like a hood, doesn't it?"

"The veins were pretty, so I made it so they'd be in front."

"...Why did you bother making them different shapes?"

"Because they're cooler that way!"

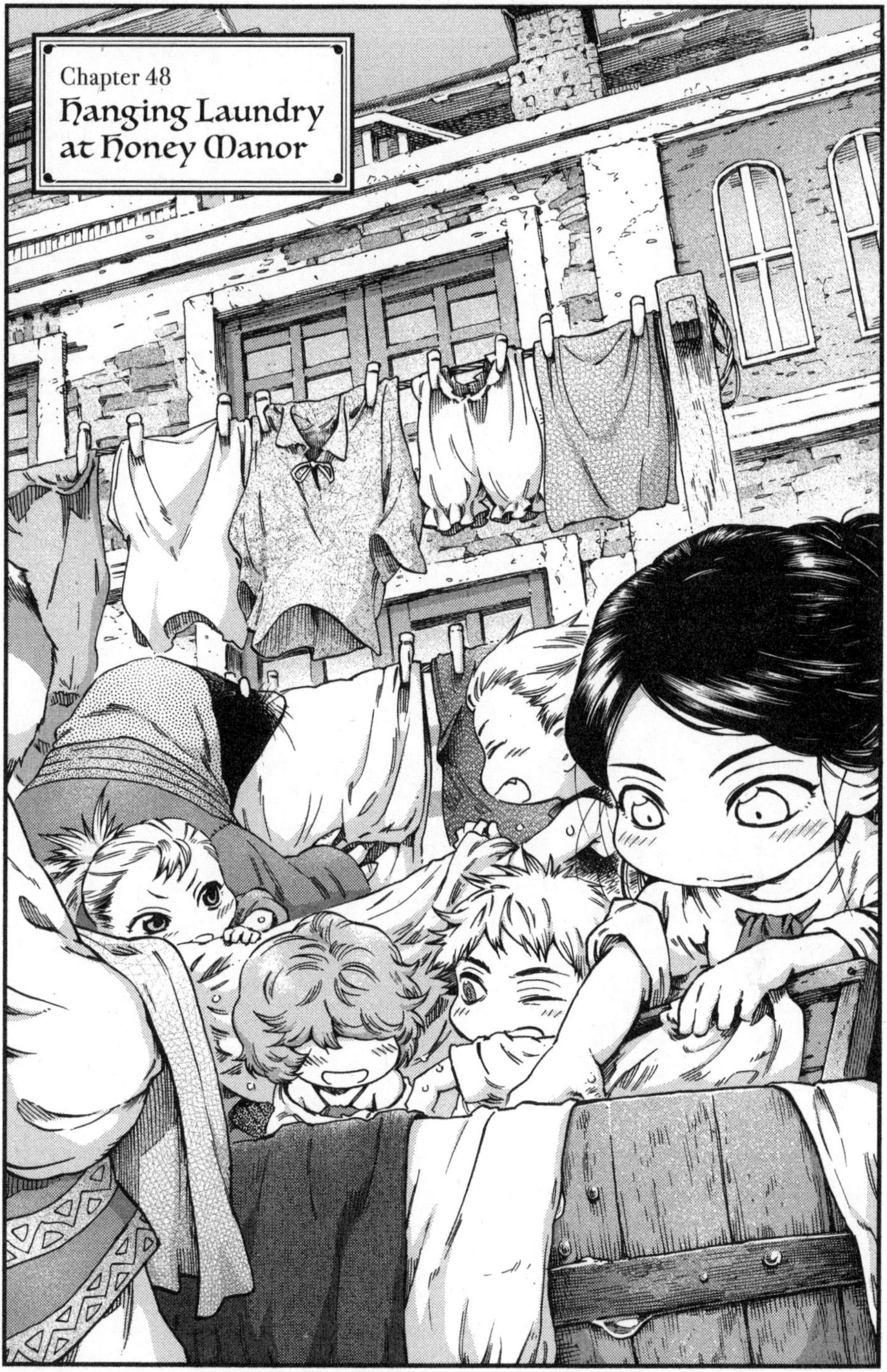
Chapter 48
Hanging Laundry at Honey Manor

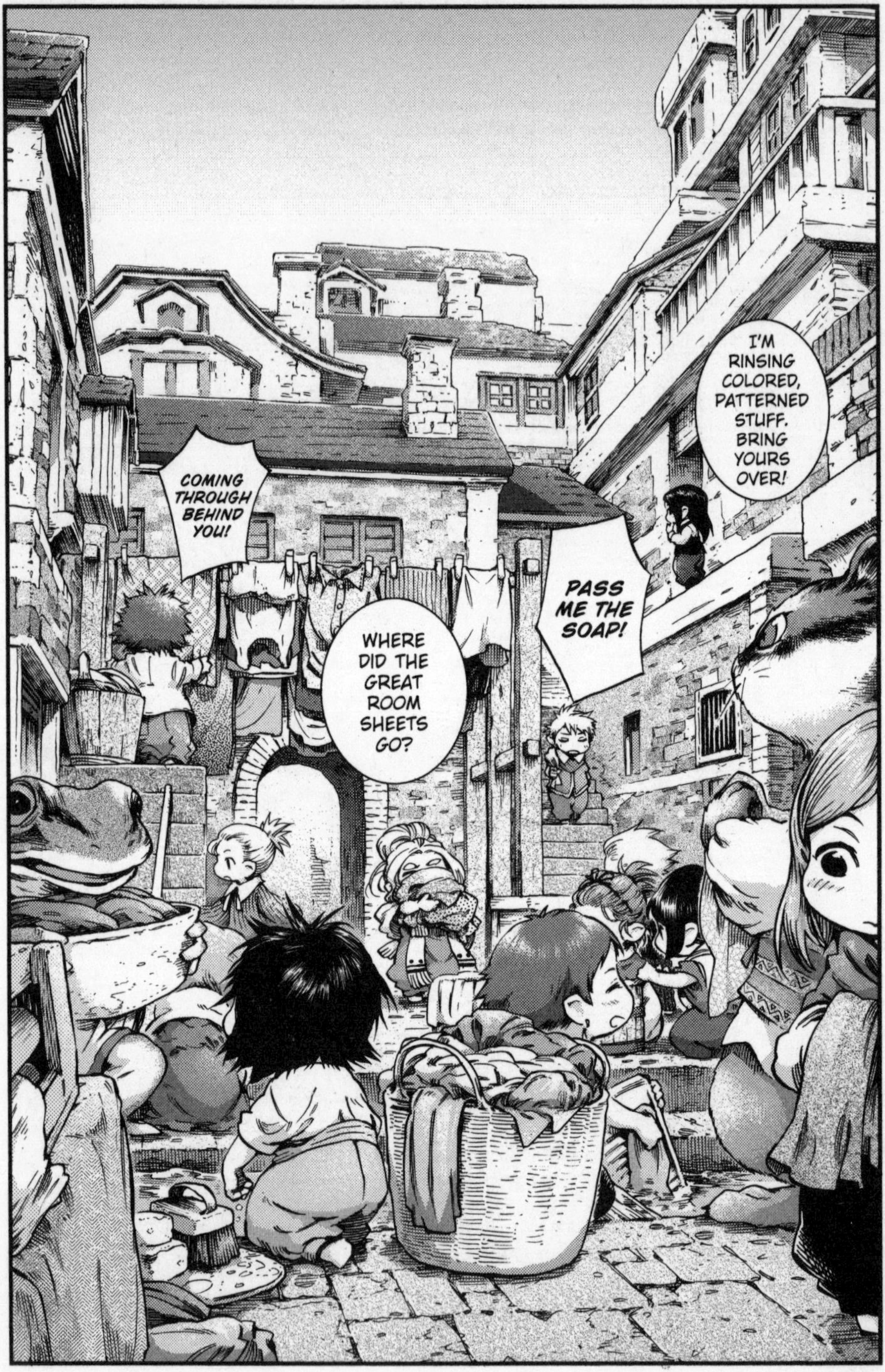
I'M RINSING COLORED, PATTERNED STUFF. BRING YOURS OVER!
PASS ME THE SOAP!
COMING THROUGH BEHIND YOU!
WHERE DID THE GREAT ROOM SHEETS GO?

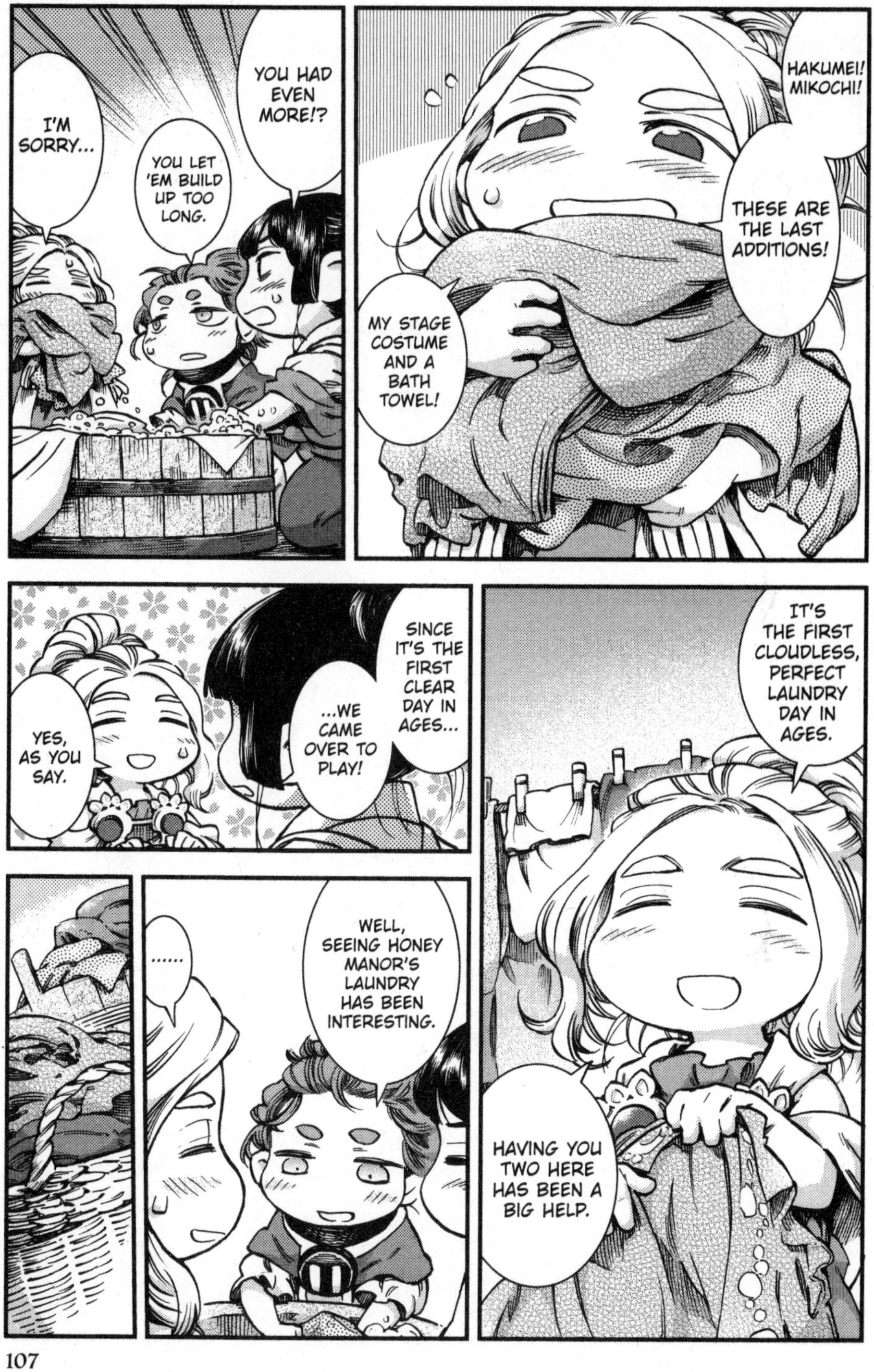

HAKUMEI! MIKOCHI!
THESE ARE THE LAST ADDITIONS!
MY STAGE COSTUME AND A BATH TOWEL!
YOU HAD EVEN MORE!?
YOU LET 'EM BUILD UP TOO LONG.
I'M SORRY...
IT'S THE FIRST CLOUDLESS, PERFECT LAUNDRY DAY IN AGES.
HAVING YOU TWO HERE HAS BEEN A BIG HELP.
SINCE IT'S THE FIRST CLEAR DAY IN AGES...
...WE CAME OVER TO PLAY!
YES, AS YOU SAY.
WELL, SEEING HONEY MANOR'S LAUNDRY HAS BEEN INTERESTING.
......

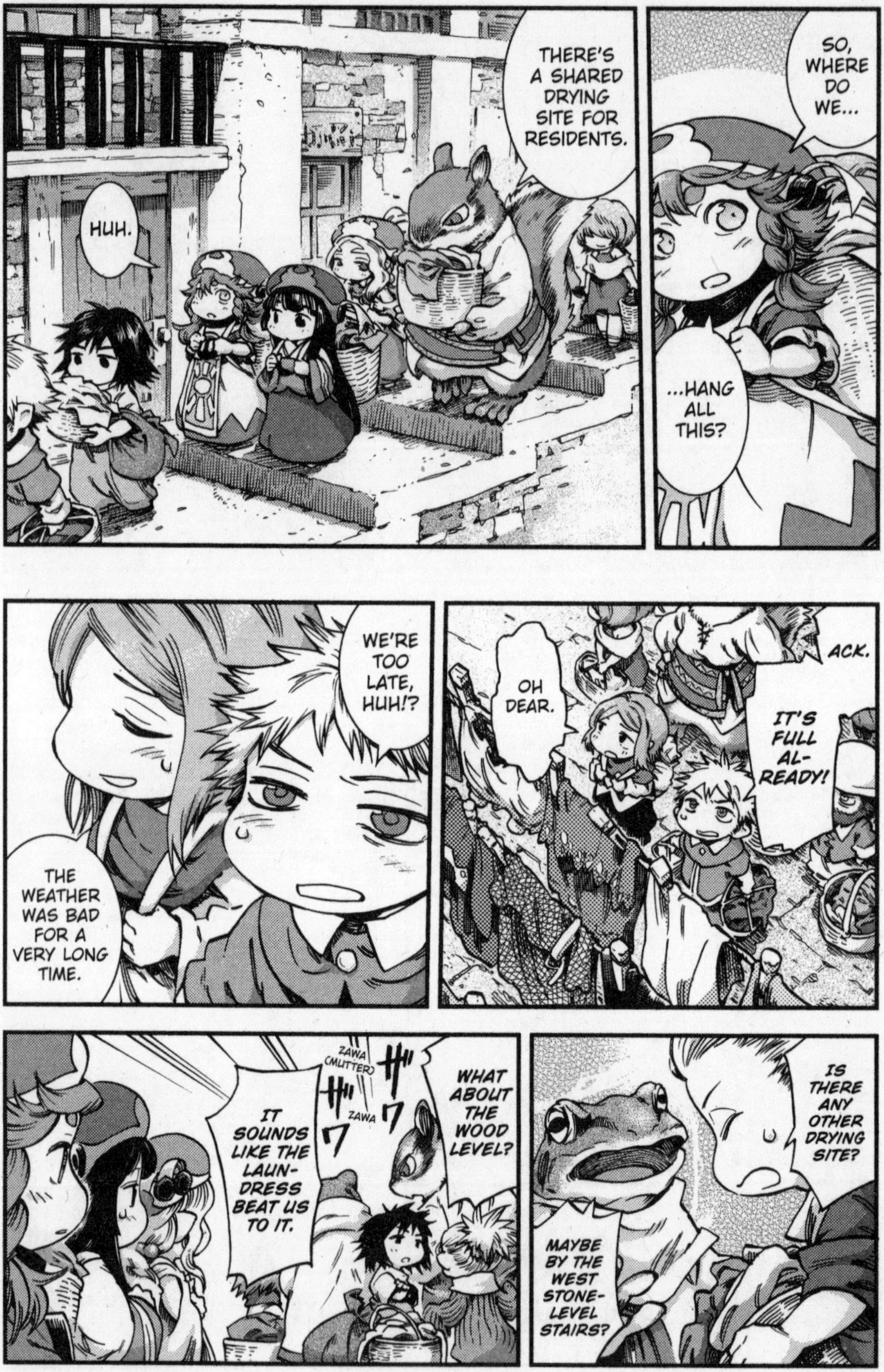
SO, WHERE DO WE...
...HANG ALL THIS?
THERE'S A SHARED DRYING SITE FOR RESIDENTS.
HUH.
ACK.
IT'S FULL AL-READY!
OH DEAR.
WE'RE TOO LATE, HUH!?
THE WEATHER WAS BAD FOR A VERY LONG TIME.
IS THERE ANY OTHER DRYING SITE?
MAYBE BY THE WEST STONE-LEVEL STAIRS?
WHAT ABOUT THE WOOD LEVEL?
ZAWA (MUTTER)
ZAWA
IT SOUNDS LIKE THE LAUN-DRESS BEAT US TO IT.

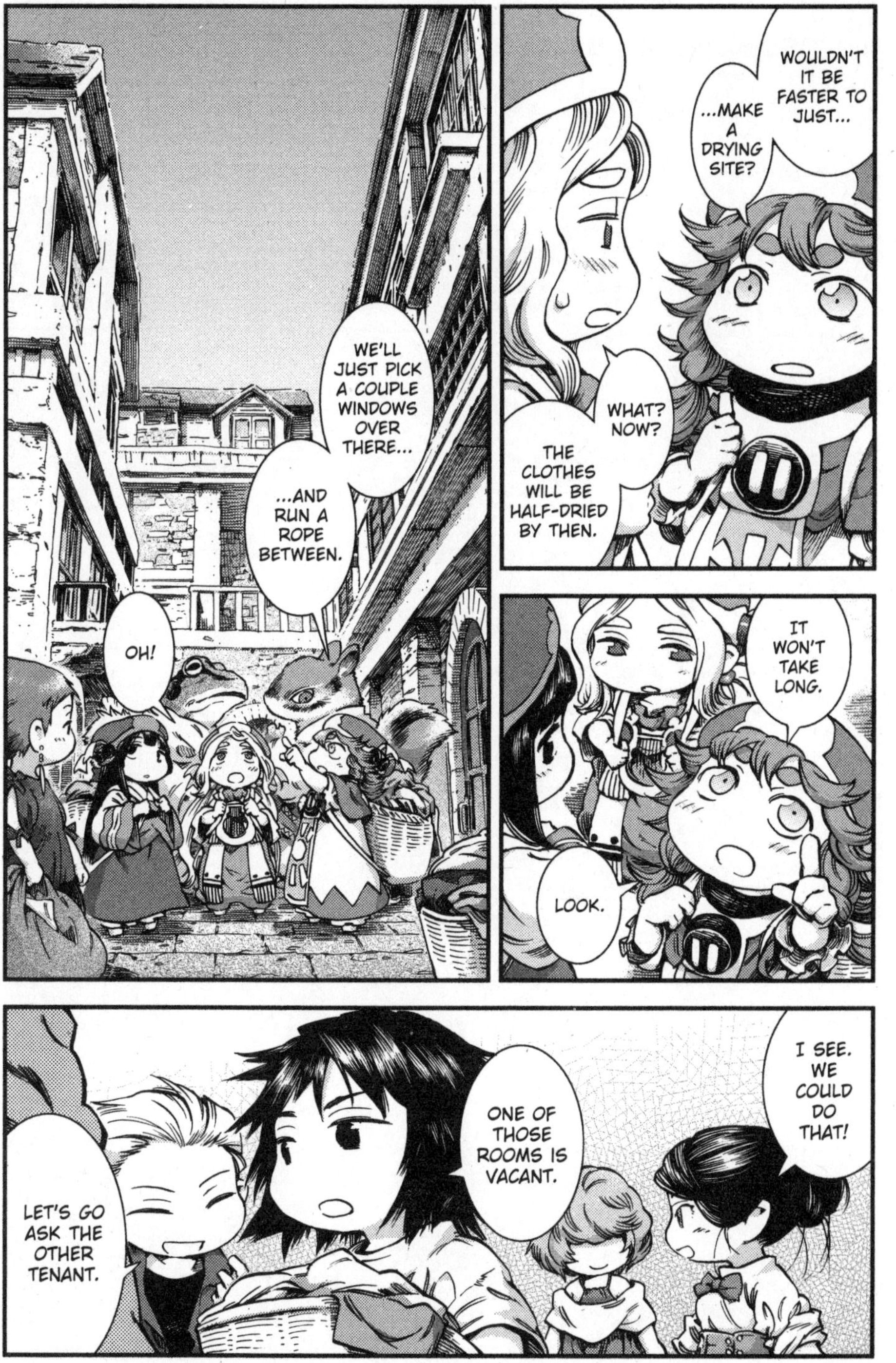
WOULDN'T IT BE FASTER TO JUST...
...MAKE A DRYING SITE?
WHAT? NOW?
THE CLOTHES WILL BE HALF-DRIED BY THEN.
IT WON'T TAKE LONG.
LOOK.
WE'LL JUST PICK A COUPLE WINDOWS OVER THERE...
...AND RUN A ROPE BETWEEN.
OH!
I SEE. WE COULD DO THAT!
ONE OF THOSE ROOMS IS VACANT.
LET'S GO ASK THE OTHER TENANT.

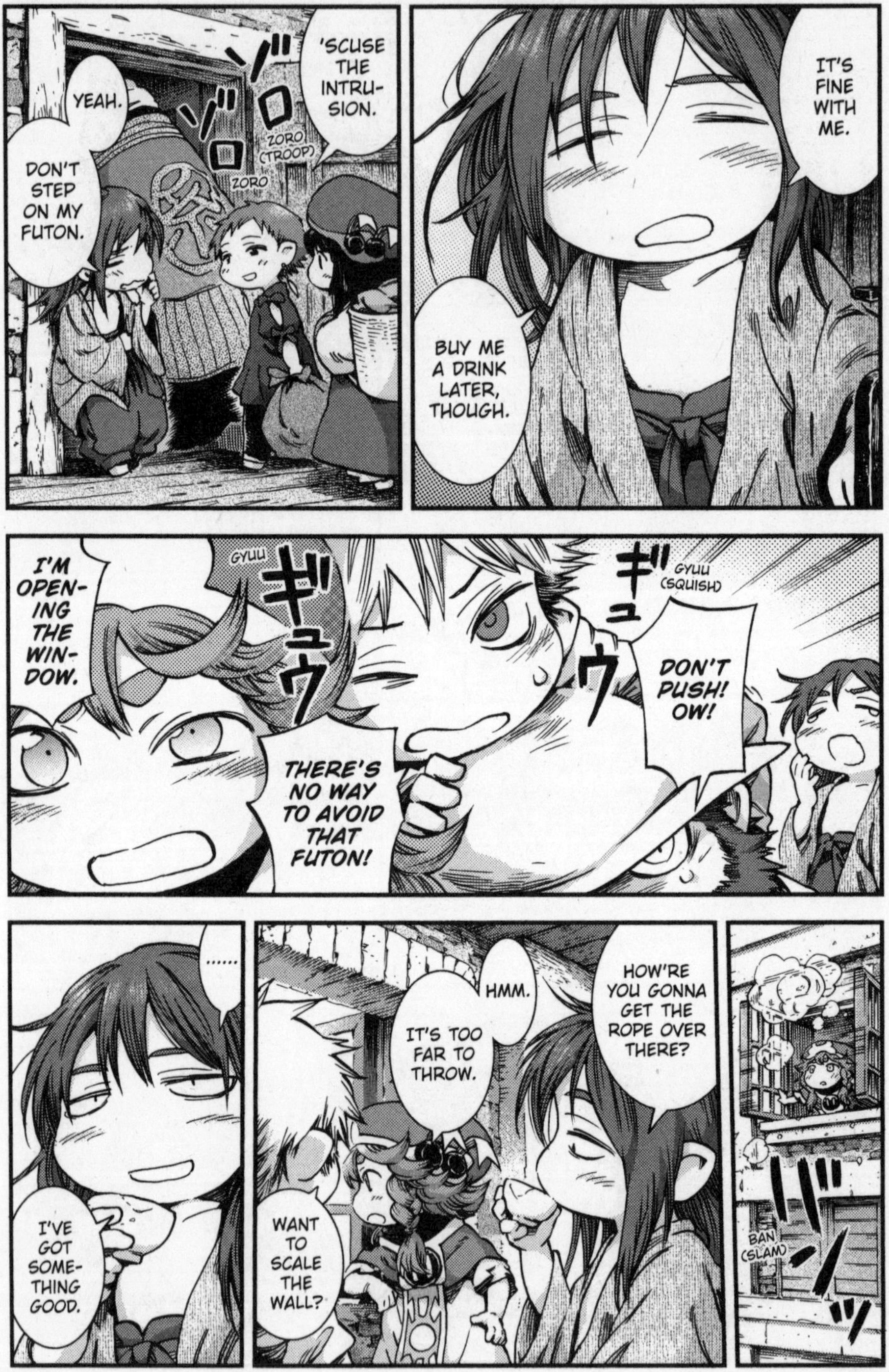
IT'S FINE WITH ME.
BUY ME A DRINK LATER, THOUGH.
'SCUSE THE INTRUSION.
ゾロゾロ
ZORO (TROOP)
ZORO
YEAH.
DON'T STEP ON MY FUTON.
ギュウ
GYUU (SQUISH)
DON'T PUSH! OW!
ギュウ
GYUU
I'M OPENING THE WINDOW.
THERE'S NO WAY TO AVOID THAT FUTON!
バン
BAN (SLAM)
HOW'RE YOU GONNA GET THE ROPE OVER THERE?
HMM.
IT'S TOO FAR TO THROW.
WANT TO SCALE THE WALL?
......
I'VE GOT SOMETHING GOOD.

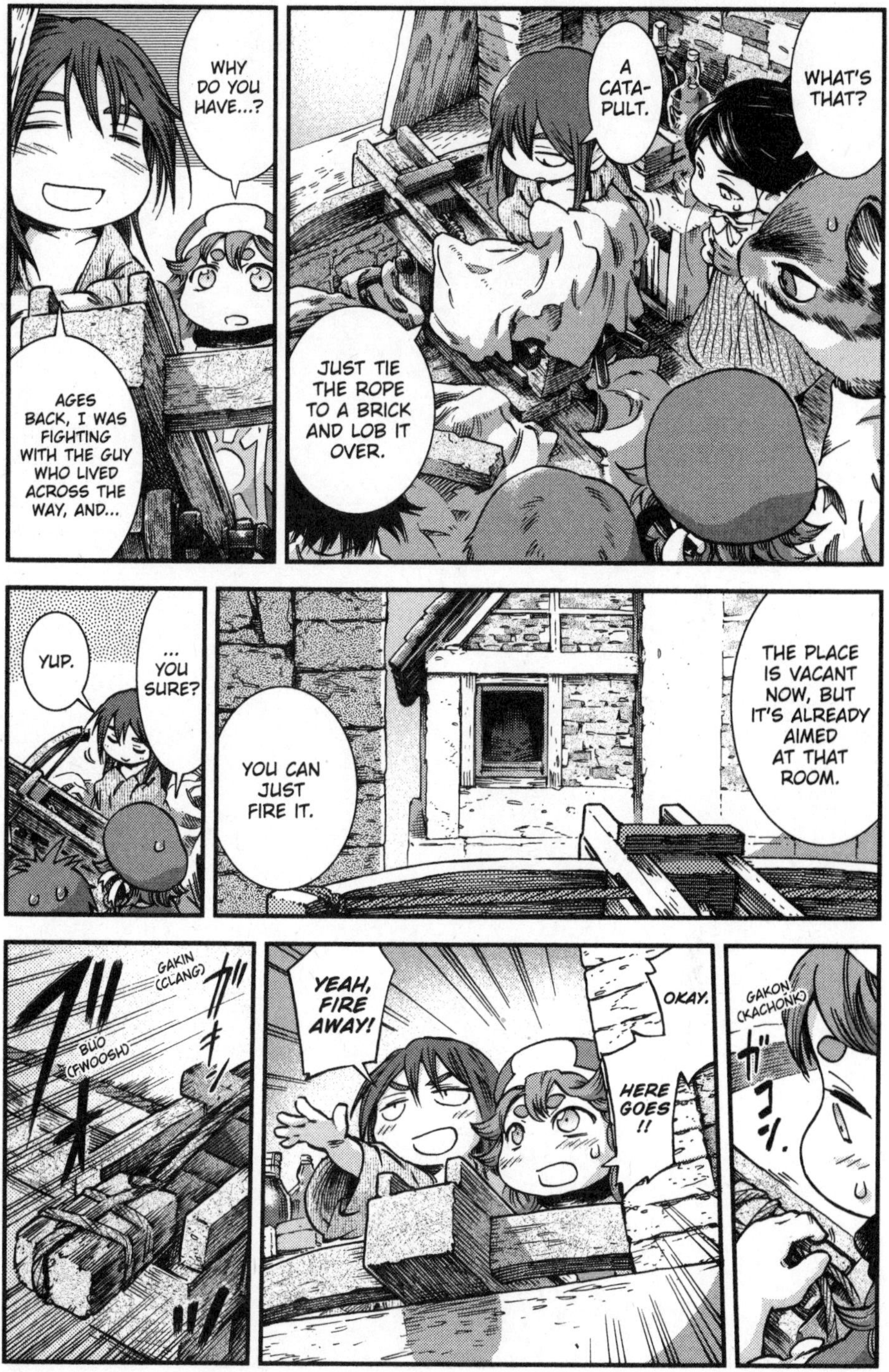

WHAT'S THAT?
A CATA-PULT.
JUST TIE THE ROPE TO A BRICK AND LOB IT OVER.
WHY DO YOU HAVE...?
AGES BACK, I WAS FIGHTING WITH THE GUY WHO LIVED ACROSS THE WAY, AND...
THE PLACE IS VACANT NOW, BUT IT'S ALREADY AIMED AT THAT ROOM.
YOU CAN JUST FIRE IT.
... YOU SURE?
YUP.
GAKON (KACHONK)
OKAY.
HERE GOES!!
YEAH, FIRE AWAY!
GAKIN (CLANG)
BUO (FWOOSH)

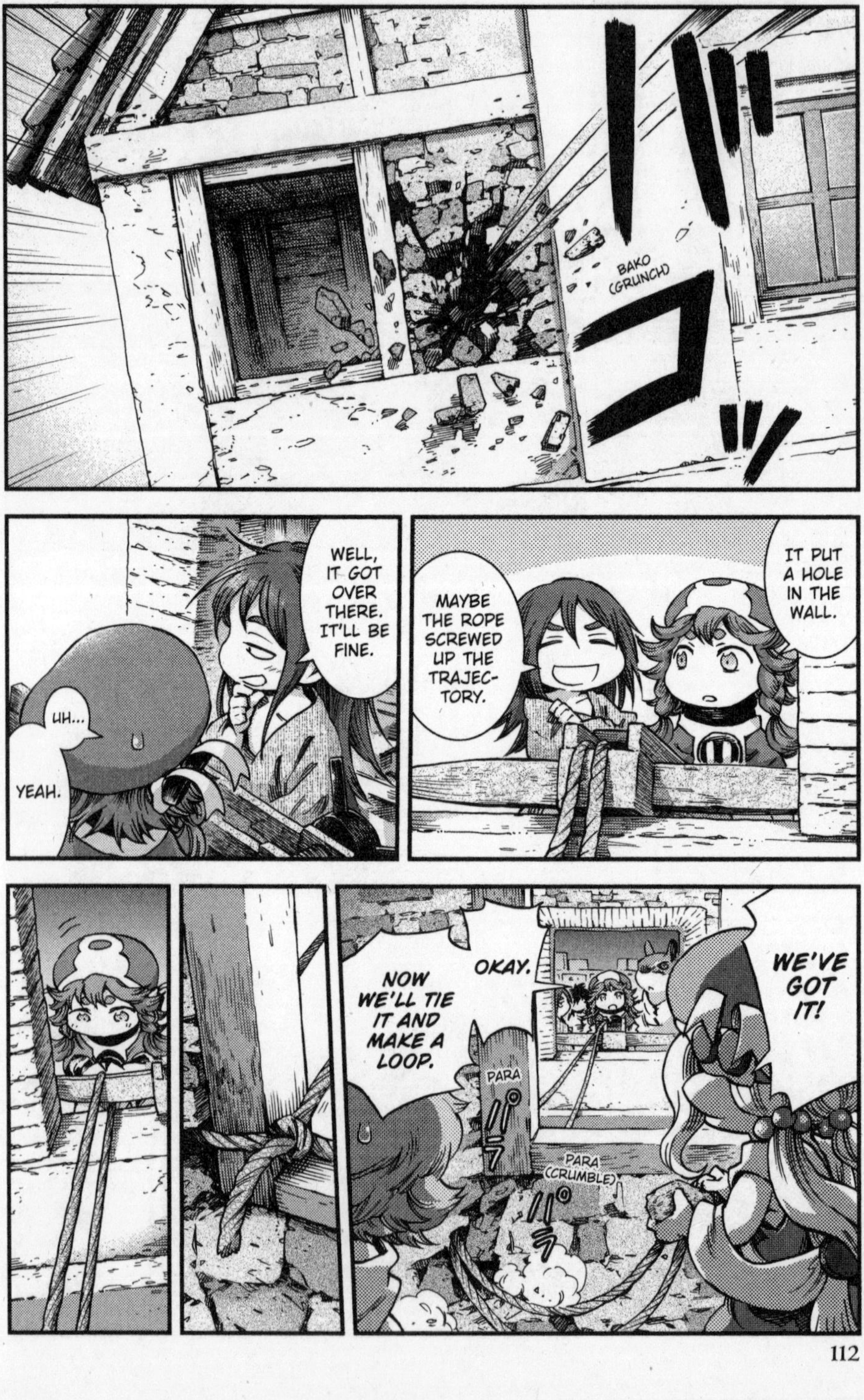
BAKO
(GRUNCH)
IT PUT A HOLE IN THE WALL.
MAYBE THE ROPE SCREWED UP THE TRAJECTORY.
WELL, IT GOT OVER THERE. IT'LL BE FINE.
UH...
YEAH.
WE'VE GOT IT!
OKAY.
NOW WE'LL TIE IT AND MAKE A LOOP.
PARA
PARA
(CRUMBLE)

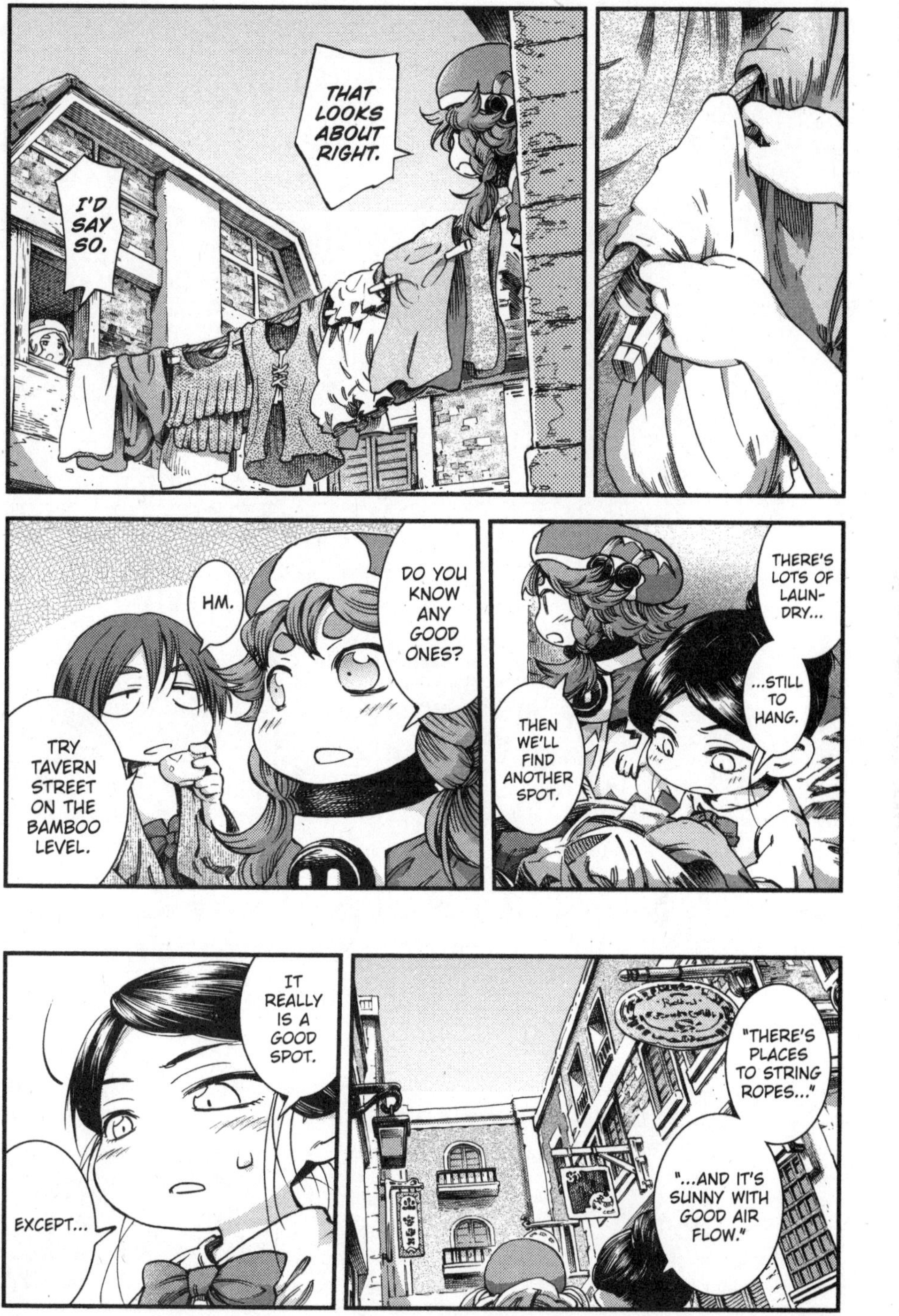
THAT LOOKS ABOUT RIGHT.
I'D SAY SO.
THERE'S LOTS OF LAUNDRY...
...STILL TO HANG.
THEN WE'LL FIND ANOTHER SPOT.
DO YOU KNOW ANY GOOD ONES?
HM.
TRY TAVERN STREET ON THE BAMBOO LEVEL.
"THERE'S PLACES TO STRING ROPES..."
"...AND IT'S SUNNY WITH GOOD AIR FLOW."
IT REALLY IS A GOOD SPOT.
EXCEPT...

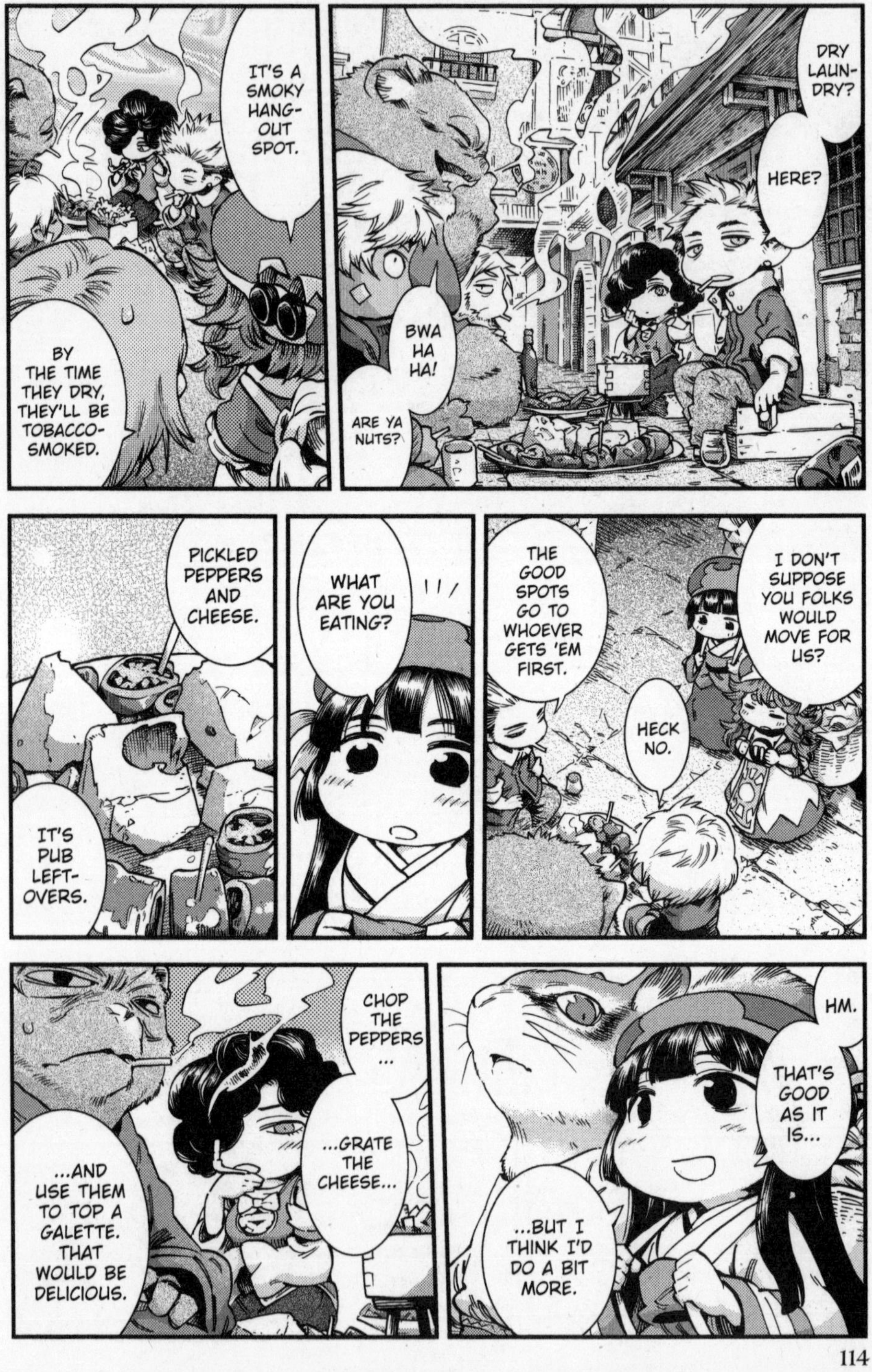
DRY LAUN-DRY?
HERE?
BWA HA HA!
ARE YA NUTS?
IT'S A SMOKY HANG-OUT SPOT.
BY THE TIME THEY DRY, THEY'LL BE TOBACCO-SMOKED.
I DON'T SUPPOSE YOU FOLKS WOULD MOVE FOR US?
THE GOOD SPOTS GO TO WHOEVER GETS 'EM FIRST.
HECK NO.
WHAT ARE YOU EATING?
PICKLED PEPPERS AND CHEESE.
IT'S PUB LEFT-OVERS.
HM.
THAT'S GOOD AS IT IS...
...BUT I THINK I'D DO A BIT MORE.
CHOP THE PEPPERS ...
...GRATE THE CHEESE...
...AND USE THEM TO TOP A GALETTE. THAT WOULD BE DELICIOUS.

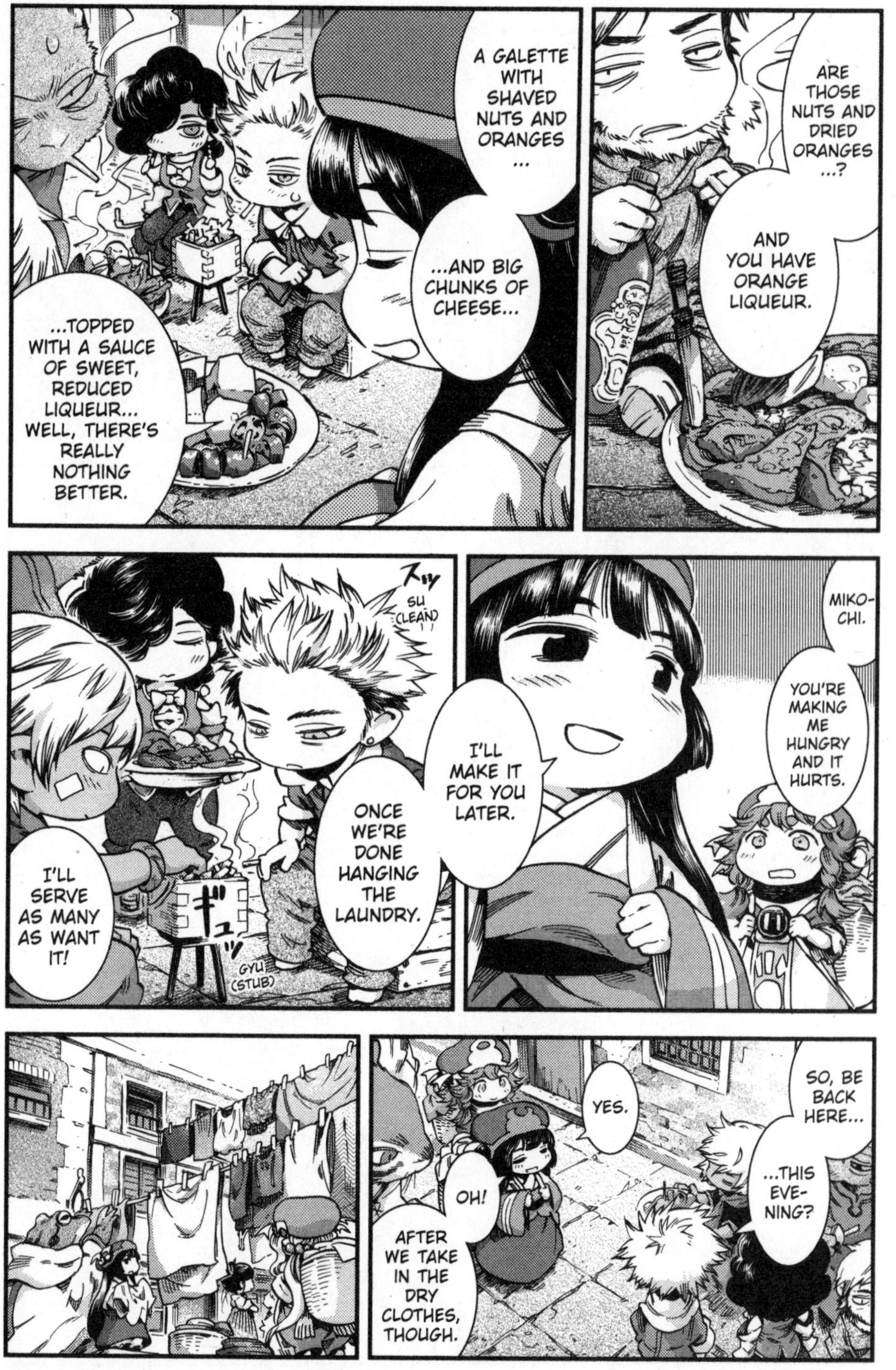
ARE THOSE NUTS AND DRIED ORANGES ...?
AND YOU HAVE ORANGE LIQUEUR.
A GALETTE WITH SHAVED NUTS AND ORANGES ...
...AND BIG CHUNKS OF CHEESE...
...TOPPED WITH A SAUCE OF SWEET, REDUCED LIQUEUR... WELL, THERE'S REALLY NOTHING BETTER.
MIKO-CHI.
YOU'RE MAKING ME HUNGRY AND IT HURTS.
I'LL MAKE IT FOR YOU LATER.
ONCE WE'RE DONE HANGING THE LAUNDRY.
スッ
SU (CLEAN)
I'LL SERVE AS MANY AS WANT IT!
ギュ
GYU (STUB)
SO, BE BACK HERE...
...THIS EVE-NING?
YES.
OH!
AFTER WE TAKE IN THE DRY CLOTHES, THOUGH.

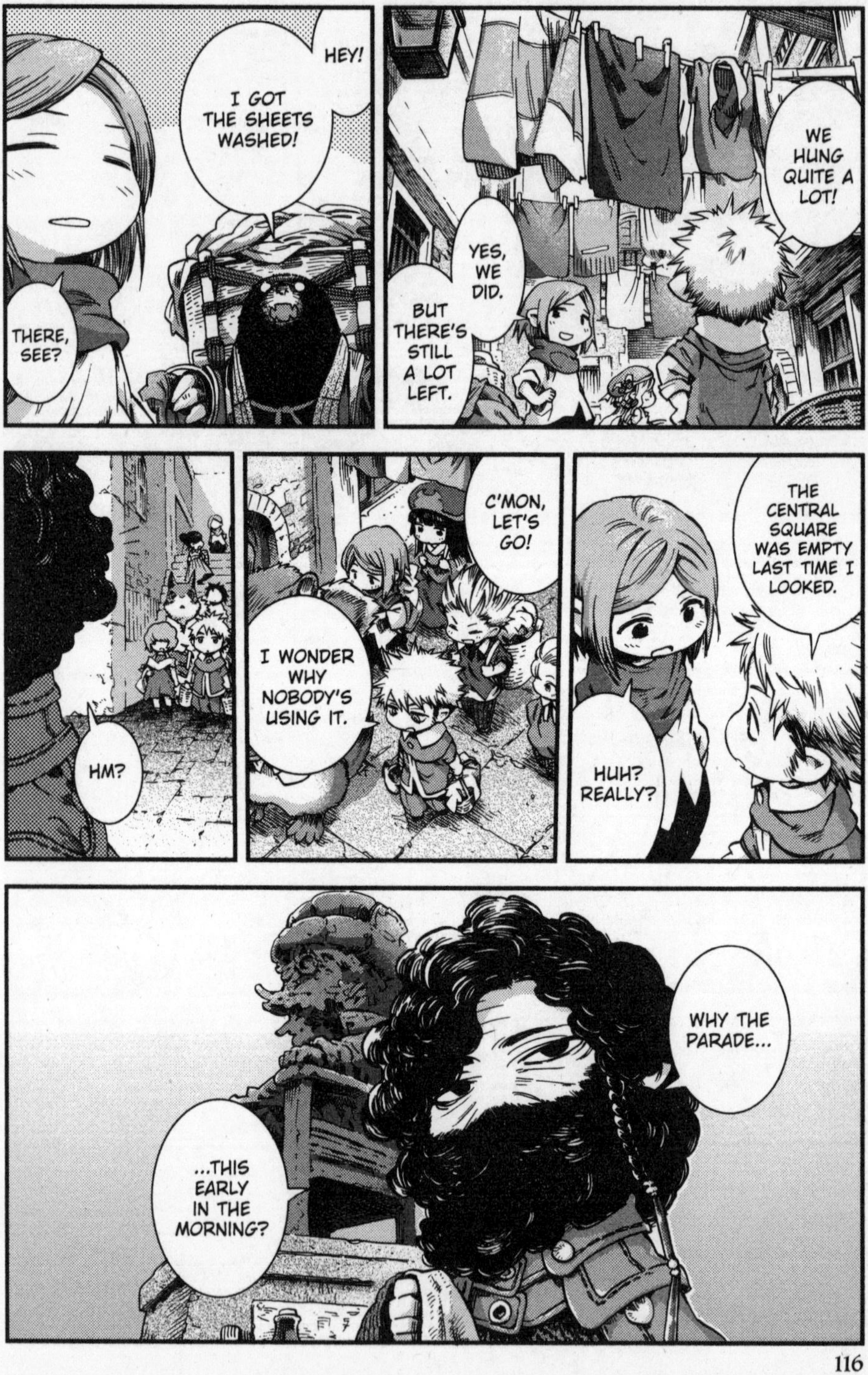
WE HUNG QUITE A LOT!
YES, WE DID.
BUT THERE'S STILL A LOT LEFT.
HEY!
I GOT THE SHEETS WASHED!
THERE, SEE?
THE CENTRAL SQUARE WAS EMPTY LAST TIME I LOOKED.
HUH? REALLY?
C'MON, LET'S GO!
I WONDER WHY NOBODY'S USING IT.
HM?
WHY THE PARADE...
...THIS EARLY IN THE MORNING?

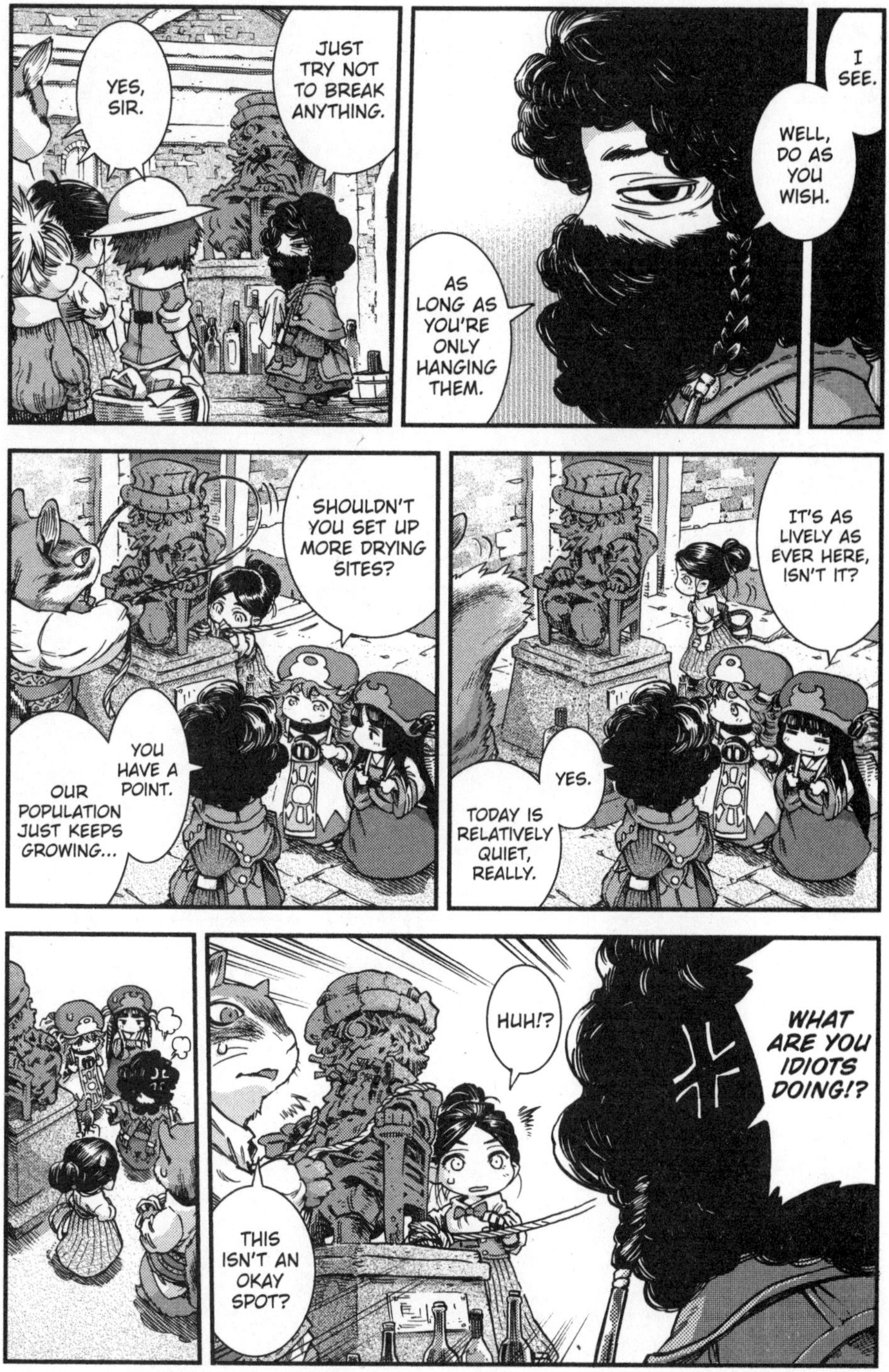
I SEE.
WELL, DO AS YOU WISH.
AS LONG AS YOU'RE ONLY HANGING THEM.
JUST TRY NOT TO BREAK ANYTHING.
YES, SIR.
IT'S AS LIVELY AS EVER HERE, ISN'T IT?
YES.
TODAY IS RELATIVELY QUIET, REALLY.
SHOULDN'T YOU SET UP MORE DRYING SITES?
YOU HAVE A POINT.
OUR POPULATION JUST KEEPS GROWING...
WHAT ARE YOU IDIOTS DOING!?
HUH!?
THIS ISN'T AN OKAY SPOT?

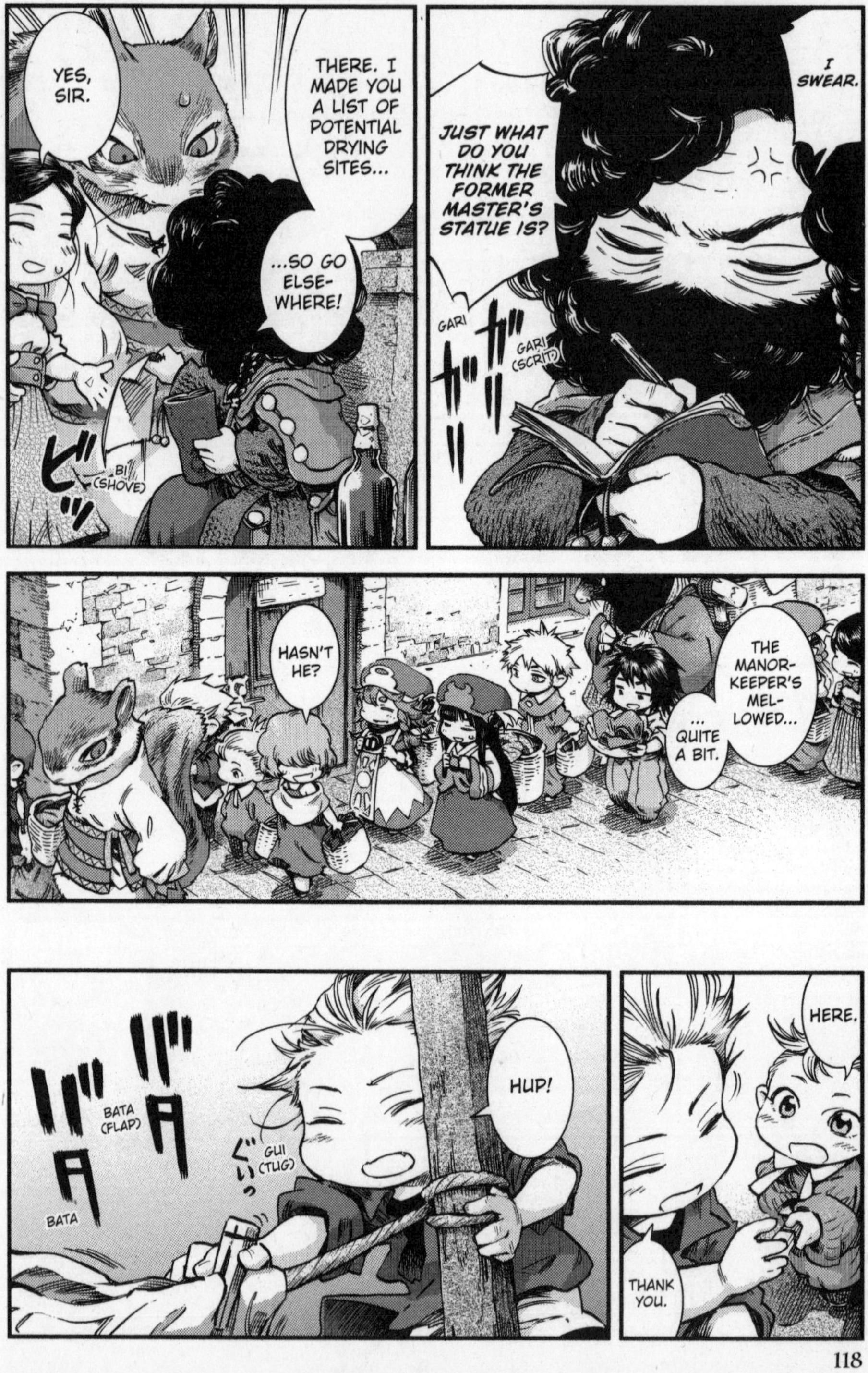
I SWEAR.
JUST WHAT DO YOU THINK THE FORMER MASTER'S STATUE IS?
GARI
GARI (SCRIT)
THERE. I MADE YOU A LIST OF POTENTIAL DRYING SITES...
...SO GO ELSE-WHERE!
YES, SIR.
BI (SHOVE)
THE MANOR-KEEPER'S MEL-LOWED...
... QUITE A BIT.
HASN'T HE?
HERE.
THANK YOU.
HUP!
BATA (FLAP)
GUI (TUG)
BATA

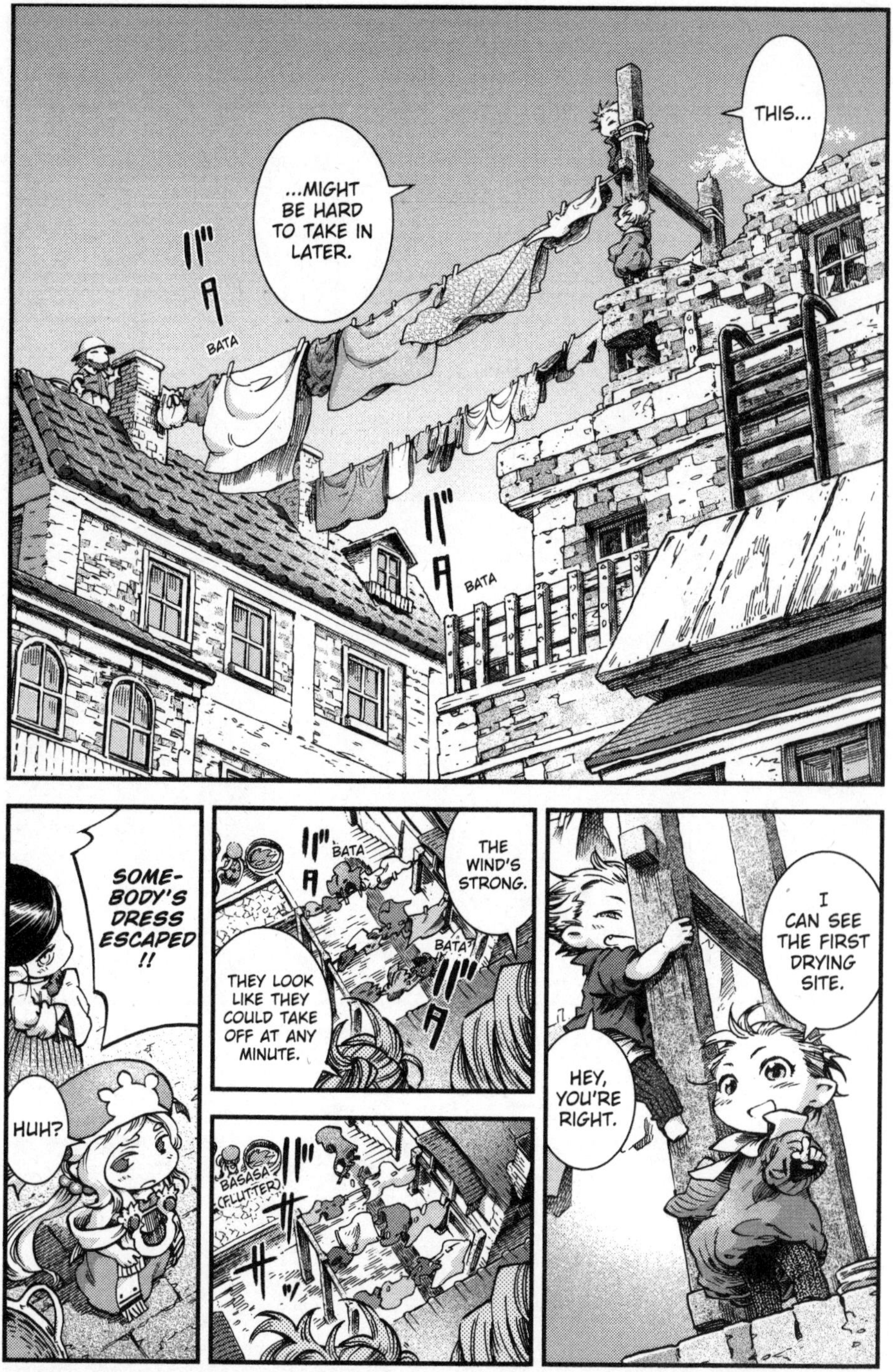
THIS...
...MIGHT BE HARD TO TAKE IN LATER.
BATA
BATA
I CAN SEE THE FIRST DRYING SITE.
HEY, YOU'RE RIGHT.
THE WIND'S STRONG.
BATA
BATA
THEY LOOK LIKE THEY COULD TAKE OFF AT ANY MINUTE.
BASASA (FLUTTER)
SOME-BODY'S DRESS ESCAPED!!
HUH?

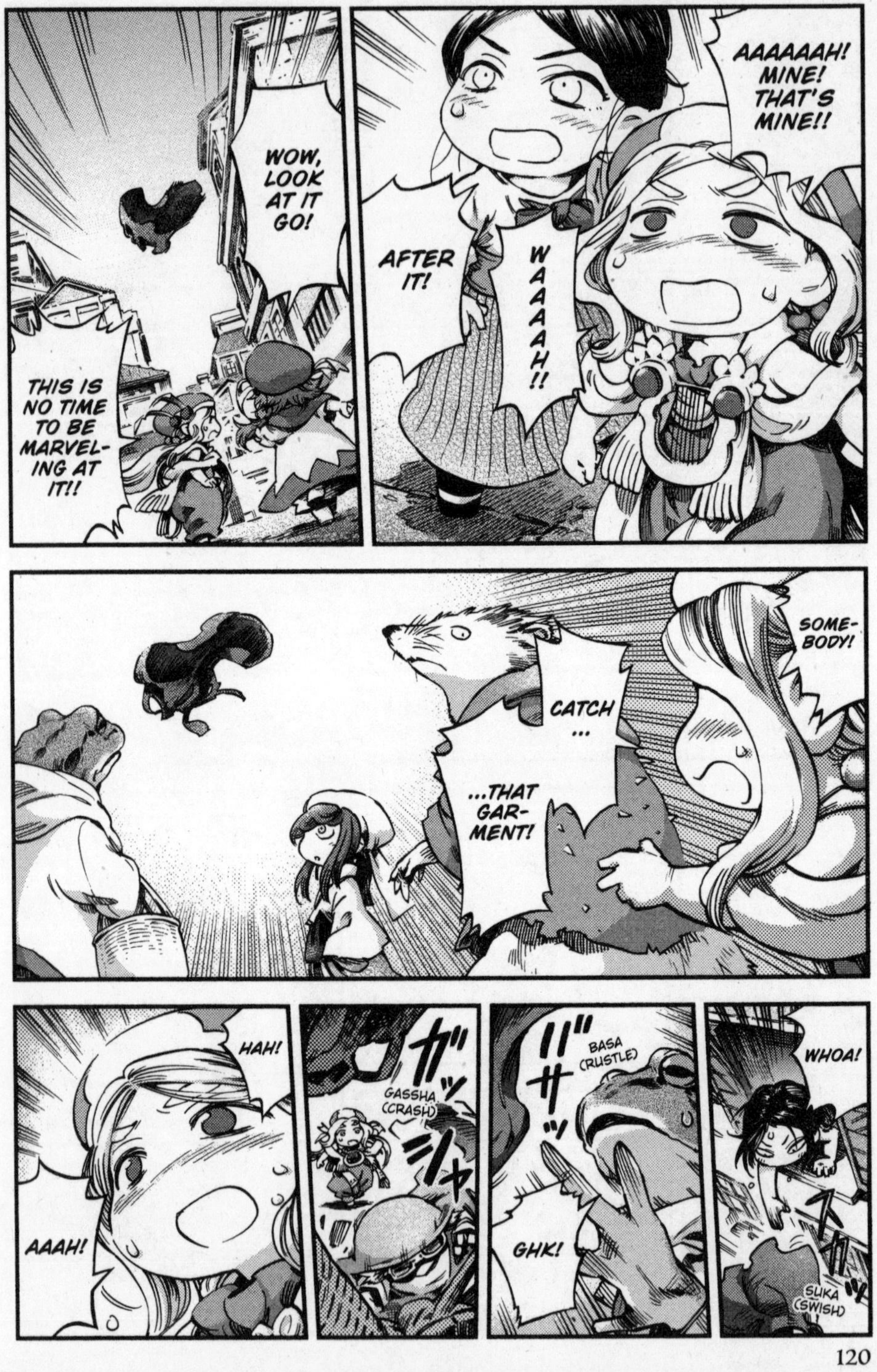
AAAAAAH! MINE! THAT'S MINE!!
WAAAAAH!!
AFTER IT!
WOW, LOOK AT IT GO!
THIS IS NO TIME TO BE MARVELING AT IT!!
SOMEBODY!
CATCH...
...THAT GARMENT!
WHOA!
SUKA (SWISH)
バサッ
BASA (RUSTLE)
GHK!
ガッ
シャ
GASSHA (CRASH)
HAH!
AAAH!

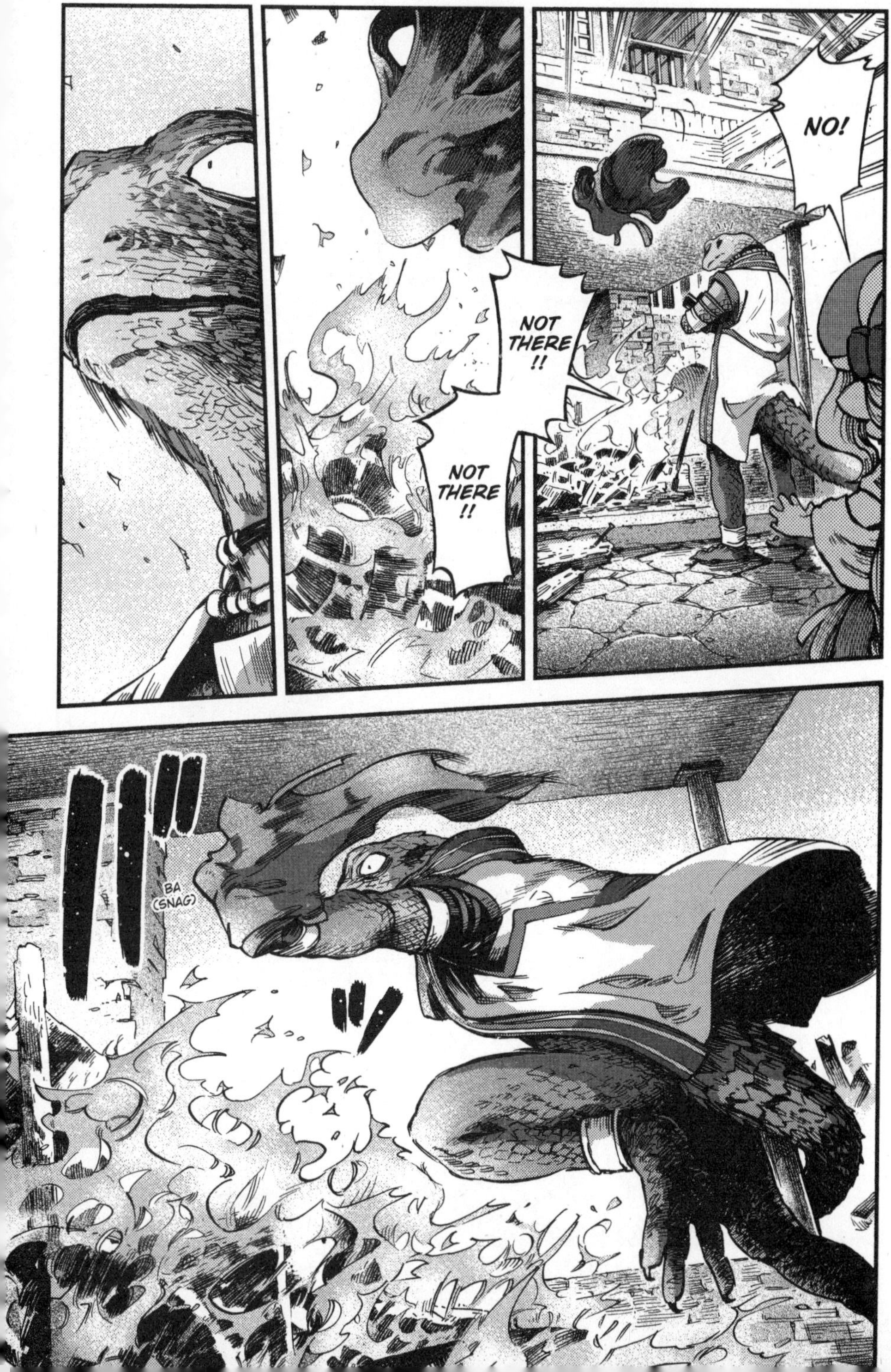
NO!
NOT THERE !!
NOT THERE !!
BA (SNAG)

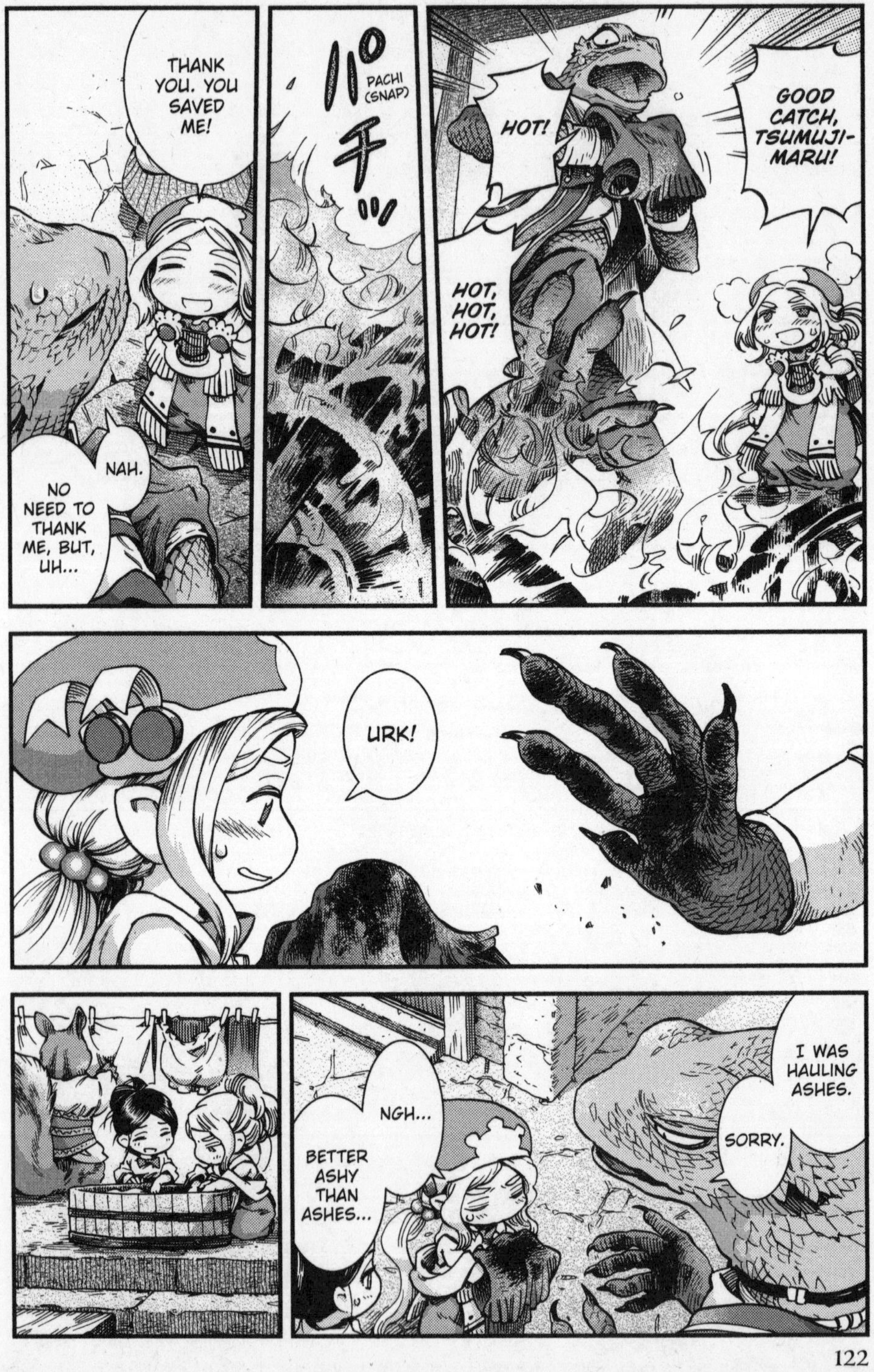
GOOD CATCH, TSUMUJI-MARU!
HOT!
HOT, HOT, HOT!
パチッ
PACHI (SNAP)
THANK YOU. YOU SAVED ME!
NAH.
NO NEED TO THANK ME, BUT, UH...
URK!
I WAS HAULING ASHES.
SORRY.
NGH...
BETTER ASHY THAN ASHES...

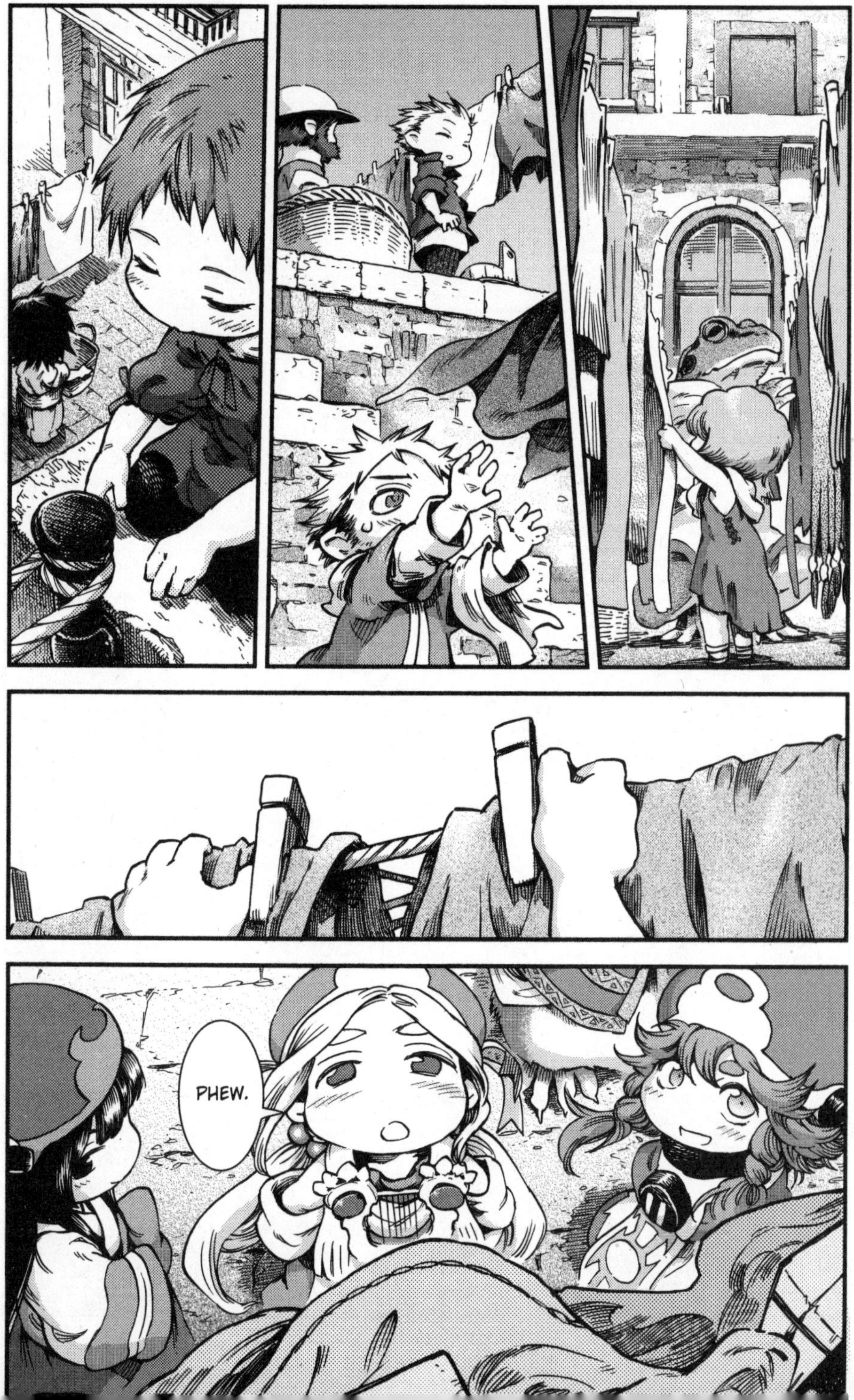
PHEW.

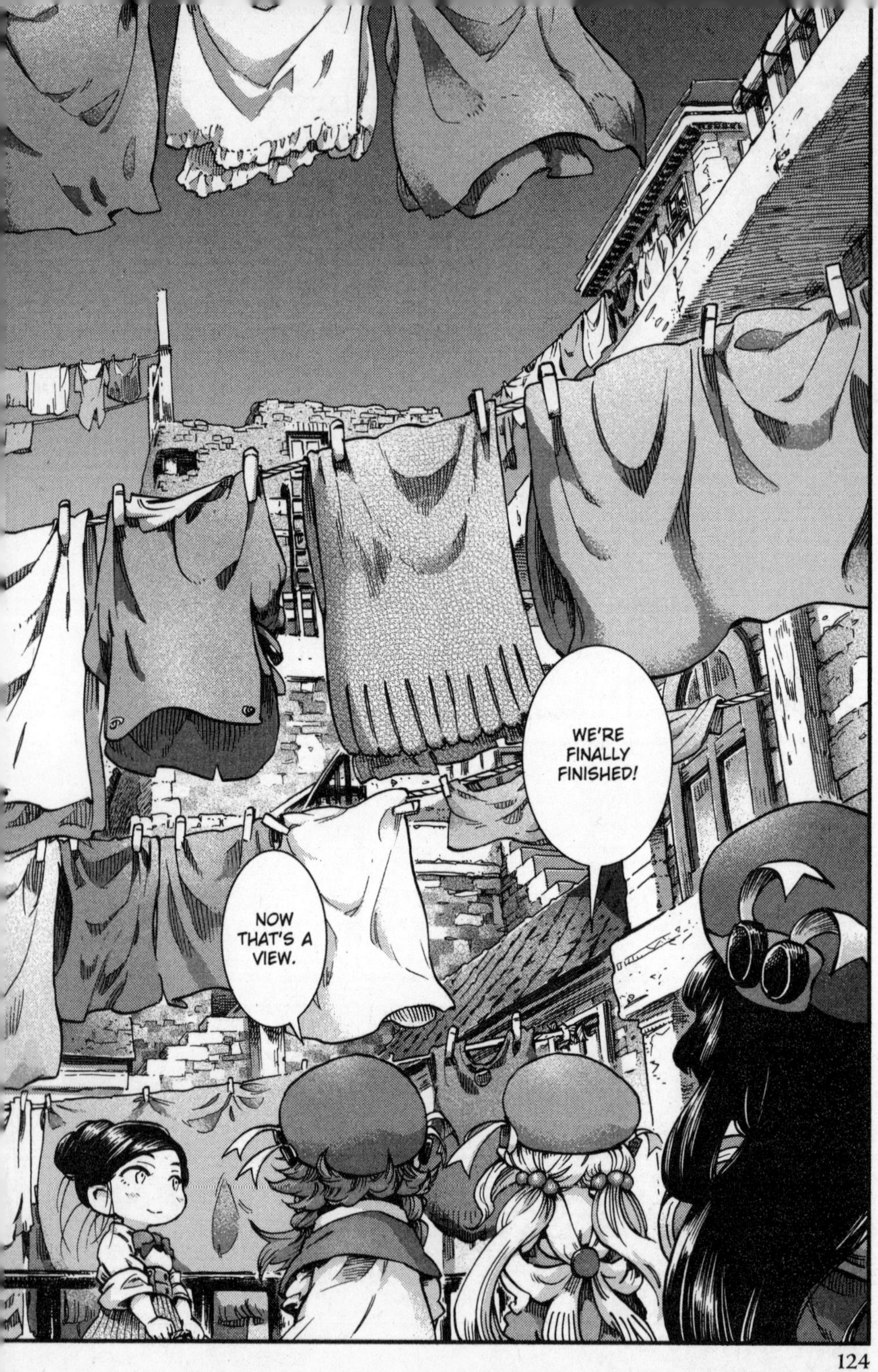
WE'RE FINALLY FINISHED!
NOW THAT'S A VIEW.

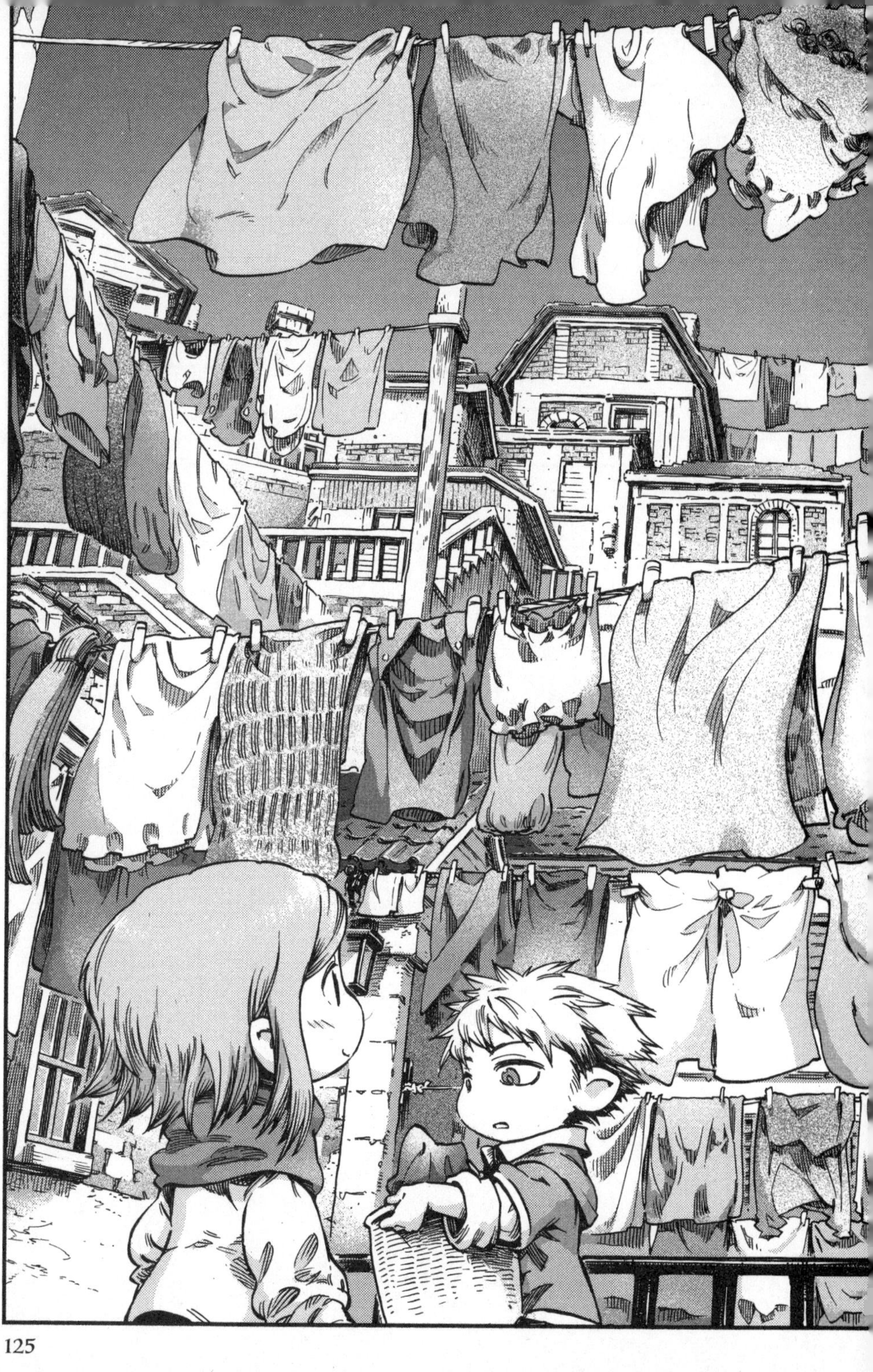

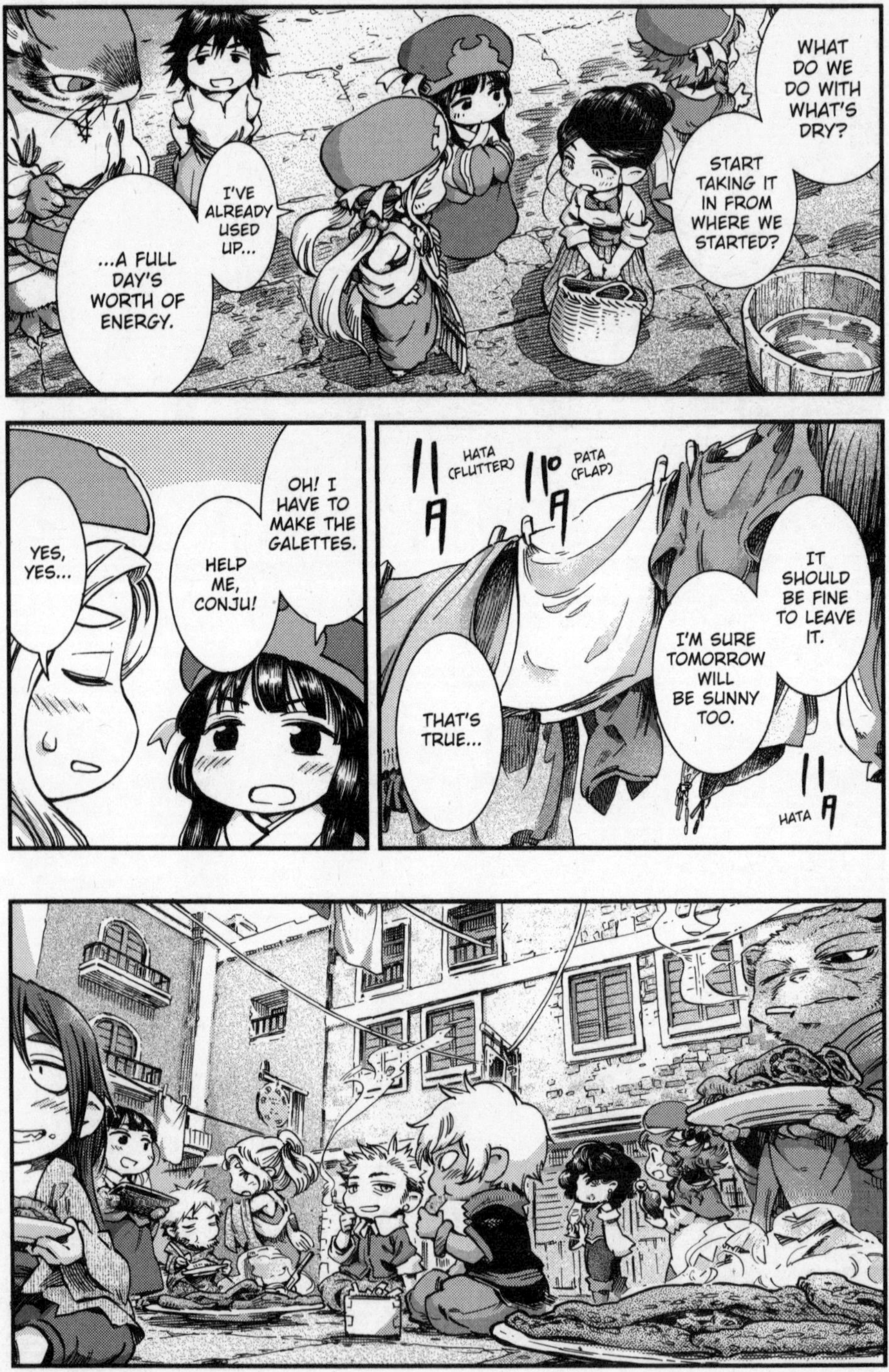
WHAT DO WE DO WITH WHAT'S DRY?
START TAKING IT IN FROM WHERE WE STARTED?
I'VE ALREADY USED UP...
...A FULL DAY'S WORTH OF ENERGY.
PATA (FLAP)
HATA (FLUTTER)
IT SHOULD BE FINE TO LEAVE IT.
I'M SURE TOMORROW WILL BE SUNNY TOO.
THAT'S TRUE...
HATA
OH! I HAVE TO MAKE THE GALETTES.
HELP ME, CONJU!
YES, YES...

Chapter 49

Farmer and Grocer

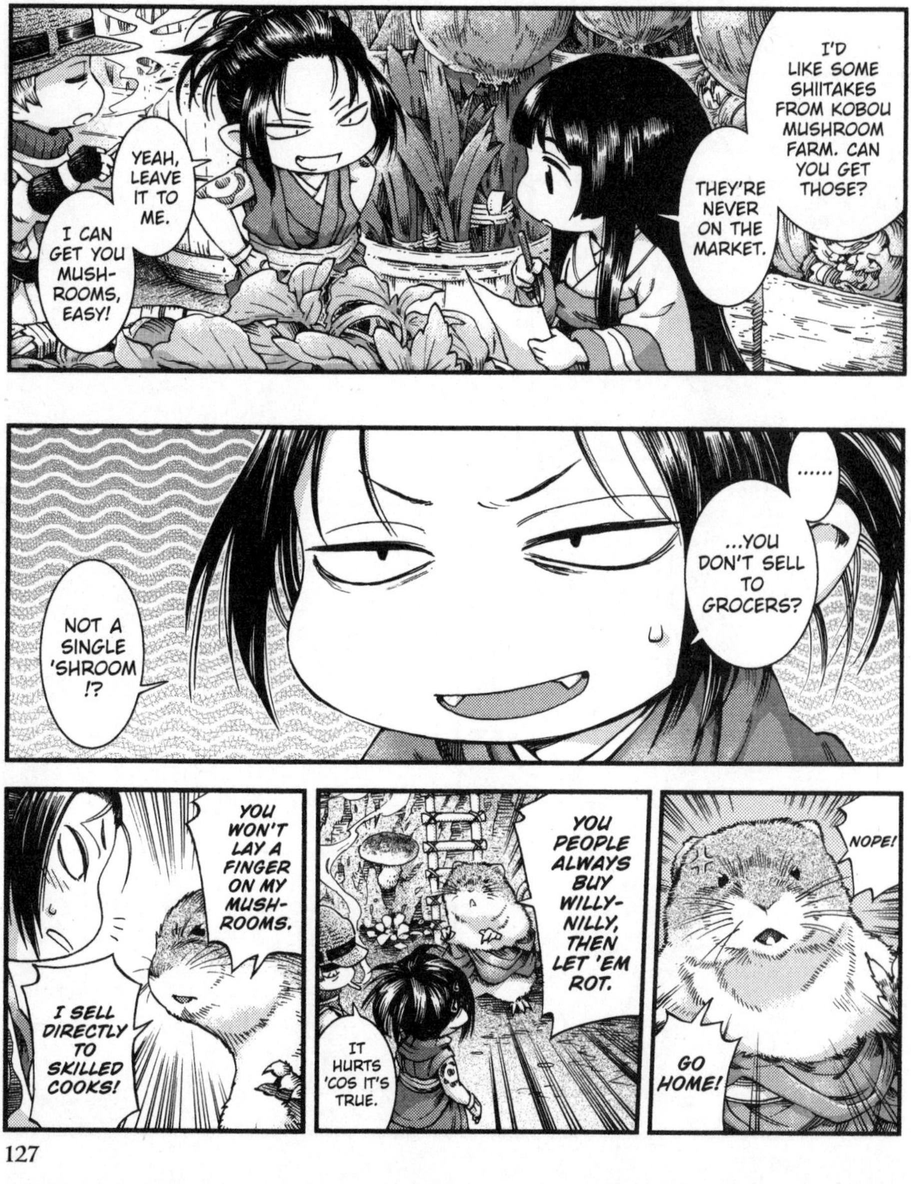
I'D LIKE SOME SHIITAKES FROM KOBOU MUSHROOM FARM. CAN YOU GET THOSE?
THEY'RE NEVER ON THE MARKET.
YEAH, LEAVE IT TO ME.
I CAN GET YOU MUSH-ROOMS, EASY!
......
...YOU DON'T SELL TO GROCERS?
NOT A SINGLE 'SHROOM !?
NOPE!
GO HOME!
YOU PEOPLE ALWAYS BUY WILLY-NILLY, THEN LET 'EM ROT.
IT HURTS 'COS IT'S TRUE.
YOU WON'T LAY A FINGER ON MY MUSH-ROOMS.
I SELL DIRECTLY TO SKILLED COOKS!

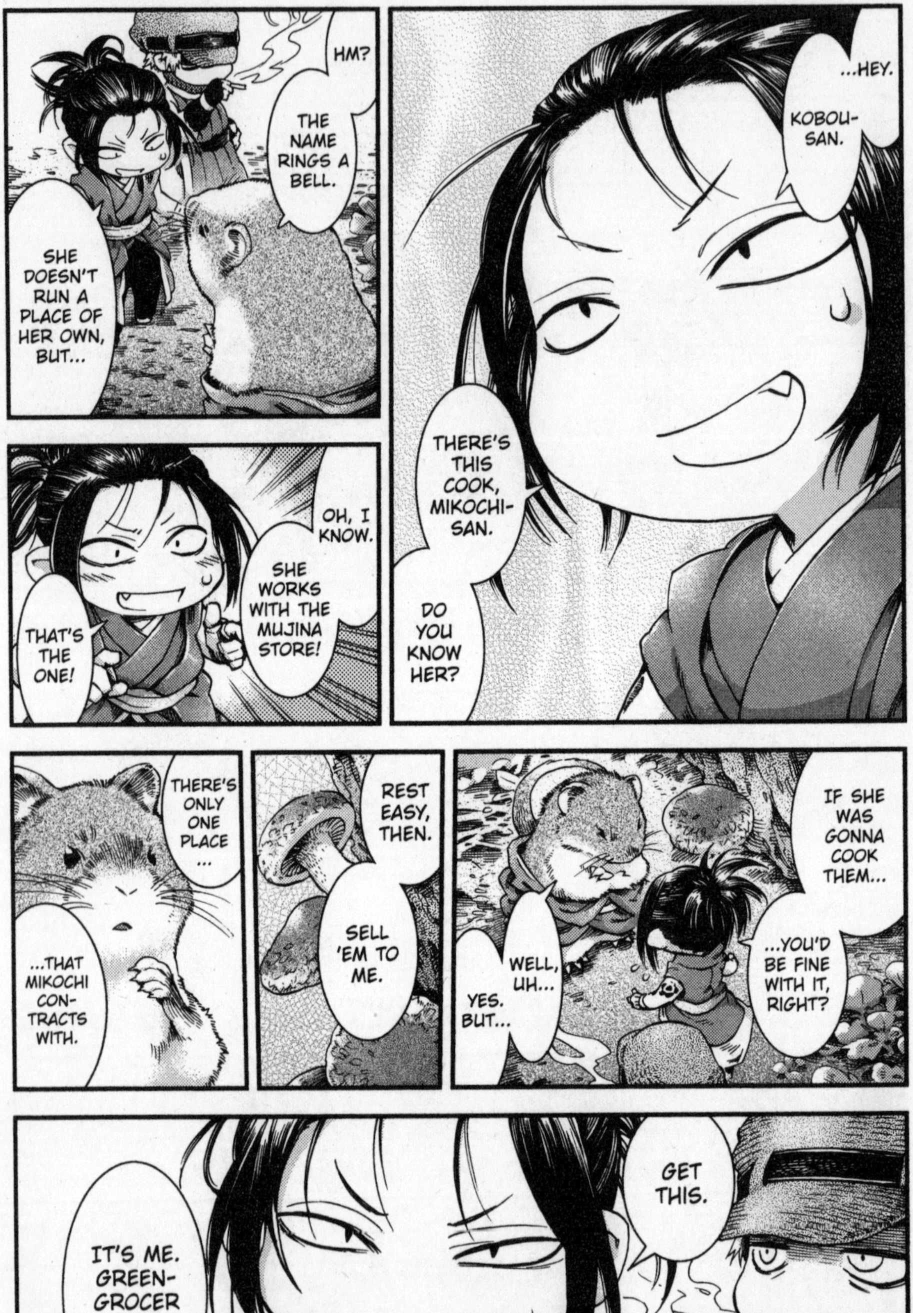
...HEY.
KOBOU-SAN.
THERE'S THIS COOK, MIKOCHI-SAN.
DO YOU KNOW HER?
HM?
THE NAME RINGS A BELL.
SHE DOESN'T RUN A PLACE OF HER OWN, BUT...
OH, I KNOW.
SHE WORKS WITH THE MUJINA STORE!
THAT'S THE ONE!
IF SHE WAS GONNA COOK THEM...
...YOU'D BE FINE WITH IT, RIGHT?
WELL, UH...
YES. BUT...
REST EASY, THEN.
SELL 'EM TO ME.
THERE'S ONLY ONE PLACE ...
...THAT MIKOCHI CONTRACTS WITH.
GET THIS.
IT'S ME. GREEN-GROCER MIKI.

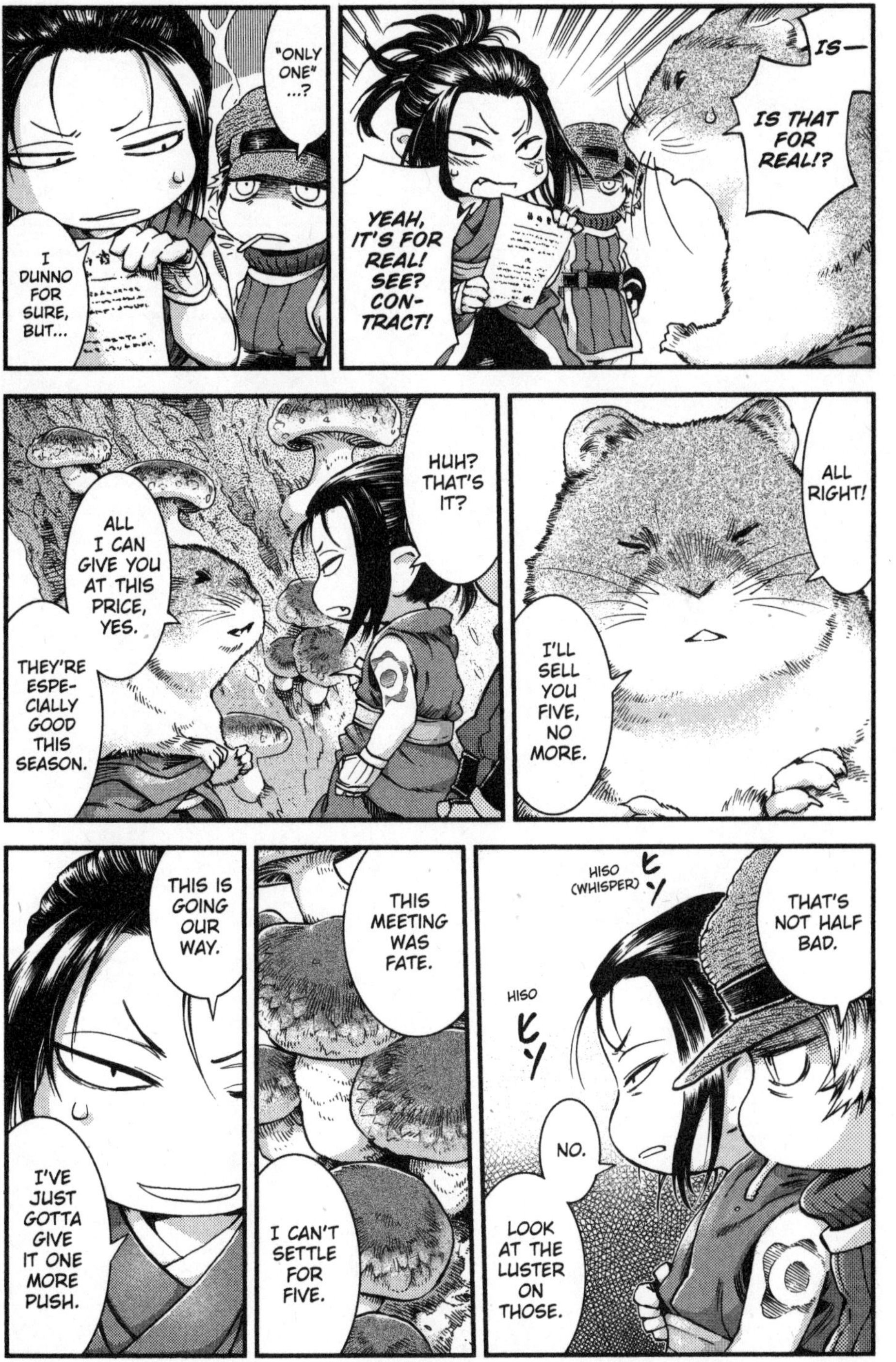
IS—
IS THAT FOR REAL!?
YEAH, IT'S FOR REAL! SEE? CON-TRACT!
"ONLY ONE" ...?
I DUNNO FOR SURE, BUT...
ALL RIGHT!
I'LL SELL YOU FIVE, NO MORE.
HUH? THAT'S IT?
ALL I CAN GIVE YOU AT THIS PRICE, YES.
THEY'RE ESPE-CIALLY GOOD THIS SEASON.
HISO (WHISPER)
THAT'S NOT HALF BAD.
HISO
NO.
LOOK AT THE LUSTER ON THOSE.
THIS MEETING WAS FATE.
I CAN'T SETTLE FOR FIVE.
THIS IS GOING OUR WAY.
I'VE JUST GOTTA GIVE IT ONE MORE PUSH.

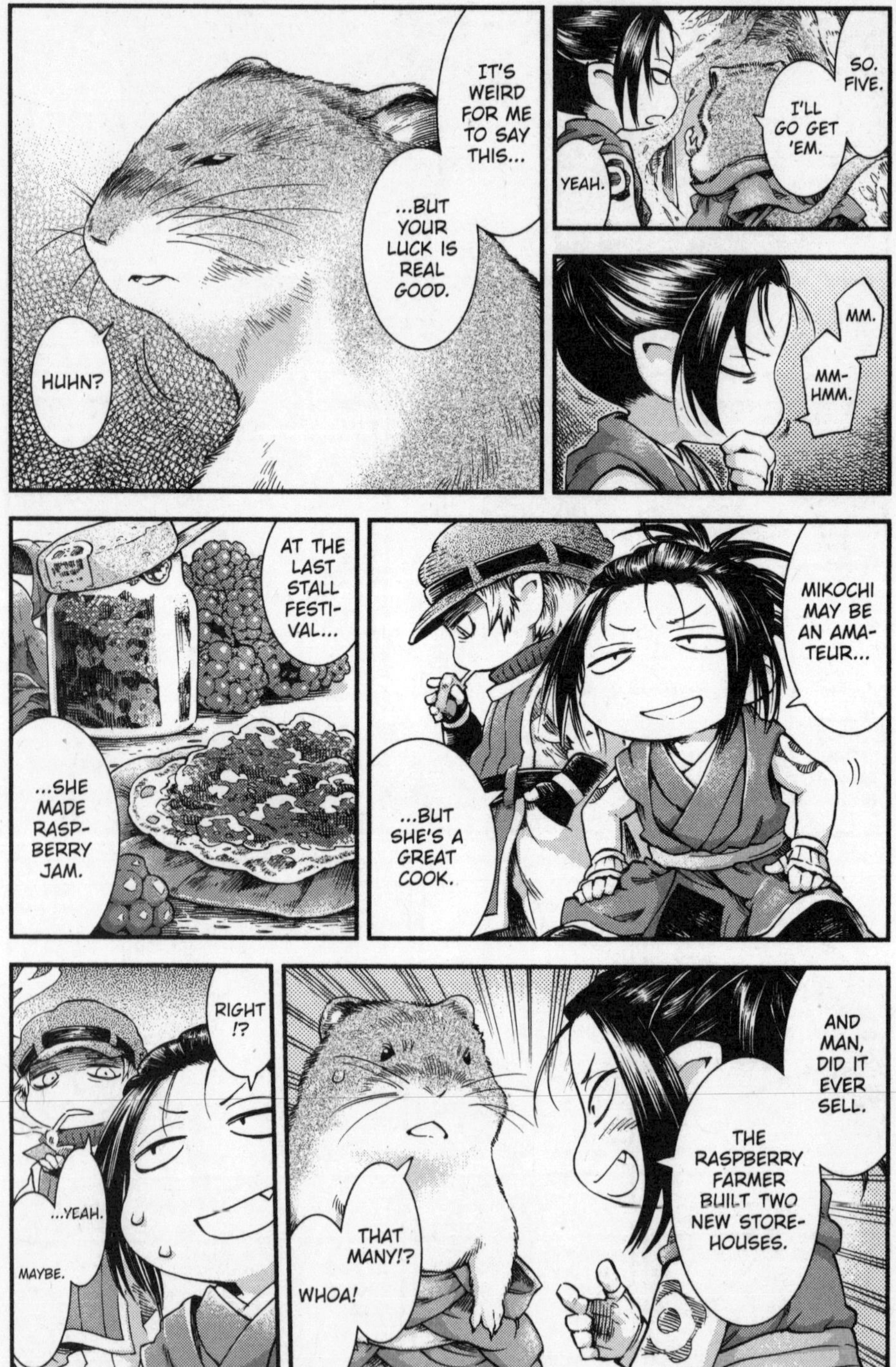
SO. FIVE.
I'LL GO GET 'EM.
YEAH.
MM.
MM-HMM.
IT'S WEIRD FOR ME TO SAY THIS...
...BUT YOUR LUCK IS REAL GOOD.
HUHN?
MIKOCHI MAY BE AN AMATEUR...
...BUT SHE'S A GREAT COOK.
AT THE LAST STALL FESTIVAL...
...SHE MADE RASPBERRY JAM.
AND MAN, DID IT EVER SELL.
THE RASPBERRY FARMER BUILT TWO NEW STOREHOUSES.
THAT MANY!?
WHOA!
RIGHT!?
...YEAH.
MAYBE.

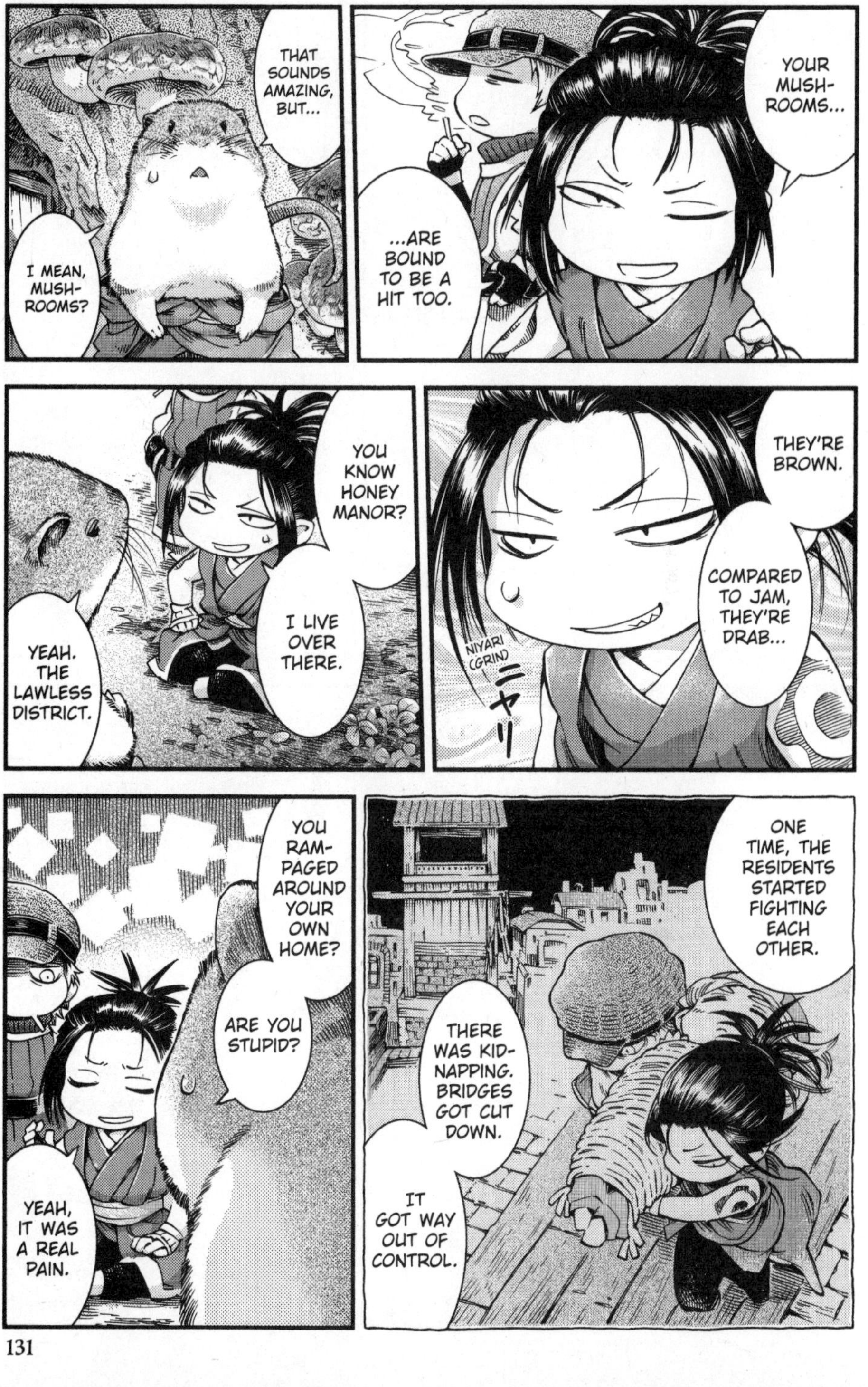
YOUR MUSH-ROOMS...
...ARE BOUND TO BE A HIT TOO.
THAT SOUNDS AMAZING, BUT...
I MEAN, MUSH-ROOMS?
THEY'RE BROWN.
COMPARED TO JAM, THEY'RE DRAB...
NIYARI (GRIN)
ニヤリ
YOU KNOW HONEY MANOR?
I LIVE OVER THERE.
YEAH. THE LAWLESS DISTRICT.
ONE TIME, THE RESIDENTS STARTED FIGHTING EACH OTHER.
THERE WAS KID-NAPPING. BRIDGES GOT CUT DOWN.
IT GOT WAY OUT OF CONTROL.
YOU RAM-PAGED AROUND YOUR OWN HOME?
ARE YOU STUPID?
YEAH, IT WAS A REAL PAIN.

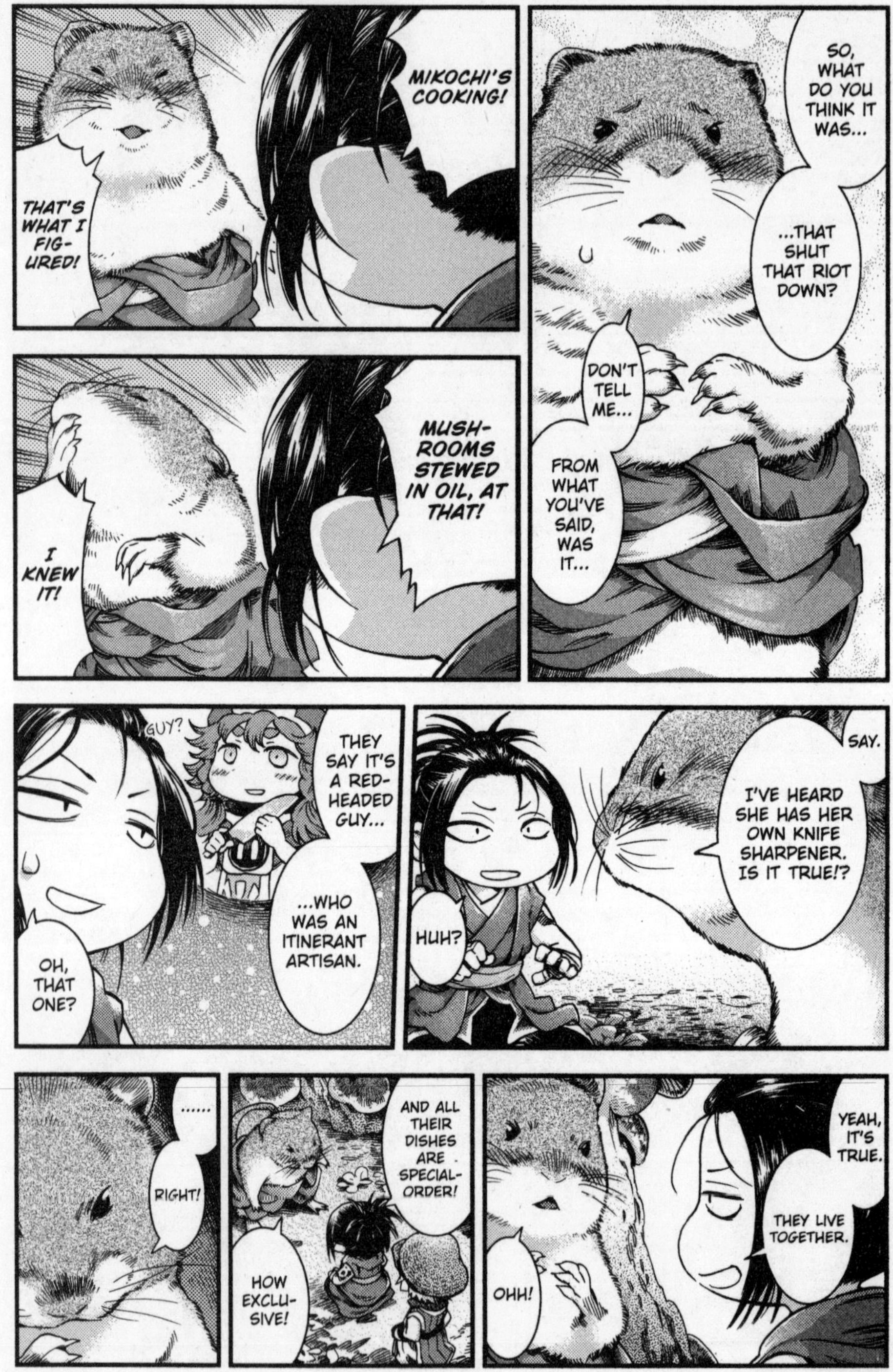
SO, WHAT DO YOU THINK IT WAS...
...THAT SHUT THAT RIOT DOWN?
DON'T TELL ME...
FROM WHAT YOU'VE SAID, WAS IT...
MIKOCHI'S COOKING!
THAT'S WHAT I FIGURED!
MUSHROOMS STEWED IN OIL, AT THAT!
I KNEW IT!
SAY.
I'VE HEARD SHE HAS HER OWN KNIFE SHARPENER. IS IT TRUE!?
HUH?
THEY SAY IT'S A RED-HEADED GUY...
GUY?
...WHO WAS AN ITINERANT ARTISAN.
OH, THAT ONE?
YEAH, IT'S TRUE.
THEY LIVE TOGETHER.
OHH!
AND ALL THEIR DISHES ARE SPECIAL-ORDER!
HOW EXCLUSIVE!
......
RIGHT!

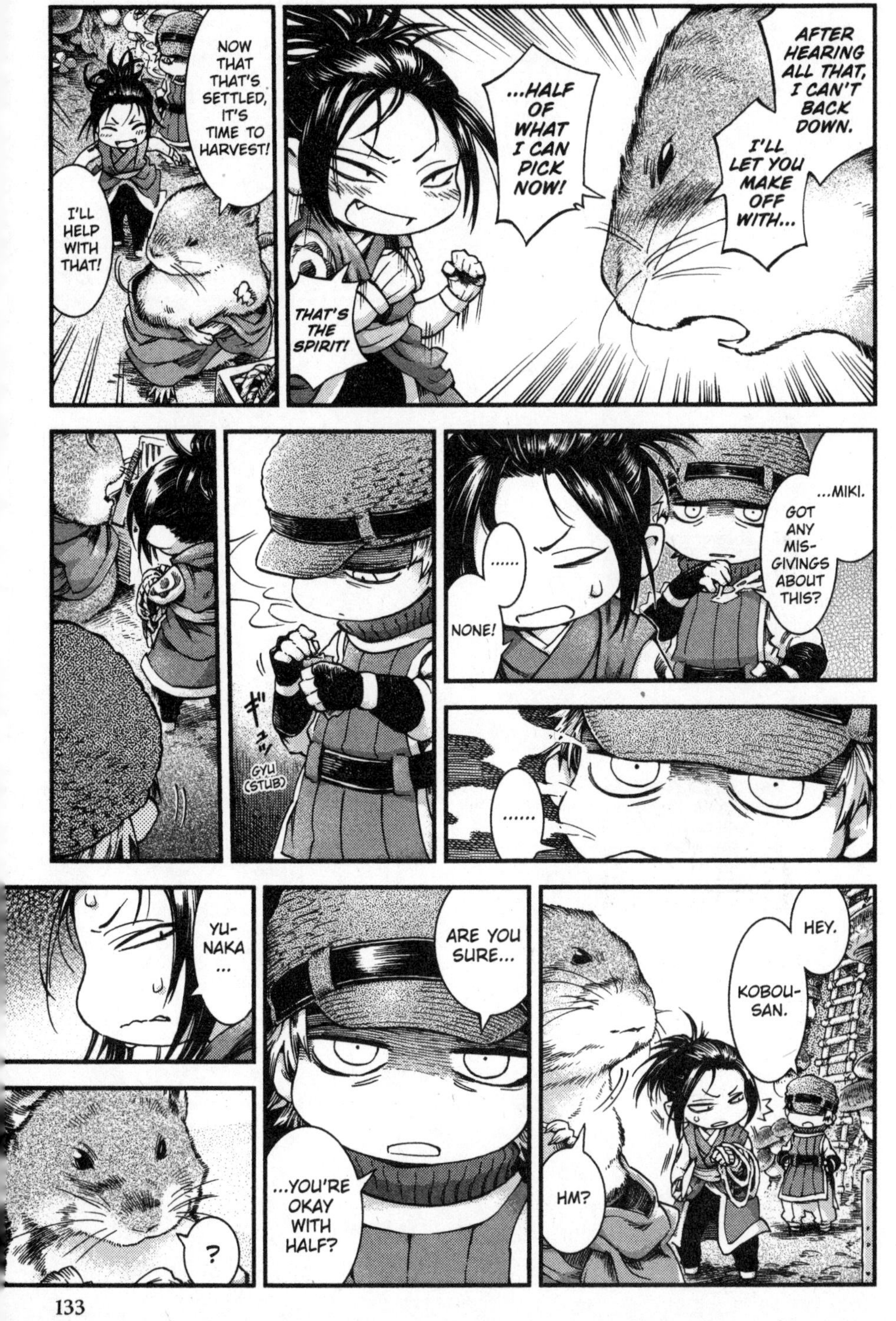
AFTER HEARING ALL THAT, I CAN'T BACK DOWN.
I'LL LET YOU MAKE OFF WITH...
...HALF OF WHAT I CAN PICK NOW!
THAT'S THE SPIRIT!
NOW THAT THAT'S SETTLED, IT'S TIME TO HARVEST!
I'LL HELP WITH THAT!
...MIKI. GOT ANY MIS-GIVINGS ABOUT THIS?
......
NONE!
......
GYU (STUB)
HEY.
KOBOU-SAN.
HM?
ARE YOU SURE...
...YOU'RE OKAY WITH HALF?
YU-NAKA ...
?

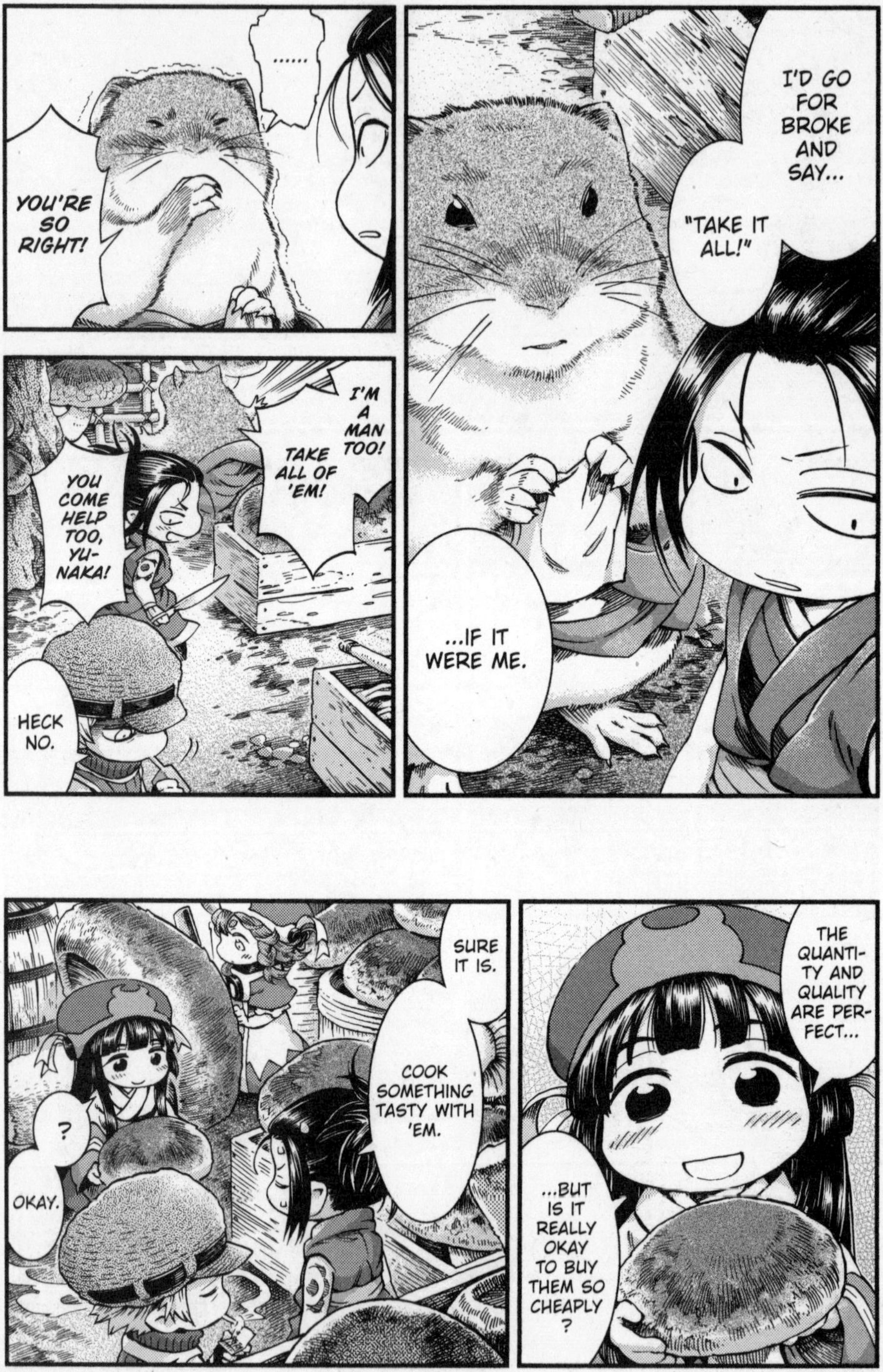
I'D GO FOR BROKE AND SAY...
"TAKE IT ALL!"
...IF IT WERE ME.
......
YOU'RE SO RIGHT!
I'M A MAN TOO!
TAKE ALL OF 'EM!
YOU COME HELP TOO, YUNAKA!
HECK NO.
THE QUANTITY AND QUALITY ARE PERFECT...
...BUT IS IT REALLY OKAY TO BUY THEM SO CHEAPLY?
SURE IT IS.
COOK SOMETHING TASTY WITH 'EM.
?
OKAY.

Chapter 49 • End

A few days ago, the Mujina Store hosted the Kobou Shiitake Festival. There were food stalls that made a variety of dishes using Kobou Mushroom Farm's shiitakes, lectures on cooking methods, and an exhibition and spot sale of preserved foods. Many mushroom lovers from Makinata and beyond attended.

Festivalgoers were as pleased as could be with the taste of Kobou shiitakes, which are almost never sold to general consumers. Many shops sold out, and the festival ended while business was still booming.

—An excerpt from *The Makinata Daily*, February 5

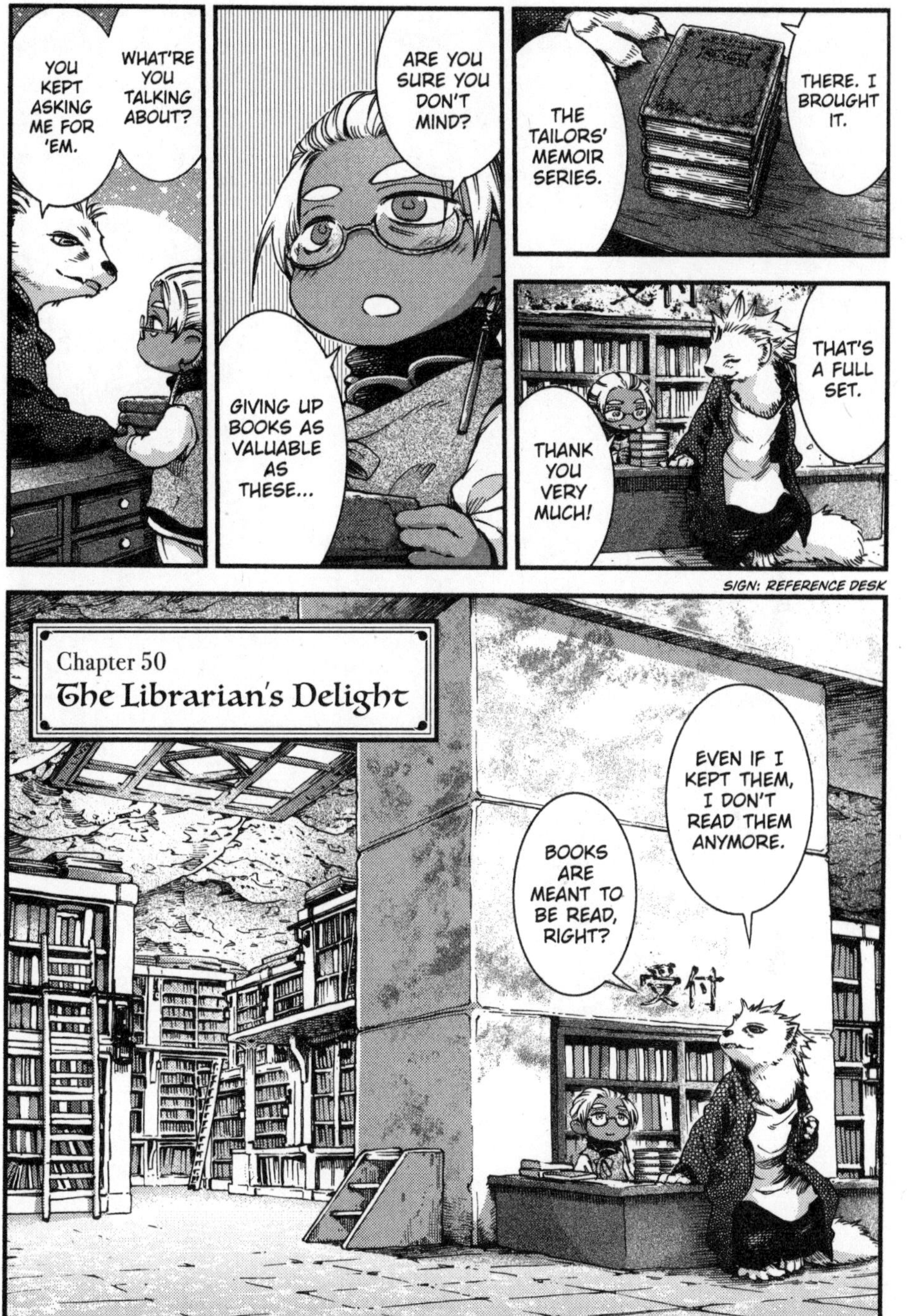
THERE. I BROUGHT IT.
THE TAILORS' MEMOIR SERIES.
THAT'S A FULL SET.
THANK YOU VERY MUCH!
ARE YOU SURE YOU DON'T MIND?
GIVING UP BOOKS AS VALUABLE AS THESE...
WHAT'RE YOU TALKING ABOUT?
YOU KEPT ASKING ME FOR 'EM.
SIGN: REFERENCE DESK
Chapter 50
The Librarian's Delight
EVEN IF I KEPT THEM, I DON'T READ THEM ANYMORE.
BOOKS ARE MEANT TO BE READ, RIGHT?
受付

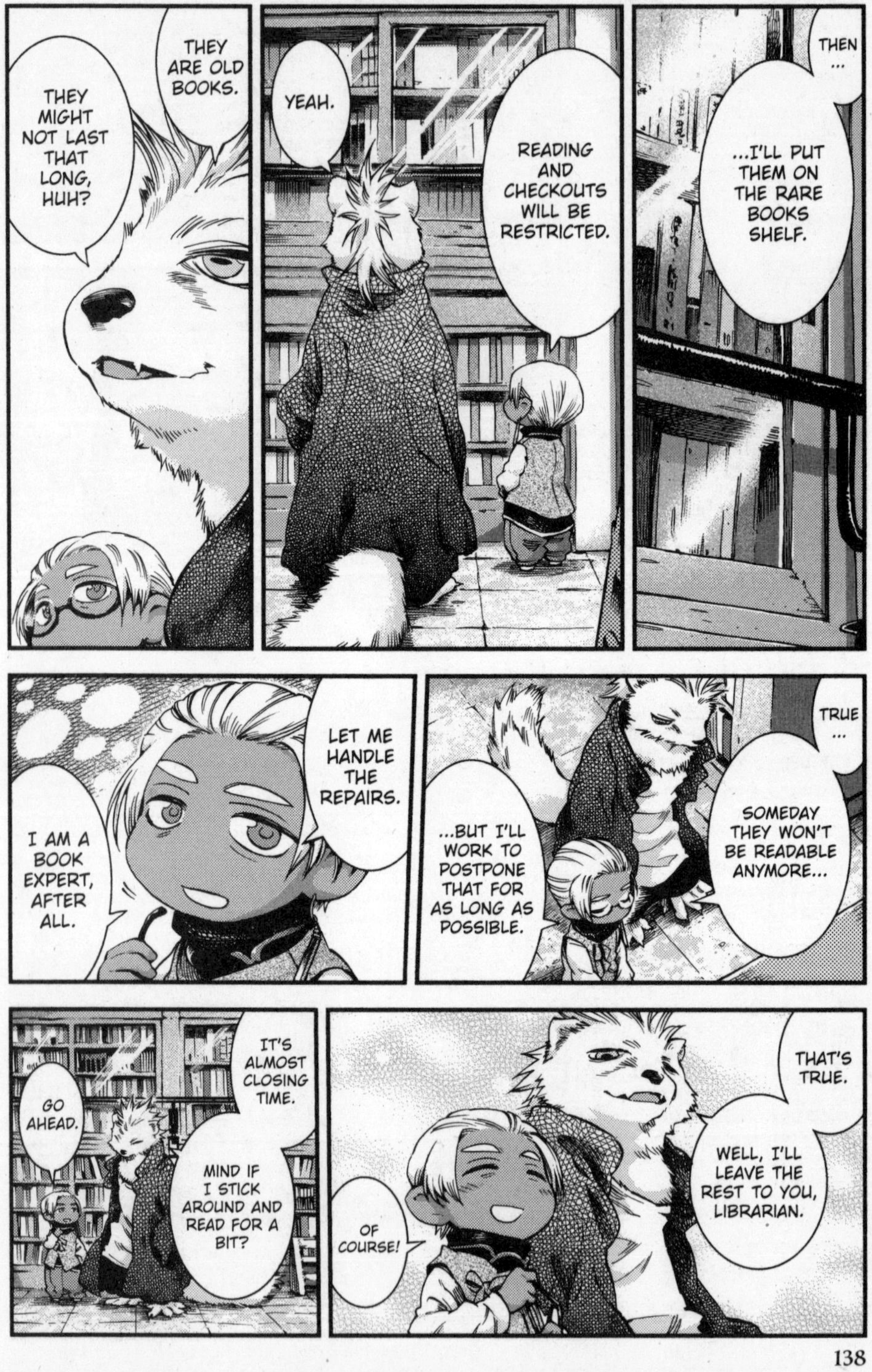
THEN ...
...I'LL PUT THEM ON THE RARE BOOKS SHELF.
READING AND CHECKOUTS WILL BE RESTRICTED.
YEAH.
THEY ARE OLD BOOKS.
THEY MIGHT NOT LAST THAT LONG, HUH?
TRUE ...
SOMEDAY THEY WON'T BE READABLE ANYMORE...
...BUT I'LL WORK TO POSTPONE THAT FOR AS LONG AS POSSIBLE.
LET ME HANDLE THE REPAIRS.
I AM A BOOK EXPERT, AFTER ALL.
THAT'S TRUE.
WELL, I'LL LEAVE THE REST TO YOU, LIBRARIAN.
OF COURSE!
IT'S ALMOST CLOSING TIME.
MIND IF I STICK AROUND AND READ FOR A BIT?
GO AHEAD.

SIGN: MAKINATA LIBRARY

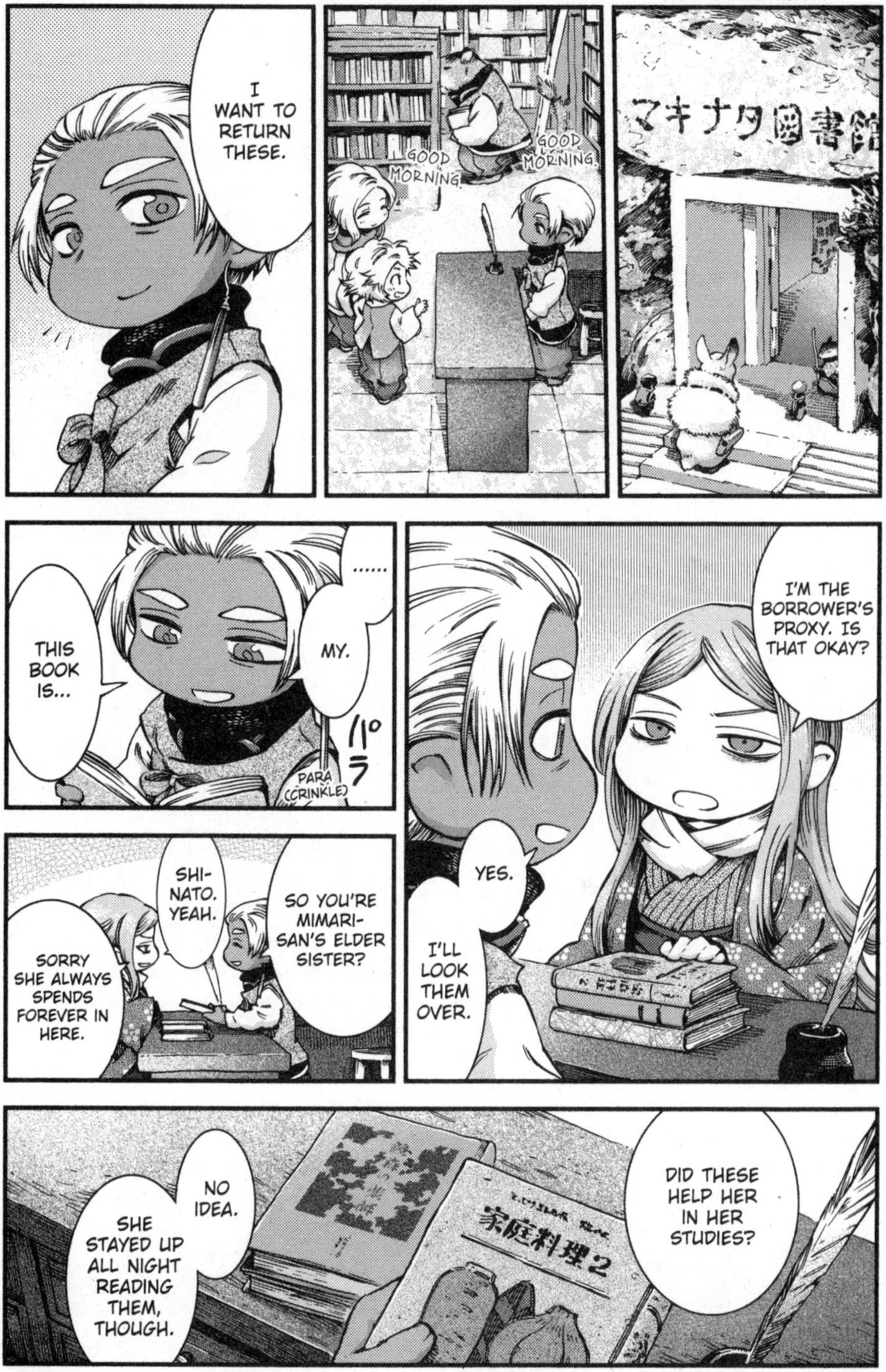
マキナタ図書館
GOOD MORNING
GOOD MORNING
I WANT TO RETURN THESE.
I'M THE BORROWER'S PROXY. IS THAT OKAY?
YES.
I'LL LOOK THEM OVER.
......
MY.
パラ
PARA (CRINKLE)
THIS BOOK IS...
SO YOU'RE MIMARI-SAN'S ELDER SISTER?
SHI-NATO. YEAH.
SORRY SHE ALWAYS SPENDS FOREVER IN HERE.
DID THESE HELP HER IN HER STUDIES?
家庭料理2
NO IDEA.
SHE STAYED UP ALL NIGHT READING THEM, THOUGH.

BOOK: HOME COOKING 2

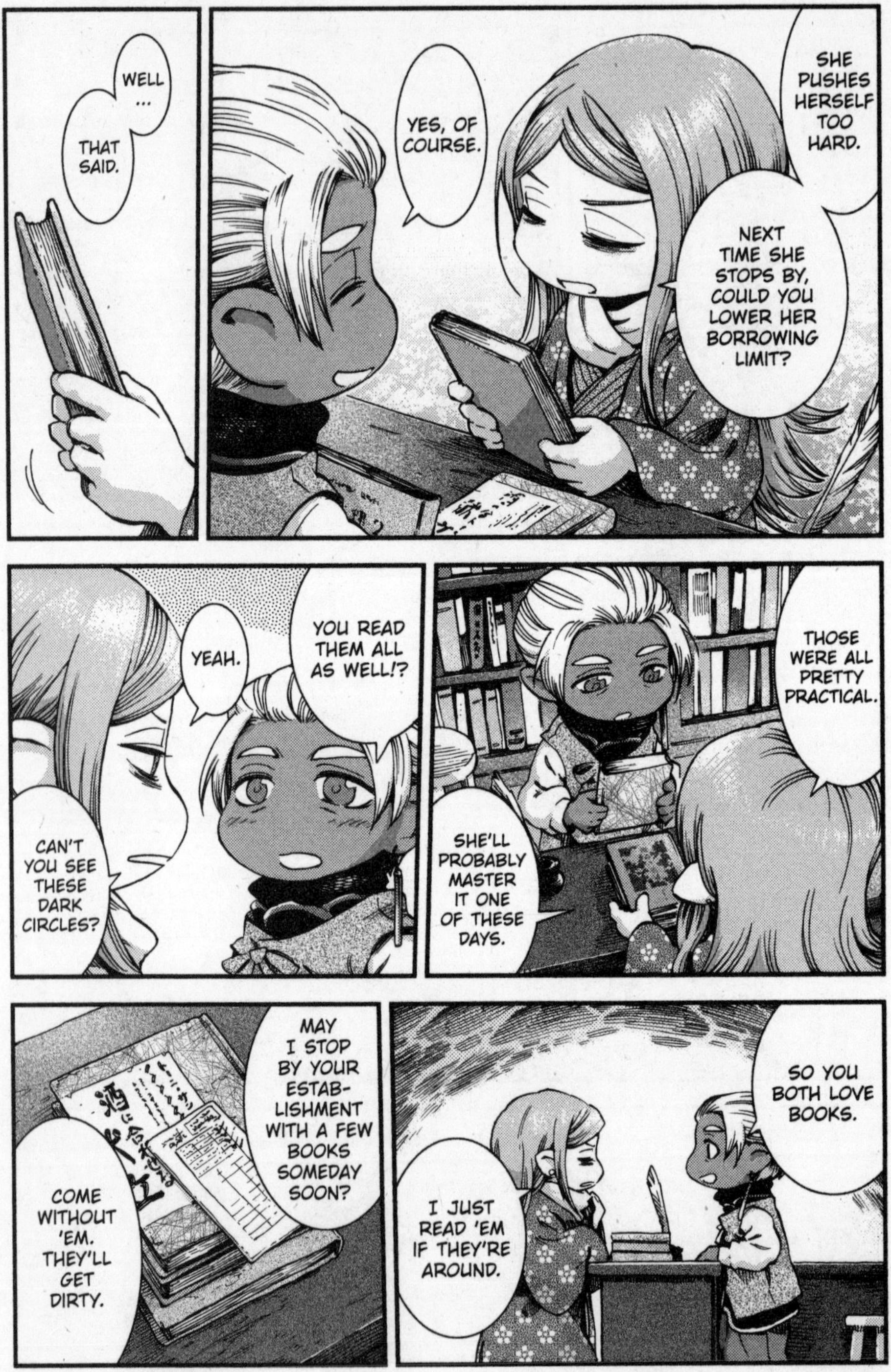
SHE PUSHES HERSELF TOO HARD.
NEXT TIME SHE STOPS BY, COULD YOU LOWER HER BORROWING LIMIT?
YES, OF COURSE.
WELL ... THAT SAID.
THOSE WERE ALL PRETTY PRACTICAL.
SHE'LL PROBABLY MASTER IT ONE OF THESE DAYS.
YOU READ THEM ALL AS WELL!?
YEAH.
CAN'T YOU SEE THESE DARK CIRCLES?
SO YOU BOTH LOVE BOOKS.
I JUST READ 'EM IF THEY'RE AROUND.
MAY I STOP BY YOUR ESTAB-LISHMENT WITH A FEW BOOKS SOMEDAY SOON?
COME WITHOUT 'EM. THEY'LL GET DIRTY.

BOOK: MENUS TO PAIR WITH SAKE

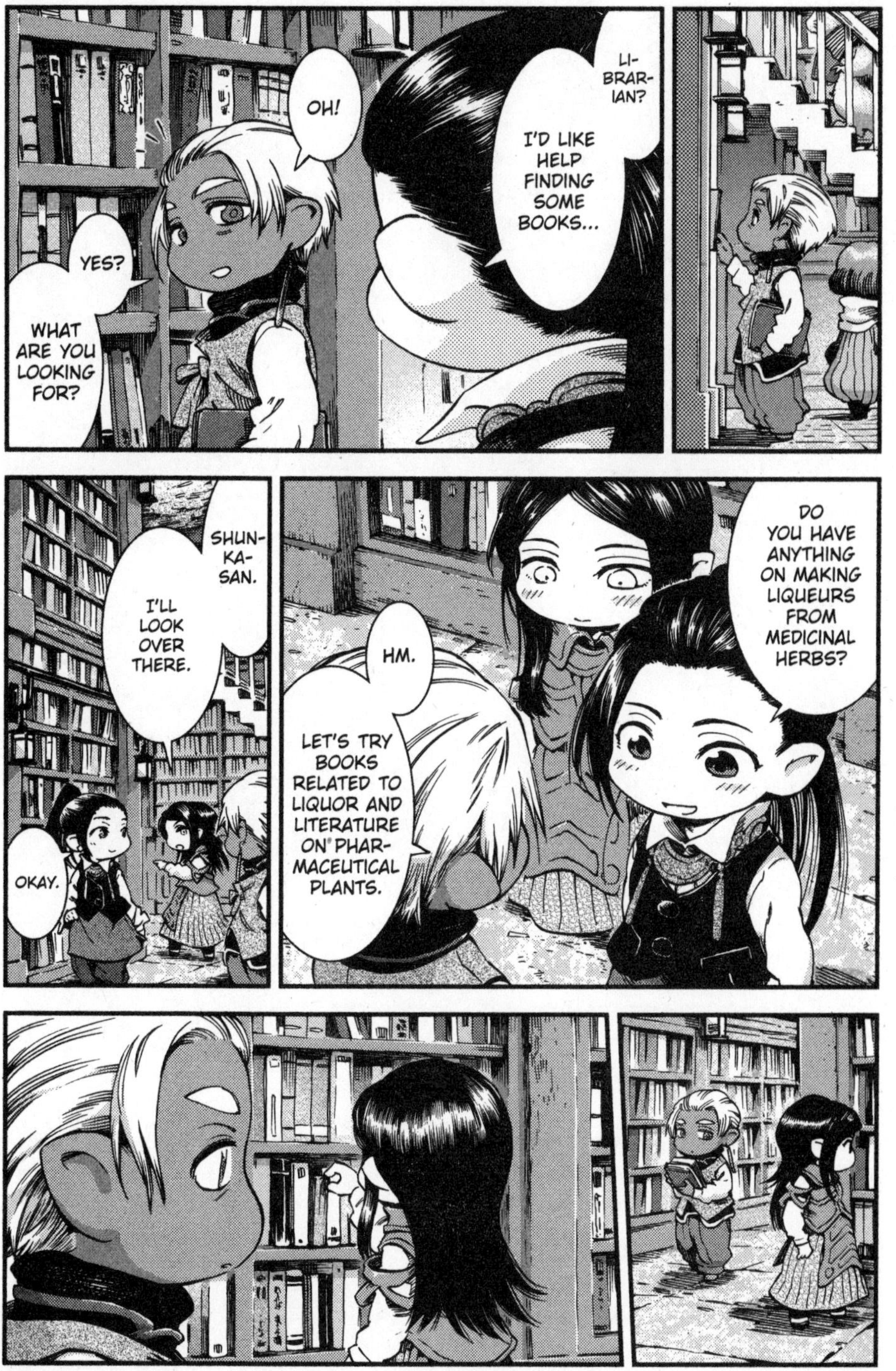
LI-BRAR-IAN?
I'D LIKE HELP FINDING SOME BOOKS...
OH!
YES?
WHAT ARE YOU LOOKING FOR?
DO YOU HAVE ANYTHING ON MAKING LIQUEURS FROM MEDICINAL HERBS?
HM.
LET'S TRY BOOKS RELATED TO LIQUOR AND LITERATURE ON PHAR-MACEUTICAL PLANTS.
SHUN-KA-SAN.
I'LL LOOK OVER THERE.
OKAY.

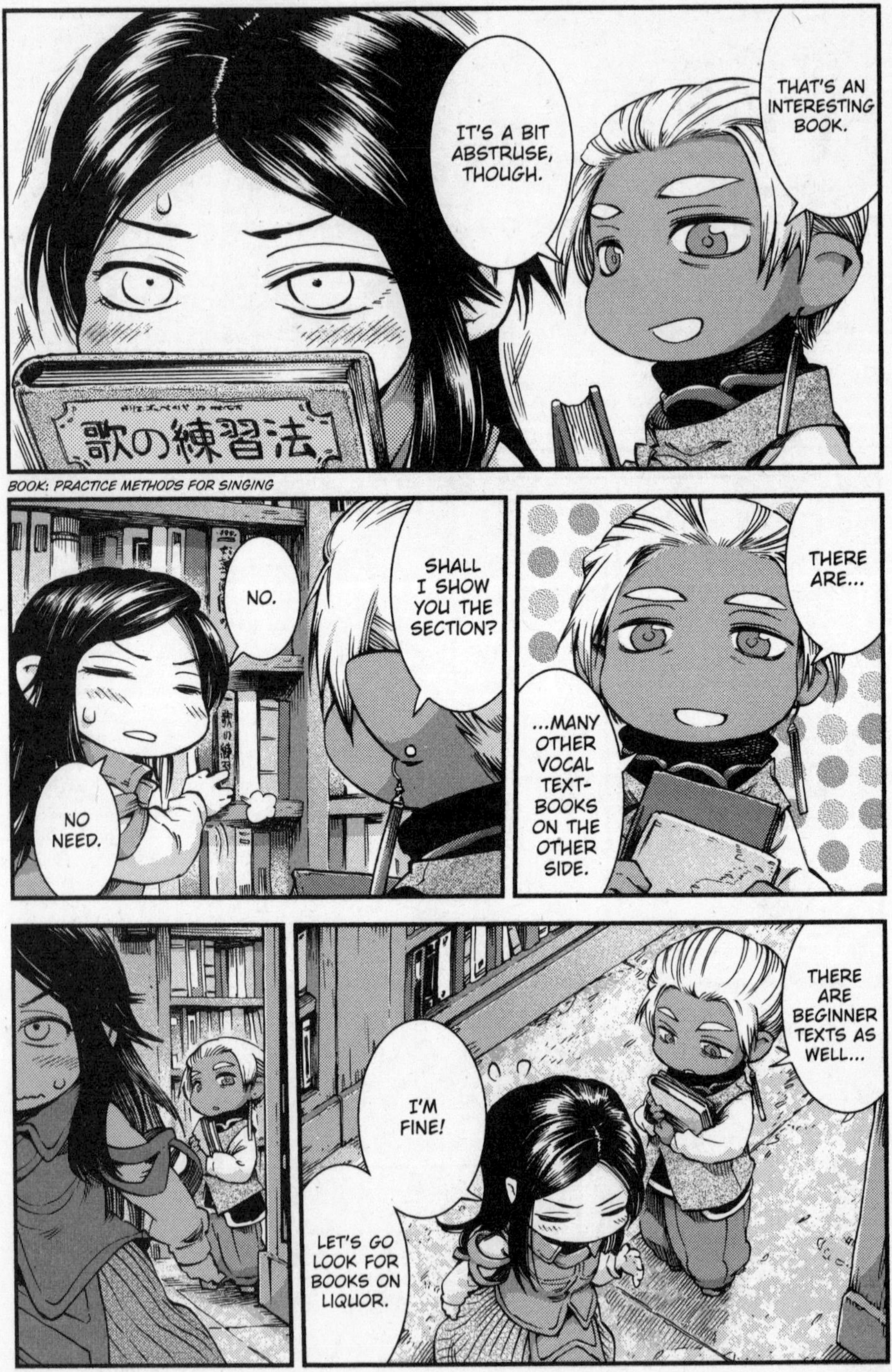
THAT'S AN INTERESTING BOOK.
IT'S A BIT ABSTRUSE, THOUGH.
歌の練習法
BOOK: PRACTICE METHODS FOR SINGING
THERE ARE...
...MANY OTHER VOCAL TEXT-BOOKS ON THE OTHER SIDE.
SHALL I SHOW YOU THE SECTION?
NO.
NO NEED.
THERE ARE BEGINNER TEXTS AS WELL...
I'M FINE!
LET'S GO LOOK FOR BOOKS ON LIQUOR.

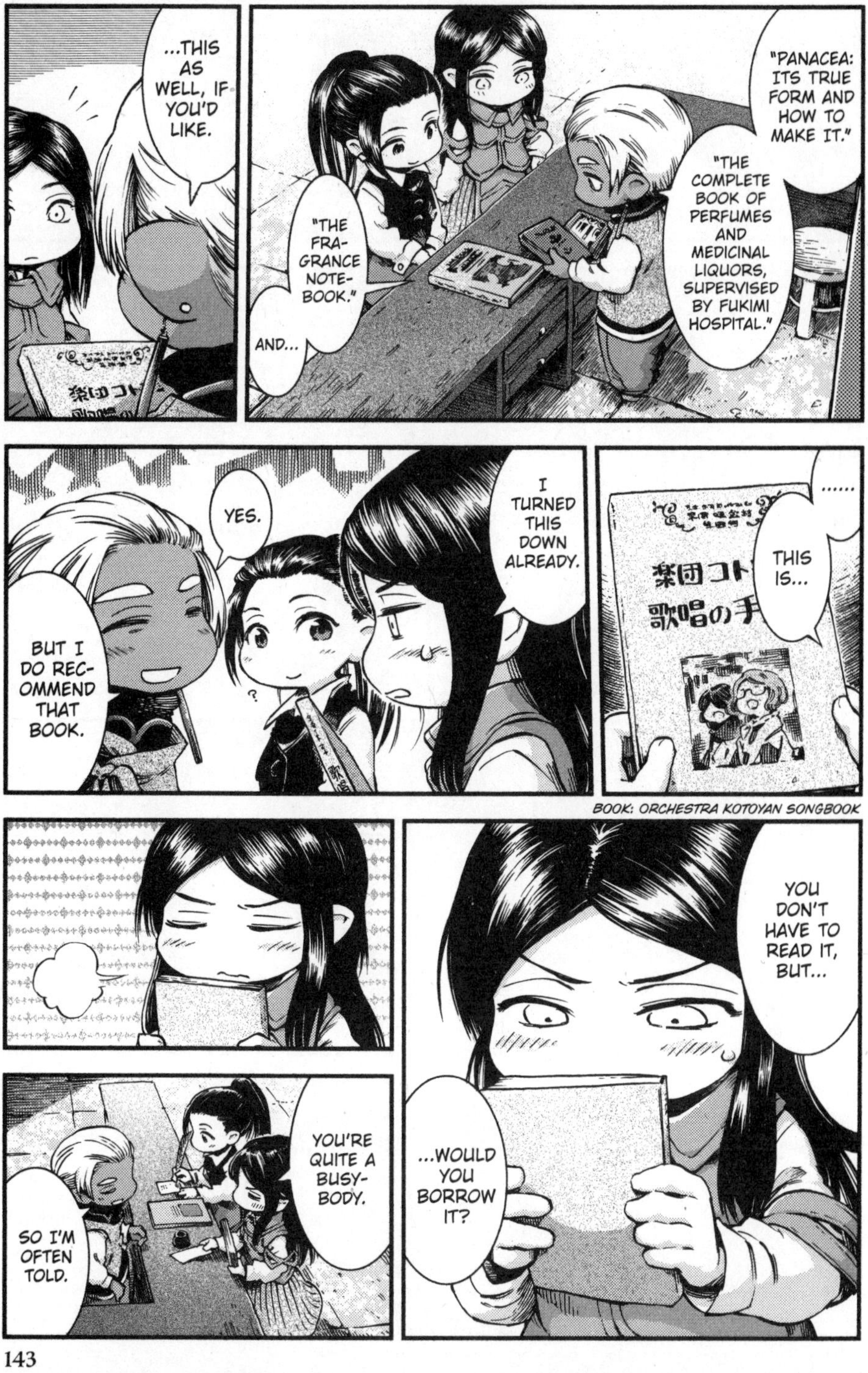
"PANACEA: ITS TRUE FORM AND HOW TO MAKE IT."
"THE COMPLETE BOOK OF PERFUMES AND MEDICINAL LIQUORS, SUPERVISED BY FUKIMI HOSPITAL."
"THE FRAGRANCE NOTEBOOK."
AND...
...THIS AS WELL, IF YOU'D LIKE.
......
THIS IS...
BOOK: ORCHESTRA KOTOYAN SONGBOOK
I TURNED THIS DOWN ALREADY.
YES.
BUT I DO RECOMMEND THAT BOOK.
YOU DON'T HAVE TO READ IT, BUT...
...WOULD YOU BORROW IT?
YOU'RE QUITE A BUSYBODY.
SO I'M OFTEN TOLD.

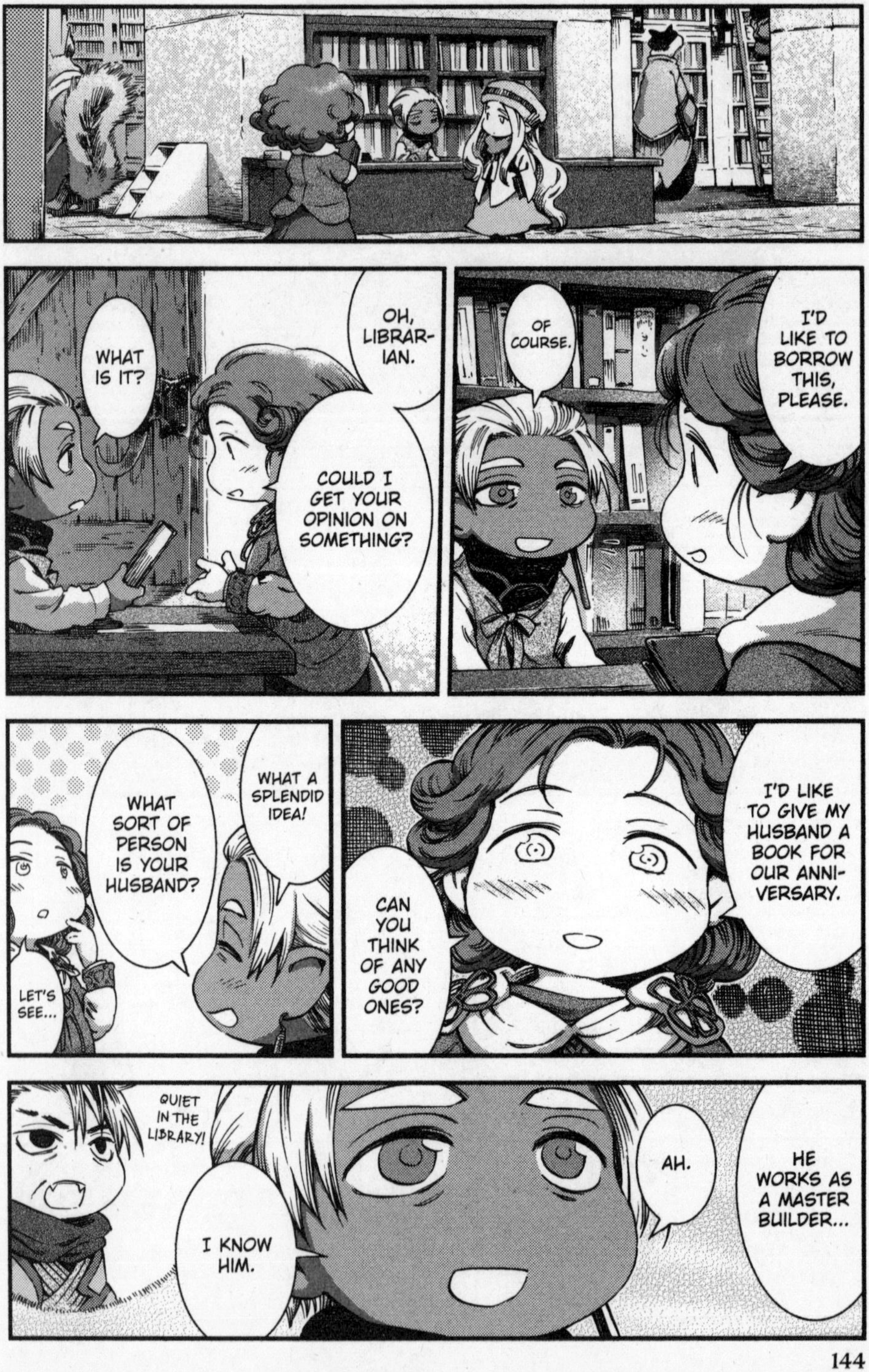

I'D LIKE TO BORROW THIS, PLEASE.
OF COURSE.
OH, LIBRARIAN.
COULD I GET YOUR OPINION ON SOMETHING?
WHAT IS IT?
I'D LIKE TO GIVE MY HUSBAND A BOOK FOR OUR ANNIVERSARY.
CAN YOU THINK OF ANY GOOD ONES?
WHAT A SPLENDID IDEA!
WHAT SORT OF PERSON IS YOUR HUSBAND?
LET'S SEE...
HE WORKS AS A MASTER BUILDER...
AH.
I KNOW HIM.
QUIET IN THE LIBRARY!

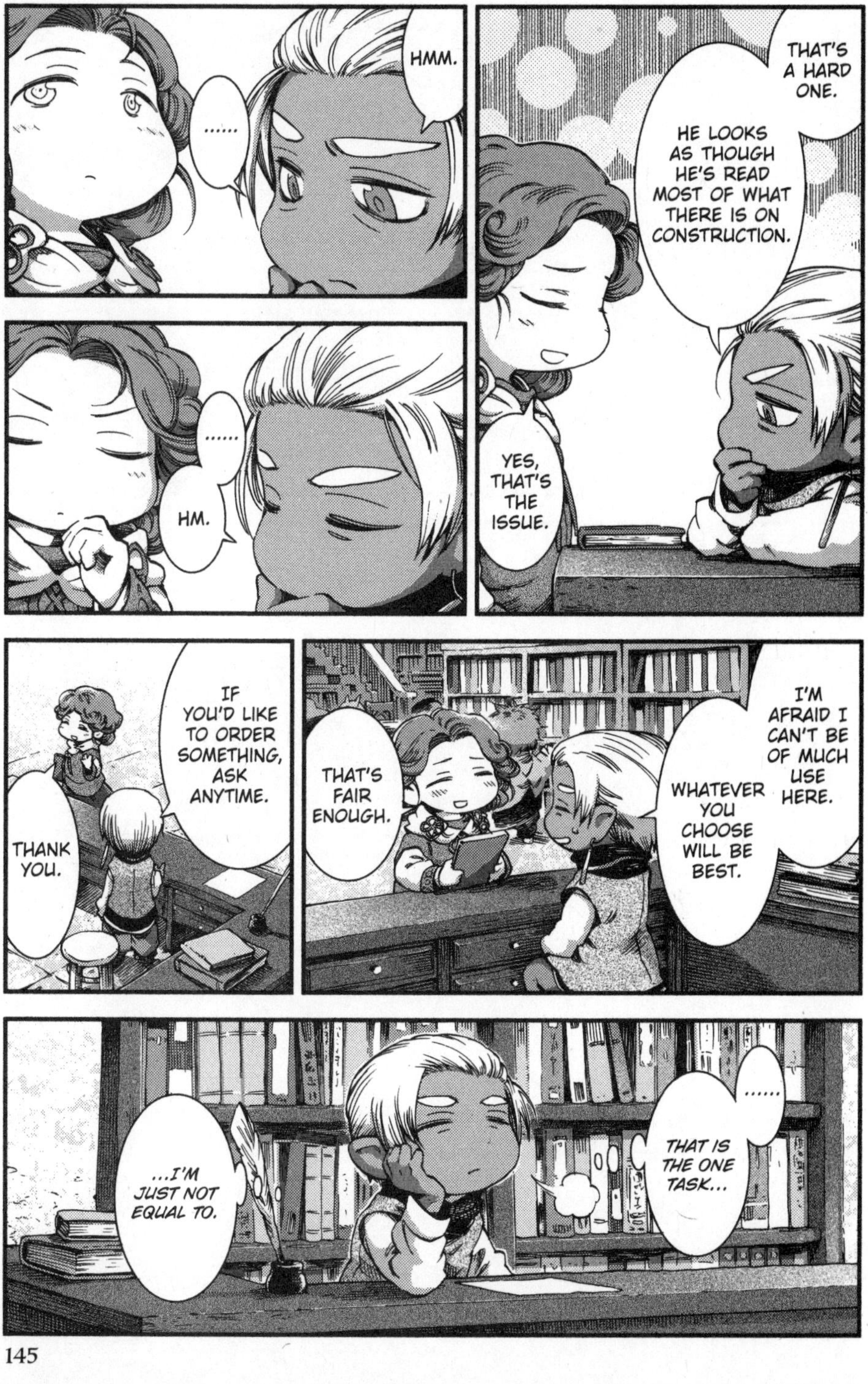
THAT'S A HARD ONE.
HE LOOKS AS THOUGH HE'S READ MOST OF WHAT THERE IS ON CONSTRUCTION.
YES, THAT'S THE ISSUE.
HMM.
......
......
HM.
I'M AFRAID I CAN'T BE OF MUCH USE HERE.
WHATEVER YOU CHOOSE WILL BE BEST.
THAT'S FAIR ENOUGH.
IF YOU'D LIKE TO ORDER SOMETHING, ASK ANYTIME.
THANK YOU.
......
THAT IS THE ONE TASK...
...I'M JUST NOT EQUAL TO.

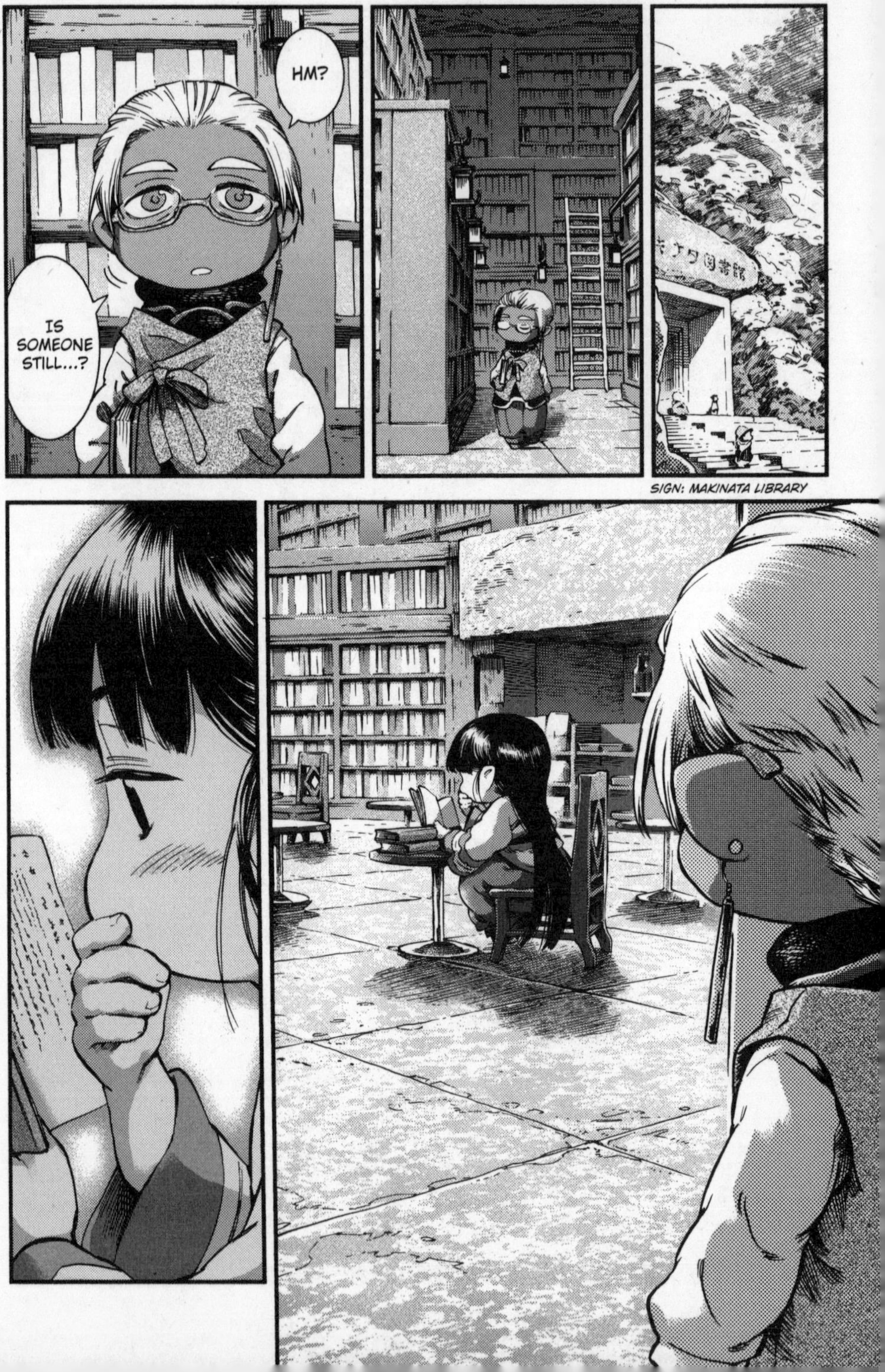
SIGN: MAKINATA LIBRARY
HM?
IS SOMEONE STILL...?

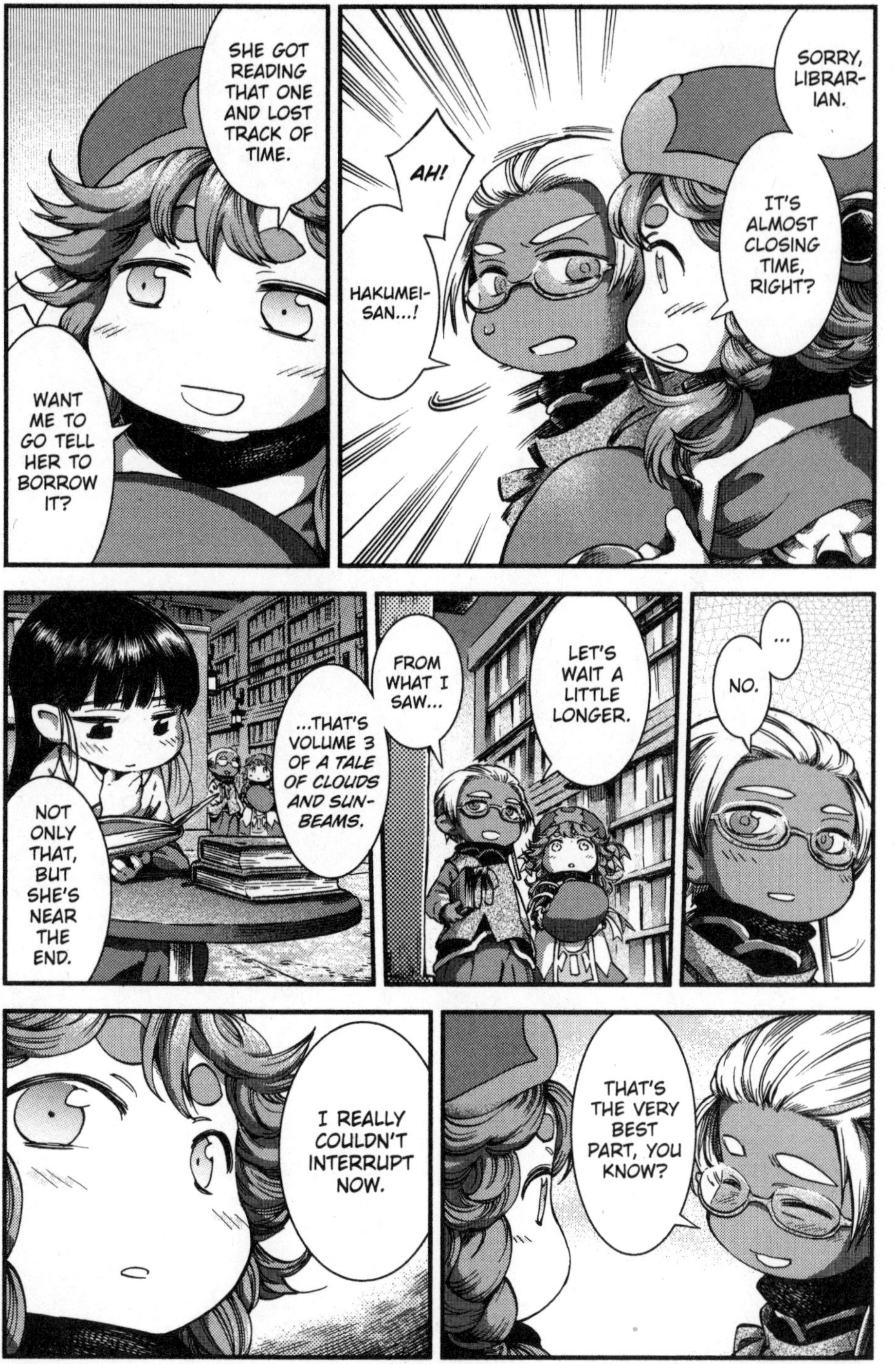
SORRY, LIBRARIAN.
IT'S ALMOST CLOSING TIME, RIGHT?
AH!
HAKUMEI-SAN...!
SHE GOT READING THAT ONE AND LOST TRACK OF TIME.
WANT ME TO GO TELL HER TO BORROW IT?
...
NO.
LET'S WAIT A LITTLE LONGER.
FROM WHAT I SAW...
...THAT'S VOLUME 3 OF *A TALE OF CLOUDS AND SUNBEAMS.*
NOT ONLY THAT, BUT SHE'S NEAR THE END.
THAT'S THE VERY BEST PART, YOU KNOW?
I REALLY COULDN'T INTERRUPT NOW.

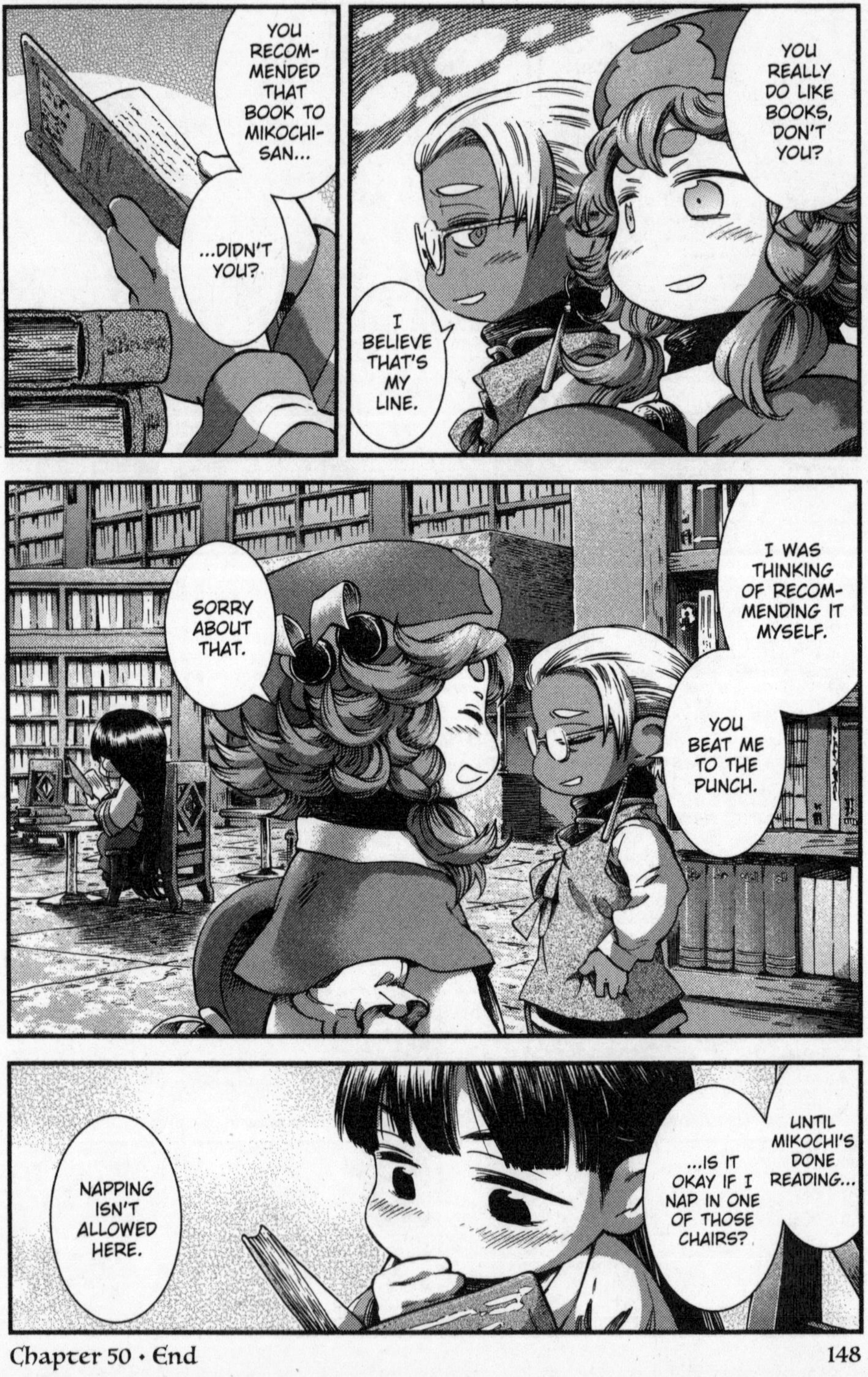
YOU REALLY DO LIKE BOOKS, DON'T YOU?
I BELIEVE THAT'S MY LINE.
YOU RECOMMENDED THAT BOOK TO MIKOCHI-SAN...
...DIDN'T YOU?
I WAS THINKING OF RECOMMENDING IT MYSELF.
YOU BEAT ME TO THE PUNCH.
SORRY ABOUT THAT.
UNTIL MIKOCHI'S DONE READING...
...IS IT OKAY IF I NAP IN ONE OF THOSE CHAIRS?
NAPPING ISN'T ALLOWED HERE.

I was handed a single bolt of white fabric, nothing more. This poplin—not enough cloth even for a single shirt, no matter how you looked at it—was the only weapon I had been given.

"Make handkerchiefs or something, then hurry on back to where you came from," my teacher spat. But for me, even that was asking too much. The fabric had a slippery sheen to it, and it seemed like top-of-the-line material. I couldn't bring myself to take my shears to it.

With no other choice, I gathered all the scraps in my workshop together, combined them with the poplin, and stitched up a misshapen dress. It was, and continues to be to this day, Luna Pescado's basic model.

—An excerpt from the Makinata Library collection
The Tailors' Memoir series, vol. 3: Luna Pescado

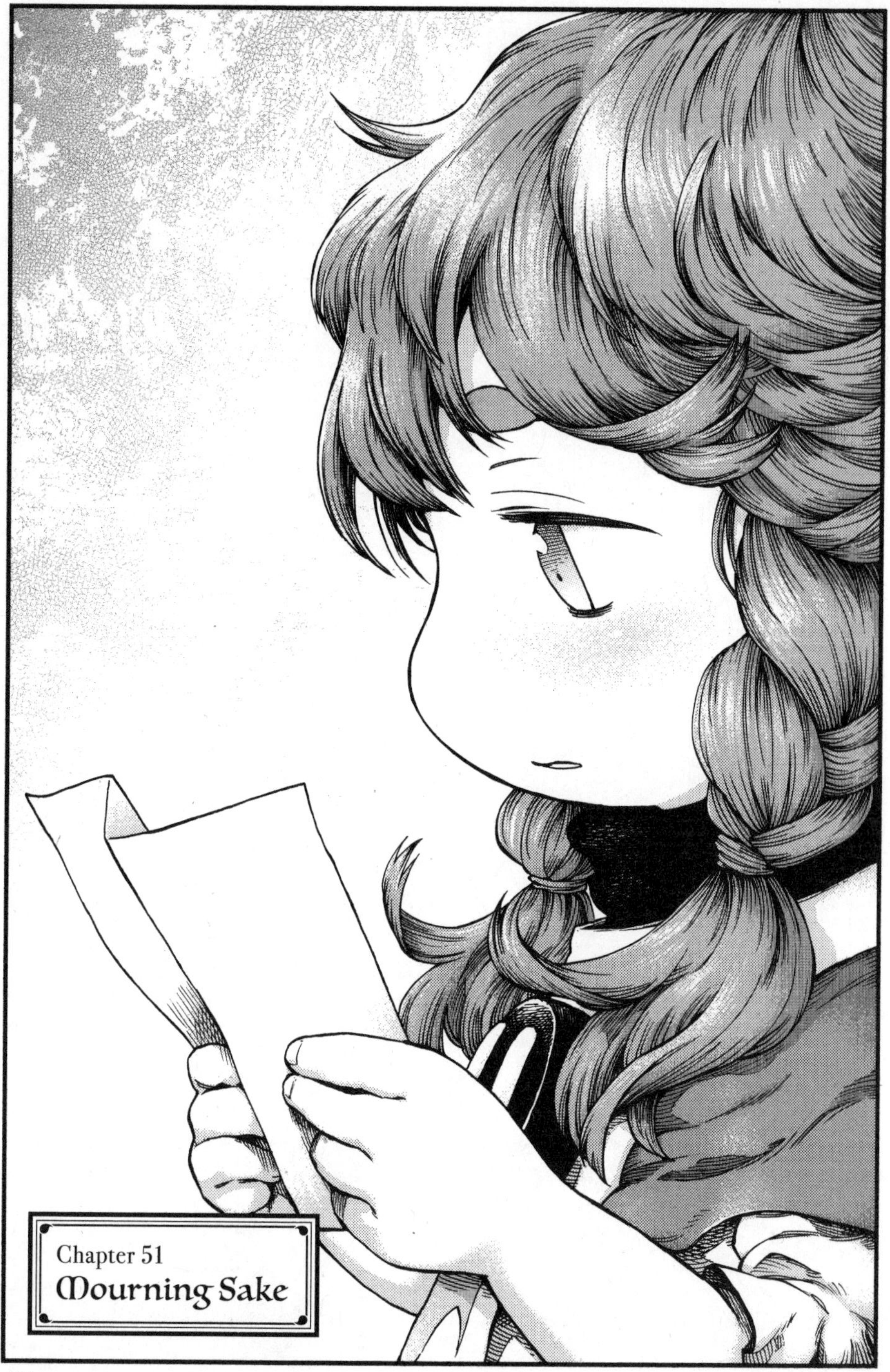

Chapter 51
Mourning Sake

IS THAT THE BOX THAT JUST CAME?

UH.

YEAH.

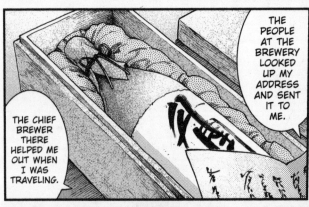

THE PEOPLE AT THE BREWERY LOOKED UP MY ADDRESS AND SENT IT TO ME.

THE CHIEF BREWER THERE HELPED ME OUT WHEN I WAS TRAVELING.

IT'S SAKE.

THIS...

...IS THE LAST THING HE WORKED ON.

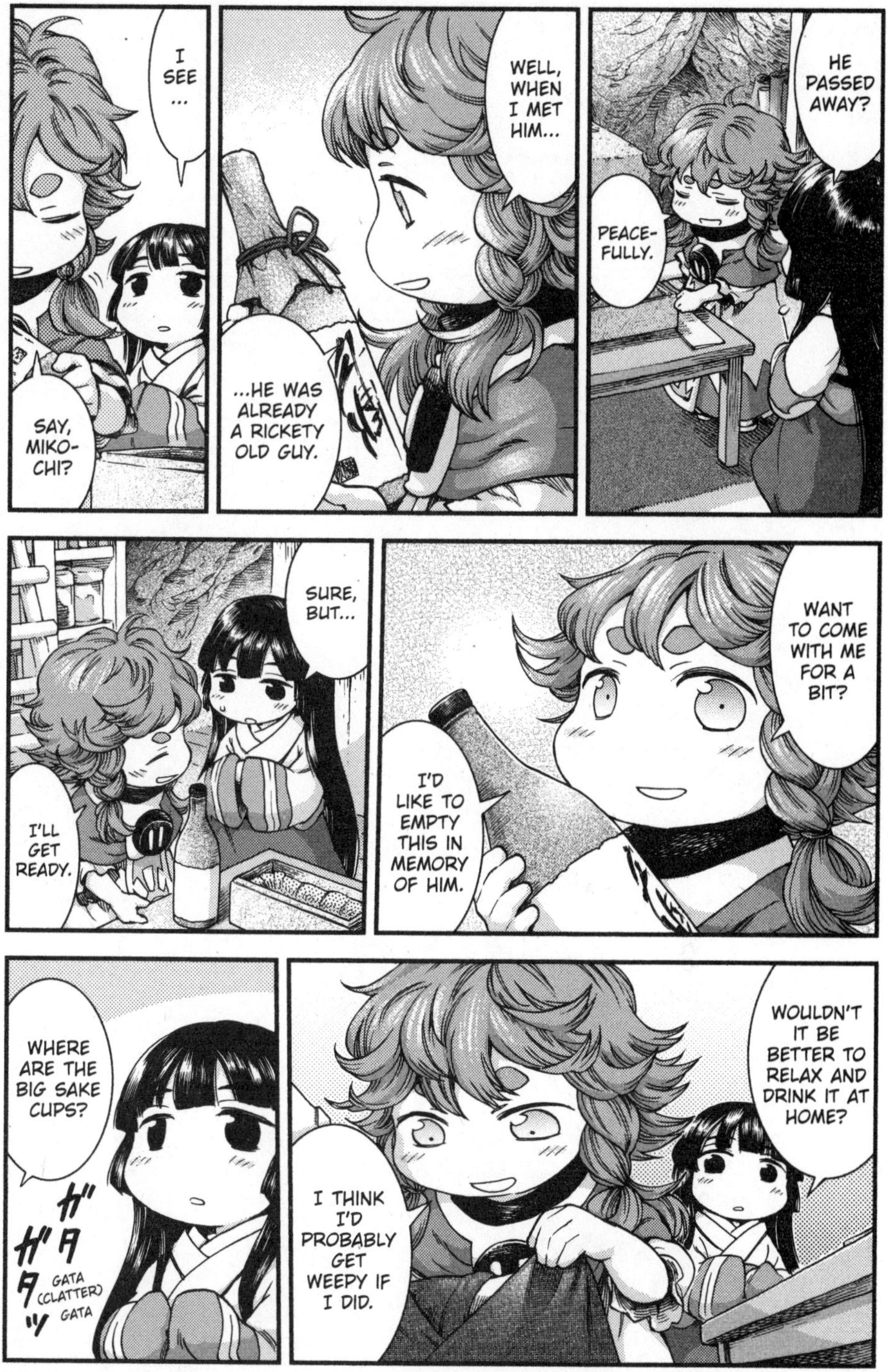
HE PASSED AWAY?
PEACE-FULLY.
WELL, WHEN I MET HIM...
...HE WAS ALREADY A RICKETY OLD GUY.
I SEE...
SAY, MIKO-CHI?
WANT TO COME WITH ME FOR A BIT?
I'D LIKE TO EMPTY THIS IN MEMORY OF HIM.
SURE, BUT...
I'LL GET READY.
WOULDN'T IT BE BETTER TO RELAX AND DRINK IT AT HOME?
I THINK I'D PROBABLY GET WEEPY IF I DID.
WHERE ARE THE BIG SAKE CUPS?
ガタガタッ
GATA (CLATTER) GATA

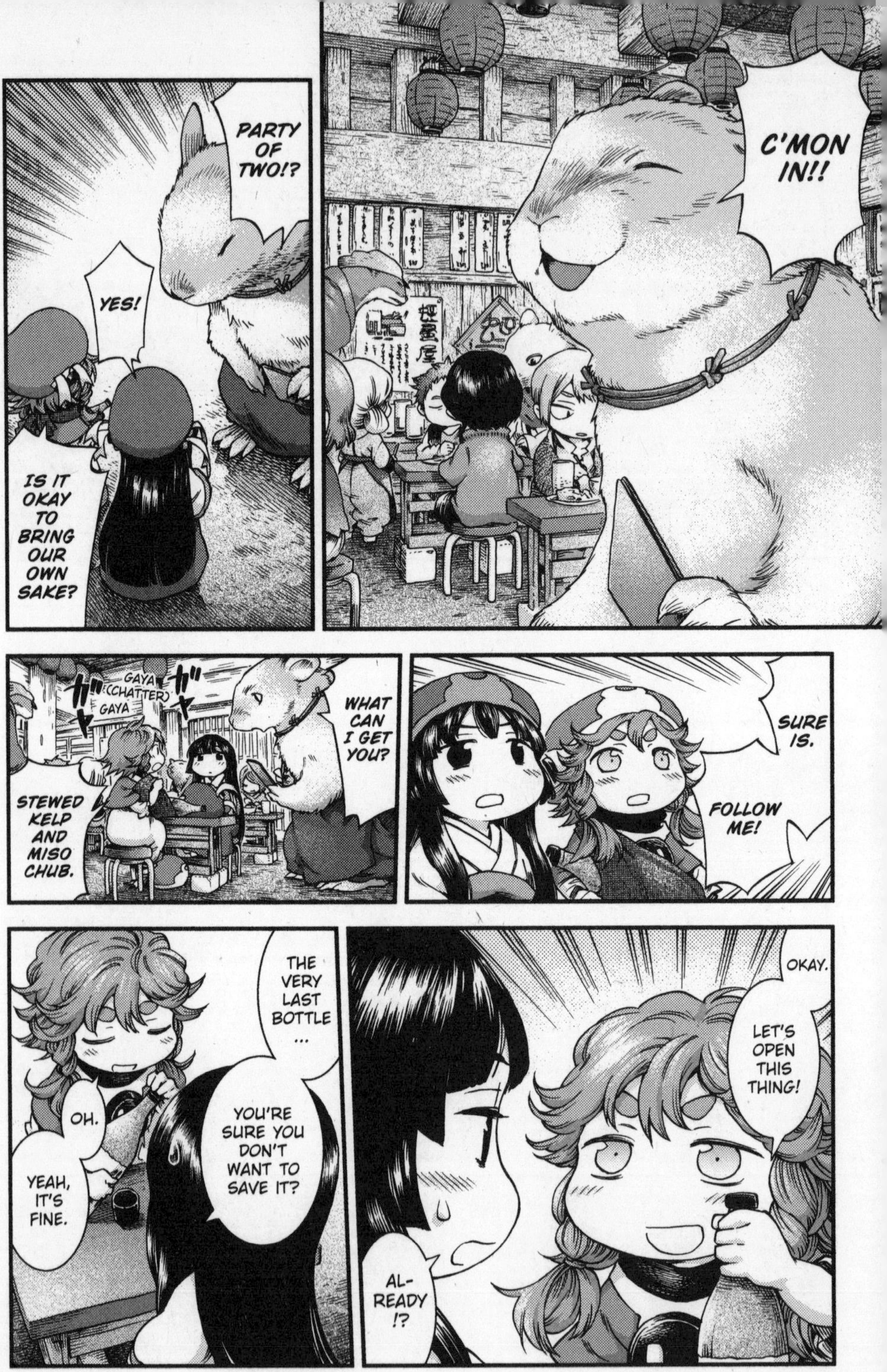
C'MON IN!!
PARTY OF TWO!?
YES!
IS IT OKAY TO BRING OUR OWN SAKE?
SURE IS.
FOLLOW ME!
GAYA (CHATTER) GAYA
WHAT CAN I GET YOU?
STEWED KELP AND MISO CHUB.
OKAY.
LET'S OPEN THIS THING!
AL-READY!?
THE VERY LAST BOTTLE...
YOU'RE SURE YOU DON'T WANT TO SAVE IT?
OH.
YEAH, IT'S FINE.

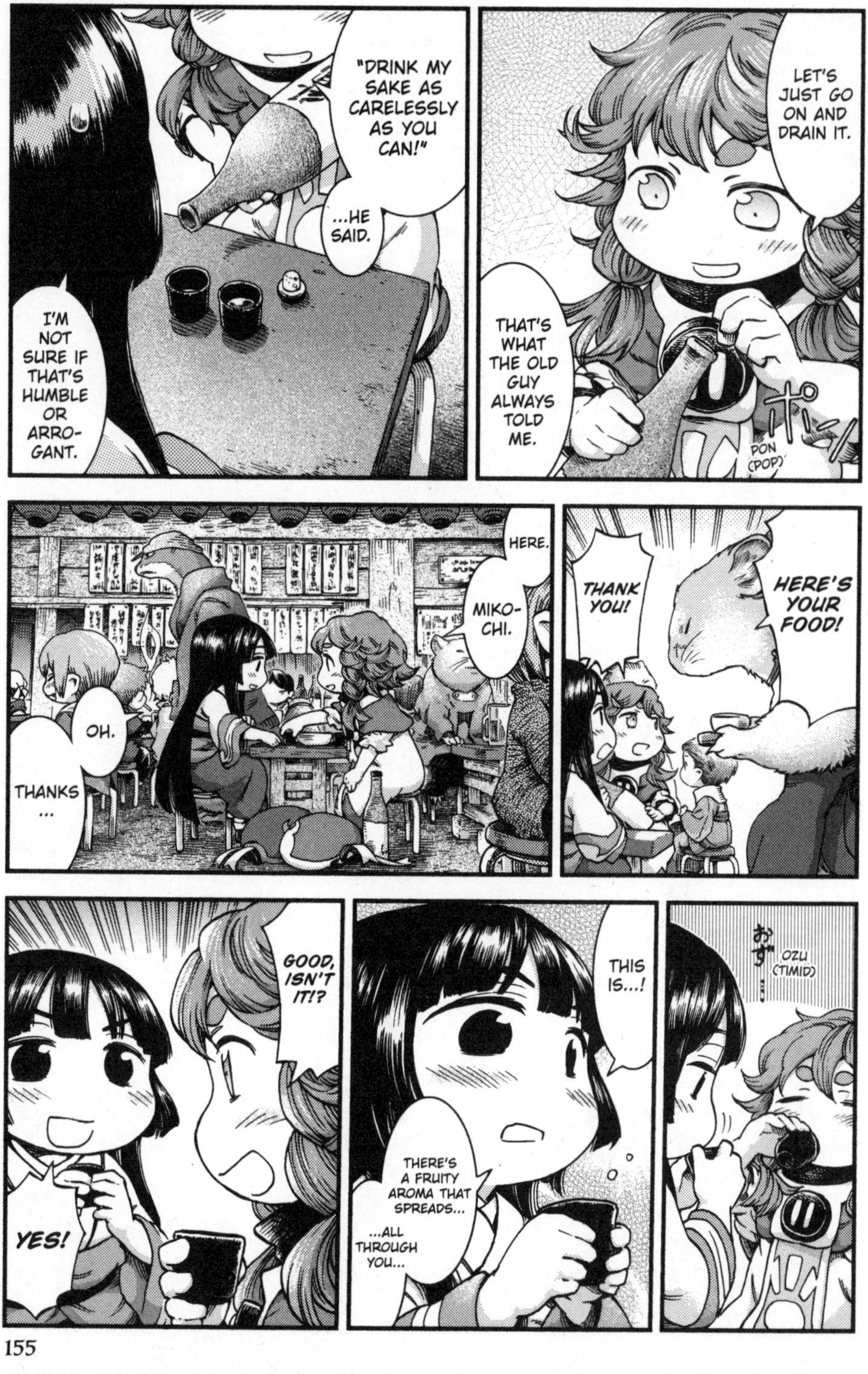
LET'S JUST GO ON AND DRAIN IT.
THAT'S WHAT THE OLD GUY ALWAYS TOLD ME.
ポン
PON (POP)
"DRINK MY SAKE AS CARELESSLY AS YOU CAN!"
...HE SAID.
I'M NOT SURE IF THAT'S HUMBLE OR ARRO-GANT.
HERE'S YOUR FOOD!
THANK YOU!
HERE.
MIKO-CHI.
OH.
THANKS ...
おず
OZU (TIMID)
THIS IS...!
THERE'S A FRUITY AROMA THAT SPREADS...
...ALL THROUGH YOU...
GOOD, ISN'T IT!?
YES!

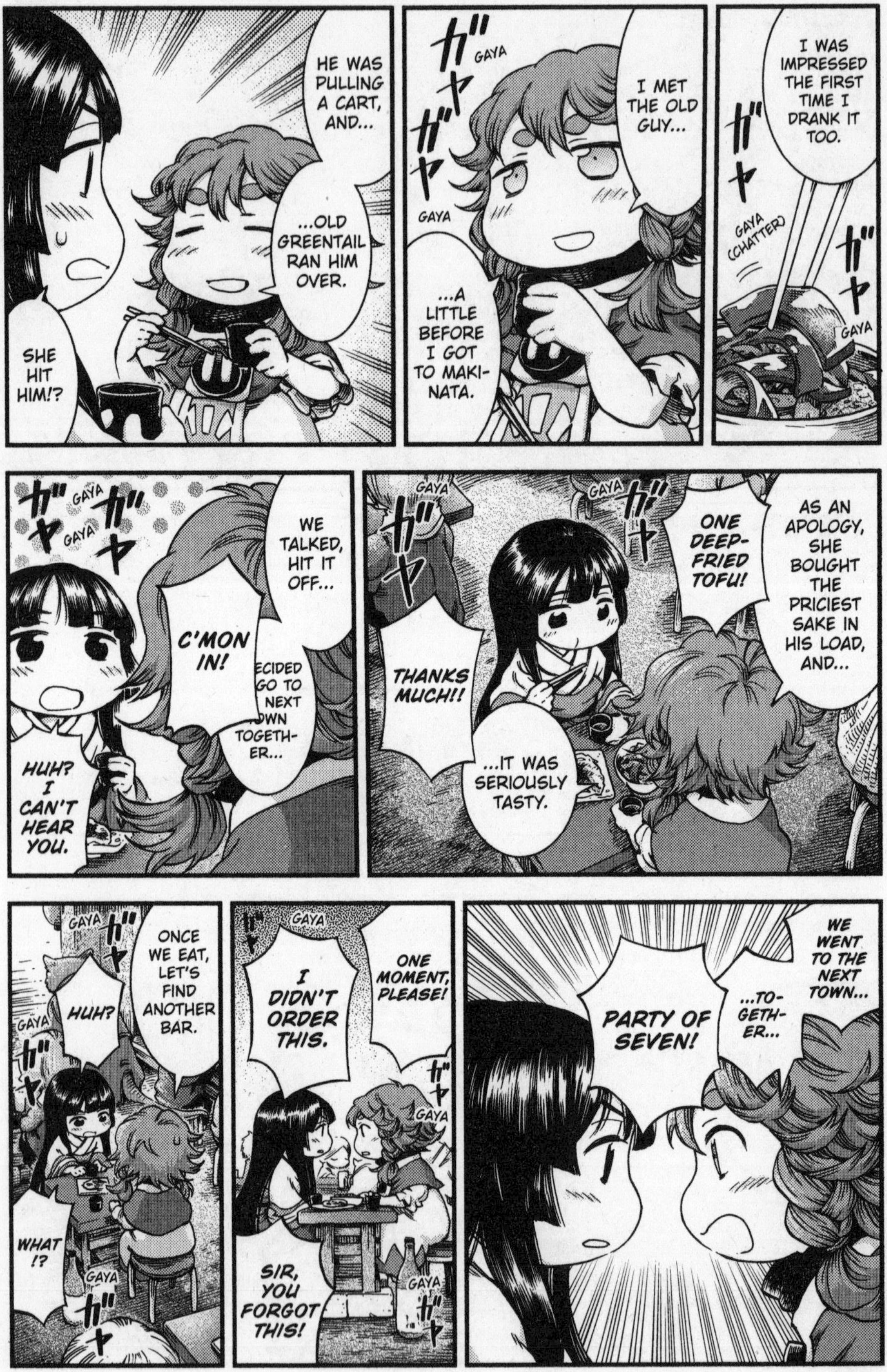
I WAS IMPRESSED THE FIRST TIME I DRANK IT TOO.
GAYA (CHATTER)
GAYA
I MET THE OLD GUY...
GAYA
...A LITTLE BEFORE I GOT TO MAKI-NATA.
GAYA
HE WAS PULLING A CART, AND...
...OLD GREENTAIL RAN HIM OVER.
SHE HIT HIM!?
AS AN APOLOGY, SHE BOUGHT THE PRICIEST SAKE IN HIS LOAD, AND...
GAYA
GAYA
ONE DEEP-FRIED TOFU!
THANKS MUCH!!
...IT WAS SERIOUSLY TASTY.
WE TALKED, HIT IT OFF...
GAYA
GAYA
C'MON IN!
ECIDED GO TO NEXT OWN TOGETH-ER...
HUH? I CAN'T HEAR YOU.
WE WENT TO THE NEXT TOWN...
...TO-GETH-ER...
PARTY OF SEVEN!
GAYA
ONE MOMENT, PLEASE!
I DIDN'T ORDER THIS.
GAYA
GAYA
SIR, YOU FORGOT THIS!
GAYA
ONCE WE EAT, LET'S FIND ANOTHER BAR.
GAYA
HUH?
WHAT!?
GAYA

SIGN: SHITSUSHITSU-YA

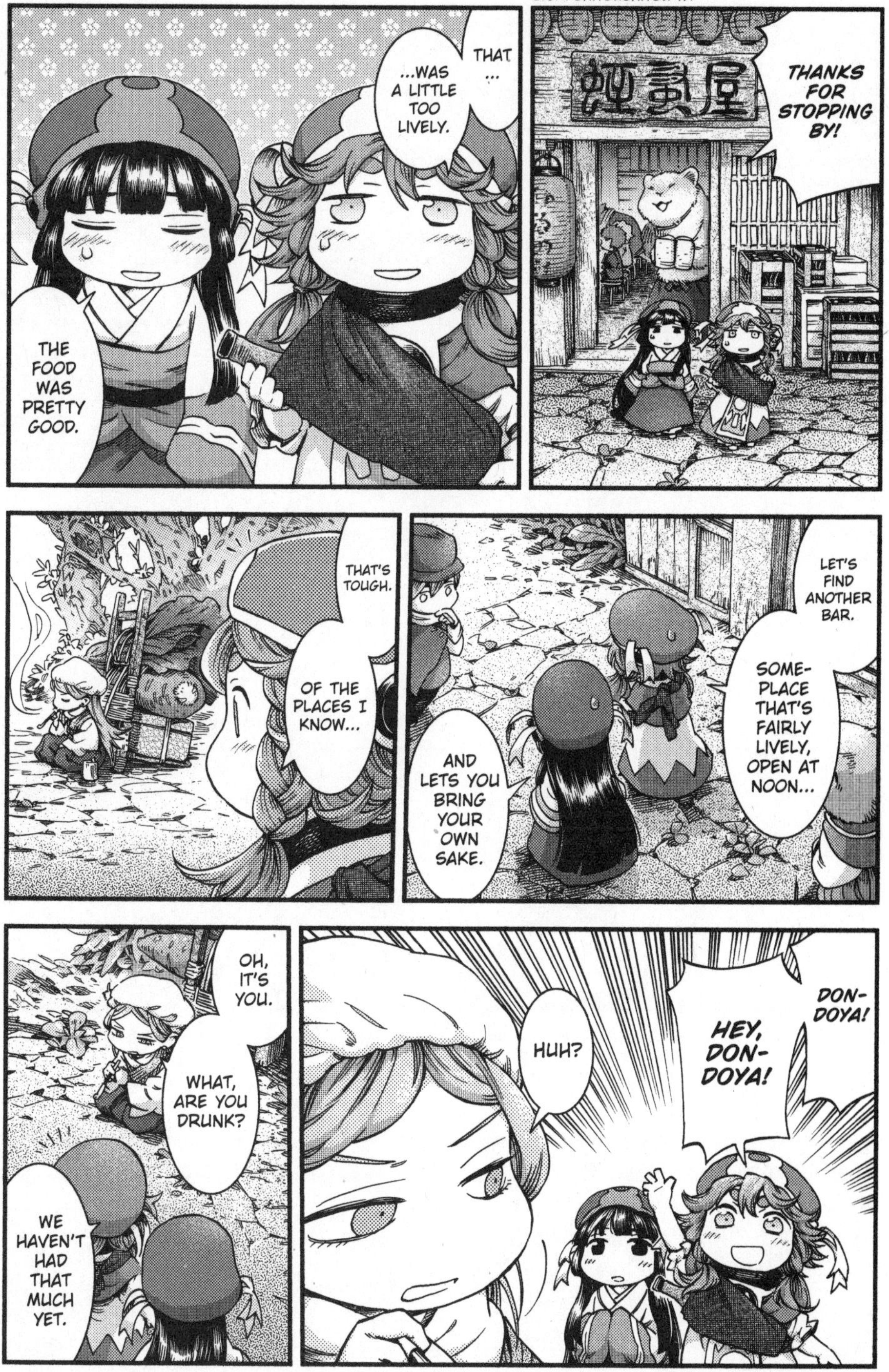
THANKS FOR STOPPING BY!
THAT ...
...WAS A LITTLE TOO LIVELY.
THE FOOD WAS PRETTY GOOD.
LET'S FIND ANOTHER BAR.
SOME-PLACE THAT'S FAIRLY LIVELY, OPEN AT NOON...
AND LETS YOU BRING YOUR OWN SAKE.
THAT'S TOUGH.
OF THE PLACES I KNOW...
DON-DOYA!
HEY, DON-DOYA!
HUH?
OH, IT'S YOU.
WHAT, ARE YOU DRUNK?
WE HAVEN'T HAD THAT MUCH YET.

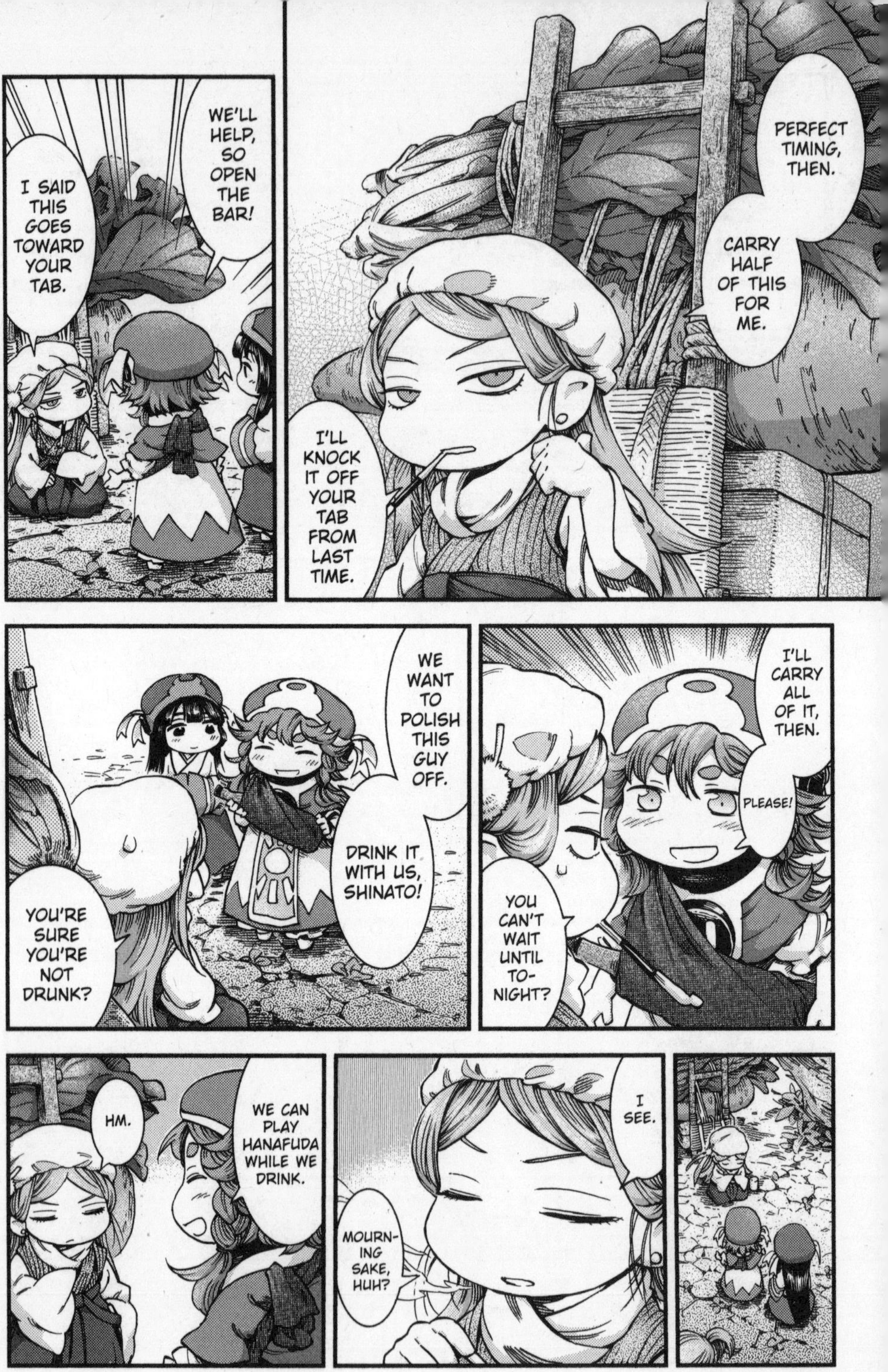
PERFECT TIMING, THEN.
CARRY HALF OF THIS FOR ME.
I'LL KNOCK IT OFF YOUR TAB FROM LAST TIME.
WE'LL HELP, SO OPEN THE BAR!
I SAID THIS GOES TOWARD YOUR TAB.
I'LL CARRY ALL OF IT, THEN.
PLEASE!
YOU CAN'T WAIT UNTIL TO-NIGHT?
WE WANT TO POLISH THIS GUY OFF.
DRINK IT WITH US, SHINATO!
YOU'RE SURE YOU'RE NOT DRUNK?
I SEE.
MOURN-ING SAKE, HUH?
WE CAN PLAY HANAFUDA WHILE WE DRINK.
HM.

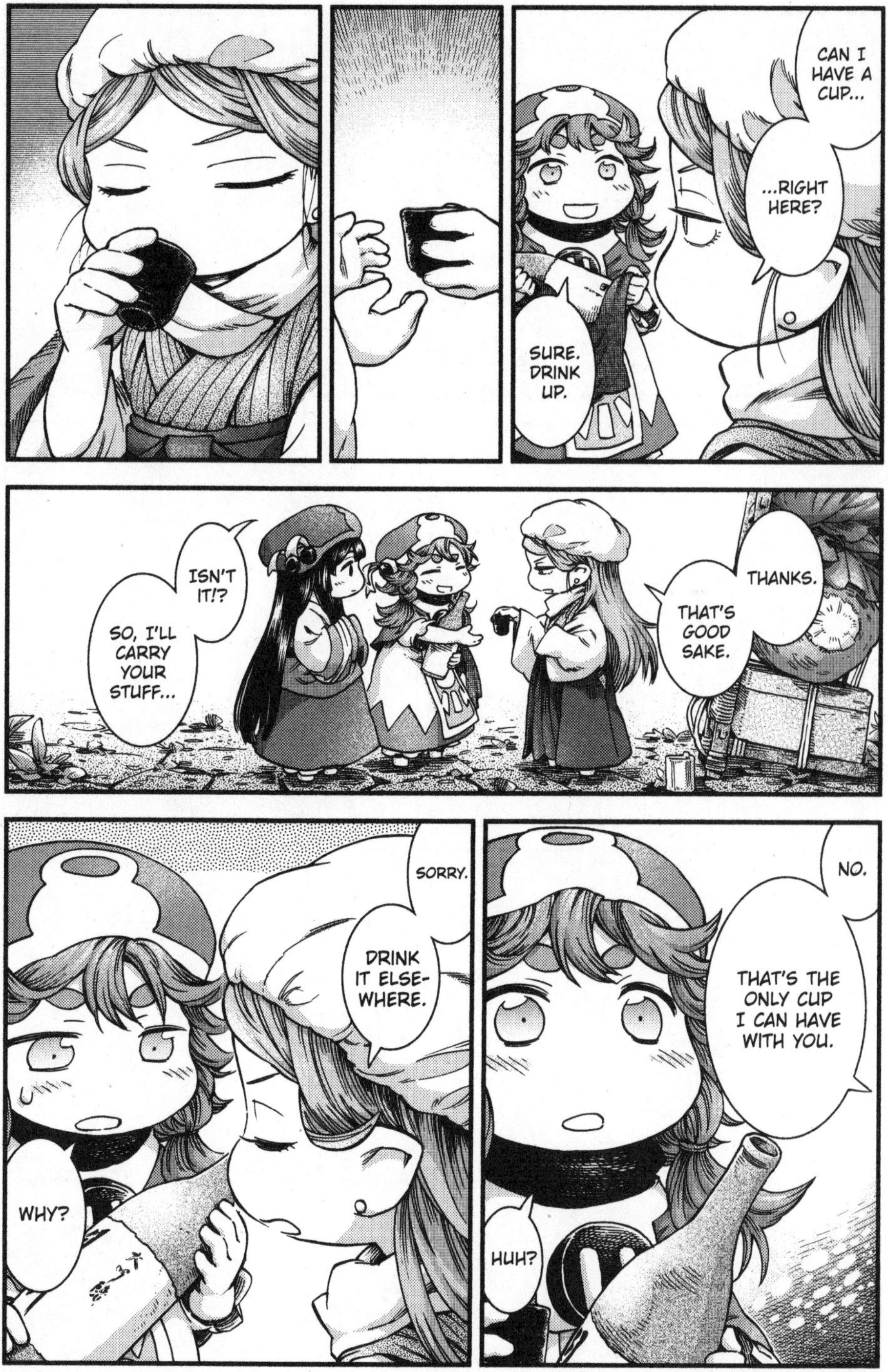
CAN I HAVE A CUP...
...RIGHT HERE?
SURE. DRINK UP.
THANKS.
THAT'S GOOD SAKE.
ISN'T IT!?
SO, I'LL CARRY YOUR STUFF...
NO.
THAT'S THE ONLY CUP I CAN HAVE WITH YOU.
HUH?
SORRY.
DRINK IT ELSE-WHERE.
WHY?

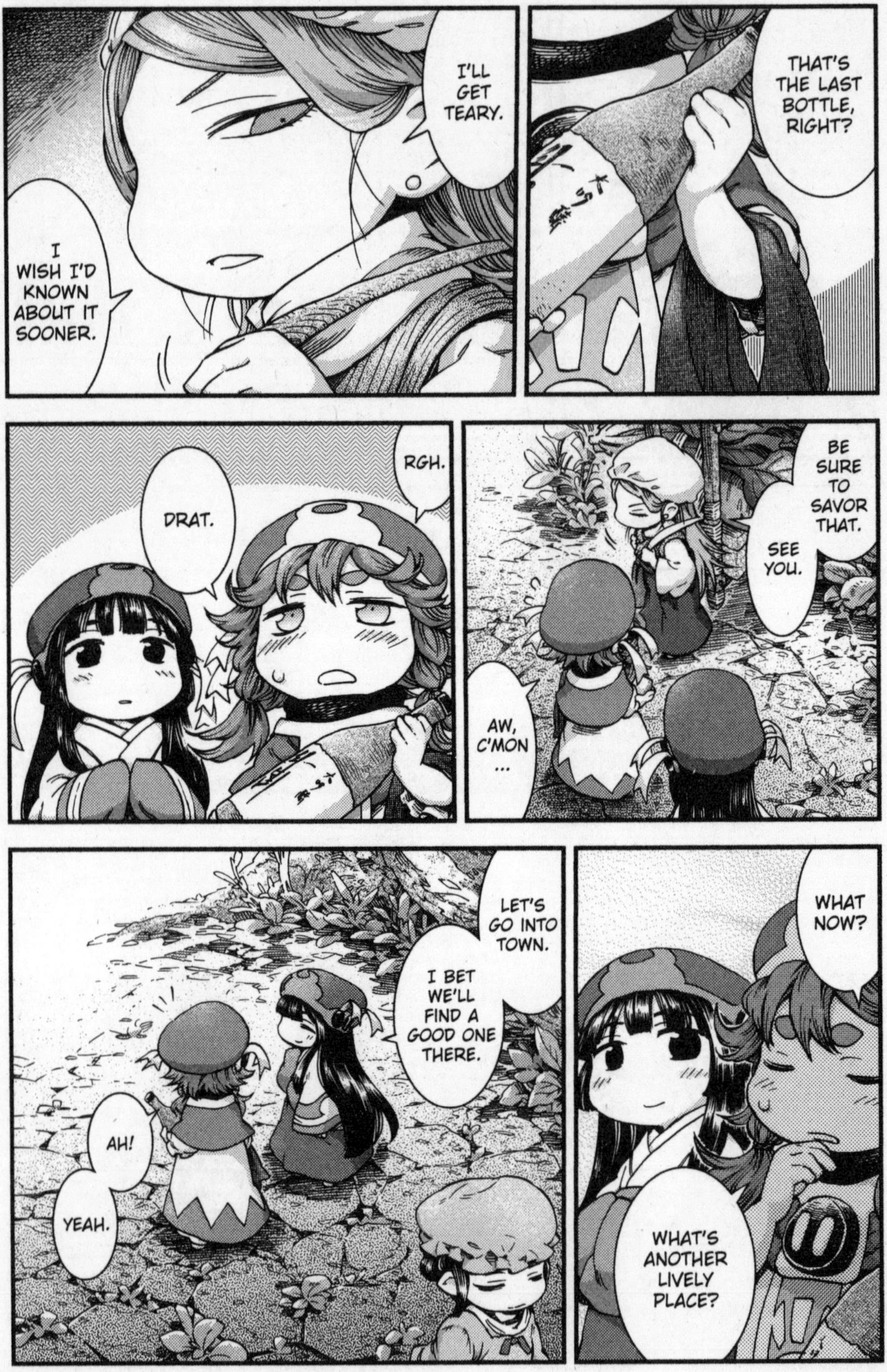
THAT'S THE LAST BOTTLE, RIGHT?
I'LL GET TEARY.
I WISH I'D KNOWN ABOUT IT SOONER.
BE SURE TO SAVOR THAT.
SEE YOU.
AW, C'MON ...
RGH.
DRAT.
WHAT NOW?
WHAT'S ANOTHER LIVELY PLACE?
LET'S GO INTO TOWN.
I BET WE'LL FIND A GOOD ONE THERE.
AH!
YEAH.

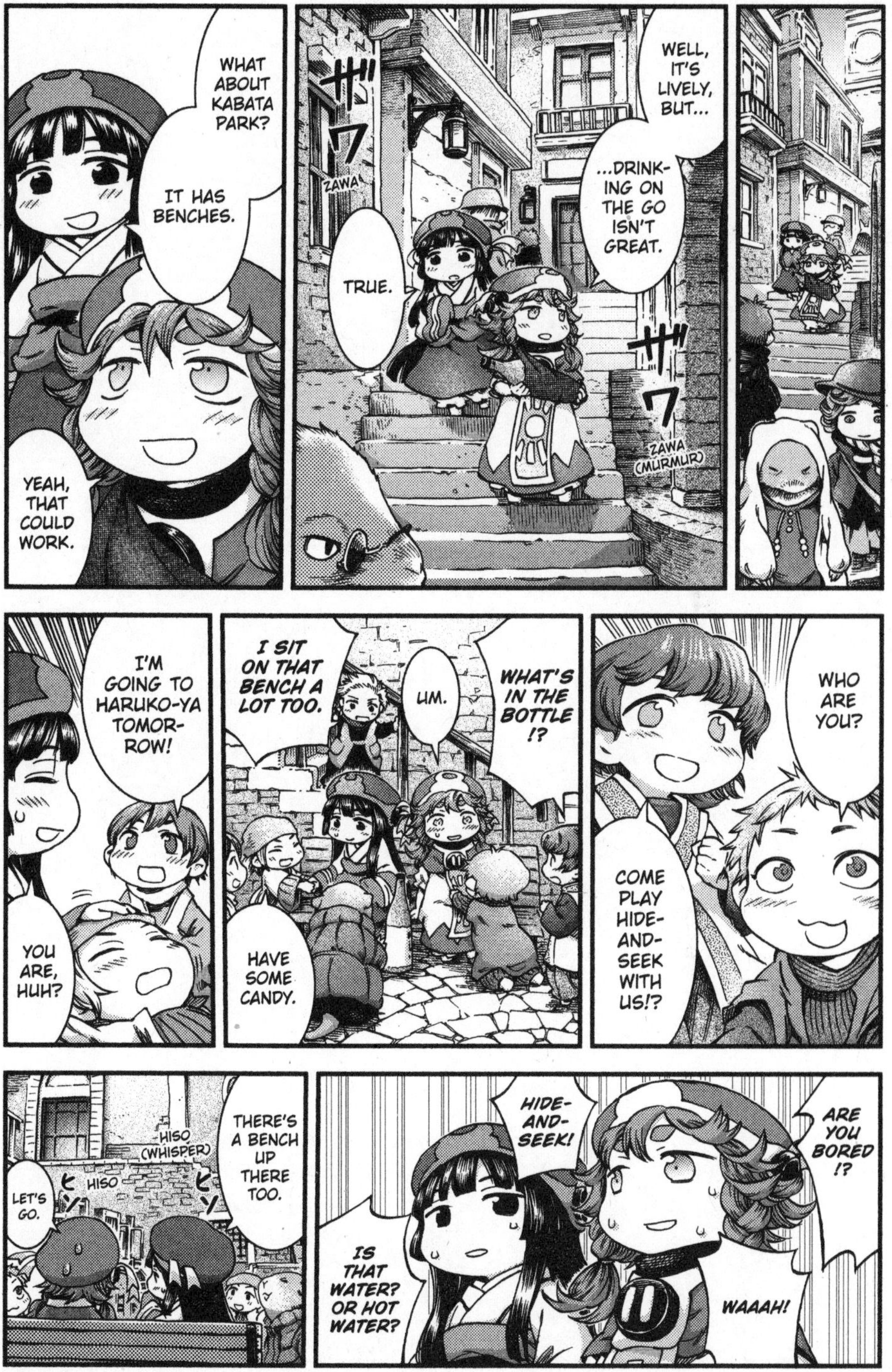
WELL, IT'S LIVELY, BUT...
...DRINKING ON THE GO ISN'T GREAT.
ZAWA
TRUE.
ZAWA (MURMUR)
WHAT ABOUT KABATA PARK?
IT HAS BENCHES.
YEAH, THAT COULD WORK.
WHO ARE YOU?
COME PLAY HIDE-AND-SEEK WITH US!?
WHAT'S IN THE BOTTLE!?
UM.
I SIT ON THAT BENCH A LOT TOO.
HAVE SOME CANDY.
I'M GOING TO HARUKO-YA TOMORROW!
YOU ARE, HUH?
ARE YOU BORED!?
HIDE-AND-SEEK!
WAAAH!
IS THAT WATER? OR HOT WATER?
THERE'S A BENCH UP THERE TOO.
HISO (WHISPER)
HISO
LET'S GO.

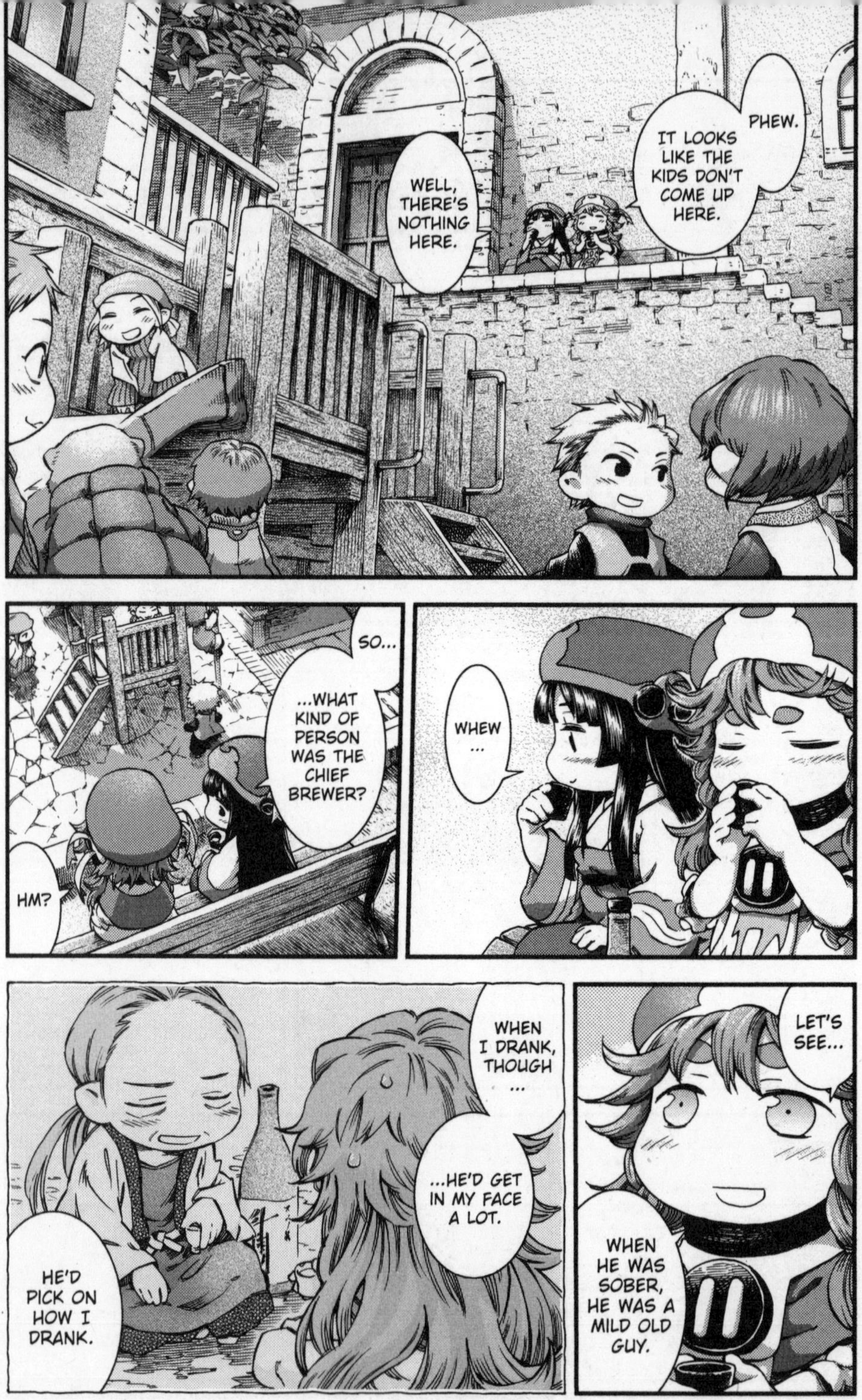
PHEW.
IT LOOKS LIKE THE KIDS DON'T COME UP HERE.
WELL, THERE'S NOTHING HERE.
WHEW ...
SO...
...WHAT KIND OF PERSON WAS THE CHIEF BREWER?
HM?
LET'S SEE...
WHEN HE WAS SOBER, HE WAS A MILD OLD GUY.
WHEN I DRANK, THOUGH ...
...HE'D GET IN MY FACE A LOT.
HE'D PICK ON HOW I DRANK.

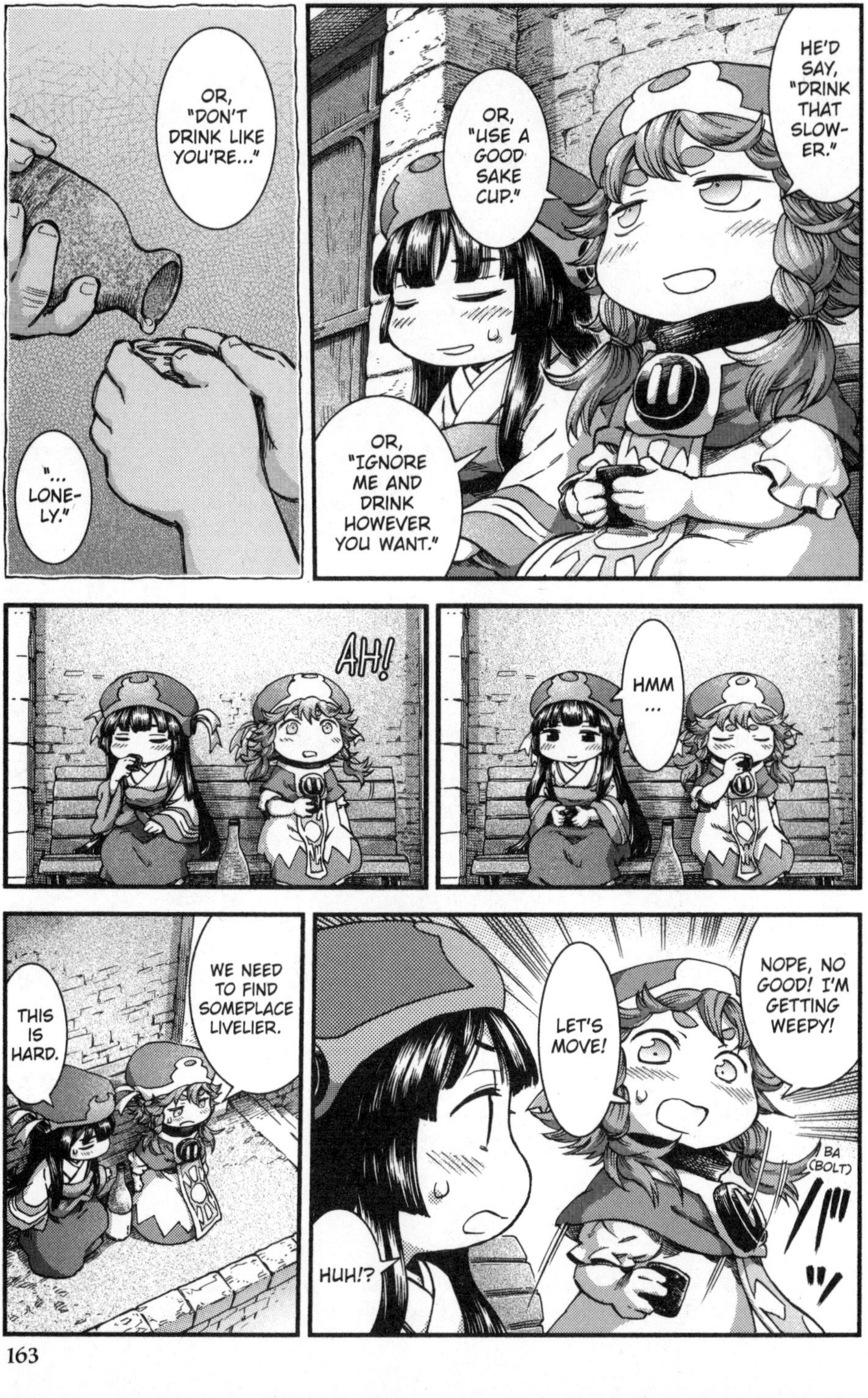
HE'D SAY, "DRINK THAT SLOW-ER."
OR, "USE A GOOD SAKE CUP."
OR, "IGNORE ME AND DRINK HOWEVER YOU WANT."
OR, "DON'T DRINK LIKE YOU'RE..."
"...LONE-LY."
HMM...
AH!
NOPE, NO GOOD! I'M GETTING WEEPY!
LET'S MOVE!
BA (BOLT)
HUH!?
WE NEED TO FIND SOMEPLACE LIVELIER.
THIS IS HARD.

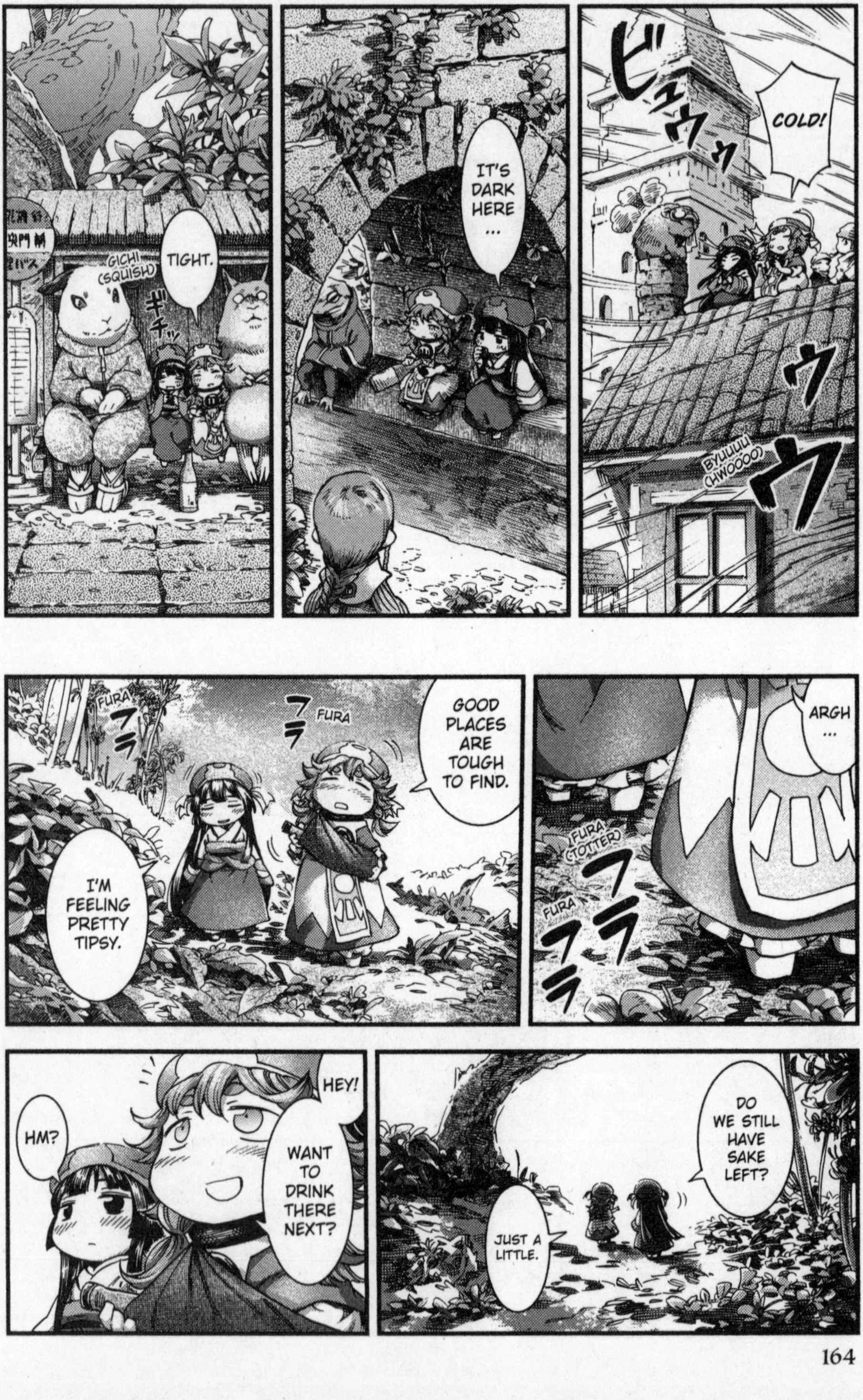
ビュウゥッ
COLD!
ウウ
BYUUUU (HWOOOO)
IT'S DARK HERE ...
TIGHT.
GICHI (SQUISH)
ギチッ
ARGH ...
FURA (TOTTER)
フラ
FURA
フラ
GOOD PLACES ARE TOUGH TO FIND.
フラ
FURA
FURA
フラ
I'M FEELING PRETTY TIPSY.
DO WE STILL HAVE SAKE LEFT?
JUST A LITTLE.
HEY!
WANT TO DRINK THERE NEXT?
HM?

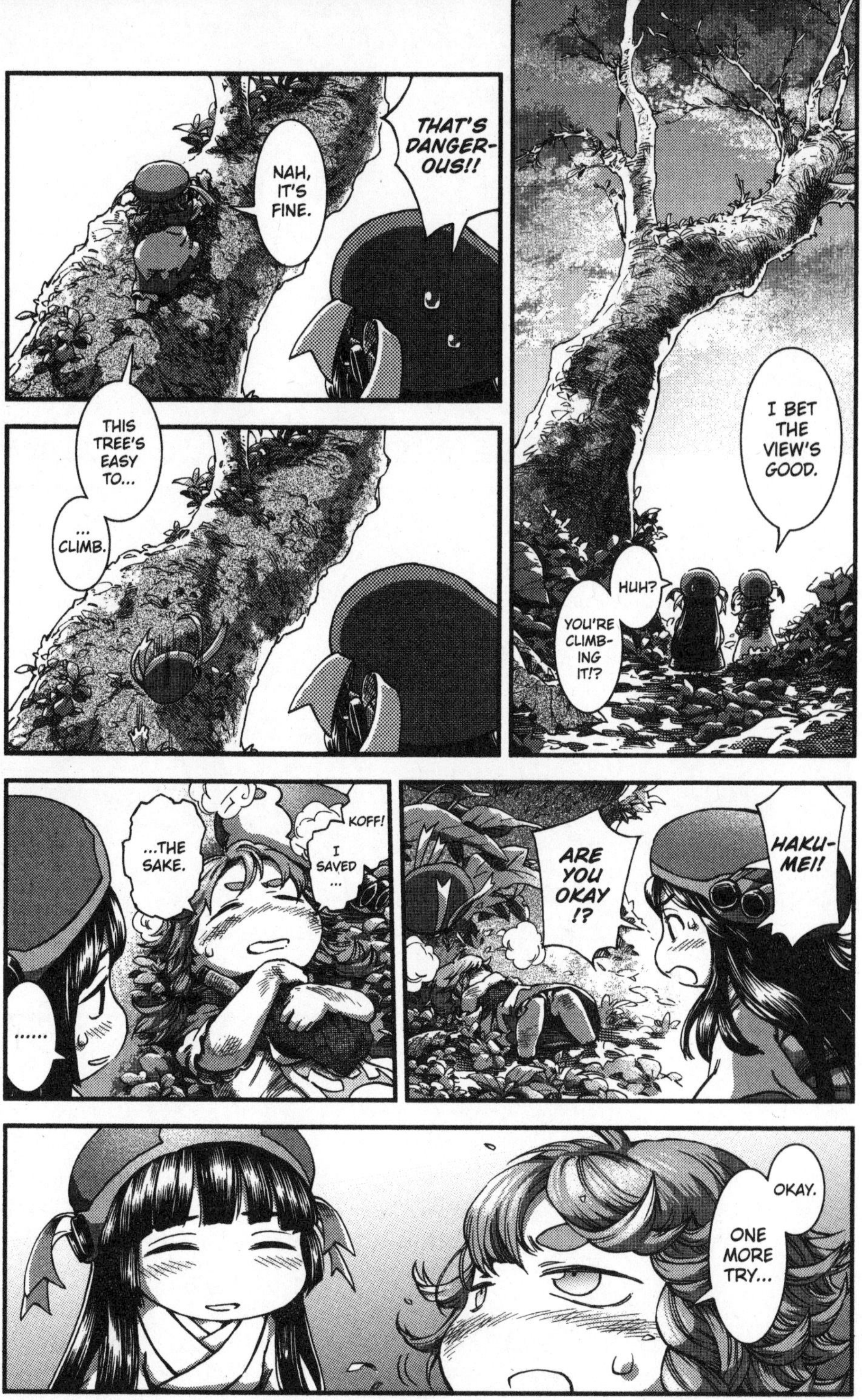
I BET THE VIEW'S GOOD.
HUH?
YOU'RE CLIMBING IT!?
THAT'S DANGEROUS!!
NAH, IT'S FINE.
THIS TREE'S EASY TO...
...CLIMB.
HAKUMEI!!
ARE YOU OKAY!?
KOFF!
I SAVED...
...THE SAKE.
......
OKAY.
ONE MORE TRY...

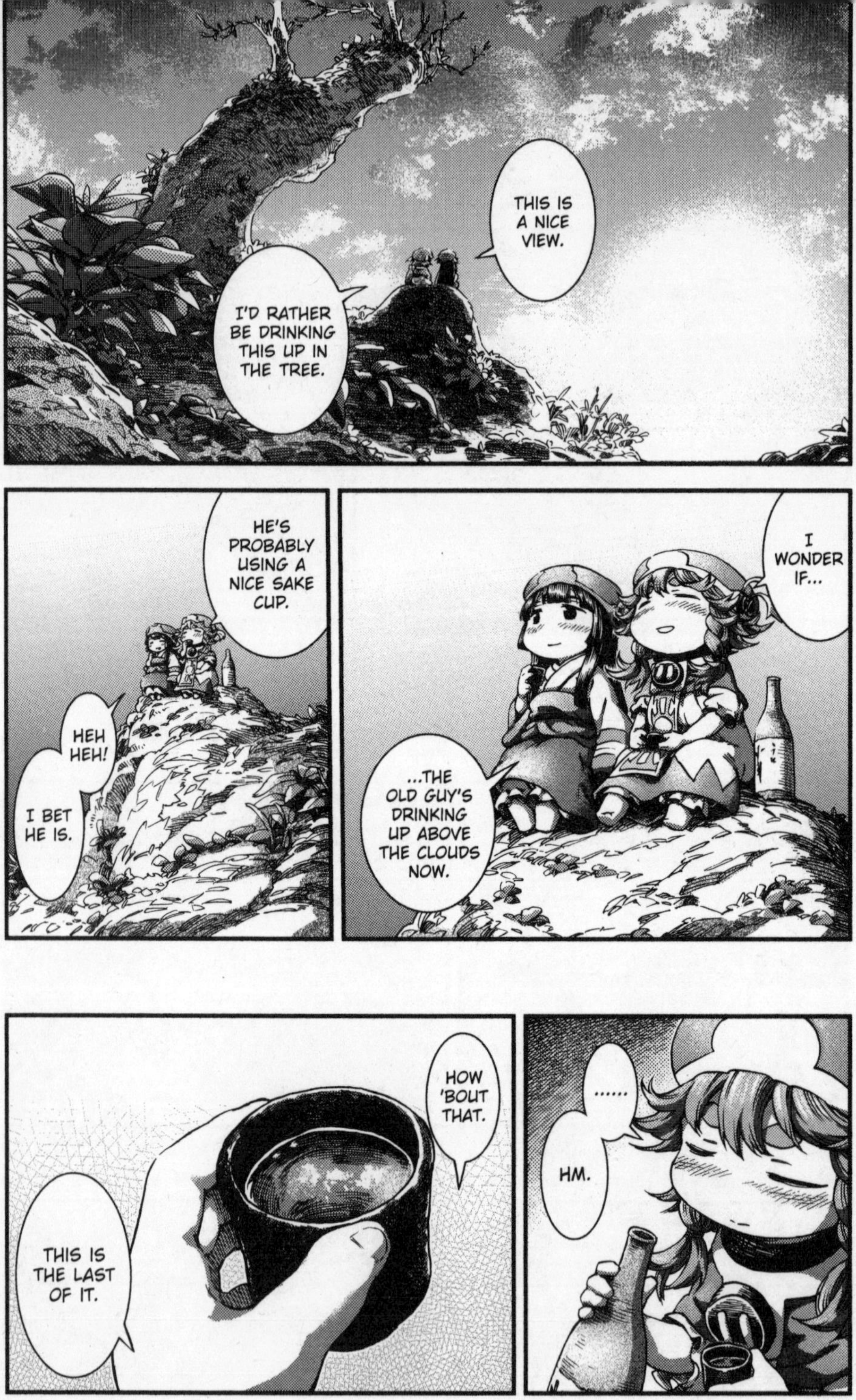
THIS IS A NICE VIEW.
I'D RATHER BE DRINKING THIS UP IN THE TREE.
I WONDER IF...
...THE OLD GUY'S DRINKING UP ABOVE THE CLOUDS NOW.
HE'S PROBABLY USING A NICE SAKE CUP.
HEH HEH!
I BET HE IS.
......
HM.
HOW 'BOUT THAT.
THIS IS THE LAST OF IT.

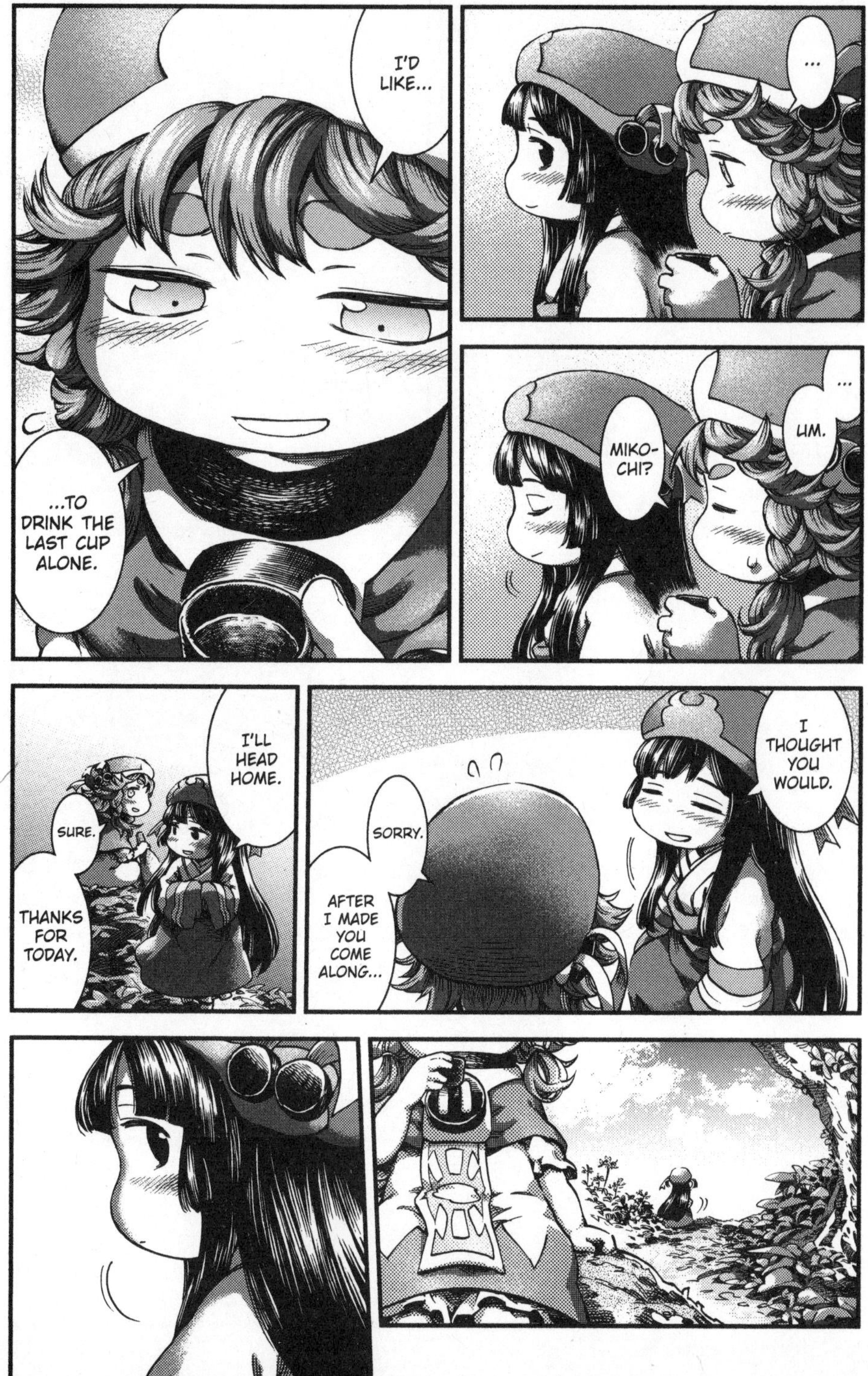
...
...
UM.
MIKO-CHI?
I'D LIKE...
...TO DRINK THE LAST CUP ALONE.
I THOUGHT YOU WOULD.
SORRY.
AFTER I MADE YOU COME ALONG...
I'LL HEAD HOME.
SURE.
THANKS FOR TODAY.

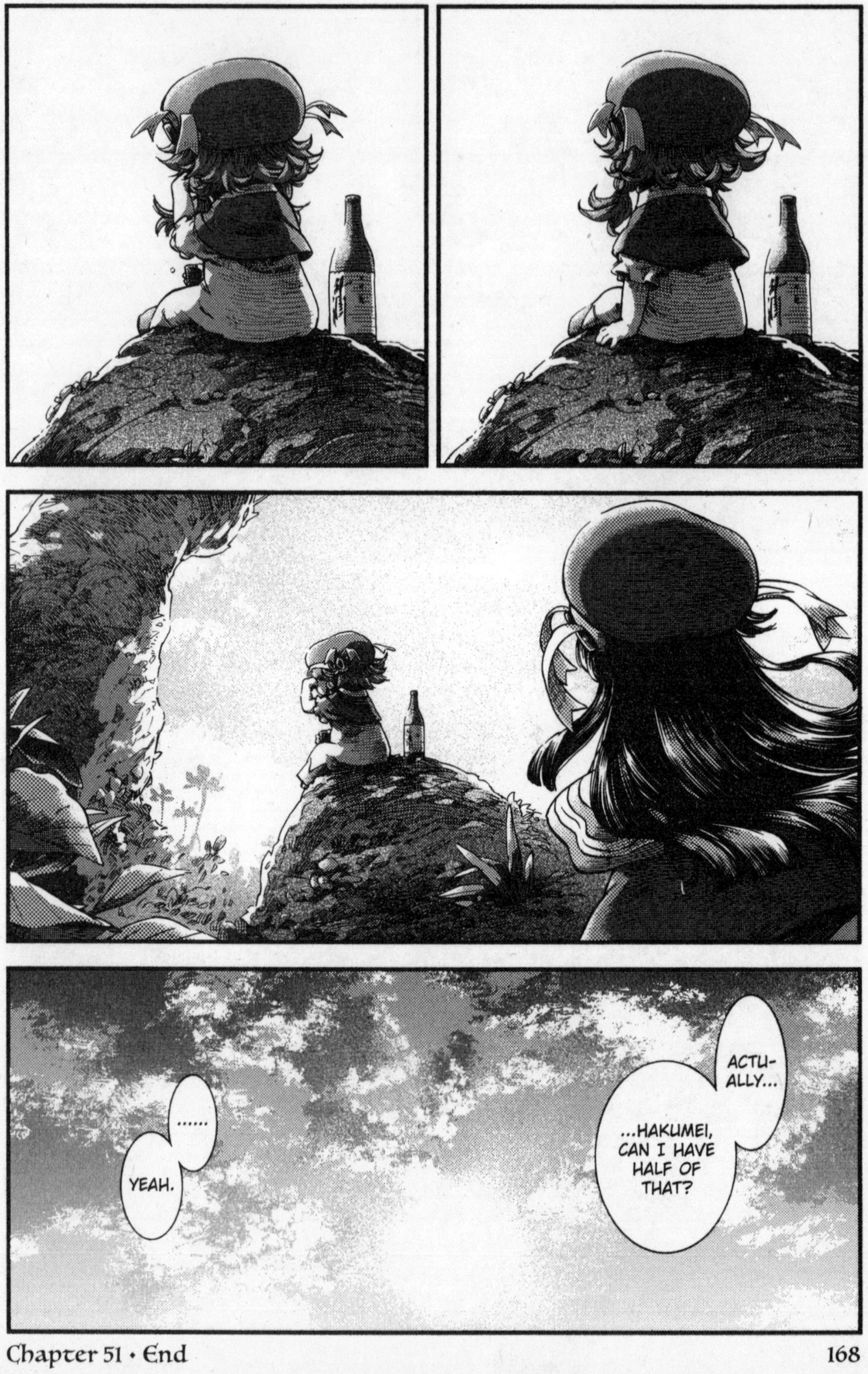
ACTU-ALLY...
...HAKUMEI, CAN I HAVE HALF OF THAT?
......
YEAH.

•*Column*• Underfoot Steps 51 / Daiginjou "Touru"

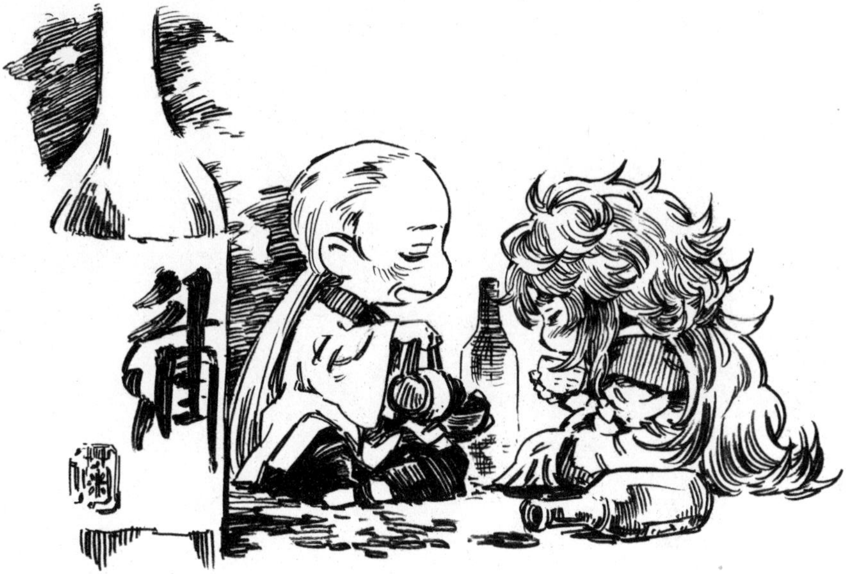

Kikuji Brewery is a venerable old sake brewery that represents the Hakegome region. This brewery, whose particular specialty is mature junmai sakes, has a unique daiginjo sake that is crisp and faintly acidic with a ginjo fragrance like young fruit.

It's said that, long ago, the chief brewer offered this sake to the water god, hoping to put him to sleep so that he could cross the Touru River. However, the sake was so clear that he couldn't get the water god even a little bit drunk.

"Gramps, that legend's gotta be a lie...urp."

"Touru gets you nice and drunk. Here, water, have some water."

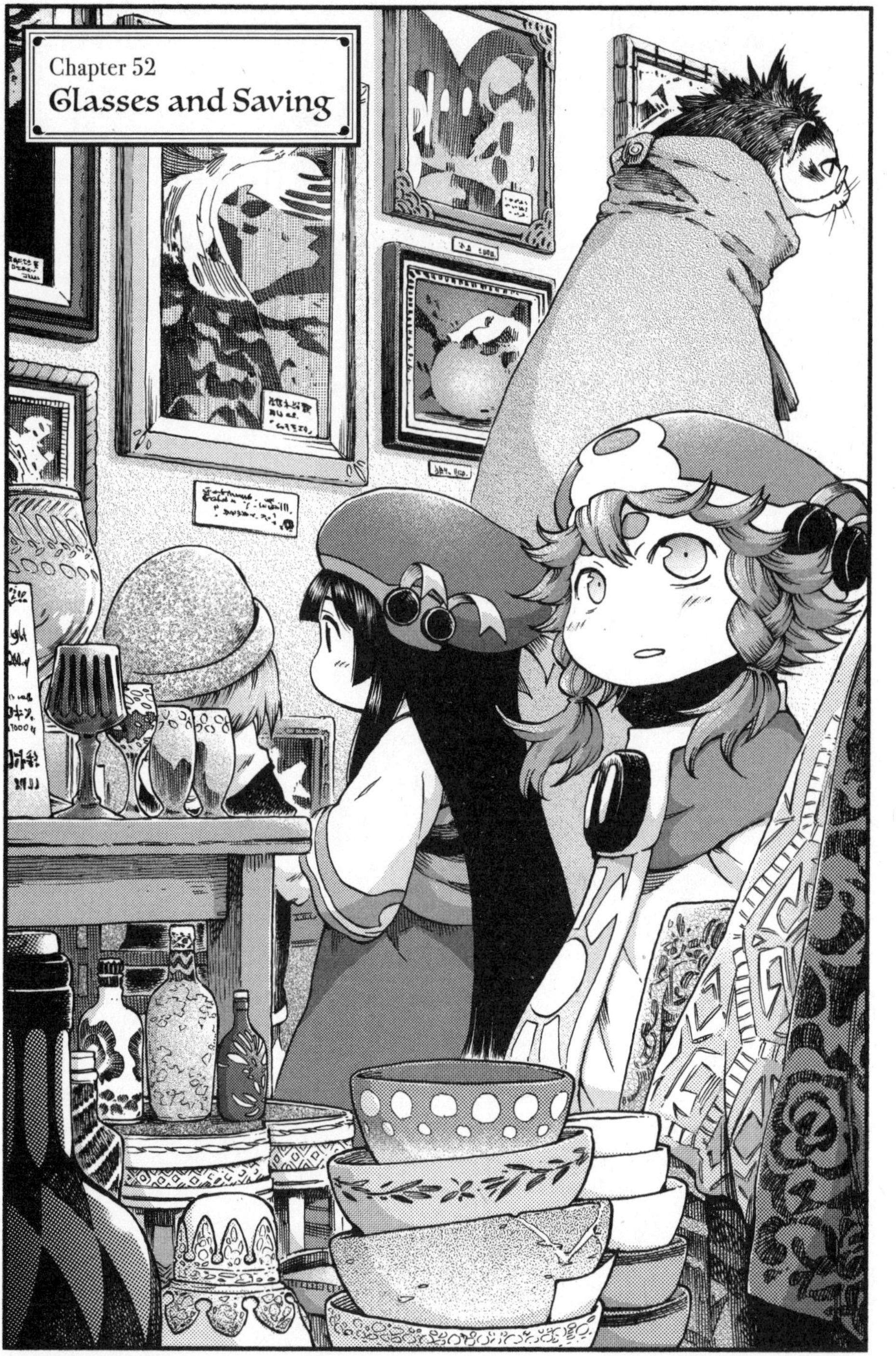
Chapter 52
Glasses and Saving

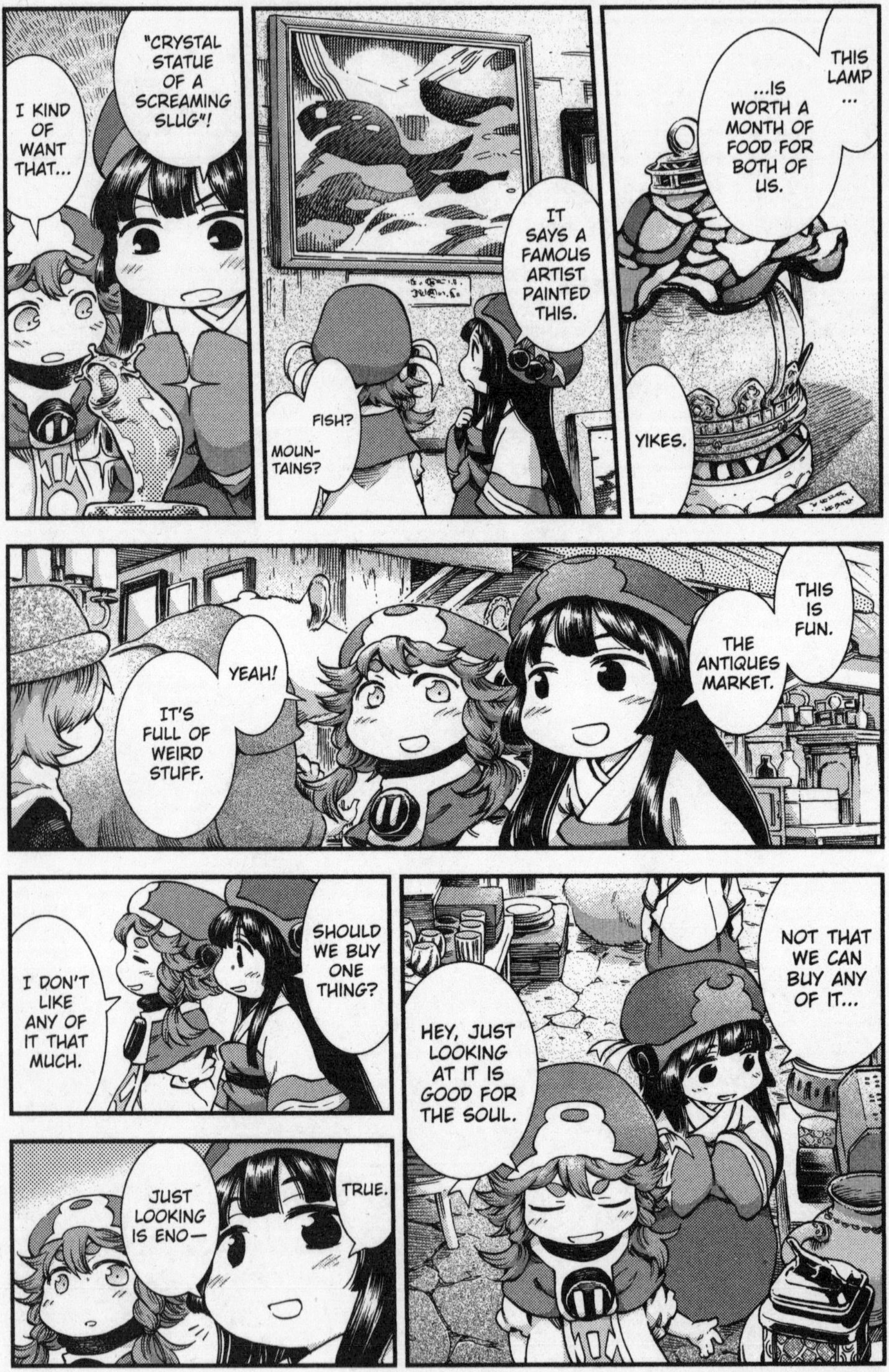
THIS LAMP ...
...IS WORTH A MONTH OF FOOD FOR BOTH OF US.
YIKES.
IT SAYS A FAMOUS ARTIST PAINTED THIS.
FISH?
MOUN-TAINS?
"CRYSTAL STATUE OF A SCREAMING SLUG"!
I KIND OF WANT THAT...
THIS IS FUN.
THE ANTIQUES MARKET.
YEAH!
IT'S FULL OF WEIRD STUFF.
NOT THAT WE CAN BUY ANY OF IT...
HEY, JUST LOOKING AT IT IS GOOD FOR THE SOUL.
SHOULD WE BUY ONE THING?
I DON'T LIKE ANY OF IT THAT MUCH.
TRUE.
JUST LOOKING IS ENO—

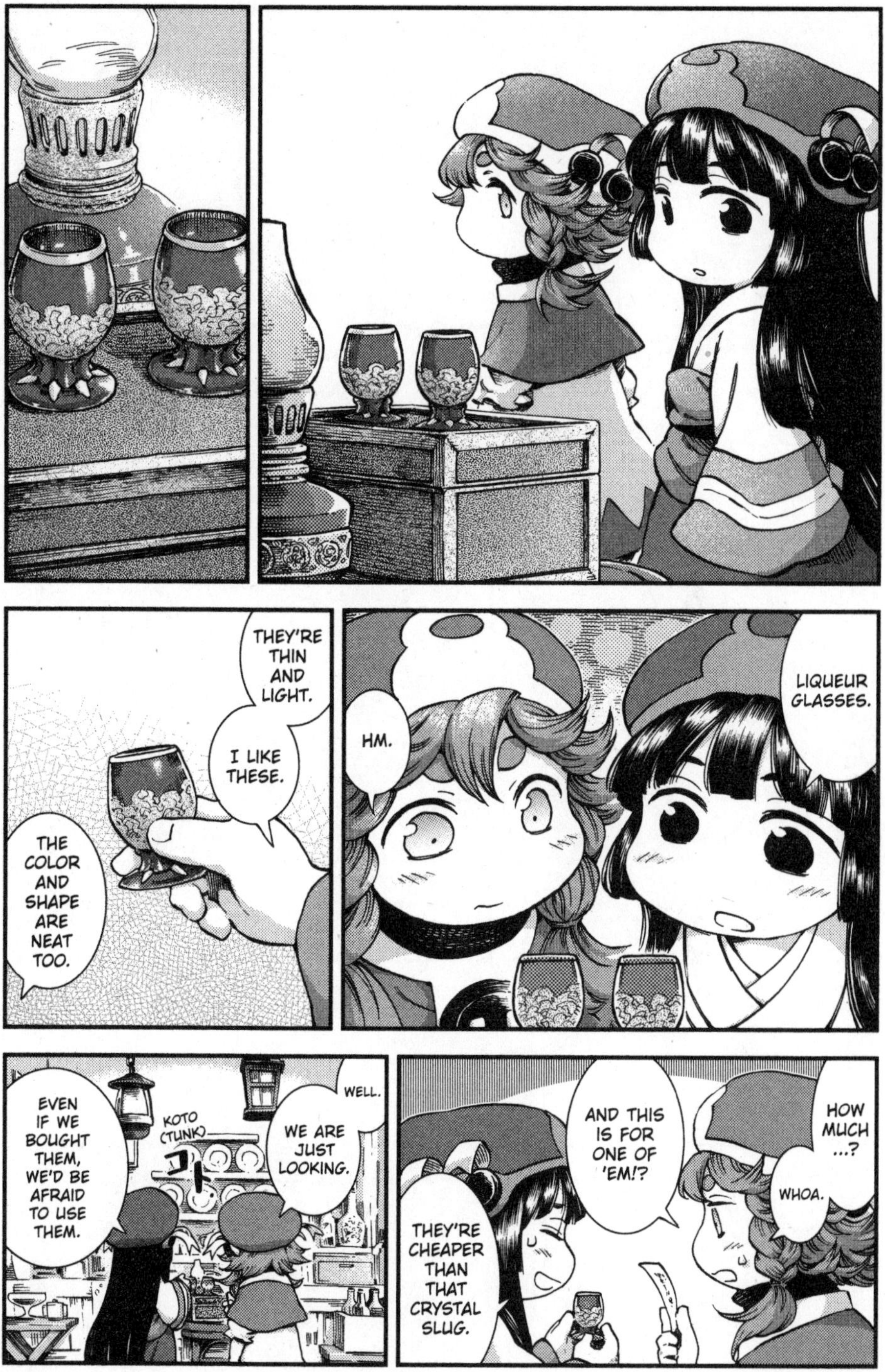
LIQUEUR GLASSES.
HM.
THEY'RE THIN AND LIGHT.
I LIKE THESE.
THE COLOR AND SHAPE ARE NEAT TOO.
HOW MUCH ...?
WHOA.
AND THIS IS FOR ONE OF 'EM!?
THEY'RE CHEAPER THAN THAT CRYSTAL SLUG.
WELL.
WE ARE JUST LOOKING.
KOTO (TUNK)
EVEN IF WE BOUGHT THEM, WE'D BE AFRAID TO USE THEM.

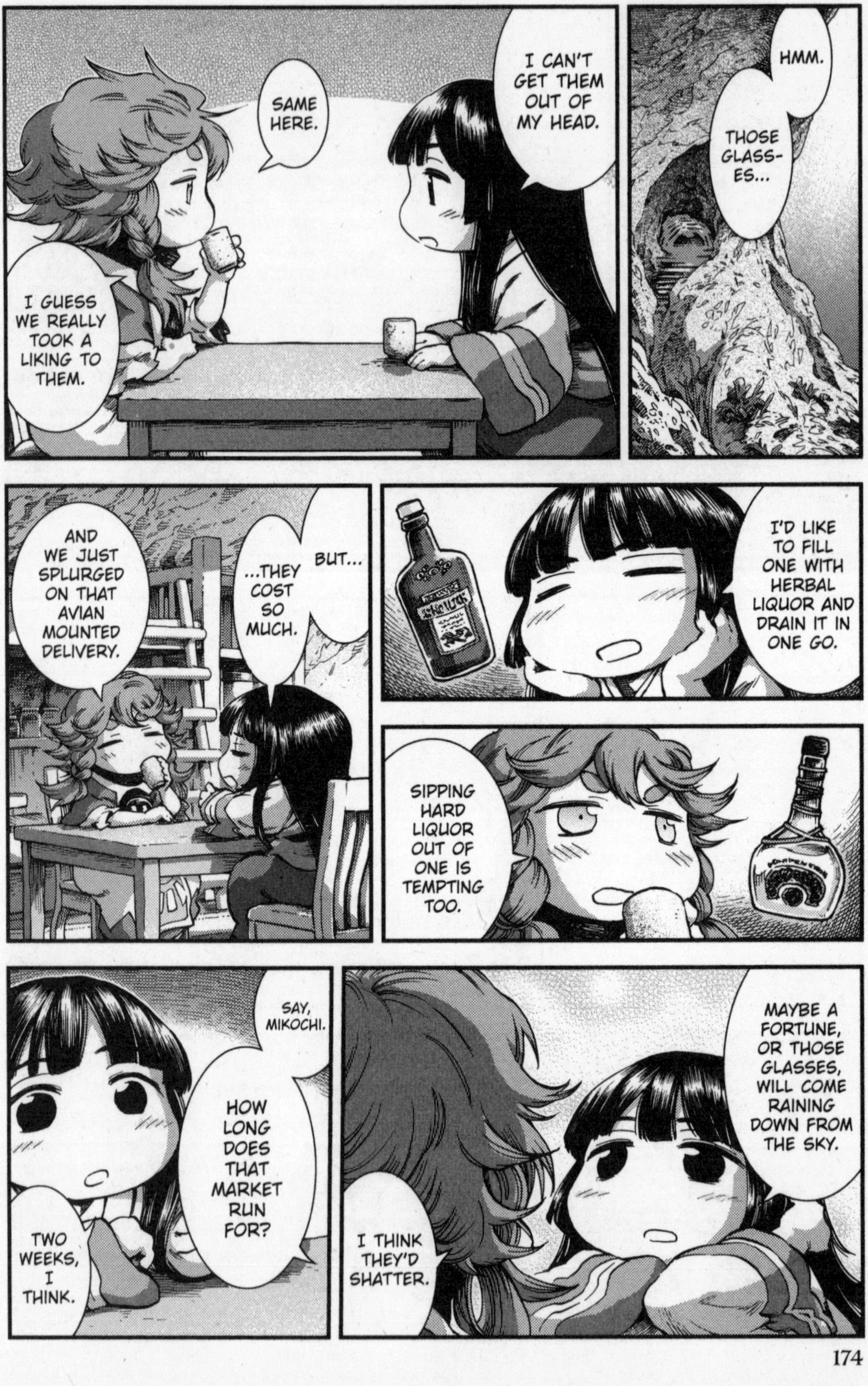
HMM.
THOSE GLASS-ES...
I CAN'T GET THEM OUT OF MY HEAD.
SAME HERE.
I GUESS WE REALLY TOOK A LIKING TO THEM.
I'D LIKE TO FILL ONE WITH HERBAL LIQUOR AND DRAIN IT IN ONE GO.
SIPPING HARD LIQUOR OUT OF ONE IS TEMPTING TOO.
BUT...
...THEY COST SO MUCH.
AND WE JUST SPLURGED ON THAT AVIAN MOUNTED DELIVERY.
MAYBE A FORTUNE, OR THOSE GLASSES, WILL COME RAINING DOWN FROM THE SKY.
I THINK THEY'D SHATTER.
SAY, MIKOCHI.
HOW LONG DOES THAT MARKET RUN FOR?
TWO WEEKS, I THINK.

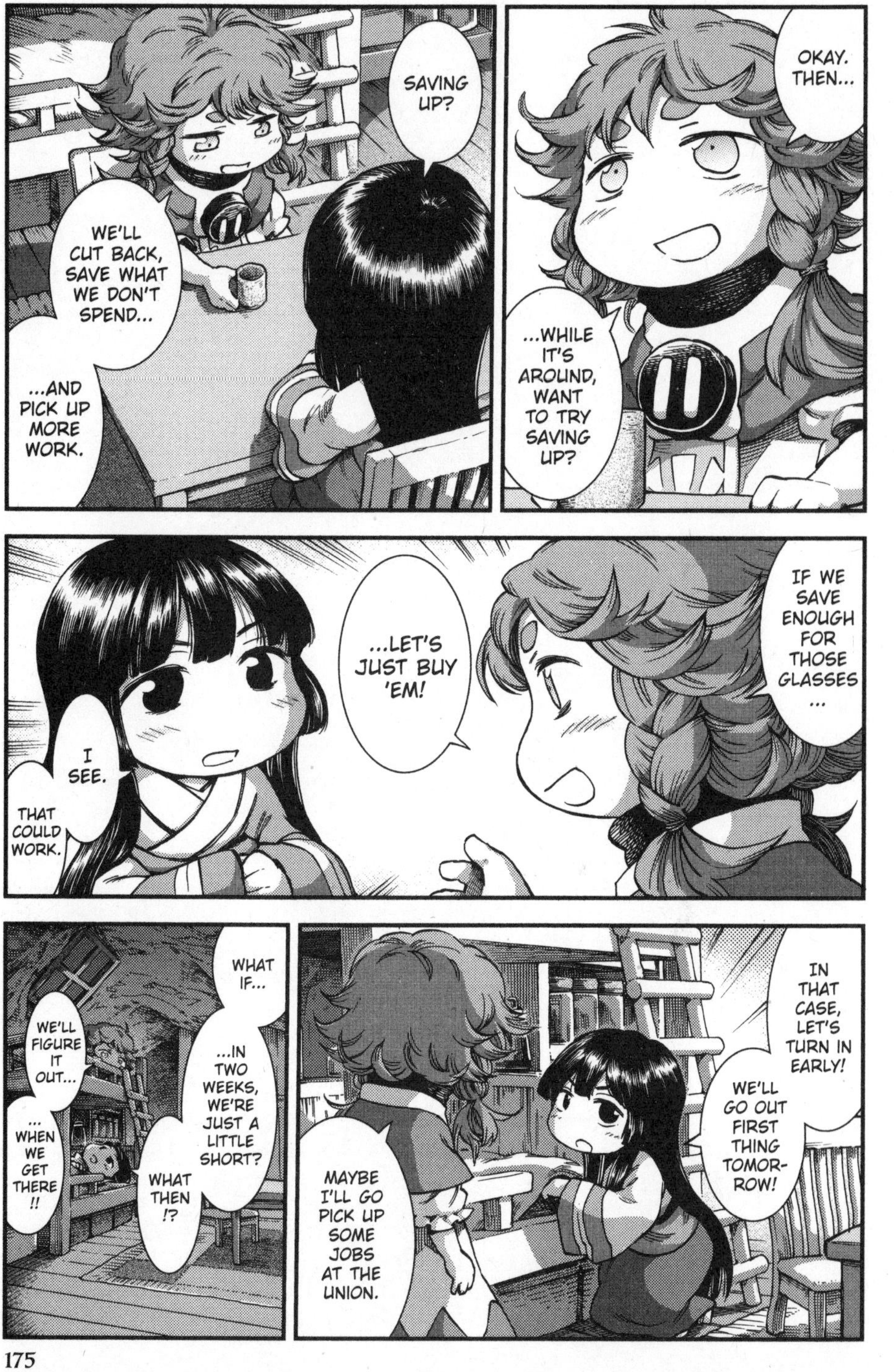
OKAY. THEN...
...WHILE IT'S AROUND, WANT TO TRY SAVING UP?
SAVING UP?
WE'LL CUT BACK, SAVE WHAT WE DON'T SPEND...
...AND PICK UP MORE WORK.
IF WE SAVE ENOUGH FOR THOSE GLASSES...
...LET'S JUST BUY 'EM!
I SEE.
THAT COULD WORK.
IN THAT CASE, LET'S TURN IN EARLY!
WE'LL GO OUT FIRST THING TOMORROW!
MAYBE I'LL GO PICK UP SOME JOBS AT THE UNION.
WHAT IF...
...IN TWO WEEKS, WE'RE JUST A LITTLE SHORT?
WHAT THEN!?
WE'LL FIGURE IT OUT...
...WHEN WE GET THERE!!

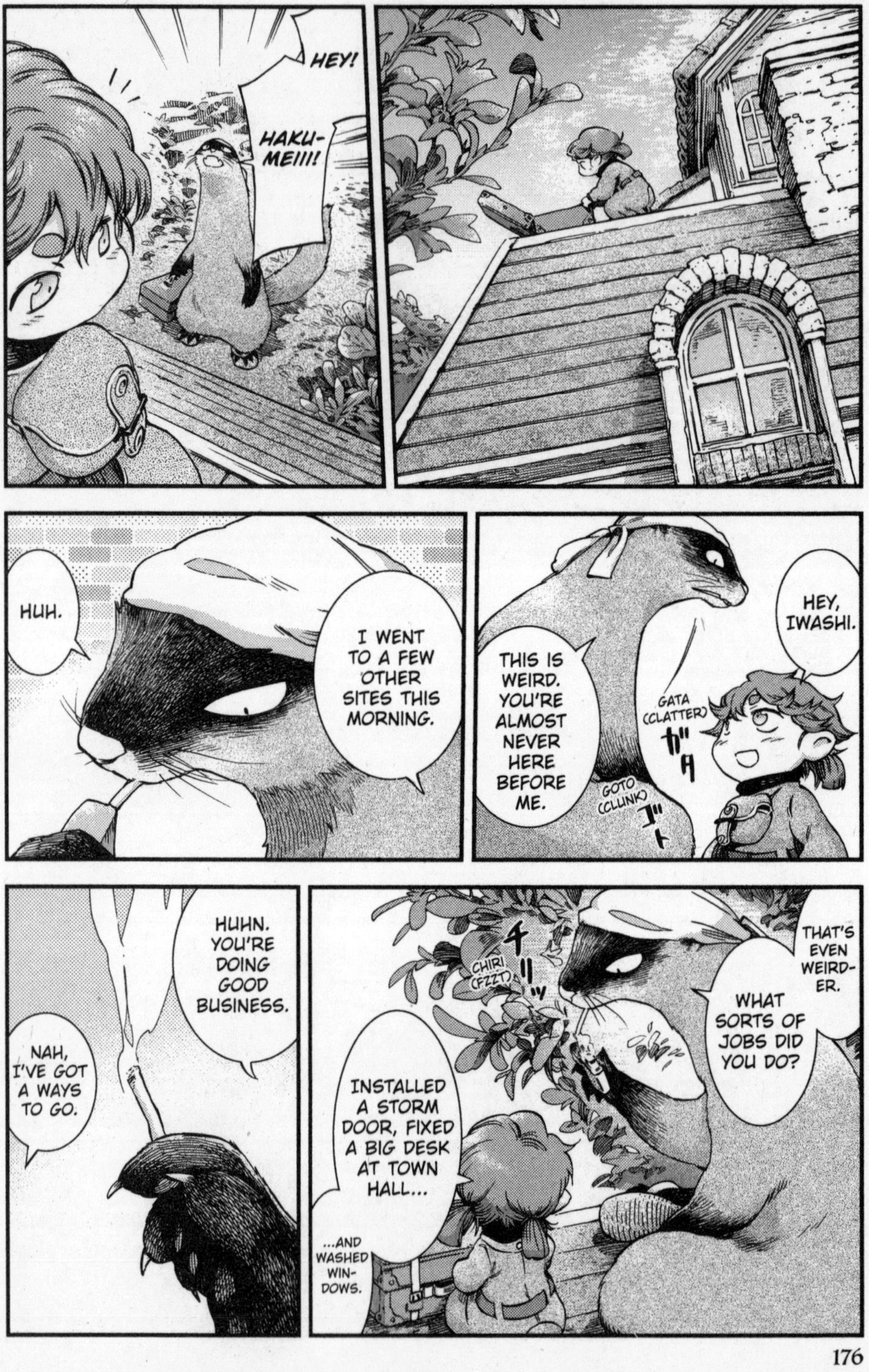
HEY!
HAKU-MEIIII!
HEY, IWASHI.
GATA (CLATTER)
ガタ
GOTO (CLUNK)
ゴト
THIS IS WEIRD. YOU'RE ALMOST NEVER HERE BEFORE ME.
I WENT TO A FEW OTHER SITES THIS MORNING.
HUH.
CHIRI (FZZT)
チリッ
THAT'S EVEN WEIRD-ER.
WHAT SORTS OF JOBS DID YOU DO?
INSTALLED A STORM DOOR, FIXED A BIG DESK AT TOWN HALL...
...AND WASHED WIN-DOWS.
HUHN. YOU'RE DOING GOOD BUSINESS.
NAH, I'VE GOT A WAYS TO GO.

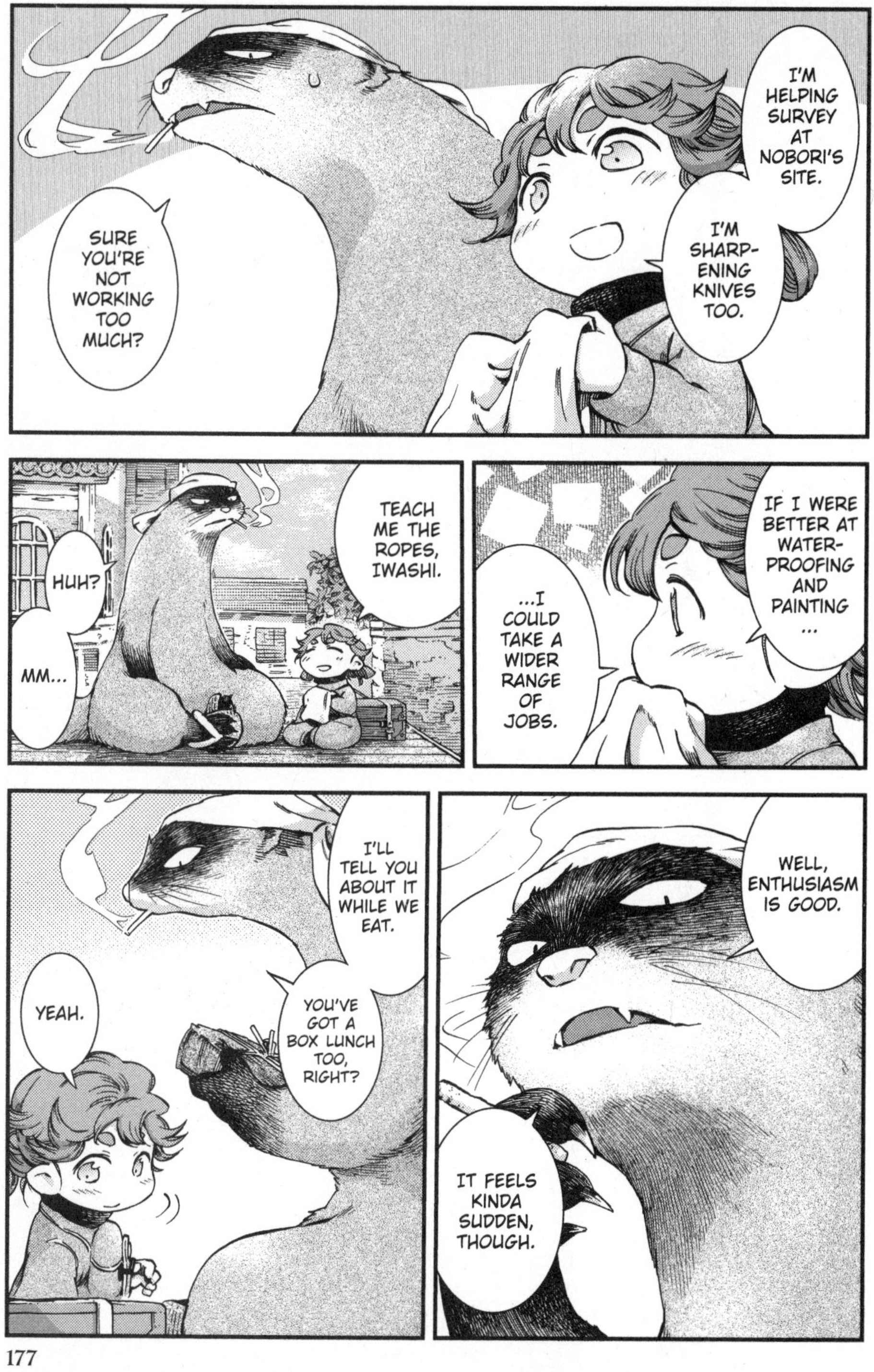
I'M HELPING SURVEY AT NOBORI'S SITE.
I'M SHARPENING KNIVES TOO.
SURE YOU'RE NOT WORKING TOO MUCH?
IF I WERE BETTER AT WATERPROOFING AND PAINTING...
...I COULD TAKE A WIDER RANGE OF JOBS.
TEACH ME THE ROPES, IWASHI.
HUH?
MM...
WELL, ENTHUSIASM IS GOOD.
IT FEELS KINDA SUDDEN, THOUGH.
I'LL TELL YOU ABOUT IT WHILE WE EAT.
YOU'VE GOT A BOX LUNCH TOO, RIGHT?
YEAH.

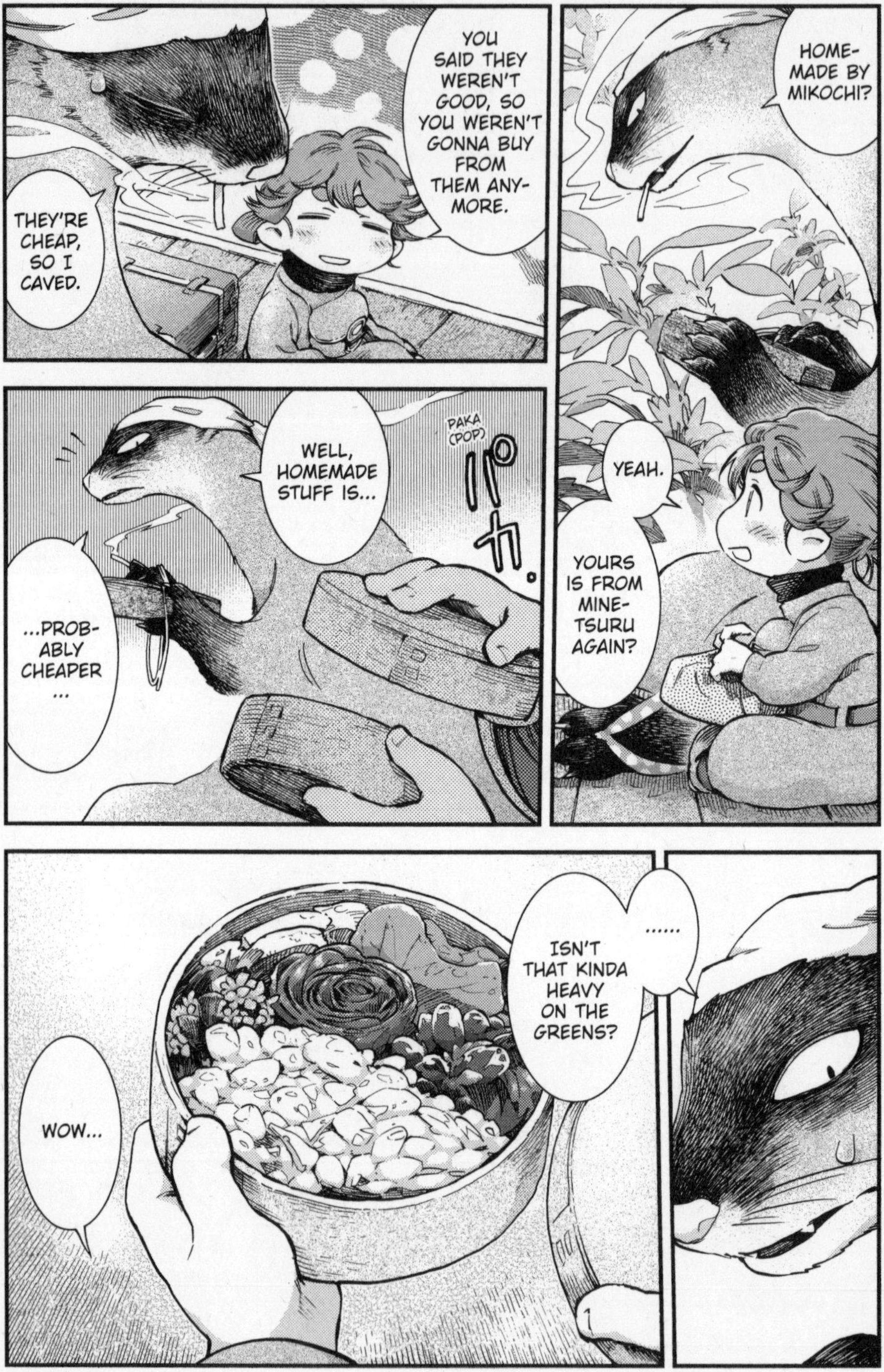
HOME-MADE BY MIKOCHI?
YEAH.
YOURS IS FROM MINE-TSURU AGAIN?
YOU SAID THEY WEREN'T GOOD, SO YOU WEREN'T GONNA BUY FROM THEM ANYMORE.
THEY'RE CHEAP, SO I CAVED.
WELL, HOMEMADE STUFF IS...
PAKA (POP)
パカ。
...PROBABLY CHEAPER...
......
ISN'T THAT KINDA HEAVY ON THE GREENS?
WOW...

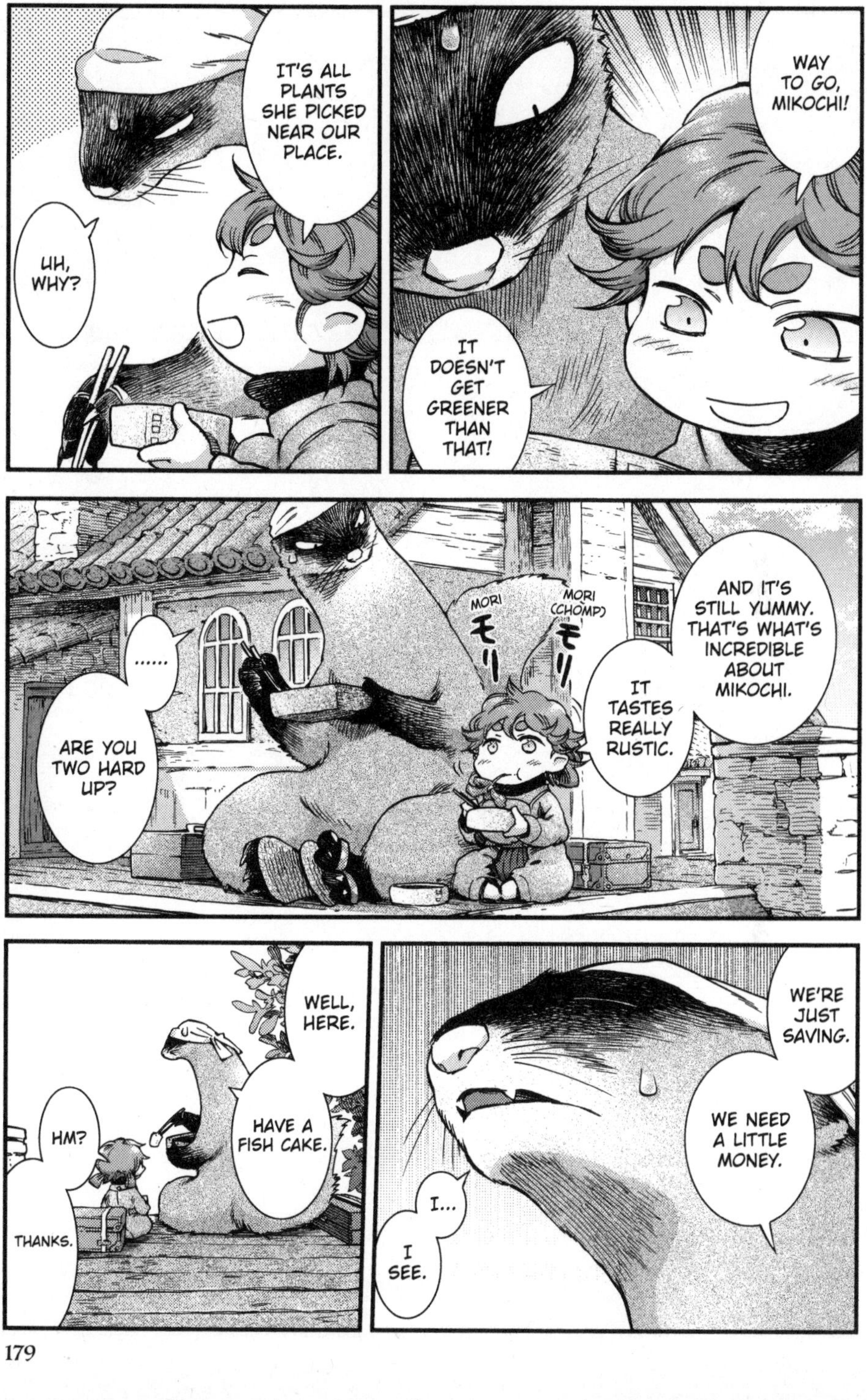
WAY TO GO, MIKOCHI!
IT DOESN'T GET GREENER THAN THAT!
IT'S ALL PLANTS SHE PICKED NEAR OUR PLACE.
UH, WHY?
AND IT'S STILL YUMMY. THAT'S WHAT'S INCREDIBLE ABOUT MIKOCHI.
IT TASTES REALLY RUSTIC.
MORI (CHOMP)
モリ
MORI
モリ
......
ARE YOU TWO HARD UP?
WE'RE JUST SAVING.
WE NEED A LITTLE MONEY.
I... I SEE.
WELL, HERE.
HAVE A FISH CAKE.
HM?
THANKS.

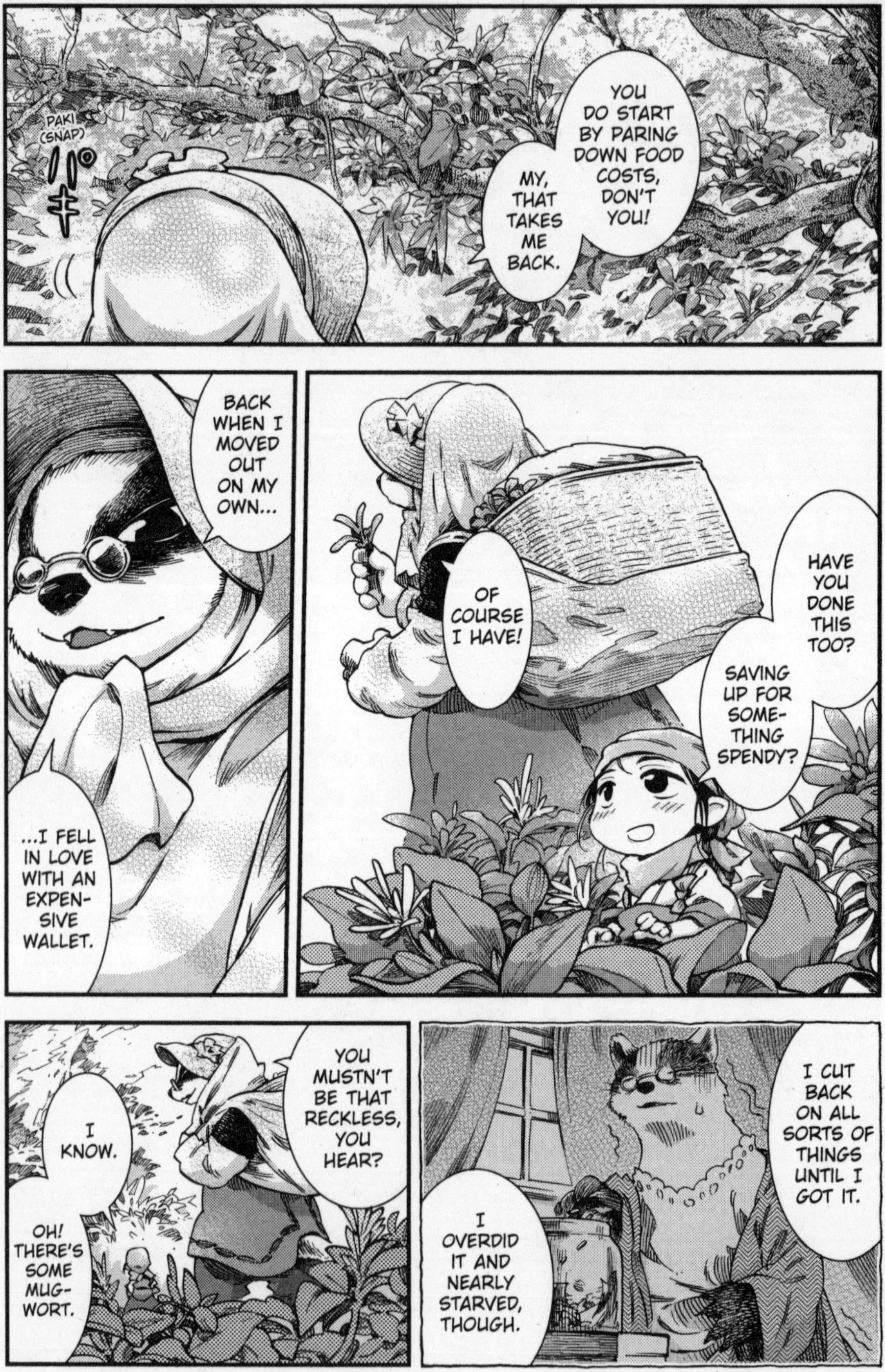
YOU DO START BY PARING DOWN FOOD COSTS, DON'T YOU!
MY, THAT TAKES ME BACK.
PAKI (SNAP)
HAVE YOU DONE THIS TOO?
SAVING UP FOR SOMETHING SPENDY?
OF COURSE I HAVE!
BACK WHEN I MOVED OUT ON MY OWN...
...I FELL IN LOVE WITH AN EXPENSIVE WALLET.
I CUT BACK ON ALL SORTS OF THINGS UNTIL I GOT IT.
I OVERDID IT AND NEARLY STARVED, THOUGH.
YOU MUSTN'T BE THAT RECKLESS, YOU HEAR?
I KNOW.
OH! THERE'S SOME MUGWORT.

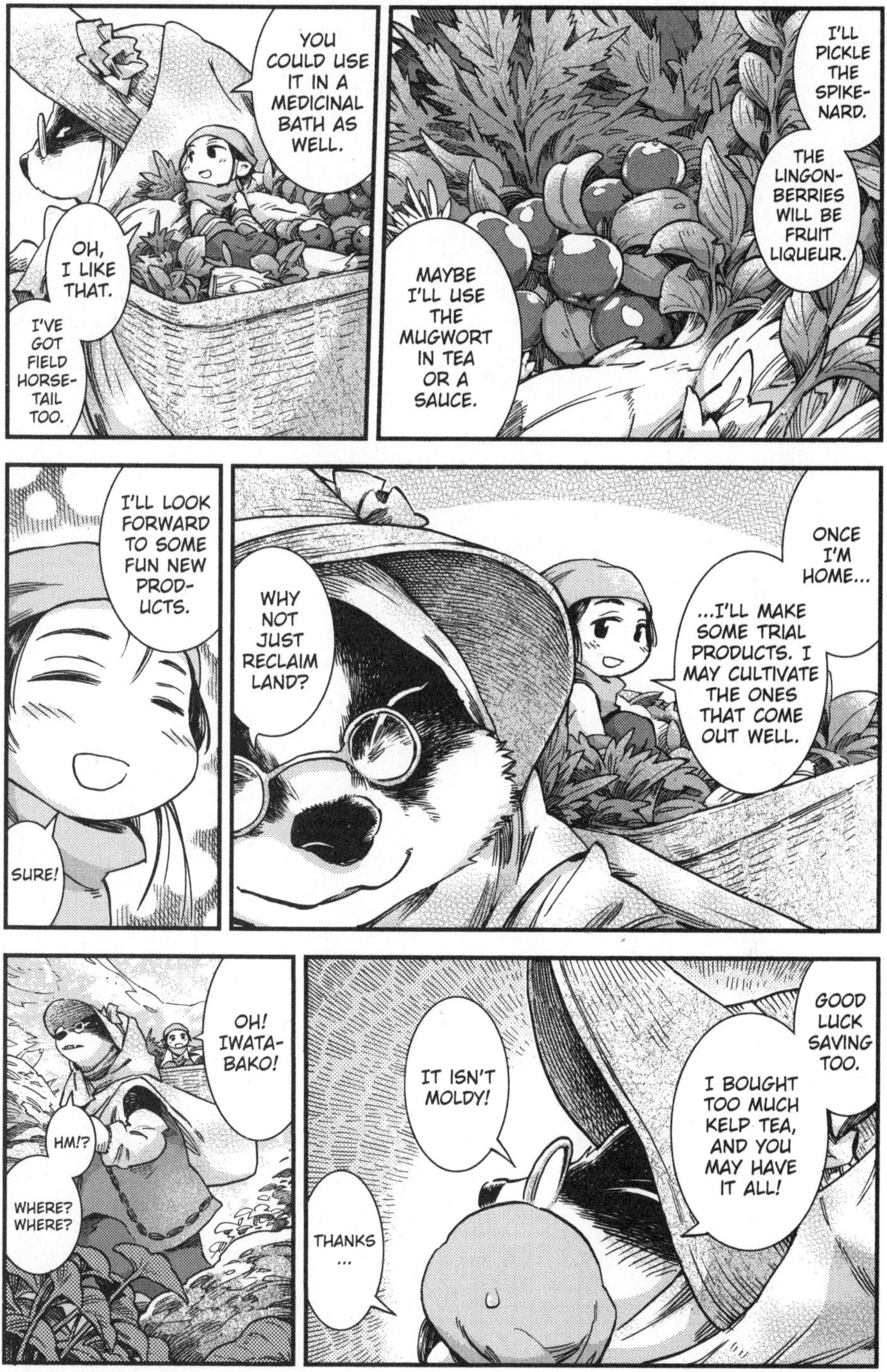
I'LL PICKLE THE SPIKENARD.
THE LINGONBERRIES WILL BE FRUIT LIQUEUR.
MAYBE I'LL USE THE MUGWORT IN TEA OR A SAUCE.
YOU COULD USE IT IN A MEDICINAL BATH AS WELL.
OH, I LIKE THAT.
I'VE GOT FIELD HORSETAIL TOO.
ONCE I'M HOME...
...I'LL MAKE SOME TRIAL PRODUCTS. I MAY CULTIVATE THE ONES THAT COME OUT WELL.
WHY NOT JUST RECLAIM LAND?
I'LL LOOK FORWARD TO SOME FUN NEW PRODUCTS.
SURE!
GOOD LUCK SAVING TOO.
I BOUGHT TOO MUCH KELP TEA, AND YOU MAY HAVE IT ALL!
IT ISN'T MOLDY!
THANKS...
OH! IWATABAKO!
HM!?
WHERE? WHERE?

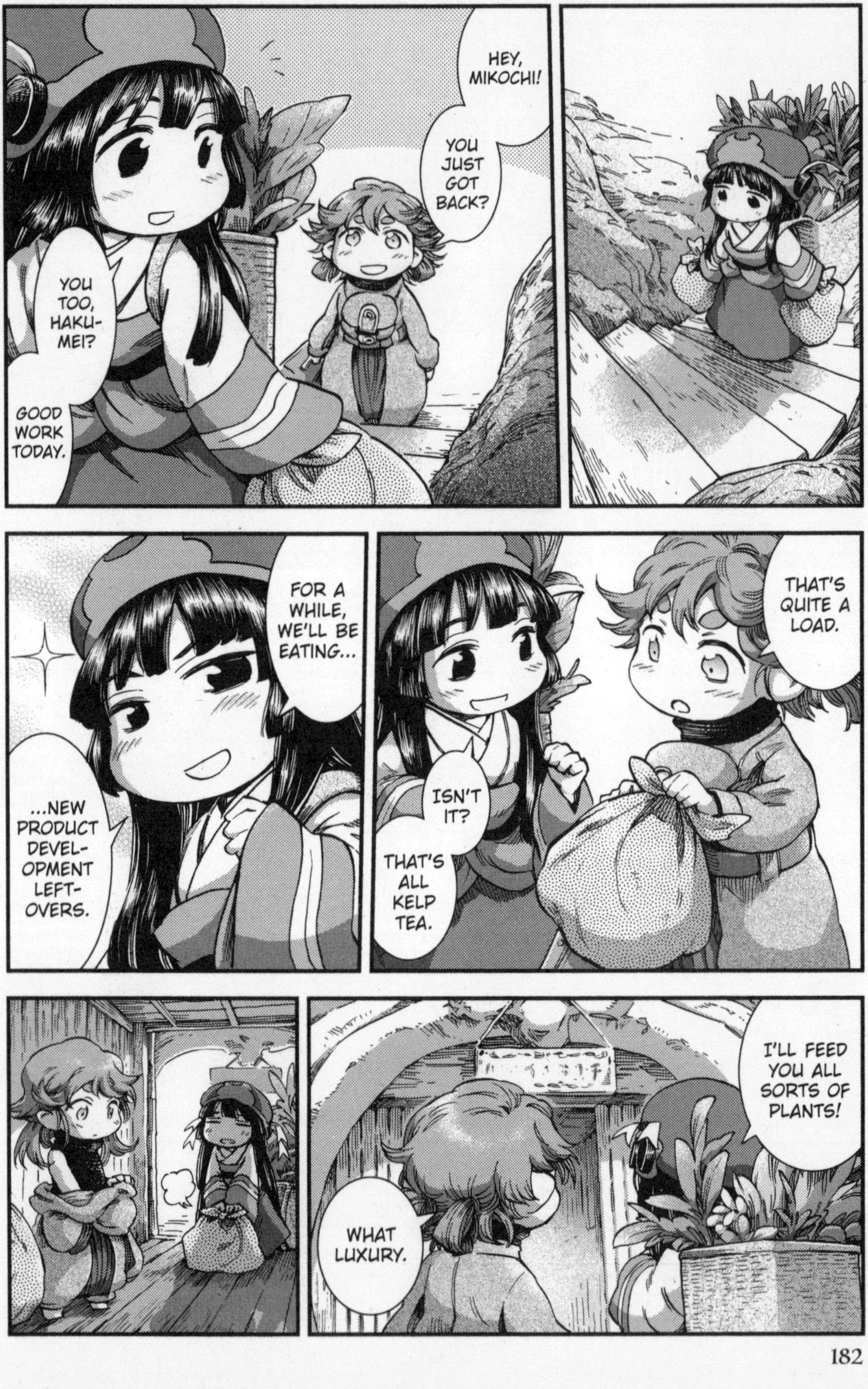
HEY, MIKOCHI!
YOU JUST GOT BACK?
YOU TOO, HAKU-MEI?
GOOD WORK TODAY.
THAT'S QUITE A LOAD.
ISN'T IT?
THAT'S ALL KELP TEA.
FOR A WHILE, WE'LL BE EATING...
...NEW PRODUCT DEVEL-OPMENT LEFT-OVERS.
I'LL FEED YOU ALL SORTS OF PLANTS!
WHAT LUXURY.

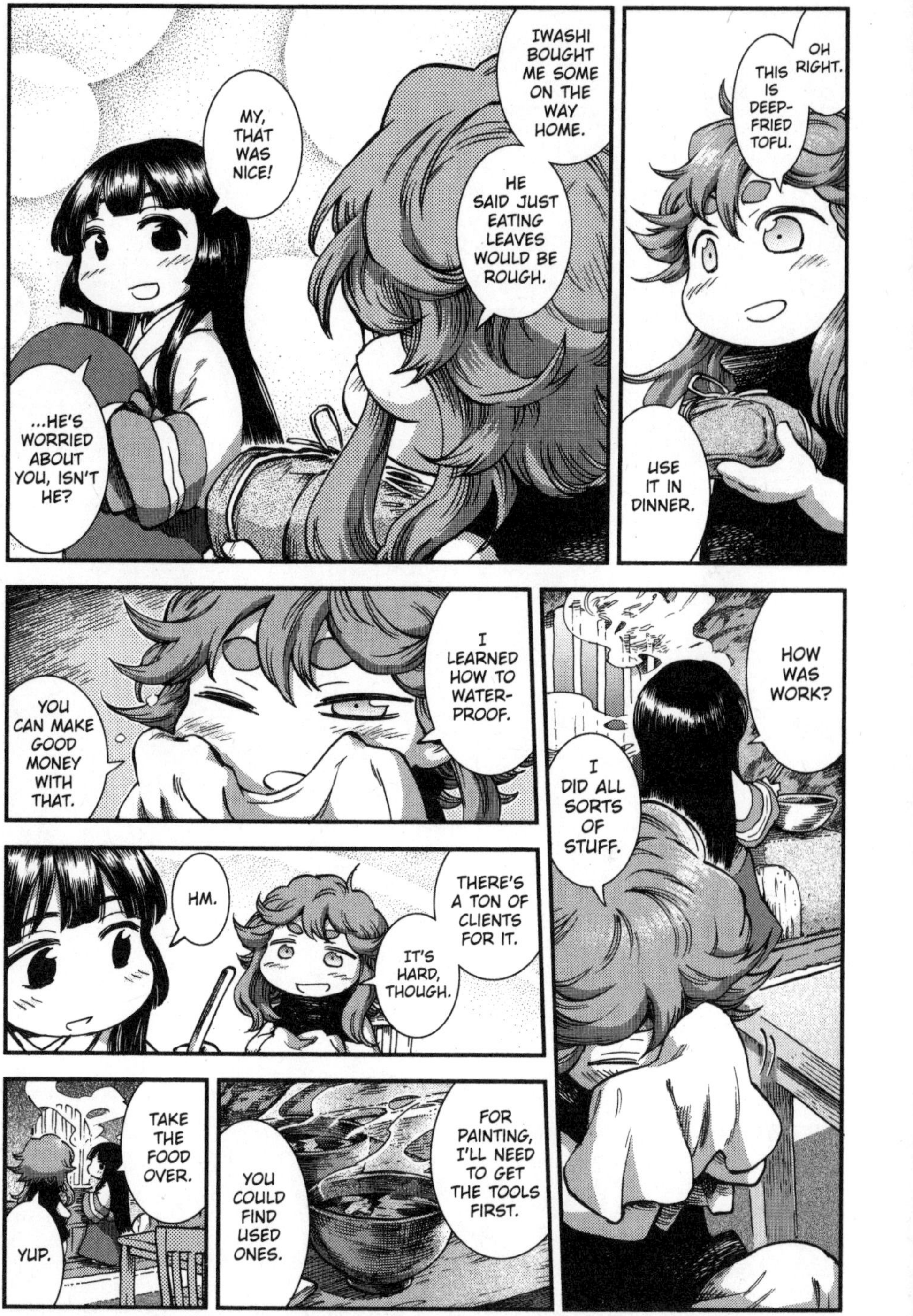
OH RIGHT. THIS IS DEEP-FRIED TOFU.
USE IT IN DINNER.
IWASHI BOUGHT ME SOME ON THE WAY HOME.
HE SAID JUST EATING LEAVES WOULD BE ROUGH.
MY, THAT WAS NICE!
...HE'S WORRIED ABOUT YOU, ISN'T HE?
HOW WAS WORK?
I DID ALL SORTS OF STUFF.
I LEARNED HOW TO WATER-PROOF.
YOU CAN MAKE GOOD MONEY WITH THAT.
THERE'S A TON OF CLIENTS FOR IT.
IT'S HARD, THOUGH.
HM.
FOR PAINTING, I'LL NEED TO GET THE TOOLS FIRST.
YOU COULD FIND USED ONES.
TAKE THE FOOD OVER.
YUP.

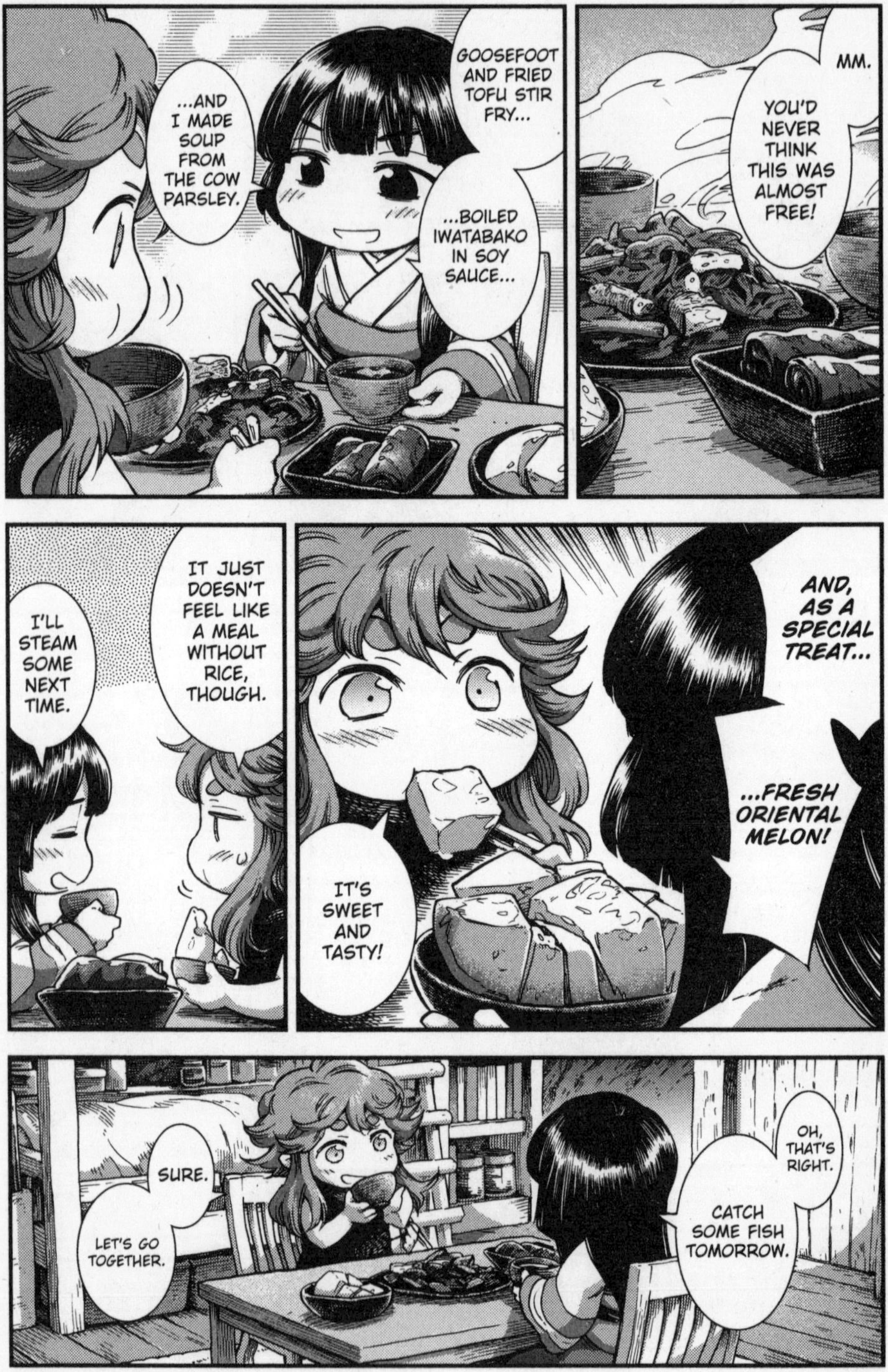
MM.
YOU'D NEVER THINK THIS WAS ALMOST FREE!
GOOSEFOOT AND FRIED TOFU STIR FRY...
...BOILED IWATABAKO IN SOY SAUCE...
...AND I MADE SOUP FROM THE COW PARSLEY.
AND, AS A SPECIAL TREAT...
...FRESH ORIENTAL MELON!
IT'S SWEET AND TASTY!
IT JUST DOESN'T FEEL LIKE A MEAL WITHOUT RICE, THOUGH.
I'LL STEAM SOME NEXT TIME.
OH, THAT'S RIGHT.
CATCH SOME FISH TOMORROW.
SURE.
LET'S GO TOGETHER.

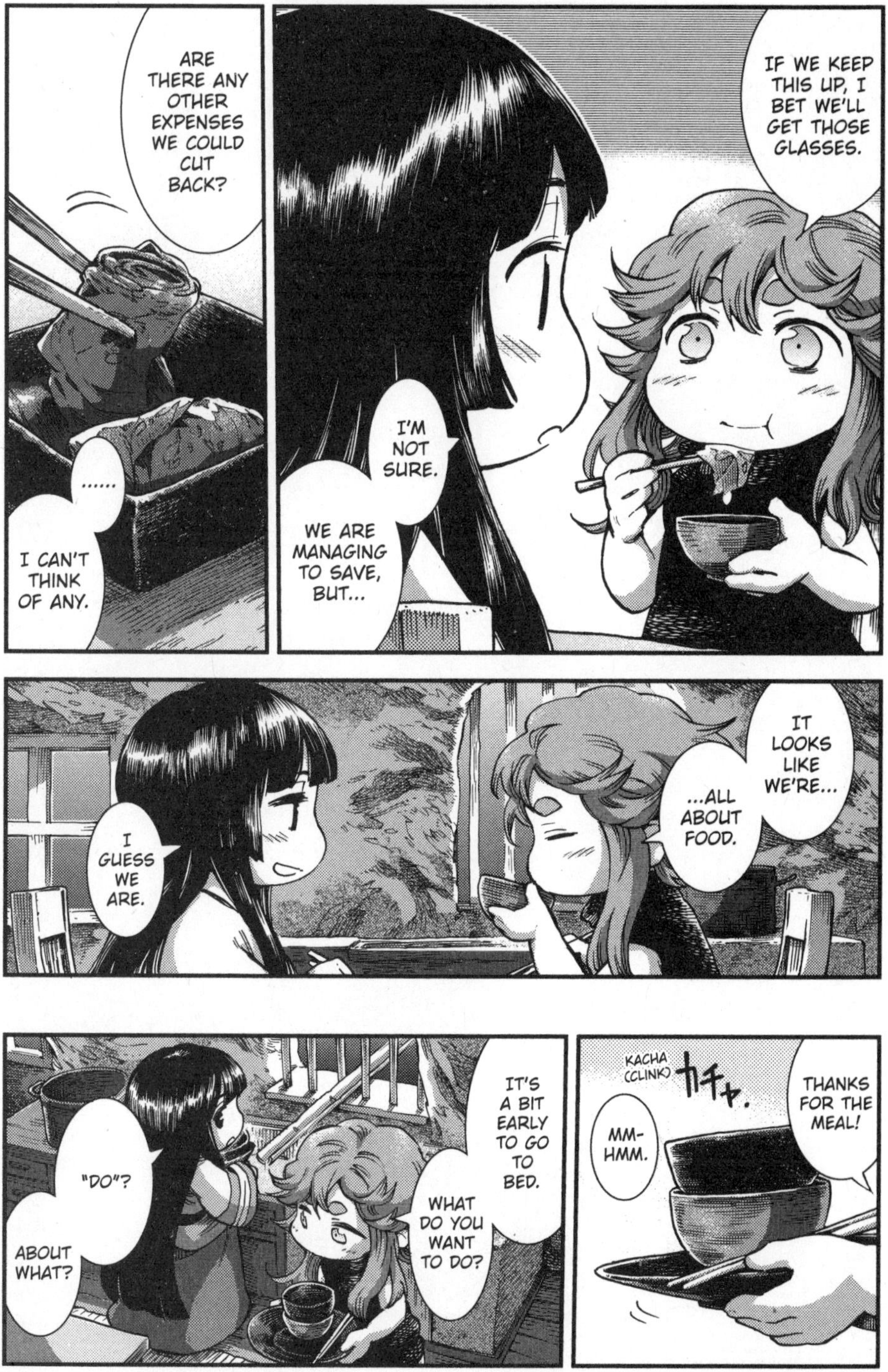
IF WE KEEP THIS UP, I BET WE'LL GET THOSE GLASSES.
I'M NOT SURE.
WE ARE MANAGING TO SAVE, BUT...
ARE THERE ANY OTHER EXPENSES WE COULD CUT BACK?
......
I CAN'T THINK OF ANY.
IT LOOKS LIKE WE'RE...
...ALL ABOUT FOOD.
I GUESS WE ARE.
KACHA (CLINK)
カチャ.
THANKS FOR THE MEAL!
MM-HMM.
IT'S A BIT EARLY TO GO TO BED.
WHAT DO YOU WANT TO DO?
"DO"?
ABOUT WHAT?

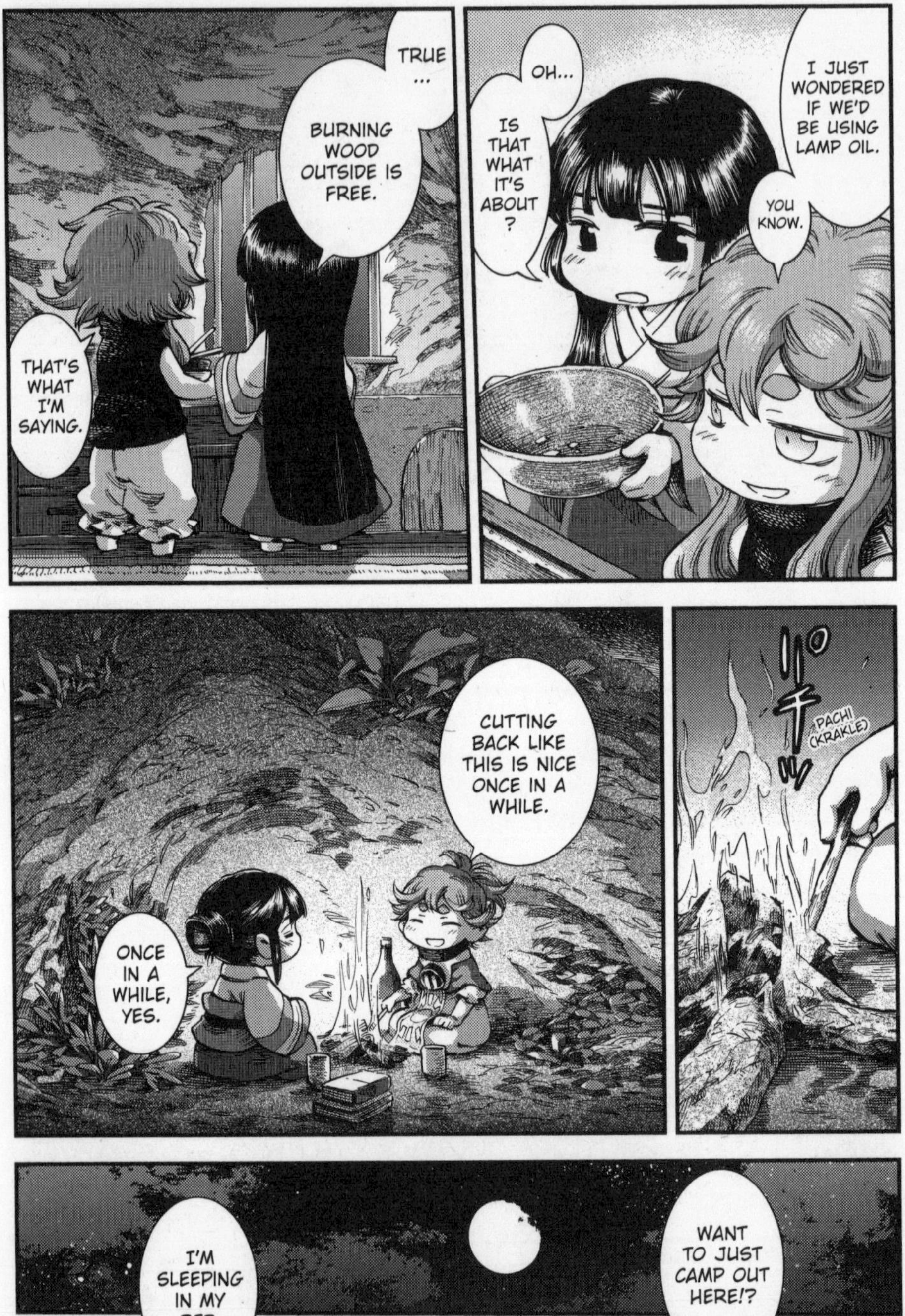
I JUST WONDERED IF WE'D BE USING LAMP OIL.
YOU KNOW.
OH...
IS THAT WHAT IT'S ABOUT?
TRUE...
BURNING WOOD OUTSIDE IS FREE.
THAT'S WHAT I'M SAYING.
PACHI (KRAKLE)
CUTTING BACK LIKE THIS IS NICE ONCE IN A WHILE.
ONCE IN A WHILE, YES.
WANT TO JUST CAMP OUT HERE!?
I'M SLEEPING IN MY BED.

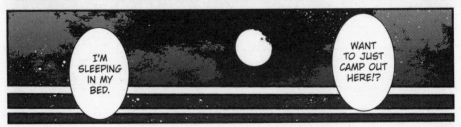

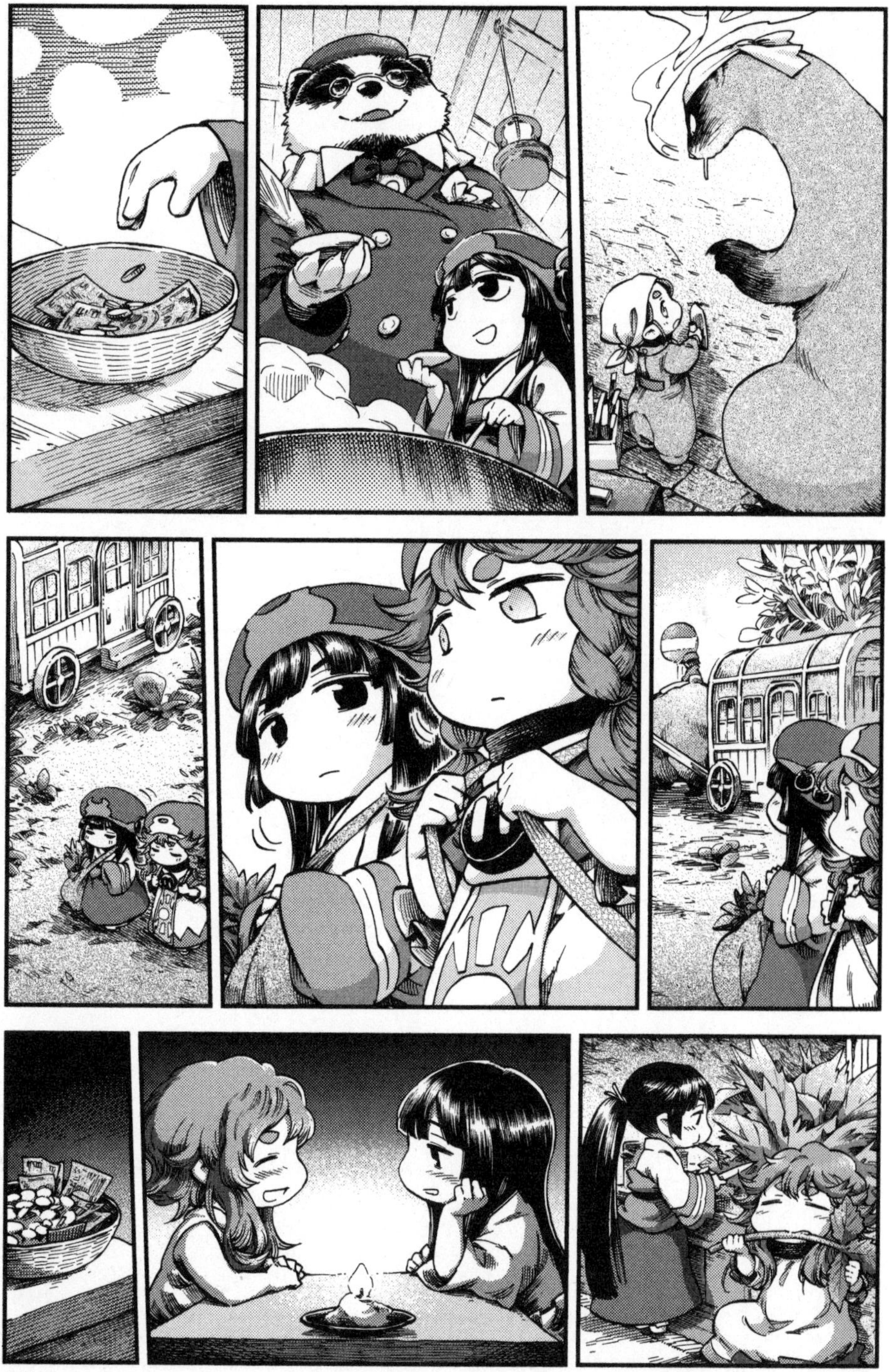

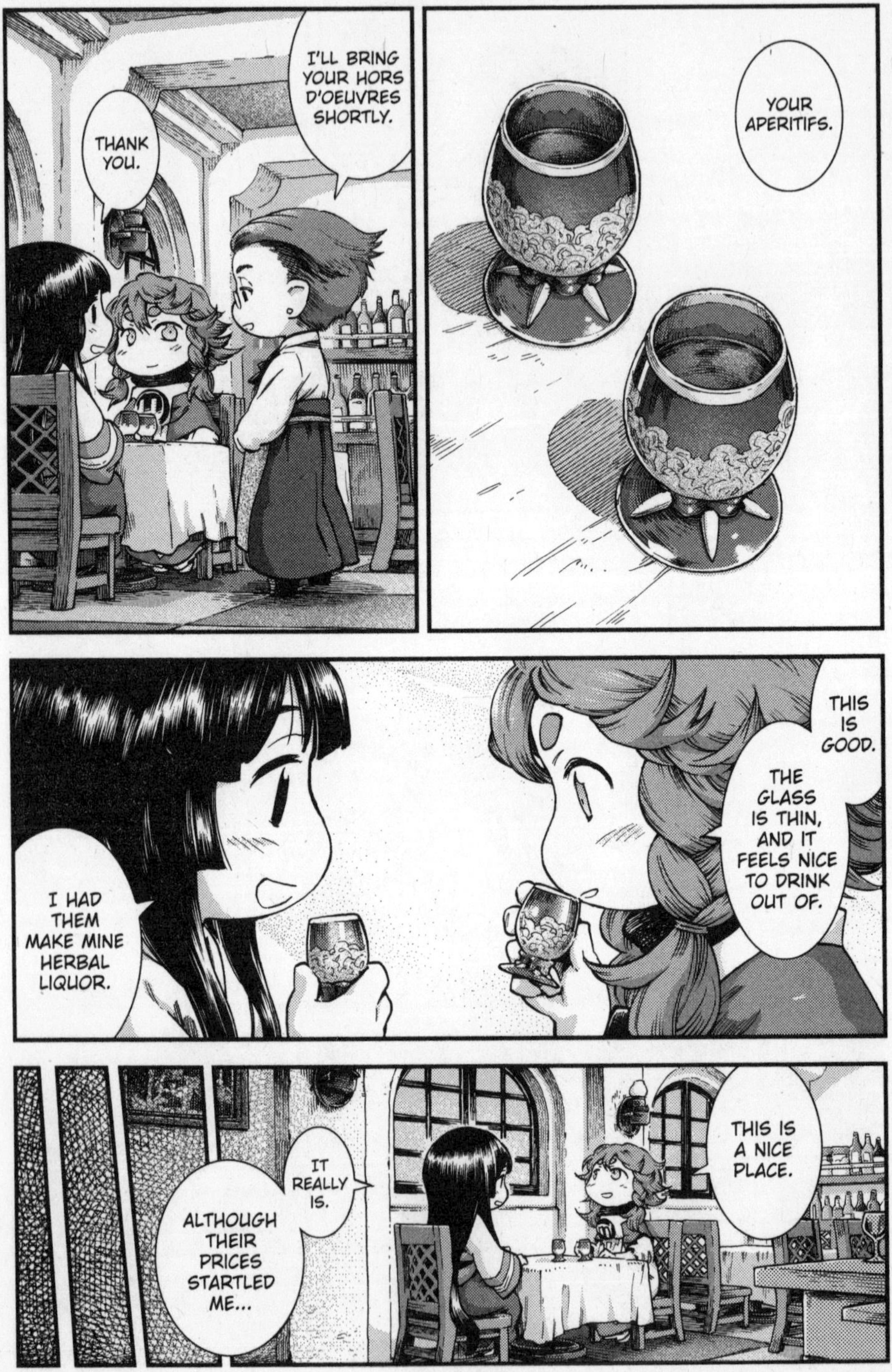
YOUR APERITIFS.
I'LL BRING YOUR HORS D'OEUVRES SHORTLY.
THANK YOU.
THIS IS GOOD.
THE GLASS IS THIN, AND IT FEELS NICE TO DRINK OUT OF.
I HAD THEM MAKE MINE HERBAL LIQUOR.
THIS IS A NICE PLACE.
IT REALLY IS.
ALTHOUGH THEIR PRICES STARTLED ME...

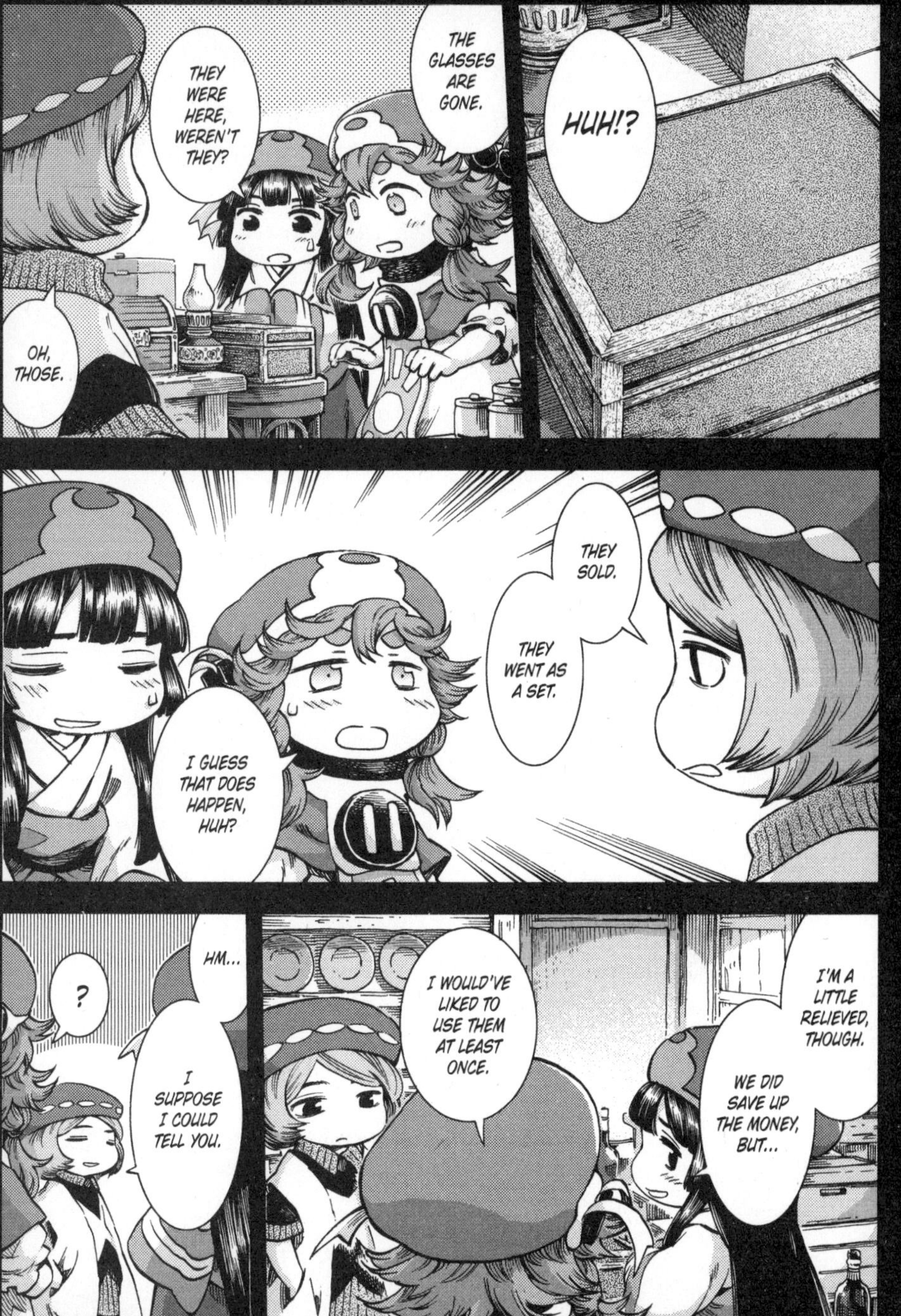
HUH!?
THE GLASSES ARE GONE.
THEY WERE HERE, WEREN'T THEY?
OH, THOSE.
THEY SOLD.
THEY WENT AS A SET.
I GUESS THAT DOES HAPPEN, HUH?
I'M A LITTLE RELIEVED, THOUGH.
WE DID SAVE UP THE MONEY, BUT...
I WOULD'VE LIKED TO USE THEM AT LEAST ONCE.
HM...
?
I SUPPOSE I COULD TELL YOU.

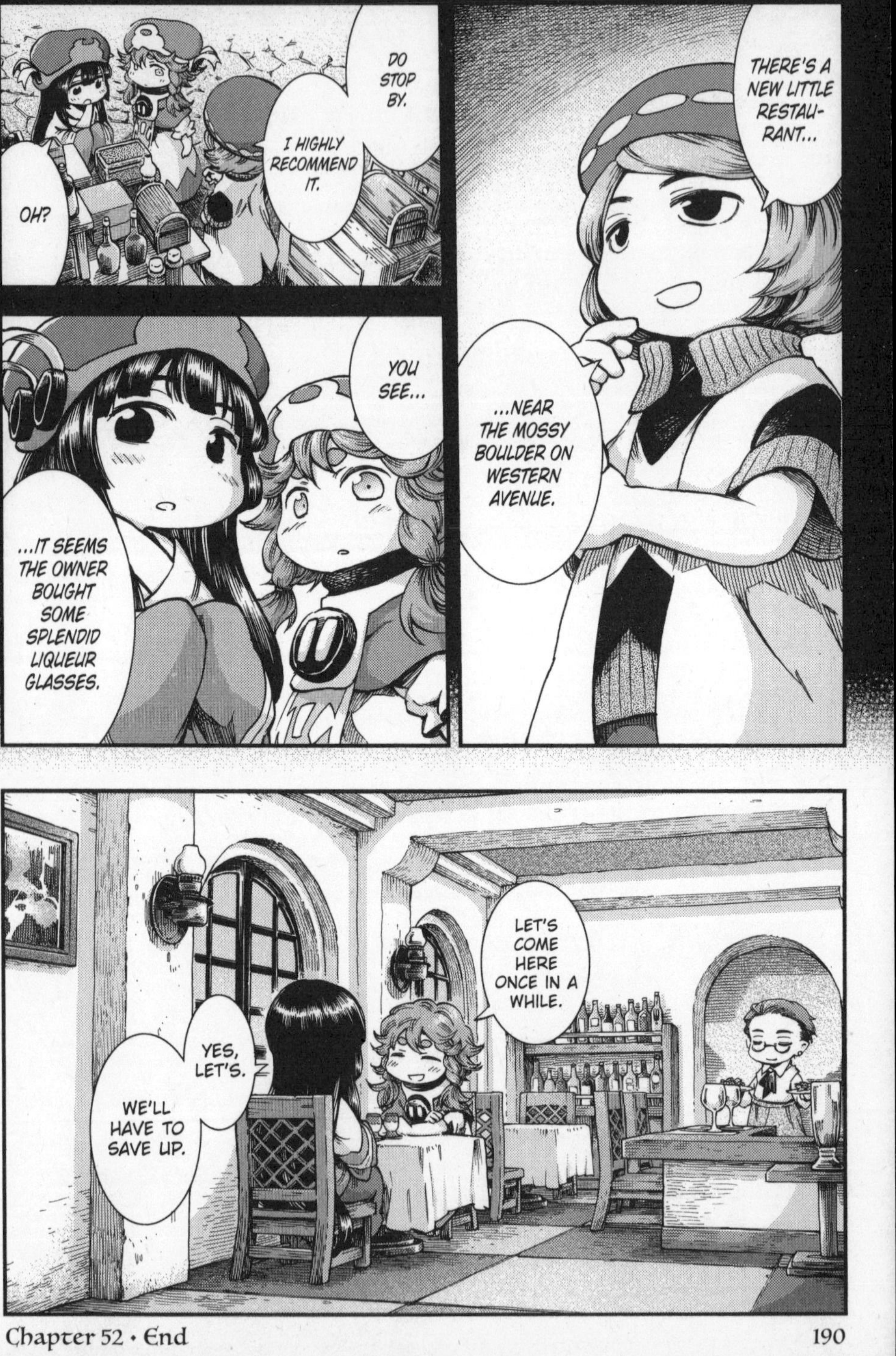
THERE'S A NEW LITTLE RESTAURANT...
...NEAR THE MOSSY BOULDER ON WESTERN AVENUE.
DO STOP BY.
I HIGHLY RECOMMEND IT.
OH?
YOU SEE...
...IT SEEMS THE OWNER BOUGHT SOME SPLENDID LIQUEUR GLASSES.
LET'S COME HERE ONCE IN A WHILE.
YES, LET'S.
WE'LL HAVE TO SAVE UP.

Chapter 52 • End

•*Column*• Underfoot Steps 52 / Crystal Statue of a Screaming Slug

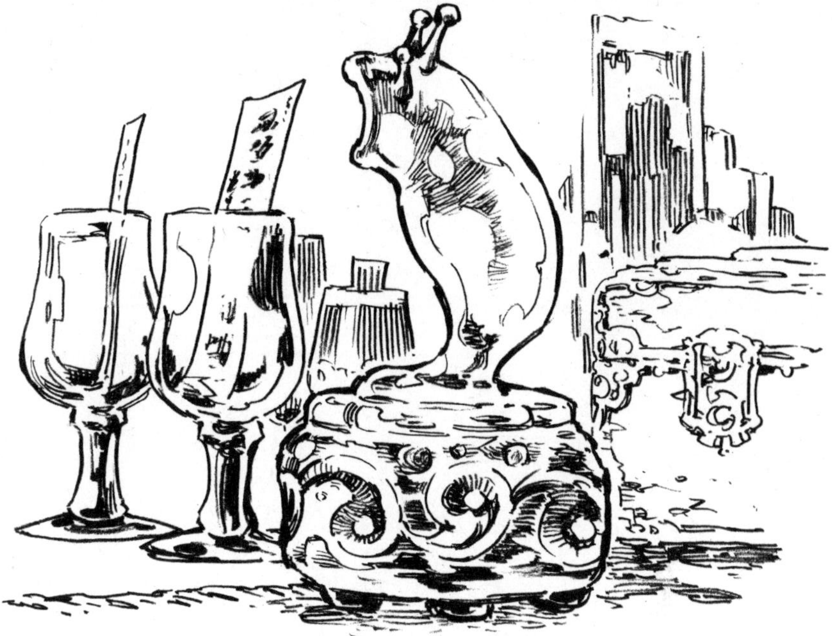

Crystal Statue of a Screaming Slug
(Manufacturer/Year of manufacture unclear)

A statue carved out of a single crystal, including the base. The stone is high-quality and perfectly clear and even detailed areas like the depths of its mouth are polished.

For a long time, it graced an old tavern in the Haruhan region, but when the establishment closed, it was put up for auction. It subsequently changed hands several times, finally coming to rest in an antique store in Makinata.

It's a lively, dynamic masterpiece, but the reason for its scream and what it might be screaming are a mystery.

*Discount negotiable

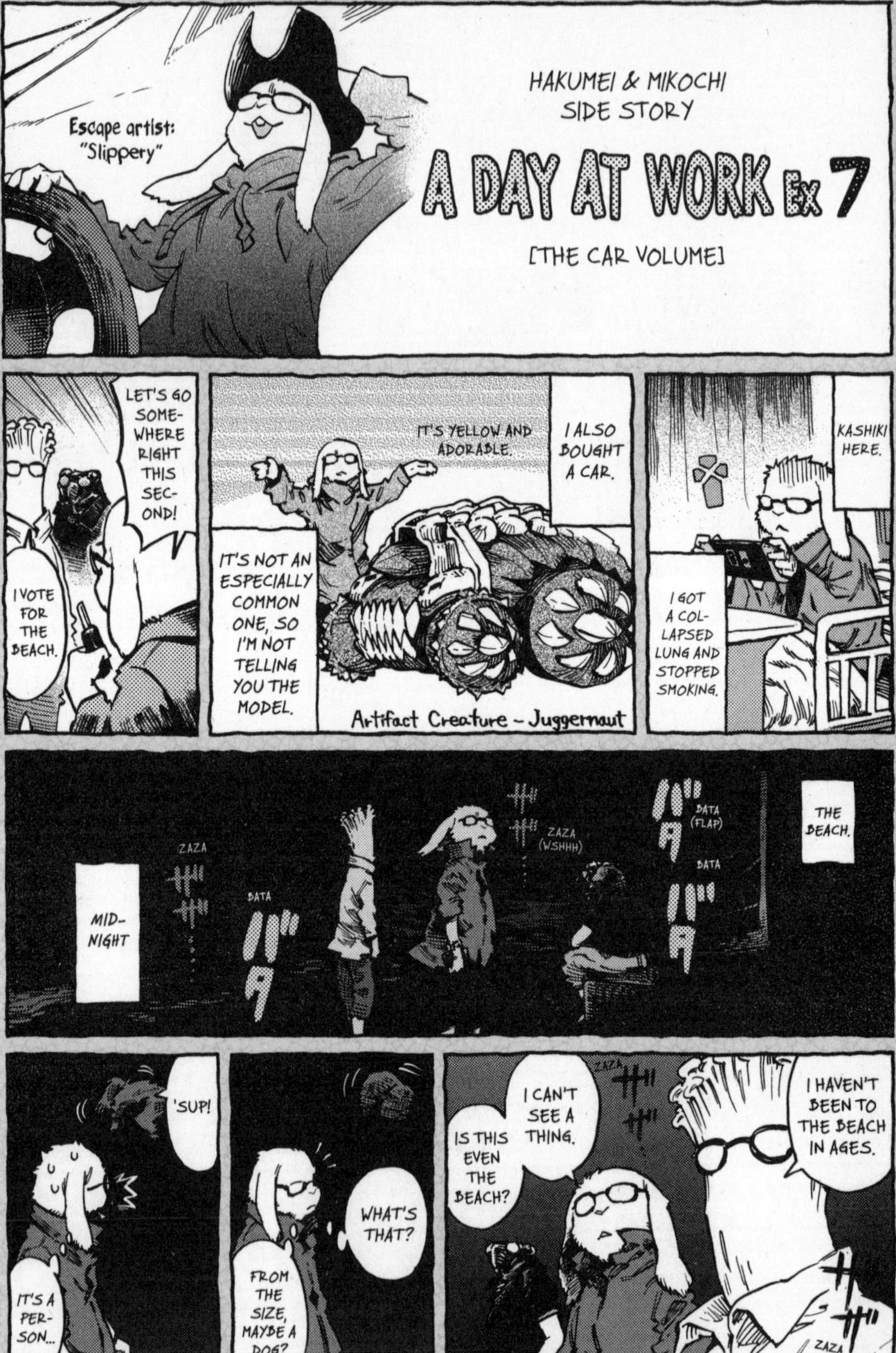
HAKUMEI & MIKOCHI
SIDE STORY
A DAY AT WORK Ex 7
[THE CAR VOLUME]
Escape artist: "Slippery"
KASHIKI HERE.
I GOT A COLLAPSED LUNG AND STOPPED SMOKING.
I ALSO BOUGHT A CAR.
IT'S YELLOW AND ADORABLE.
IT'S NOT AN ESPECIALLY COMMON ONE, SO I'M NOT TELLING YOU THE MODEL.
Artifact Creature - Juggernaut
LET'S GO SOMEWHERE RIGHT THIS SECOND!
I VOTE FOR THE BEACH.
THE BEACH.
BATA (FLAP)
BATA
ZAZA (WSHHH)
ZAZA
BATA
MIDNIGHT
I HAVEN'T BEEN TO THE BEACH IN AGES.
ZAZA
I CAN'T SEE A THING.
IS THIS EVEN THE BEACH?
ZAZA
WHAT'S THAT?
FROM THE SIZE, MAYBE A DOG?
'SUP!
IT'S A PERSON...

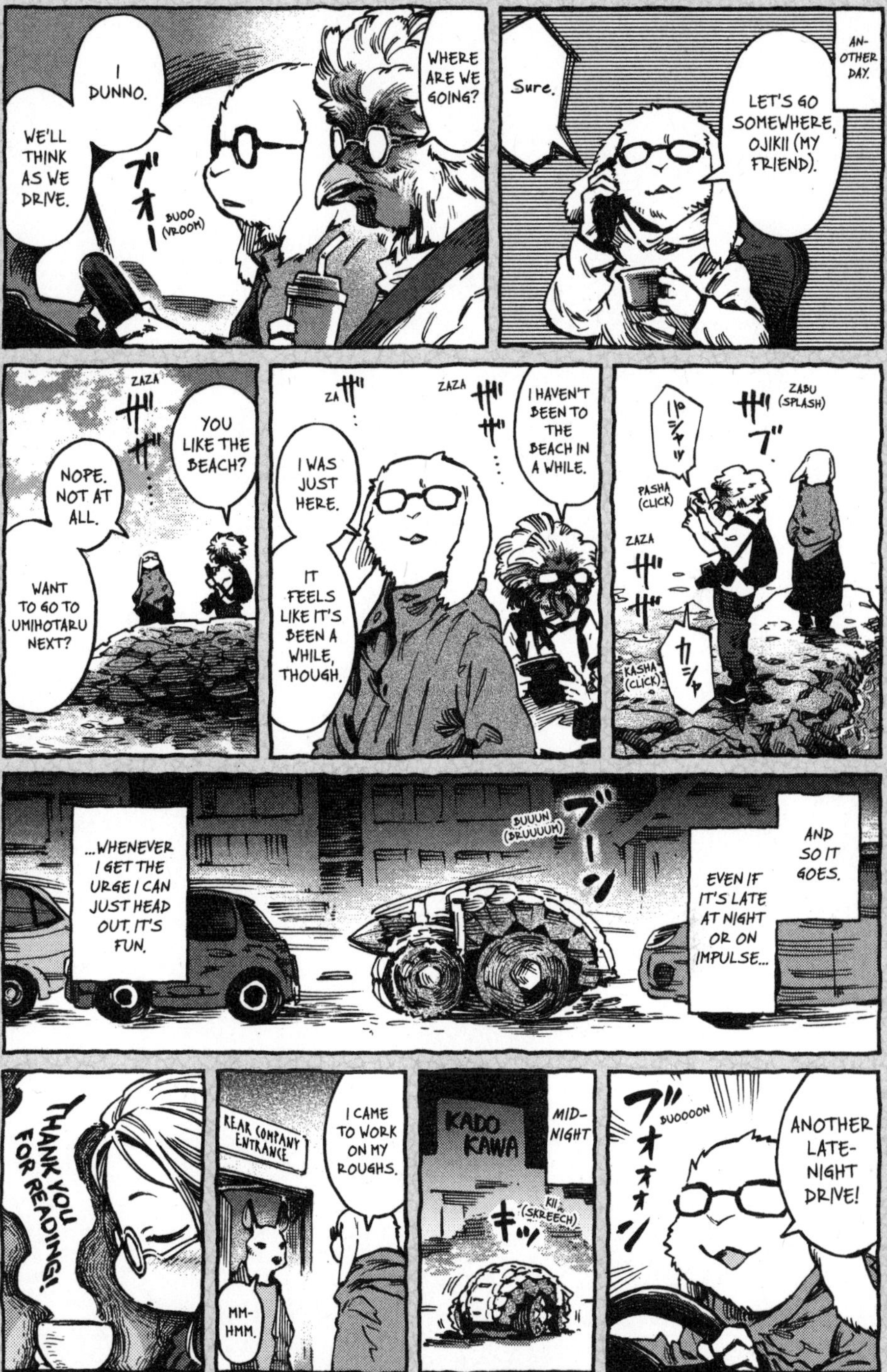
AN-OTHER DAY.
LET'S GO SOMEWHERE, OJIKII (MY FRIEND).
Sure.
WHERE ARE WE GOING?
I DUNNO.
WE'LL THINK AS WE DRIVE.
ブオー
BUOO (VROOM)
ザブ
ZABU (SPLASH)
パシャッ
PASHA (CLICK)
ZAZA
ザザ
カシャ
KASHA (CLICK)
I HAVEN'T BEEN TO THE BEACH IN A WHILE.
ZAZA
ザザ
ZA
ザ
I WAS JUST HERE.
IT FEELS LIKE IT'S BEEN A WHILE, THOUGH.
ZAZA
ザザ
YOU LIKE THE BEACH?
NOPE. NOT AT ALL.
WANT TO GO TO UMIHOTARU NEXT?
AND SO IT GOES.
EVEN IF IT'S LATE AT NIGHT OR ON IMPULSE...
BUUUN (BRUUUUM)
ブーン
...WHENEVER I GET THE URGE I CAN JUST HEAD OUT. IT'S FUN.
ブオオオン
BUOOOON
ANOTHER LATE-NIGHT DRIVE!
MID-NIGHT
KADO KAWA
キッ
KII (SKREECH)
I CAME TO WORK ON MY ROUGHS.
REAR COMPANY ENTRANCE
MM-HMM.
THANK YOU FOR READING!

To Be Continued...

Hakumei
&
Mikochi
Tiny Little Life in the Woods

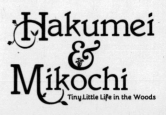

Special Content

Assorted
HakuMiko

• *Morgen Harta* •

A reader participation project from the main *Harta* magazine; artists drew situations suggested by the readers. Sentences inside brackets are requests, artist comments follow.

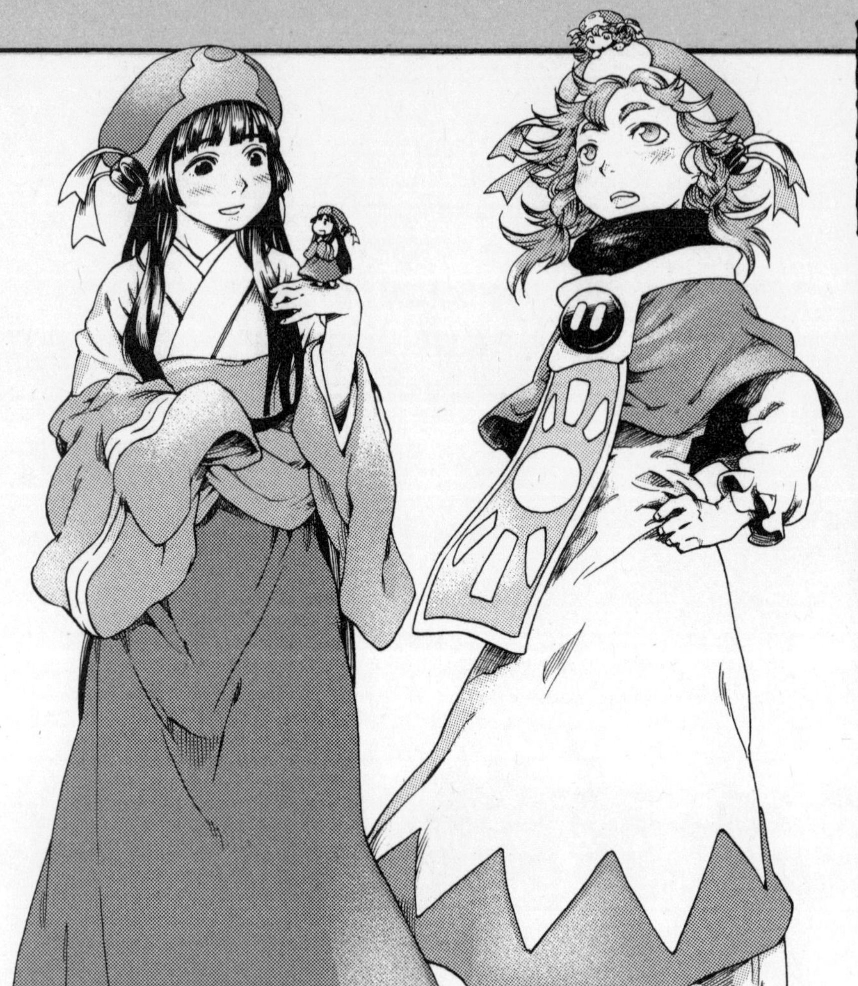

❶**[Draw their human-sized versions]** Somebody please cosplay these. ❷**[Hakumei and Mikochi in human society, playing on Kashiki-san's desk]** Even a smartphone has a massive, spectacular screen. I'm jealous. ❸**[Draw them in each other's clothes]** Hakumei looks like she works at a traditional inn. ❹**[I want to see them playing in the ocean]** Even if they went to the beach, neither of them seems likely to swim much. ❺**[Hakumei as a maid! High school girl Mikochi!]** It would be fun to dress them in all sorts of things, wouldn't it? Like bunny-ear coats or space suits. ❻**[When they're drunk after drinking too much]** Don't mix your drinks, all right? ❼**[I bet Mikochi gets called "Michiko" by mistake a lot, so I'd like to get defiant about it and see Hakumei and Michiko!]** It's Mikochi. Everybody remember that!

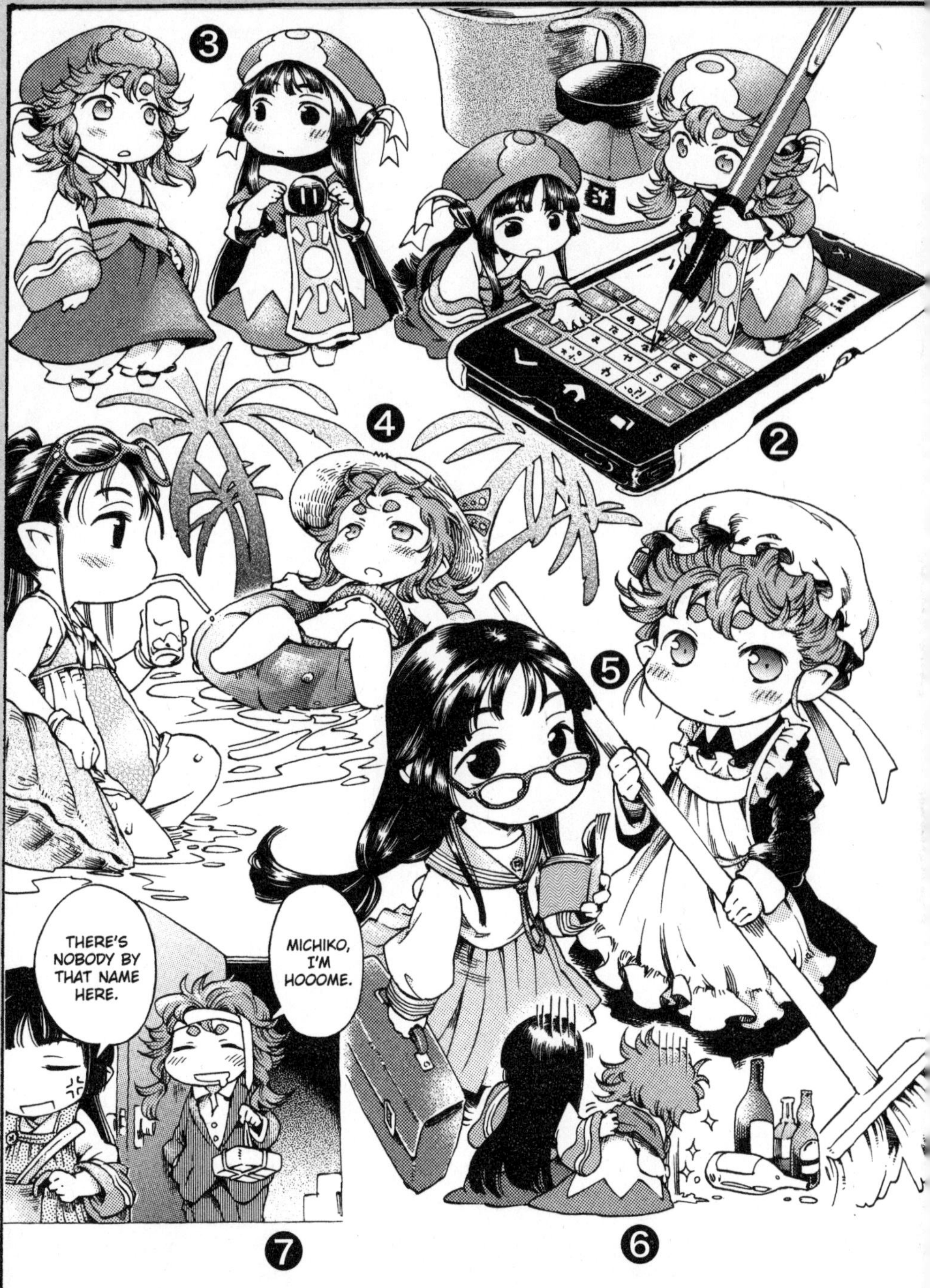
MICHIKO, I'M HOOOME.
THERE'S NOBODY BY THAT NAME HERE.

PUT IT TO WORK!
THE HARTA CASE

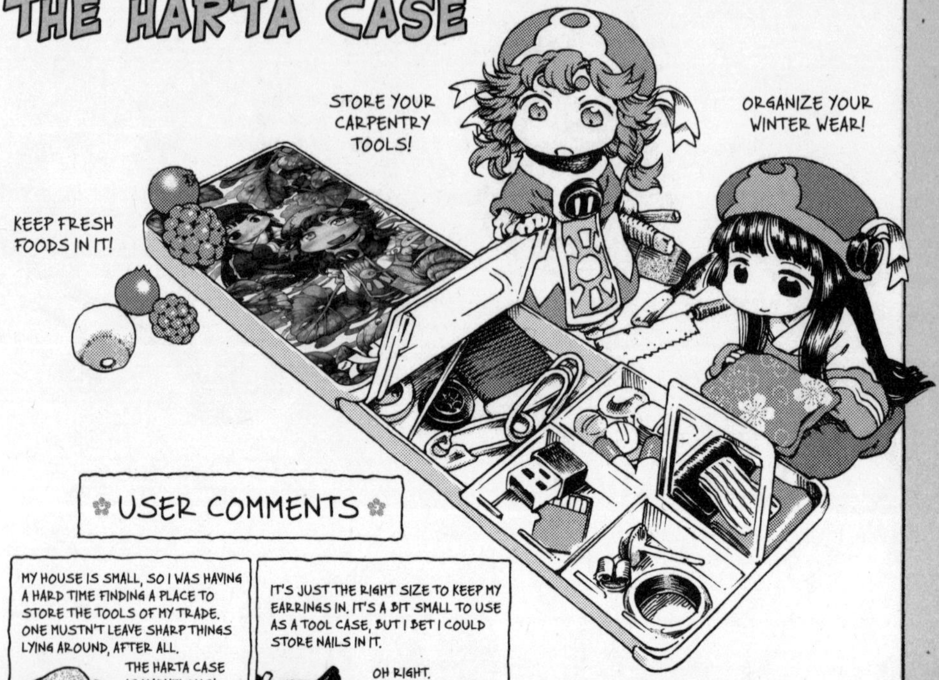
STORE YOUR CARPENTRY TOOLS!
ORGANIZE YOUR WINTER WEAR!
KEEP FRESH FOODS IN IT!

USER COMMENTS

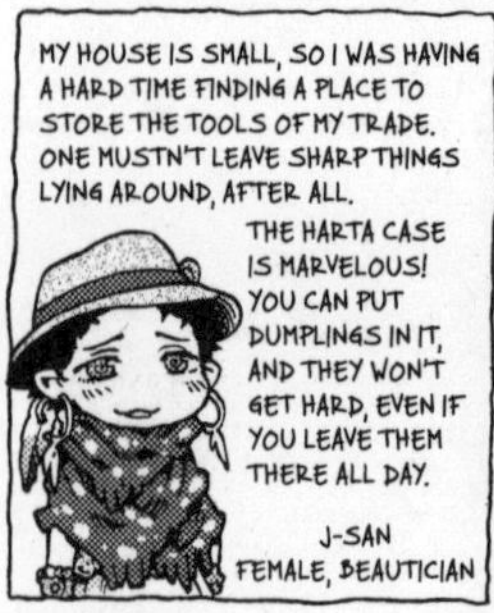
MY HOUSE IS SMALL, SO I WAS HAVING A HARD TIME FINDING A PLACE TO STORE THE TOOLS OF MY TRADE. ONE MUSTN'T LEAVE SHARP THINGS LYING AROUND, AFTER ALL.
THE HARTA CASE IS MARVELOUS! YOU CAN PUT DUMPLINGS IN IT, AND THEY WON'T GET HARD, EVEN IF YOU LEAVE THEM THERE ALL DAY.
J-SAN
FEMALE, BEAUTICIAN

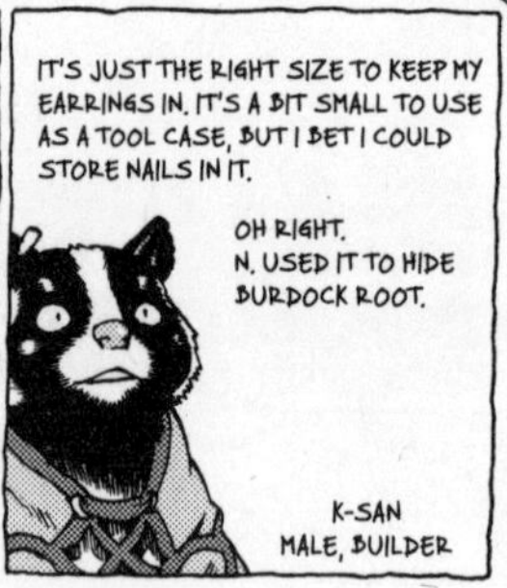
IT'S JUST THE RIGHT SIZE TO KEEP MY EARRINGS IN. IT'S A BIT SMALL TO USE AS A TOOL CASE, BUT I BET I COULD STORE NAILS IN IT.
OH RIGHT. N. USED IT TO HIDE BURDOCK ROOT.
K-SAN
MALE, BUILDER

A column introducing a special gift (accessory case) for people who submitted survey postcards to *Harta* magazine.

An illustration printed on a Japanese-style teacup. Given to people who visited all seven locations in a stamp rally held at an event.

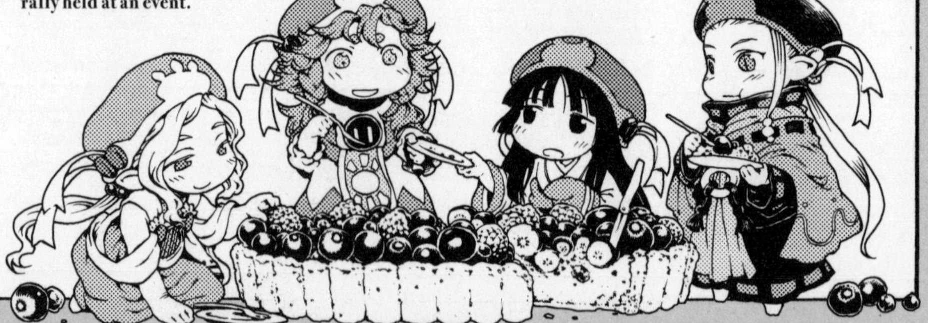

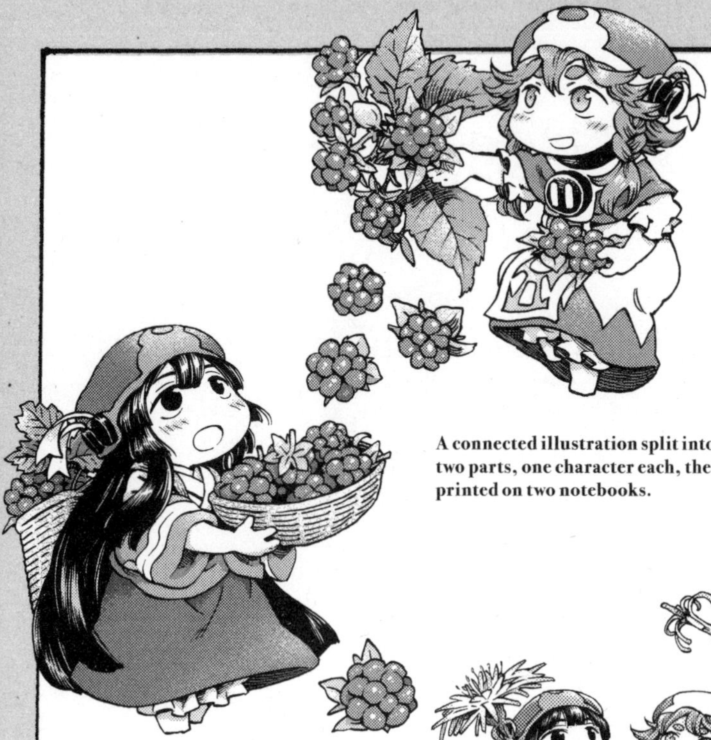

A connected illustration split into two parts, one character each, then printed on two notebooks.

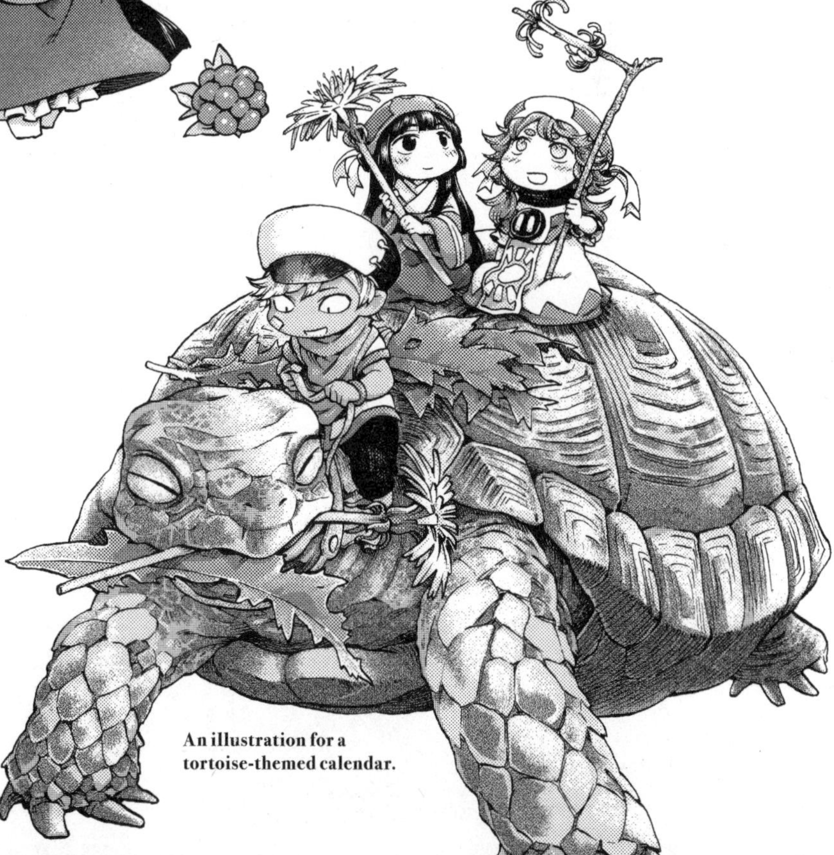

An illustration for a tortoise-themed calendar.

● Assorted HakuMiko: First Appearances ●

pages 197, 202

Harta, December 2017, Volume 50 Bound-in booklet, "HakuMiko Koro Koro"

pages 198, 199

Harta, November 2014, Volume 49 Morgen Harta

page 200

Top: *Harta*, March 2015, Volume 22

Bottom: *Machi★Asobi Vol. 11*, "Find the Little People! Hakumei and Mikochi Stamp Rally" prize

P. 201

Top: *Harta*, October 2017, Volume 48 Purchaser bonus illustration: Hakumei

Middle: *Harta*, November 2017, Volume 49 Purchaser bonus illustration: Mikochi

Bottom: "Perpetual Calendar," 2018 present exclusively for regular *Harta* buyers

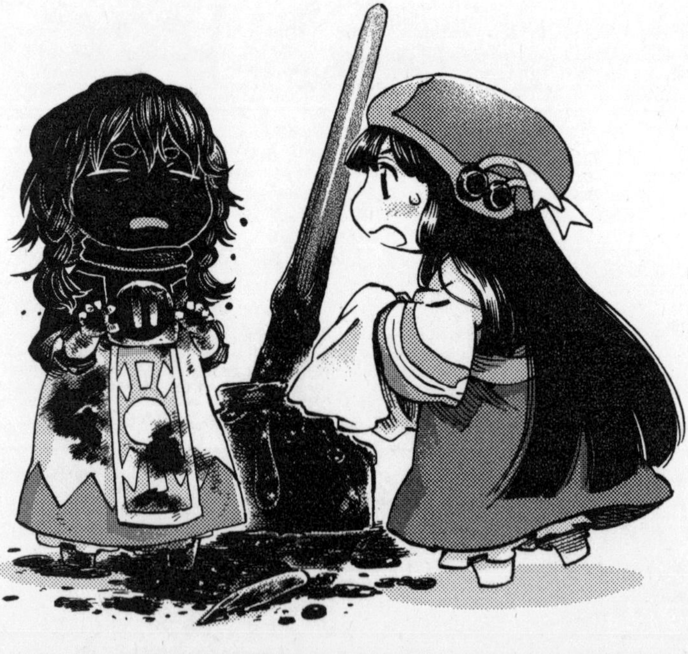

The End

Hakumei & Mikochi

Tiny Little Life in the Woods

Translation Notes

Common Honorifics
no honorific: Indicates familiarity or closeness; if used without permission or reason, addressing someone in this manner would constitute an insult.
-san: The Japanese equivalent of Mr./Mrs./Miss. If a situation calls for politeness, this is the fail-safe honorific.
-chan: An affectionate honorific indicating familiarity used mostly in reference to girls; also used in reference to cute persons or animals of either gender.
-senpai, Senpai: An honorific used when addressing upperclassmen or more experienced coworkers.

Currency conversion: Although exchange rates fluctuate daily, a good general estimate is ¥100 to 1USD.

Page 12: *Agarwood* is the heartwood of *Aquilaria* trees that have been infected with a type of mold. The infection provokes the production of a dark, fragrant resin, and the wood infused with this resin is used in incense and perfumes. Top-grade agarwood is one of the world's most expensive natural raw materials.

Page 29: Tea leaves were very expensive and not readily available to the common people before the late Edo period (1603–1868). Prior to that, most people drank **plain boiled water**. In the last few years, it's made a comeback as a health drink in Japan; it's said to warm you up from the inside out, improve digestion, and speed up your basal metabolism. Of course...that isn't why Kiyomoto is serving it here.

Page 51: There's a superstition taught to children in Japan that, when you hear thunder, you have to hide your **belly button** or the thunder god will take it. Attempts at practical explanations for the superstition range from the fact that thunderstorms bring cooler air and leaving your stomach exposed could lead to illness, to the fact that covering your belly button generally involves lowering your head and leaning down at least a little, making you marginally less likely to be struck by lightning.

Page 56: *Hanafuda*, or "flower cards," are traditional Japanese playing cards used in a variety of games. The deck consists of 48 cards in 12 suits (each suit featuring a different flower and representing a month of the year), with four cards in each suit. Fun fact: The Nintendo company (yes, that one) started out as a hanafuda manufacturer.

Page 60: *Kuragakoi* refers to a mature sake that has been stored in a dirt cellar at room temperature, in the dark, for a little over a year.

Page 74: *Amazake* is a rather thick, sweet drink made from fermented rice. It's either nonalcoholic or has a very low alcohol content.

Page 92: Mountain yam is astonishingly slimy when raw. It doesn't have much flavor, so it's added to foods for this texture. It's usually served grated raw, and either chilled or at room temperature.

Page 114: In this case, **galette** refers to a savory pancake made with buckwheat flour.

Page 143: Vagarshak Kotoyan was an Armenian classical composer who lived between 1921–1992 and was known for their contributions to Armenian choral and vocal music. The **Orchestral Kotoyan Songbook** is likely a collection of their work.

Page 169: *Daiginjo* sake is ultra high-quality sake brewed from rice grains polished to 50 percent of their weight or below. *Ginjo* sake is high-quality sake brewed by low-temperature fermentation from rice grains polished to 60 percent. *Junmai* sake is sake that's made without added alcohol or sugar.

Page 181: *Iwatabako* is an alpine gesneriad (*Conandron ramondioides*), a species of small flowering plant. Its name means "rock tobacco" due to the fact that its leaves resemble tobacco leaves. It's native to east Asia and grows on rock faces, in forests, or beside streams.

Page 193: While there is a crustacean known as *umihotaru*, or "sea firefly," Kashiki is talking about the **Umihotaru Parking Area**, a rest area/mall built on an artificial island in Tokyo Bay near the Chiba side.

Page 196: Hakumei and Mikochi is serialized in the manga magazine *Harta*, which releases ten issues per year.

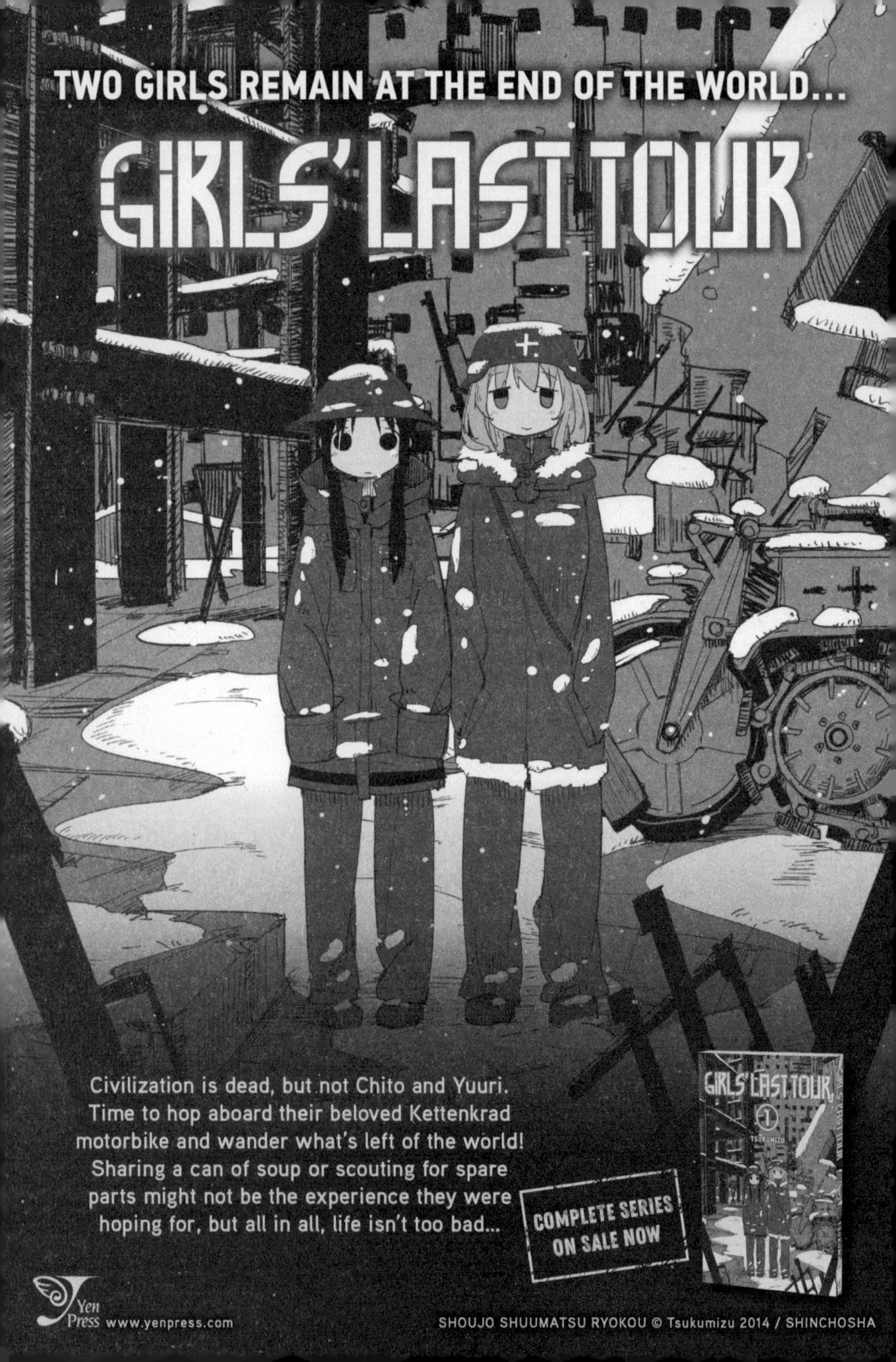
TWO GIRLS REMAIN AT THE END OF THE WORLD...
GIRLS' LAST TOUR
Civilization is dead, but not Chito and Yuuri. Time to hop aboard their beloved Kettenkrad motorbike and wander what's left of the world! Sharing a can of soup or scouting for spare parts might not be the experience they were hoping for, but all in all, life isn't too bad...
COMPLETE SERIES ON SALE NOW
GIRLS' LAST TOUR
1
TSUKUMIZU
Yen Press www.yenpress.com
SHOUJO SHUUMATSU RYOKOU © Tsukumizu 2014 / SHINCHOSHA

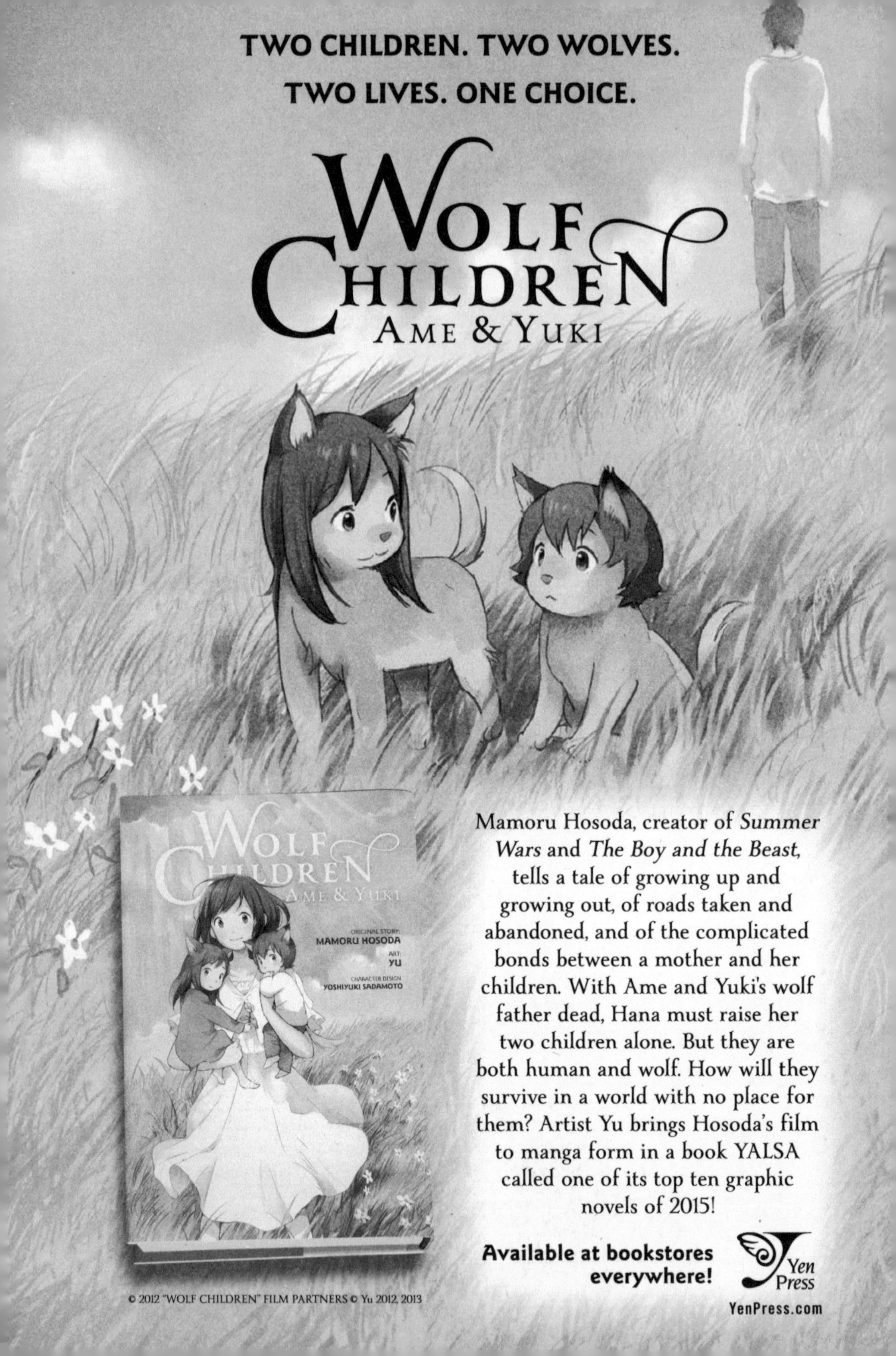
TWO CHILDREN. TWO WOLVES.
TWO LIVES. ONE CHOICE.
WOLF CHILDREN
AME & YUKI
WOLF CHILDREN
AME & YUKI
ORIGINAL STORY: MAMORU HOSODA
ART: YU
CHARACTER DESIGN YOSHIYUKI SADAMOTO
Mamoru Hosoda, creator of *Summer Wars* and *The Boy and the Beast*, tells a tale of growing up and growing out, of roads taken and abandoned, and of the complicated bonds between a mother and her children. With Ame and Yuki's wolf father dead, Hana must raise her two children alone. But they are both human and wolf. How will they survive in a world with no place for them? Artist Yu brings Hosoda's film to manga form in a book YALSA called one of its top ten graphic novels of 2015!
Available at bookstores everywhere!
Yen Press
YenPress.com
© 2012 "WOLF CHILDREN" FILM PARTNERS © Yu 2012, 2013

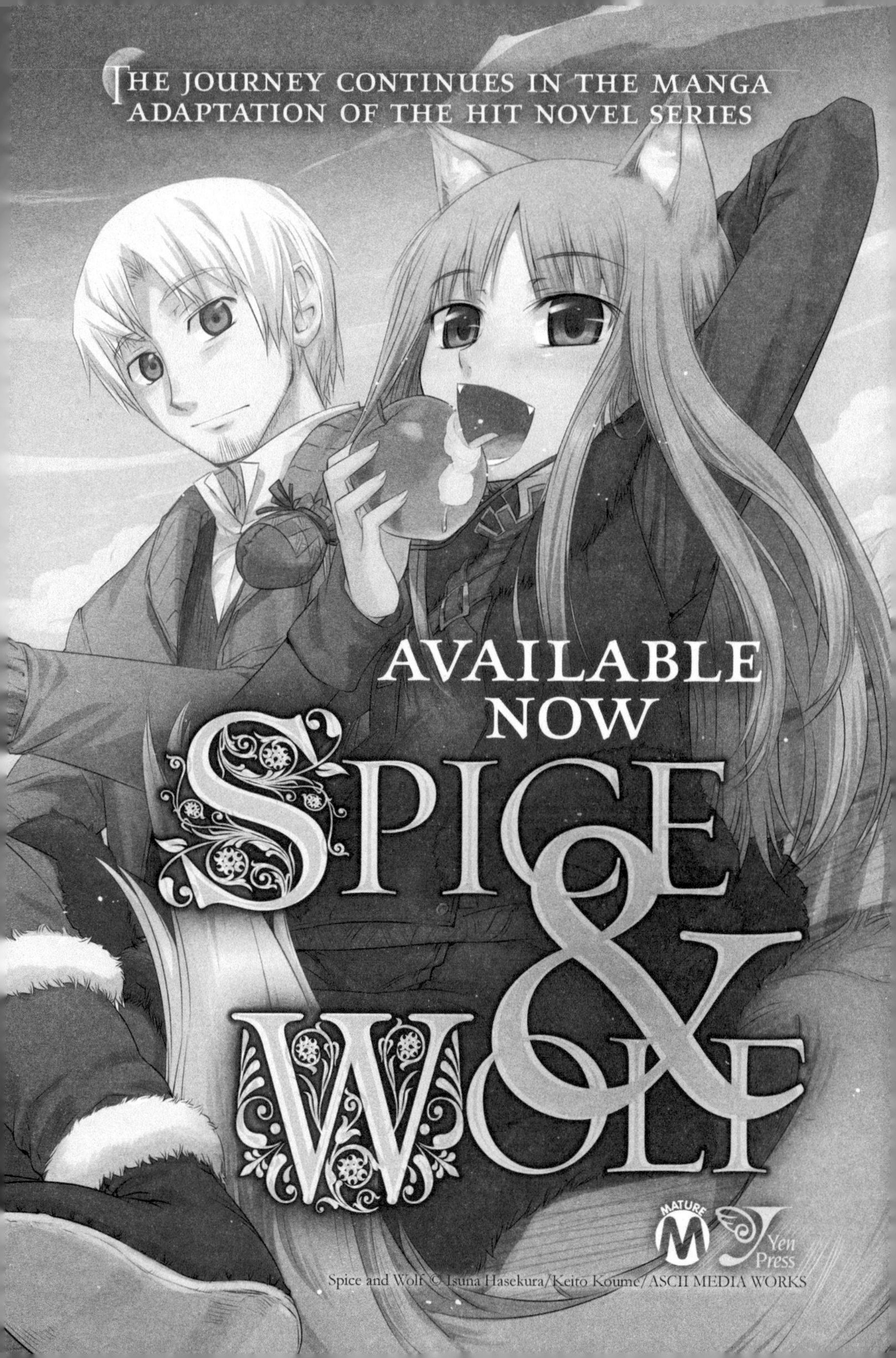
THE JOURNEY CONTINUES IN THE MANGA
ADAPTATION OF THE HIT NOVEL SERIES
AVAILABLE
NOW
SPICE
&
WOLF
MATURE
M
Yen
Press
Spice and Wolf © Isuna Hasekura/Keito Koume/ASCII MEDIA WORKS

Hakumei & Mikochi 7
Tiny Little Life in the Woods

� Takuto Kashiki ✿

Translation: TAYLOR ENGEL **Lettering: ABIGAIL BLACKMAN**

HAKUMEI TO MIKOCHI Volume 7
© Takuto Kashiki 2019
First published in Japan in 2019 by KADOKAWA CORPORATION, Tokyo.
English translation rights arranged with KADOKAWA CORPORATION, Tokyo through TUTTLE-MORI AGENCY, Inc., Tokyo.

Yen Press
150 West 30th Street, 19th Floor
New York, NY 10001

Visit us at yenpress.com
facebook.com/yenpress
twitter.com/yenpress
yenpress.tumblr.com
instagram.com/yenpress

First Yen Press Edition: September 2019

Library of Congress Control Number: 2018941284

ISBN: 978-1-9753-3231-0

10 9 8 7 6 5 4 3 2 1

WOR

Printed in the United States of America